Catherine Cookson was born in Tyne Dock, the illegitimate daughter of a poverty-stricken woman, Kate, whom she believed to be her older sister. She began work in service but eventually moved south to Hastings where she met and married Tom Cookson, a local grammar-school master. At the age of forty she began writing about the lives of the working-class people with whom she had grown up, using the place of her birth as the background to many of her novels.

Although originally acclaimed as a regional writer – her novel *The Round Tower* won the Winifred Holtby award for the best regional novel of 1968 – her readership soon began to spread throughout the world. Her novels have been translated into more than a dozen languages and more than 50,000,000 copies of her books have been sold in Corgi alone. Fifteen of her novels have been made into successful television dramas, and more are planned.

Catherine Cookson's many bestselling novels established her as one of the most popular of contemporary women novelists. After receiving an OBE in 1985, Catherine Cookson was created a Dame of the British Empire in 1993. She was appointed an Honorary Fellow of St Hilda's College, Oxford in 1997. For many years she lived near Newcastle-upon-Tyne. She died shortly before her ninety-second birthday in June 1998.

'Catherine Cookson's novels are about hardship, the intractability of life and of individuals, the struggle first to survive and next to make sense of one's survival. Humour, toughness, resolution and generosity are Cookson virtues, in a world which she often depicts as cold and violent. Her novels are weighted and driven by her own early experiences of illegitimacy and poverty. this is what gives them power. In the specialised world of women's popular fiction, cookson has created her own territory Helen Dunmore, *The Tim*

BOOKS BY CATHERINE COOKSON

NOVELS

Kate Hannigan
The Fifteen Streets
Colour Blind
Maggie Rowan
Rooney
The Menagerie
Slinky Jane
Fanny McBride
Fenwick Houses
Heritage of Folly
The Garment
The Fen Tiger
The Blind Miller
House of Men
Hannah Massey
The Long Corridor
The Unbaited Trap
Katie Mulholland
The Round Tower
The Nice Bloke
The Glass Virgin
The Invitation
The Dwelling Place
Feathers in the Fire
Pure as the Lily
The Mallen Streak
The Mallen Girl
The Mallen Litter
The Invisible Cord
The Gambling Man
The Tide of Life
The Slow Awakening
The Iron Façade
The Girl
The Cinder Path
Miss Martha Mary Crawford
The Man Who Cried
Tilly Trotter

Tilly Trotter Wed
Tilly Trotter Widowed
The Whip
Hamilton
The Black Velvet Gown
Goodbye Hamilton
A Dinner of Herbs
Harold
The Moth
Bill Bailey
The Parson's Daughter
Bill Bailey's Lot
The Cultured Handmaiden
Bill Bailey's Daughter
The Harrogate Secret
The Black Candle
The Wingless Bird
The Gillyvors
My Beloved Son
The Rag Nymph
The House of Women
The Maltese Angel
The Year of the Virgins
The Golden Straw
Justice is a Woman
The Tinker's Girl
A Ruthless Need
The Obsession
The Upstart
The Branded Man
The Bonny Dawn
The Bondage of Love
The Desert Crop
The Lady on My Left
The Solace of Sin
Riley
The Blind Years
The Thursday Friend

THE MARY ANN STORIES

A Grand Man
The Lord and Mary Ann
The Devil and Mary Ann
Love and Mary Ann

Life and Mary Ann
Marriage and Mary Ann
Mary Ann's Angels
Mary Ann and Bill

FOR CHILDREN

Matty Doolin
Joe and the Gladiator
The Nipper
Rory's Fortune
Our John Willie

Mrs Flannagan's Trumpet
Go Tell It To Mrs Golightly
Lanky Jones
Nancy Nutall and the Mongrel
Bill and the Mary Ann Shaughnessy

AUTOBIOGRAPHY

Our Kate
Catherine Cookson Country

Let Me Make Myself Plain
Plainer Still

HERITAGE OF FOLLY
&
THE FEN TIGER

Catherine Cookson

CORGI BOOKS

HERITAGE OF FOLLY & THE FEN TIGER
A CORGI BOOK : 055214701X
9780552147019

PRINTING HISTORY
This Corgi collection first published 1999

7 9 10 8

Copyright © Catherine Cookson 1999
including

HERITAGE OF FOLLY
Originally published in Great Britain by
Macdonald and Jane's (Macdonald & Co) (Publishers) Ltd.
Copyright © Catherine Cookson 1961

THE FEN TIGER
Originally published in Great Britain by
Macdonald & Jane's Ltd.
Copyright © Catherine Cookson 1963

Set in 12pt Bembo by
Phoenix Typesetting, Ilkley, West Yorkshire.

Corgi Books are published by Transworld Publishers,
61–63 Uxbridge Road, London W5 5SA,
a division of The Random House Group Ltd,
in Australia by Random House Australia (Pty) Ltd,
20 Alfred Street, Milsons Point, Sydney, NSW 2061, Australia,
in New Zealand by Random House New Zealand Ltd,
18 Poland Road, Glenfield, Auckland 10, New Zealand
and in South Africa by Random House (Pty) Ltd,
Isle of Houghton, Corner of Boundary Road & Carse O'Gowrie,
Houghton 2198, South Africa.

Penguin Random House is committed to a sustainable future for
our business, our readers and our planet. This book is made from
Forest Stewardship Council® certified paper.

Printed and bound in Great Britain by Clays Ltd, Elcograf S.p.A.

Heritage of Folly

Catherine Cookson

CORGI BOOKS

1

It was after the bus had left Morpeth and had passed through Ulgham and Widdrington that the landscape changed. The farm-lands now gave place to bare, scree-covered slopes with small fields bordered by drystone walls. Here and there when the road dipped into a sheltered valley the earth seemed to promise softness, but the promise was not kept. The whole tone of the land was cold and lonely, and this, Linda thought as she gazed through the bus window, was but a reflection of how she was feeling inside. Her heart was cold with fears of what lay ahead, and she was lonely as she had never been lonely before.

In a short while the bus would reach Surfpoint Bay and she would meet her future employer. This alone would have filled her with some apprehension had she been on time, but she was arriving two hours late. Her train having been held up owing to fog, she had lost the bus that would have got her to her destination at two o'clock.

She hoped he wouldn't be annoyed, it was important that she got off to a good start . . . a good start was everything. What if she made a mess of things? She closed her eyes on this thought and her father's voice became loud in her ears, saying,

'A waste of money sending her to an agricultural college . . . a waste of money keeping her at school until she was eighteen . . . a waste of everything. Look at her. Does she look cut out for farm work? A land girl! Never heard tell of such nonsense.'

But for once in her life her mother had had her own way and she was given the chance to shape a desire into hard reality. And farming was hard reality; even the short stays on the farm which her uncle managed in Crowborough had taught her that much.

Before proceeding for a two-year course at an agricultural college it was essential that she have a year of practical training on a farm. The farm in Crowborough did not offer her this as it was given over wholly to the breeding of Galloway cattle, but the owner had been instrumental in getting her fixed up on a farm in Northumberland. And with her mother's blessing and her father's prophetic warning of failure she had early this morning left London; and now the journey was nearly over.

The stage . . . a model . . . or even a shop and I could have understood it. Her father's voice was still going on, and she moved impatiently on the bus seat and almost exclaimed aloud, 'Oh, be quiet.' If only the interview was over . . . that was really what was worrying her, the first meeting with her employer. Perhaps this was because she knew that Mr Batley would have preferred a male student. And there was the letter he had written to her; it had been stiff, but then it was a business letter and you couldn't get much idea of a person from a business letter. Well, she told herself, there wouldn't be much longer to worry now, for the journey was almost over, in fact they had arrived. When she shivered she admonished herself strongly, 'Don't be silly, he can't swallow you.'

The light of the November day was fading and it wasn't until the bus was running on the flat at the bottom of the hill that she realised that what had appeared to be a cluster of houses was in reality only two. Both grey-stoned, they stood tall and stark, dominating about twenty chalets. When the bus drew to a stop, Linda, standing on the platform, saw that the larger of the two houses was an inn, The Wild Duck, and outside it was standing a small, very fat woman, a white apron round her middle and her arms bare to the elbows. Near her stood a little girl of about seven. There was no sign of a man of any sort waiting.

'Kept fine for you.' The woman spoke to the driver who had now alighted from the bus and was stretching his arms above his head.

'Aye, it's all right here, Mrs Weir,' he answered, 'but it was as thick as clarts when we left Newcastle.'

'No!' Her eyebrows slid up her smooth brow.

'Aye, Mrs Weir, it was.' The conductor endorsed his mate's statement.

During this exchange Linda stood aside and looked about her, but she had only time to notice the great expanse of sand with white-collared waves

9

rolling on to it when the woman said, 'And you, me dear, you're for Batley's aren't you?'

'Yes, I am.' Linda brought her eyes eagerly to the woman.

'Well, he was down here for the last one and of course you weren't on it.'

'My train was late, I lost the connection . . . is it far to the farm?'

'Well, it all depends what you mean by far. Ten miles is nowt to some folks, then to others a mile's enough.'

'Is it ten miles?' Linda could not stop her eyes from stretching in surprise.

'No, it's only me way of putting things. Look, you could do with a cup of tea, I bet. Come along in. Yours is ready for you, lads,' she nodded to the conductor and driver. 'You know your road . . . You come this way, Miss.'

Linda followed her into a little parlour, so warm, shining and comfortable that for a moment she wished she had reached her journey's end and could sit here and relax and not think or worry about employers or farms or futures.

As Mrs Weir poured out the tea she talked. 'Now if he's not here within the next ten minutes your best plan is shanks's pony. You'll do it in twenty minutes or so and get there afore it's really dark . . . Oh, I know what. Katie'll climb the knoll and see if the car's coming over the cliff. Katie!' Mrs Weir's voice filled the house, and when the child came running, saying, 'Yes, Auntie?' Mrs Weir said, 'Go, climb the knoll and see if Batley's wagon's coming along the road. Be careful now.'

'Yes, Auntie.' The child was away, and Mrs Weir explained, 'There's steps up the cliff just beyond the house. Her legs are young, she can do it. You can see along the top from there.' She handed the cup to Linda and almost without drawing breath she went on, 'You don't look cut out for the part. Would never say you were a farm girl if I had put a name to you. You're thin. You could do with a bit of this.' She thumped her stomach.

This quick change in the conversation made Linda smile and she said, 'I'm much stronger than I look.'

'Well, you'll need to be to stick farming. And up there an' all. Wild it is up there. Bad enough down here, but we're sheltered a bit. Cut you into slices up there. You know Ralph Batley?'

'No.'

'Oh, thought you might.'

It was on the point of Linda's tongue to say, 'Tell me, what's he like?' but she checked herself. Women were women all the world over, and this woman, as kind as she was, might inform him of her enquiries the next time they met. She didn't want that to happen.

A few minutes later Katie came panting into the kitchen saying, 'I can't see the car, Auntie.'

'Aw well . . .' Mrs Weir turned to Linda, 'it looks like he's been held up or he might be thinking you're not for coming the day, or

11

his Jeep's broken down . . . and that'll be no surprise . . . anything could have happened to stop him.'

'Yes . . . yes.' Linda was on her feet; the picture that Mrs Weir presented was sending her spirits down to zero again. By this time of the day she should have met her employer and know, at least, to some extent, what he was like. But here she was, darkness not far off and the meeting with him still to come.

'My man's taken the van into Amber, or he would have run you up there like a shot, but my advice to you is to start off now . . . not that I'm hurrying you, mind. If the lines weren't down I'd ring up and that would bring him, but the day afore yesterday we had a fair storm here, took part of the cliff away and a couple of poles an' all. They should be right by the morrow but the morrow isn't the day, is it?'

Mrs Weir was leading the way to the door again and now she said brightly over her shoulder, 'But I can tell you one good thing – your luggage has come: a trunk and two cases . . . that was it, wasn't it?'

'Oh, have they? That's good. That's something, anyway.' Linda found herself laughing as she looked down into the big moon face of Mrs Weir. 'And they've gone up?'

'Aye. He took them back this afternoon with him.'

The fact that her luggage had arrived at its destination cheered her somewhat and she took leave of garrulous Mrs Weir and Katie with the promise that she would surely look in on them again soon. They had come to the end of the second house with her, which was a shop but which was now shuttered, and Mrs Weir's voice sent her on her way crying, 'You can't go wrong, keep to the road.'

She walked quickly to the end of the sea wall, which formed a sort of promenade, and there she turned and looked back. Mrs Weir and Katie were still standing watching her and when they waved she answered their salute gaily. She liked these people . . . Oh, she did.

Once she had left the promenade the road branched away from the sea and steeply upwards. At one point it was just a broad cleft cut out of the rock, and she wondered how a car could ever get through it. As she walked hurriedly out of the gully, the road widened and quite suddenly, as if she had been propelled there by a lift, she found herself on top of the cliff. There to the left of her lay the sea, deep green to where, in the far distance, a strip of fire edged the horizon. It was like an echo of the afterglow, and although it was breathtakingly beautiful and demanded that she stand entranced for a moment in awe-filled admiration, it also told her there was need for hurry. It had not taken her more than five minutes to reach this point and if the journey to the farm was, according to Mrs Weir, a twenty-minute walk, then if she wanted to get there before it was really dark she must put a spurt on.

It was at this point that she was confronted with a problem that almost made her retrace her steps back to the inn. Mrs Weir had said, keep to the road, but which road? Before her the road divided itself into two; one side, she noticed, and not without a slight shudder, wound its way perilously near the edge of the cliff, and it was bordered on its right side by a wire fence with a treble row of barbed wire for good measure running along its top. This undoubtedly was to keep the cattle from going over the cliff. But surely it couldn't be the road. She looked towards the other branch. This looked really nothing more than a lane, yet there was the print of car wheels on the rough grass that bordered it, whereas on the cliff path the rocky surface showed no indication of it having been used by a vehicle. Anyway, she considered, no-one in their right senses would take that cliff path. As for bringing a farm vehicle along there, you wouldn't do that unless you wanted to commit suicide. Without further hesitation she found herself taking the road to the right and after only a short way she felt that her choice had been the right and sensible one, for it broadened out into a sort of carriageway which was apparently kept in reasonable repair, for she saw that here and there the potholes had recently been made up with broken rock.

Exactly twenty minutes after she had left Mrs Weir she was still on the road and there was no farm in sight. Just a little tremor of panic rose in her from the region of her stomach. Soon it would be quite dark, she hadn't a torch, she was feeling cold, and her light case had taken on a lead-like weight now. There was only one thing she was thankful for at the moment and that was she had been wise enough to put on her flat-heeled shoes. The path now was winding steeply downhill and she had the impression that she was descending into the cove again at Surfpoint Bay, but knew that this was impossible for this path had led away from the cliffs and the cove. Wherever she was she was well inland. Then, rounding one sharp twist in the path, she saw the light. The relief that surged through her brought her to a halt and she found that she was biting her lip to stop its trembling. She was here, she had arrived. There below her lay the farm, with lights shining out from the farmhouse itself. She could only make out the dim shape of the buildings but she knew in her heart that it was a beautiful farm. She had to stop herself from running the last few yards down the hill.

Walking somewhat sedately, she left the cliff path, crossed over an intersecting road, through a white gate, up a broad-flagged path to some still broader steps which led on to what looked like a terrace flanking the house, and to the front door. It was a massive door of weathered oak, its blackness intruding into the fading light.

As her hand went up to the knocker she heard laughter coming from somewhere within the house and a woman's voice shouting a name. 'Rouse! Rouse!'

She lifted the knocker and tapped rather timidly on the door. The knock seemed to cut off the woman's laughter and there followed a period of silence before the door was opened.

The woman was standing with her back to the light and Linda could not make out her face distinctly; she only knew that she was tall, as tall as herself, and thin, even thinner than she was, and she was dark, as dark as she herself was fair.

'Yes?' The word was a question that seemed laboured with surprise.

'I'm . . . I'm Linda Metcalfe.'

The woman moved slowly forward now and peered into Linda's face. And then she said, 'Are you looking for someone?'

The sickly feeling that was creeping through Linda now told her without further words what had happened. She had come to the wrong farm.

'What's the matter?' A deep, thick voice came from behind the woman, and the voice seemed to suit the man now standing in the doorway. Then as Linda was about to speak he switched an outside light on, and as she blinked and looked into his heavy red face she stammered, 'I . . . I'm afraid I've come to the wrong place.'

'Yes? Where are you making for . . . the Bay, Surfpoint Bay?'

'No, no, I've just come from there. I was on my way to Fowler Hall Farm and I must have taken the wrong turning.'

Although the couple before her neither moved nor altered their expressions, Linda was vitally aware that her words had come as a shock to them.

How long the silence continued she did not know, but it was broken by another male voice from somewhere in the house, calling, 'Where are you?'

'Come here a minute.' The woman spoke over her shoulder but without taking her eyes off Linda, and when into the scene came a young man whose thinness, colouring and height proclaimed him to be the woman's son, she said to him, 'This young lady's lost her way, she's making for . . . up there.' The last two words seemed to cause her some effort, and she accompanied them with a heavy sideways lift of her head.

The young man was standing not more than a foot from Linda now and over his dark, bold, appraising gaze there fell, like a sheet, a look of startled surprise.

Again silence enveloped them all.

'What made you take this road? The road you wanted lay along the cliff.' It was the elder man speaking, his voice rough and harsh, and when Linda answered, 'It didn't look safe somehow,' there was a quick exchange of glances between the three people opposite her.

Then the woman seemed to take charge of the situation. 'You'd better come in,' she said, 'until we see what can be done. You can't get there in the dark . . . not alone.' On this she turned and walked into the house and the men stood one on each side of the doorway waiting for Linda to pass between them, and as she did so she had the oddest feeling, which made her want to lower her eyes as if from their naked virility.

Once past them she entered a glass-partitioned lobby, and from there stepped into a large hall which was evidently used as a lounge. Immediately she saw it was a beautiful room, so beautiful that she hesitated to walk into it in her outdoor shoes. Red rugs on a light oak floor, flanked by white walls, the white broken here and there by flashes of scarlet, heavy velvet scarlet curtains, a great fire burning in an open fireplace and, fronting it, a deep couch. But dominating all this was the staircase. Bare oak, it wound its way out of the hall to the right to form a balcony flanking the end wall. The whole was like an expensive Christmas card, but strangely out of place with its owners, at least with the two men. It was the woman, Linda thought, who would be solely responsible for this room, for like her it was colourful yet dignified. The woman was wearing a red wool dress and her black hair was straight and pulled tightly back from her forehead, and like her own hair it was long and dressed almost in the same style, lying in a bun on the nape of her neck.

'Sit down . . . will you have a cup of tea?' The woman looked towards the table set with tea things standing to the side of the couch, and Linda, taking the seat indicated on the sofa, replied quietly, 'No, thank you, I had some tea in the village . . . at the inn.'

'Why couldn't Weir have taken you up?'

'He had gone out with the car.' Linda looked up at the elder man.

'He would . . . What're you doing in these parts . . . you've no connection with the Batleys, have you?'

'No, I'm going to study farming. I'm going as a student for a year with Mr Batley.'

The three pairs of eyes were on her again and she turned hers from the older man to the woman and then to the son, but brought them back quickly to the man again as he exclaimed, 'God in heaven!'

What was behind this remark she didn't know, and she hadn't time to ponder, for at that moment the woman turned to her son and said, 'You'll have to run her up in the car.'

'Wh–a–t!' The younger man's whole expression was one of protest. Then as if realising the effect of his attitude on the uninvited guest he turned to Linda and said hastily, 'I'm sorry, but you see . . .'

'Rouse! Come here a minute.' The woman was walking away across the wide hall towards a doorway. But the young man didn't follow her until his father jerked his head sharply, then very reluctantly he moved away across the room in his mother's wake.

Now the man came and took his position on the hearthrug with his back to the fire. He was dressed in kneebreeches, tweed coat and slippers and he joined his hands under the tail of his coat before he said, 'You know what you're in for? Farming in this county, particularly this end of it, is tough.'

'I like being out of doors. I'm used to all weathers.'

'You may be, but there's weather and weather; we don't just get weather here.' His eyes were moving over her now, from her mushroom-coloured, small fur hat right down to her feet. And he seemed amused at what he saw for he began to chuckle. It was a low, rumbling chuckle, it was a spiteful sound and it brought the colour flooding up into Linda's face. And then to her amazement he threw his head back and laughed. He laughed until the tears sprang from his eyes.

Linda had risen to her feet. She was embarrassed, hurt and angry, but more angry than anything else, and when the woman came hurrying into the room again, this must have appeared evident to her, for after admonishing her husband with a sharp 'Stop that, John!' she turned to Linda and said, 'He's not laughing at you, don't take offence.'

Linda was standing stiffly looking at the man, and now he returned her gaze and spoke to her in an enigmatic way, but the meaning of his words she fully comprehended. 'He was wanting a cart-horse and he gets a year-old filly,' he sneered.

'John!'

The word was a command, but he flapped his hand at his wife and ignored her as he added, 'Fowler's Folly, indeed!'

Up to now Linda had liked everybody she had met on her journey through this county, but now the pleasant mood of the day had changed and to her surprise she found that the emotion she was feeling was akin to hate and the strength of it both startled and shocked her. She could only give herself one word to express this man's character and that was spiteful. He imagined her employer had let himself in for a bundle of uselessness and he was revelling in the thought. Well, he would see. She felt that she wanted to do something, and at this very moment, to demonstrate her capabilities, yet she knew that if the opportunity had presented itself she would have failed dismally, for here was a man who could use a sneer, a laugh or a sarcastic remark with devastating effect.

'My son Rouse is going to take you up.'

Linda turned to the woman but did not answer her, for she found that she was trembling with her anger.

'You know what this might lead to.' The man was speaking to his wife now . . . his voice without laughter was brittle . . . and she answered without looking at him as she led Linda towards the front door, 'He'll drop her at the top gate.'

The woman led the way across the terrace, down the steps and along the garden path to the road, where stood a small open car with the son, Rouse, already seated at the wheel. He did not get out and usher her into the seat, it was the mother who opened the car door and indicated that she should get in. Then when she had banged the door closed again she gave no word of farewell, merely inclining her head in a nod before the car spurted forward.

Linda, her anger still bubbling in her, sat silent, and she had been in the car some minutes before her companion spoke. As he gave a swift turn to the wheel to round a sharp bend he said abruptly, 'Our name's Cadwell.' Then after a moment, during which Linda made no reply, he added, 'May I ask what yours is?'

'Linda Metcalfe.' Her tone was not conducive to further conversation. She didn't intend it should be.

On the bend they ran into a strong wind and she heard him repeating her name as if he was calling across a valley, and as he shouted, 'I'm Rouse, as I suppose you've already learnt,' she did not answer, for at this stage she was having her work cut out to get her breath and hold on to her hat at the same time.

Down in the sheltered valley there had been little wind, but now they were climbing up steeply into it and at one point the car slowed to a crawl in low gear. Then suddenly as she felt herself pushed forward she knew they were out of the valley and on high, exposed, level ground again. At one time she thought she recognised the main road on which she had travelled towards Surfpoint Bay in the bus, but she couldn't be sure, and she reasoned against this. If Fowler Hall Farm was only twenty minutes' walk from the Bay surely the car should do it in a matter of minutes.

On and on the car went now and no words passed between them. Then after she had been on the road for what she felt must be fifteen minutes at least, she sat up straight and asked, 'Where are we going?'

'Fowler Hall, Batley's place. That's where you want to go, isn't it?'

'Yes, but I understood it was only a short walk from Surfpoint Bay.'

'Yes, it is, but not this way. Don't worry, I'm not trying to kidnap you or anything in that line.'

'I wasn't suggesting that you were.' Her tone was cutting, and now the dark eyes flashed sideways at her and she saw he was laughing at her. After a moment he asked evenly, 'What part of the country are you from?'

'Sussex.'

'Oh, Silly Sussex by the sea?'

This remark she considered was too stupid and she didn't deign to answer it.

With a sudden jolt the car came to a halt and he turned slowly towards her and said, 'That was an inane thing to say. The fact is I've never been to Sussex, only heard that saying somewhere.'

This touch of humility in him changed her feelings toward him somewhat and she said with a softening of her tone, 'If you've never been there, it's a pleasure you must give yourself, it's a wonderful county.'

'Yes, I've heard that an' all . . . Well, you've arrived.'

Linda peered about her, but there was no house within the radius of the headlights, and when she stood on the road she was somewhat appalled to find herself confronted with nothing more than a five-barred gate, a field gate.

'Where is the house?'

As she spoke a fierce gust of wind pulled at her hat and swelled her clothes into a bell about her legs, and as she pressed down the skirt of her coat with one hand and clung on to her hat with the other, his hand came on to her arm and steadied her. Then after a moment he led her towards the gate and, pointing into the darkness, he said, 'Over there, those are the farm buildings. Can you see that flicker of light?'

So faint was the light that she would not have noticed it had he not focused her attention upon it, but just as she caught sight of it, it disappeared.

'The house is beyond. It looks as though there's someone in the yard. You'll be all right. There's a cart track leads round this field, it will take you right into the yard . . . Have you a torch?'

'No . . . well, not with me.'

'Here . . .' he put his hand into the pocket of his duffel coat and pulled out a torch, 'take this.'

'Oh, thank you.'

He unlatched the gate but stood with it in his hand before opening it, and then he said, 'Well, good luck.'

Again Linda felt kindly disposed towards him for he sounded, unlike his father, as if he really did wish her good luck. She held out her hand, saying

'Goodbye, and thank you very much for helping me.'

The fingers that closed round hers were hard and the grip was tight. 'I want my torch back, mind.' He was smiling.

'Of course, I'll leave it at your house.'

He released her hand as he said, 'No, don't do that.' Then he added quickly, 'Not because you wouldn't be welcome; don't judge us on how my father reacted today, I'm only saying this for your own sake . . . It'll be better for you not to have us on your visiting list.'

'Why? Aren't you friends with Mr Batley?' She asked the question pointedly.

'Huh! You'll find out soon enough . . . But don't you fret, I'll get my torch back. I'll look out for you.'

His tone had changed and its quality was slightly too familiar and she wanted to say, 'Please don't. I'll send it through the post,' but she let it go. 'Goodbye,' she said again, 'and thank you.'

He said nothing further but pushed the gate open and she passed through it, and when a few minutes later she turned the corner of the field, she saw that the car was still there but with the headlights pointing in the opposite direction now, and in a way she felt comforted that he was waiting until she reached the farmyard.

Her torch picked out a dark huddle of buildings and then an archway, and before she passed through this she turned her eyes across the field again but there was no sign of the headlights now. As she entered the farmyard she wondered for a moment if there were dogs about . . . she was very fond of dogs but dogs weren't usually very fond of strangers . . . and when almost immediately she heard the sound of muffled barking which indicated it was coming from somewhere indoors, she sighed thankfully.

She flashed her torch around the familiar sight of a farmyard and noticed with pleasure that it was clean. She'd heard tell that some of these out-of-the-way farms could be shockers. From a door to the right of the yard came a chink of light and with her heart now thumping heavily against her ribs she made her way towards it and after only a moment's hesitation she lifted the latch and pushed open the door.

She was looking into a single cow byre. The smell that met her was warm and sweet, like incense, and there before her on a heap of fresh straw lay a small Galloway cow. The animal was on its side and kneeling on the ground stroking its face and talking to it was a man with his back towards her. The inflection of his voice was rising and falling in a gentle murmur. He was talking as if the animal was a child, a sick child, saying, 'There, there. There, there. It's all right, it'll soon be over. There, there. It won't be long now, take it easy . . . we'll have her on the mat before you in no time. Is that you, Michael?'

He did not turn round, and Linda found she could not answer him one way or the other.

'Did you find Uncle Shane?'

At this point she coughed and the sound brought him sharply round on his hunkers. She saw his mouth drop open in surprise before he jerked himself to his feet. He was standing at the front of the byre staring at her as if he thought she was not real, and just when she felt she could not stand his concentrated gaze for a second longer, he passed his hand over his eyes and slowly down his face.

'I'm sorry . . .' the voice came from between his fingers where his hand was resting against his mouth, 'it went clean out of my head . . . with Sarah here.' He jerked his head in the direction of the cow.

'That's quite all right.' She felt a wave of relief as she moved slowly into the light towards him. This then was Mr Batley. He was quite different from the picture which she had created of him and which had taken on something of a sinister quality since her meeting with the Cadwells. He wasn't as old as she had thought, under thirty-five. He was tall, very tall, perhaps six foot two, and his breadth owed nothing to flesh. As she looked into his face she could not help being struck by the sparseness of flesh on it. There was something about his face that gave her the impression that he might, sometime recently, have passed through a grave illness. His hair was dark but not of the black darkness of the Cadwell men. What caught her attention immediately were his eyes, the eyes that were hard on her again. They were grey, clear and without warmth. They did not seem to belong to the man whom she had heard talking softly to the cow. She knew that in his look there was something of the same ingredient as had been in Mr Cadwell's and in a wave of anxiety she recalled Mr Cadwell's words: 'He was wanting a cart-horse and he gets a year-old filly.'

To disabuse him of this impression and put herself immediately in the picture, she looked down at the cow and giving silent thanks for the little knowledge of cattle she had picked up on the Crowborough farm she said, 'You stock Galloways then?'

'Yes.' He was still looking at her.

'Is it her first?'

'Yes.' This question brought his attention to the animal again, and he turned and was about to kneel down beside her when he twisted his long length round and as if speaking his thoughts aloud demanded, 'But how did you manage to get here? Didn't you go to the house?'

'No, I came across a field from the roadway.'

'Who brought you up there? Mr Weir?'

'No.' As she returned his gaze something within her warned her not to mention the name of Cadwell, yet she couldn't see how else she could explain her arrival, so she prevaricated by saying, 'I went to the wrong house. They . . . they brought me to the gate.'

There came upon them a silence that she recognised, it was the same kind of silence that had followed the name of Batley when she had spoken it to the Cadwells. He was standing stiff and straight now, looking at her.

'What was the name of the people who brought you?'

She swallowed once before answering, 'I think it was Cadwell.'

Was it hate she watched spring into his face, or pain, or fury, or all three? But in an instant he was transformed before her eyes, and she had to tell herself firmly that it was her imagination and that he was not menacing her.

The cow at this moment gave a cry, and its moving uneasily on the straw had the power to bring his attention from her. Her heart was racing as she watched him close his eyes then swallow hard before turning away and on to his knees again.

She stood helplessly watching him for some moments as his hands moved over the animal, then more out of nervousness than a desire to help at this stage, for she had never seen a calving, she heard herself saying, 'Can I . . . can I do anything?'

So long was he in answering her that it would appear he hadn't heard her or that he could not bring himself to speak. Then the words seemed to be squeezed through his lips as he said, 'You'll . . . get . . . messed . . . up.'

'Oh, that doesn't matter.' Her relief sounded in her voice, and the next minute she was pulling off her coat and hat and hanging them on a nail at the side of the byre. His eyes flicked towards her as she stepped on to the straw, but they were raised no further than the skirt of her soft blue woollen dress.

'There's an apron there.' Again his words came reluctantly as he thrust one hand out behind him indicating the corner of the byre.

Following his directions she took from a nail a large piece of clean sacking, and when she had tied it around her waist she again entered the box.

'Go to her head. Keep your voice low, keep talking to her, her name's Sarah . . . She's not easy.'

As he finished this staccato information she was virtually aware that he was still consumed by a turmoil of feeling. He rose and went to a steaming bucket just outside the byre and plunged his arms up to his elbows into the white-coloured liquid, then taking a file from a tray standing on a shelf, he began methodically and quickly to clean his nails before he came again to the animal.

Kneeling on the straw Linda touched the cow's head, but when she began to talk to the animal the sound of her own voice seemed to embarrass her and she was hesitant. Then suddenly self was forgotten, submerged before the miracle that was taking place.

She was talking softly and rapidly to Sarah now and fondling her head as if she herself had reared her, and the man delivering the calf was her Uncle Chris. 'There, there, Sarah, you'll be all right. There, there, that's a dear. It's nearly over, good . . . dear Sarah.' Then she looked to where her employer was holding across the palm of his hand two quivering little hooves, the forelegs of the calf. She could only see part of what he was doing but she knew by his actions that he was rolling back the bag of skin that enveloped the calf. It was as if he was pulling the baby out of a stocking. Sarah squirmed, and he said to her in a voice that Linda could not associate with the glowering man of a few minutes ago, 'Gently, Sarah, gently, gently.'

At this point the byre door was thrust open and a thick Irish voice cried, 'Begod! Ralph, has it come upon her? I was away up at the . . .'

'Stay still, keep quiet.'

The command had more power than any shouted order. It was soft yet grinding, as if every word was being strained through steel filings.

Linda watched an old man with grey hair approach the byre on tiptoes and by his side a small boy of not more than seven or eight. The eyes of both the old man and boy were fixed on her and not on the progress of the birth.

The old man's mouth had dropped into a gape, and when he finally closed it it was to mutter, 'Mother of God!'

'Uncle Shane!' It was another command, still soft, and the old man whispered back quietly, 'All right, Ralph, all right, I'll hold me whisht.'

Sarah's body looked a contortion of pain and Linda could feel the strain under her hands. Pity for the animal swelled in her so much that she had to crush her teeth into her lower lip to stop herself from moaning in sympathy.

'Keep talking.' It was an unusually quiet request.

Unselfconsciously now she looked down into the soft, melting, pain-filled eyes of Sarah, but her voice was unsteady as she talked to the animal.

An oath from Ralph Batley brought her head up, and as she looked in concern towards him the old man whispered low, 'What's wrong, Ralph?'

After a moment the reply came. 'The head's turned back.'

'Aw, Holy Mother, will it be a vet job?'

There was no answer to this and, fascinated, she watched her employer gently inserting his arm up to the elbow into the cow.

Quickly and softly she talked to Sarah now. Stroking the animal's sweating face and forgetting herself and those about her entirely, she poured out endearments saying, 'Darling, darling. There, sweet . . . there. All over, all over.'

Suddenly Sarah gave a very human sigh and, when her body began to sink in and her muscles relax and she sighed deeply again, Linda sighed with her and her sigh released a smile. Then with her forearm she wiped the sweat from her own brow.

'Oh, bejapers! What a beauty. She's a beauty, Ralph.'

Ralph Batley now silently motioned Linda to her feet and out of his way, and when she had obeyed him she watched him wipe down the new baby with a wisp of straw before placing it near its mother's head, and when she saw Sarah's black tongue come out and lovingly lick her daughter, she experienced a wondrous feeling of happiness. She had witnessed her first calving. She couldn't explain it but there would never be another calving like it.

She was loosening the apron from about her waist when she became aware that the boy and the old man were gazing at her fixedly. Methodically she dusted the straw from the sacking before hanging it up on its nail again, and taking down her coat and hat. Then shyly she turned and faced the pair and after returning their scrutiny for a second or so she smiled, and almost immediately her smile was returned by the old man. But the boy's face remained solemn and full of enquiry, not untouched with wonder.

'Tell me, how did you come? Did Weir bring you?' The old man was standing near her now, his eyes shining up at her like beams through the rough stubble of hair that covered most of his face.

Before Linda could make any reply Ralph Batley's voice cut in sharply from just behind her shoulder, saying, 'This is my uncle . . . Mr MacNally, and this,' the hand came past her and rested on the boy's head, 'this is my nephew, Michael.' Before she could acknowledge the introductions in the conventional way or otherwise he went on, 'Take Miss Metcalfe up to the house, Uncle, I'll be there in a moment or two.'

'Aye, Ralph. Yes, I'll do that. Will you come along now?' The old man backed away from her, one arm extended in a courtly gesture as if she was some personage he was ushering into a banquet. She felt inclined to laugh. She liked this old man. From first impressions she didn't think she would get many laughs from her employer, but this old man seemed to be bubbling with a peculiar sense of joy, and she found her heart reaching out to him as if it was aching to come within the orbit of such warmth.

The boy Michael was going ahead of her towards the byre door, when Ralph Batley's voice crying sharply, 'Michael!' brought him round, and whatever signal he received from behind her he immediately stood to one side and allowed her to pass out through the door which Shane was now holding open for her.

In the yard the wind tore at them, and as the old man steadied her with his hand on her elbow he yelled, 'Have you long come? I've been away up in the top field, the fence is flat.'

'No, I've just arrived.'

'Then you haven't been in the house at all?' His voice was high with surprise.

'No.'

She could feel his bewilderment and it came over strongly as he said, 'I wondered about your case there. By the way, pass it over here.' He put out his hand for it, and she did not protest that she could carry it, but let him take it from her.

'Did Weir bring you up? You didn't say.'

'No, Mr Weir was out.'

'You couldn't have got here afore dark then?'

'No, I lost my way and I arrived at another farm. The name . . .' She paused, then went on,

34

'The name was Cadwell.' She gave this information briefly.

The old man came to an abrupt stop and his hand came off her arm and she was forced to stand with her head and shoulders pressed back against the wind while he turned to the boy and said, 'Michael. Here, take hold of this case and go on up.' He pushed the case and the lamp into the boy's hands, then added, 'Away with you now.' And it wasn't until the child had moved off that he said quickly, 'Don't tell me that a Cadwell brought you up here?'

'Yes, the young man, Rouse, I think his name was.'

'You didn't tell him that . . . Ralph, back there?'

'Yes, I'm afraid I did. I didn't see any reason not to.' This wasn't strictly true but Linda could not explain how it had been impossible for her to withhold the means by which she had arrived here.

'Name of God!'

'What have I done wrong?' There was a tremor of apprehension in her voice. 'I didn't know that Mr Cadwell and Mr Batley were at loggerheads, it was unfortunate that I should go there. I wouldn't have had this happen for the world, I'm terribly sorry if I've caused—'

'That's all right, that's all right, you weren't to know, girl. Now we must go in . . . I don't know how Maggie will take this . . . his mother. Come.' He took hold of her arm again. 'I'll take you round to the front door, she'd never forgive me for taking you in by the back way. Visitors must always come in the front door.'

Linda did not protest that she did not come within the category of a visitor, for she was now too disturbed and distressed with the thought that even before she had reached her destination she had gathered up the threads of a feud and trailed them along with her to this very house, and this fact was bound to have a dampening effect upon her reception.

They were walking along a broad, flagged terrace now and the wind was meeting them head-on, and when they reached the porch they both stood panting for a moment, before the old man said, 'I'll take off me boots, Maggie would brain me if I went in with me boots on.' Then bending towards her he whispered, 'Wipe your feet, there on that mat. Wipe them hard. Mud you know, it treads in.'

Very like a child, and feeling at this moment not far removed from one, she did as she was requested, while she watched him hop from one stockinged foot to the other over the cold stone flags to the door. Then when he opened the door it was immediately made plain to her why her feet should be as clean as possible, for the floor on to which she stepped was shining. It was polished as she had never before seen a floor polished, except in an advertisement. But her attention was lifted from the floor to the hall which opened out before her, for in size and shape it was an exact replica of the hall of the Cadwells' house. There was the same large, open fireplace. There was the same winding staircase but going off to the left with the balcony running from it along the entire length of the far wall; yet for all the similarity the hall was as different from the Cadwells' as chalk from cheese, for it had nothing of its elegance or charm. This room, Linda saw at once, was used as a general room. Being so, it recalled to her mind Mrs Weir's parlour, yet because of its size it lacked the cosiness of that small room. A long black oak refectory table ran lengthwise down the hall. Standing with her back to its head was a woman. She was of medium height with greying hair and had two patches of red high on her cheek bones. Her eyes were round, brown and bright, and her expression checked Linda's progress.

The Cadwells had looked at her each in their own way. Ralph Batley's appraisal had shown her his surprise, and she did not think that it was of a pleasant nature to him. The old man Shane had greeted her gleefully, the boy with wonder; but this woman's look was different. Linda was conscious of her gaze sweeping her from head to foot. It seemed as if she was being called upon to make a quick decision and was finding the progress difficult. The boy Michael had evidently prepared her to some extent, for he was standing by her side biting at his thumbnail, looking up at the same time from under his brows towards Linda.

'Well, she's come, Maggie.' Shane's voice was high again. 'Found her way here in the dark.'

The woman was now coming towards Linda, her eyes still holding her gaze.

37

'I'm sorry you've had to find your way. When you didn't come at two he thought maybe . . . anyway, he couldn't leave the calving.' The woman's voice was soft and thick and pleasant, but before Linda could reassure her that it was perfectly all right, she had turned on the old man, crying, 'It's your fault. Where d'you think you've been, you could have gone down.'

'Now, Maggie, whisht a while, I was up in the top field with the railings as flat as a pancake. You wouldn't have had me leave them and the cattle get through, now would you?'

'Oh.' She moved her head impatiently then turned to Linda saying, 'Well, come in, come in. Here, let me have your coat. You'll be frozen.'

As Linda took off her coat Shane, tripping towards the fireplace like an aged gnome, said with evident pleasure, 'She's got her hand in already, Maggie, she's been helping with the calving. Now what d'you think of that? It's come, it's a fine heifer although her head was back.'

'Helping with the calving?' The woman held Linda's coat across her hands and looked up at her incredulously and Linda, going hot with what she knew was to come, said hesitantly, 'Apparently I came in the back way. I saw the light in the byre.'

'You came in the back way? From the main road?'

'Yes.'

'Oh.' She nodded at Linda, a smile now softening her face. 'Mr Weir brought you.'

38

'No.'

'No, Weir didn't bring her.' They all turned their eyes towards a door under the balcony through which Ralph Batley was entering the room. It was evident that he had heard his mother's question, and as he came slowly across the hall he said to no-one in particular, 'She took the wrong road.' Then throwing a cold, grey glance at her, he added, 'Didn't you, Miss Metcalfe?'

'Yes, I did.'

Even to herself she sounded on the defensive. It was as if she had committed a crime by taking the wrong road. She watched him reach up to the high mantelshelf and take a pipe from out of a wooden rack, then knocking the bowl into the palm of his hand he turned to his mother. But his eyes remained on the pipe as he said heavily, 'She forked right at the cliff end.'

Linda was not looking at Mrs Batley, but Mrs Batley was looking at her son. Her brown eyes were wide and unmistakably there was fear in them.

Ralph Batley turned from his mother's gaze to the fire now and lifting his foot he thrust it into the heart of the blazing logs. A shower of sparks sprayed around the chimney and fell on to the gleaming copper kettle that stood on one side of the hearth and on to the great black-leaded kettle resting on a stand near the bars. Then taking a home-made spill from out of a bunch that filled a rack on the brick wall and putting it towards the blaze he said, 'Our neighbours were kind enough to bring her to the top gate.'

39

With a feeling of utter helplessness Linda watched the older woman's eyes come towards her again, in their depth such a look of pain now that she wanted to cry out, 'What have I done?' but her attention was drawn to Ralph Batley, for he was giving her evidence as to the extent he was disturbed for he was attempting to light an empty pipe. Realising this he threw the spill into the fire and thrust the pipe into his pocket, and as if to cover up his mistake his tone and manner changed and he said with a poor attempt at lightness, 'I'm forgetting, you haven't met my mother.'

It seemed a little late for a formal introduction, but she forced a smile to her face and inclined her head towards the older woman.

Mrs Batley's response to this was to say quietly, 'You'll be wanting a wash, will you come up?' She turned about and walked across the hall, Linda's coat still on her arm, and Linda, picking up her case, followed her up the stairs, along the balcony to the far end. There Mrs Batley opened a door, saying over her shoulder, 'I hope you'll be comfortable.'

Linda moved into the room. Then turning quickly about she looked at the older woman appealingly and said under her breath, 'I'm sorry, Mrs Batley, I seem to have done something wrong. I'm sorry.'

Mrs Batley stared at her for a moment, then stepping into the bedroom and closing the door behind her, she continued to look at Linda for some seconds before she said, 'I'm sorry too, my dear. I'm sorry you had to start like this. One thing

I'll ask of you, keep away from the . . .' she paused here as if the name was too painful to utter, then brought out, 'the Cadwells.' She shook her head back and forth in small movements as she went on, 'If you want to work here and in peace, don't even mention their name. And another thing I would ask you, do your best for him, will you? I'll have to say this quickly for I wouldn't like him to think I was talking, but you see he never wanted a woman on the place, he was against it. But I was for it, and you're not quite what I expected.' She held up her hand in a gesture of appeal. 'No offence meant, but you don't look exactly cut out for this life. Still, time will tell . . . Come down when you're ready.' She turned about and went quickly out of the room, leaving Linda staring at the closed door in bewilderment.

Her mind was in a whirl. Unintentionally she had stirred up a hornets' nest and naturally she was getting stung. Then everyone she had met since coming off the bus had told her in one way or another that she was unsuitable, at least for the part she hoped to play on a farm. And now, Mrs Batley's words, 'He didn't want a woman on the place.'

Slowly she turned and looked about her, and what she saw was pleasing and held some comfort, for there was a wood fire burning in the grate, the furniture was old-fashioned but solid and shining. The bed was a single brass one, with large knobs dominating each corner. On it was a patchwork quilt but a patchwork with a difference for the patches had been made into a design which spoke

41

of countless hours of labour. The floor was bare wood and again highly polished and before the hearth and by the side of the bed were two clippie rugs, and in the corner near the black-faced wardrobe stood her trunk and two cases. This then was her room. It was comfortable and homely. And this house was to be her home for the coming year. She should be bubbling with happiness but all she wanted to do was sit down and cry.

She did not unpack but merely washed herself and combed her hair. She used little make-up at any time, but tonight she was more sparing with it than ever. Yet fifteen minutes later when she went quietly down the stairs it could have been that she had come down dressed for a ball, for all their eyes turned and watched her approach.

The table was set now with a white cloth and was laden with food and she said apologetically, 'I hope I haven't kept you waiting.'

'No, no, we're just going to start. Come and sit down.' Mrs Batley took her seat at one end of the table and indicated a chair to the right of her. On her left sat Uncle Shane and next to him Michael, and at the head of the table Ralph Batley took his seat.

'Say your grace.' Mrs Batley's head dropped forward as she spoke, and Shane and Michael's followed suit, but as Linda's head moved downwards she knew without looking at him that her employer's remained erect.

'Bless us, O Lord, and these Thy gifts which we

receive through Thy bounty, through Christ our Lord, Amen . . . Now would you like bacon and egg pie and a bit of ham, or this salted pork?' Mrs Batley pointed to a large flat dish.

'You have some of that, Maggie salts it herself.' This was Uncle Shane speaking, his fork pointing to the dish.

'I'll have some bacon and egg pie, please. Yes, and a little pork . . . thank you.'

Linda had always considered that she had a good appetite although she may not have shown it in her figure, but she could not attempt to eat half of the dishes that were offered to her. There was little talking during the meal except at one stage when Mrs Batley asked, 'Have your parents ever been in farming?'

'No, never . . . except my uncle, my mother's brother, he manages a farm in Sussex.'

'What is your father?'

'He's an accountant.'

'An accountant?' Mrs Batley made a small motion with her head, and Shane said, 'An accountant. Now there's a fine job for you, you don't soil your hands at that. No going out in the rain, hail and snow and getting the skin whipped off your nose. What possessed you to go in for this?'

'I'm fond of animals and I've always spent my holidays with my uncle and aunt, on the farm.'

No-one made any comment on this but Ralph Batley must have moved on his chair for the leg squeaked on the polished floor and Mrs Batley put in quickly, 'Well, if you've all had sufficient you can make a move to the fire.'

'I'll help you to clear.'

Linda's help was accepted by Mrs Batley without comment, and carrying a tray of dishes she followed the older woman to the door through which Ralph Batley had entered the hall and into what she found was a large kitchen.

Michael trotted back and forth carrying plates, and each time he entered the kitchen he cast his eyes shyly towards Linda, which she found both endearing and amusing.

When some time later she was standing at the sink drying the dishes that Mrs Batley had washed and was searching in her mind for something to say to break the awkward silence that was hanging over them, Mrs Batley said softly but with startling suddenness, 'Were you inside the house?'

'You mean . . . you mean the Cadwells'?' Linda's voice too was quiet.

'Yes.' Mrs Batley's hands moved rapidly in the water.

'Yes, I was in the hall.'

'Oh, you were.' The older woman flicked her hands downwards into the sink with a violent movement, and with a harsh bitterness but still under her breath she said, 'And I suppose you're comparing it with ours? We haven't got a hundred-pound carpet or a Parker-Knoll suite, nor all the fal-dals.'

Linda looked at Mrs Batley, who was now thrusting the china noisily into the cupboard.

44

She was not hurt at the attack, rather she found herself pitying this woman, and she lied as she said softly, 'I didn't notice how the place was furnished. All that I can remember about it is that the hall is somewhat similar in shape to yours with the stairs and balcony at the end . . . But one thing I did notice and that was the floor and furniture, they didn't gleam as yours do.'

Even if this latter had not been true she would have been bound to say it, for the woman before her, she felt, needed comforting. There was a loneliness emanating from her that touched some chord in Linda's own heart, for in spite of her youth she, too, knew what it was to feel lonely. The love in her own home had been so divided that it had never been able to bear fruit. Because of her father's jealousy her mother's affection towards her had only been doled out at opportune times. Her father, she had realised long ago, was a man who should never have had any family for he claimed the undivided attention of his wife. It had been painful to her to realise that her parents' life together was easier when she was out of the way, for her father was a different man when her mother did not show her any undue attention. You had to taste loneliness before you could recognise the form it took in others.

All Mrs Batley's movements were quick and jerky, and her voice was of the same pattern, and now, taking off her apron and flattening down her hair from its centre parting with both hands and making no reference to Linda's flattering remark, she said, 'Come along and sit down.'

As she spoke Ralph Batley came into the kitchen. He looked neither at his mother nor at Linda but went straight to the back door and, lifting his coat off it, he thrust his arms into it, and he was on his way out when his mother said, 'Will she do?'

For a moment Linda had the awful sensation that the question referred to herself, but when the reply came, 'She'll do all right,' she was forced to smile. It was the calf they were speaking about. It had yet to be proved whether she herself . . . would do all right.

For the first time Linda saw a flicker of a smile pass over the older woman's face as she turned to her and said, 'That's one mercy.' She said this as if the calf was a precious addition to the stock, not just another head to be counted.

In the living-room Shane was sitting with his feet stretched out to the blaze but he heaved himself up with rare courtesy on her arrival, saying, 'Sit yourself here, it's the best chair in the house.'

'No, no, I'll sit here next to you.'

'Do what he says, he's getting selfish enough.'

On this Shane MacNally turned on his stepsister, saying, 'Now, now, Maggie, tell all me sins but don't pin that one on me. I wouldn't be where I am this day if I could claim that quality.' The old man's jocular tone was tinged with sadness and Mrs Batley said briskly, 'Sit yourself down, man, and stop being sorry for yourself.'

'Aw, Maggie.' He was laughing again.

Mrs Batley was busy now setting up a framework to the side of the fireplace and Linda saw it was a half-finished rug. She watched her bring a carrier bag from a cupboard under the stairs and drop it on Shane's knee, saying, 'Get yourself busy, that'll keep you out of mischief. I've run out of clippings.'

'Oh, I'll help, Gran. I'll roll the balls.' The boy scrambled from the rug where he had been reading and took up a position, not next to the old man but to the side of Linda's feet. It wasn't the best position for catching the strip of cloth that Shane was cutting, and every now and again he had to lean his elbow on the floor and reach across her to grab at a fresh strip. He was methodically rolling the cloth into a ball when he spoke to her but still without looking at her. 'I lit your fire,' he said.

'Did you? That was kind of you, it was lovely to see a fire in my bedroom.' Linda smiled gently down on his bent head.

A short silence followed, broken only by the sound of the progger as Mrs Batley thrust it through the hessian. Then the boy's voice came again, scarcely above a whisper now. 'That was my mummy's room.'

'Michael, leave that be and get on with your reading.' The command came from Mrs Batley, and the boy, his head drooping, said, 'Yes, Gran,' then crawled slowly across the floor to the mat and lay down on his stomach. But he didn't pull his book towards him again. His elbow dug into the mat, his head resting on the palm of his hand, he lay gazing into the fire, and Linda's eyes went wonderingly to him. So she was in his mother's room . . . Where was his mother? At this moment her thoughts were lifted from the child as her employer once again came into the room. He was in his shirt-sleeves and wearing slippers now, and when the firelight fell full on his face it lent to it a warm colour. Linda found herself thinking as she looked at him that he could be good looking, almost handsome, yet he wasn't, his face was too stiff, too expressionless. Except for the moment in the cow byre when he had almost frightened her with the look in his eyes, his expression was fixed, embedded in a cold reserve.

Before he took his seat in the winged leather chair against the chimney wall he glanced down at the boy on the rug, then lifting his eyes quickly to his mother he tapped his cheekbone.

Linda had not guessed that the boy was crying, for from taking up his position on the mat he had not moved, not even his head. She had been watching him. But Ralph Batley apparently knew the signs.

Now she saw Mrs Batley nod quickly towards Shane and Shane look towards the boy. Following this the old man coughed and pulling himself slowly up in his chair he turned towards her and said in an off-hand way, 'Have you been about at all in your time . . . travelled much?'

Linda shook her head. 'Not a lot, I'm afraid. I've been to France twice and Italy, but I have usually spent my holidays on the farm as I said.'

'Ah, it's a pity. Now there's me, I've travelled

the world. I've been a bit of everything, cowboy, pirate, aye and sheriff. Aye, I have that, I've been a sheriff. I nearly hung a man once, I did an' all, and I nearly got hung meself into the bargain, for the fellow I was going to hang got away and if I hadn't had the fastest horse in Mexico it wouldn't be me here this night telling you.'

Although the old man was nodding at her and looking her full in the face he did not seem to be seeing her, nor did he seem to notice the boy as he turned from the fire and looked towards her. Yet she knew it was precisely for the boy's sake that he was talking. But as he went on she found herself becoming enthralled with his tales. She did not know whether to believe what she was hearing or not. Some of his exploits were of the giant-killer type, yet she felt there must be an element of truth in them. Mrs Batley was prodding at the canvas and her face looked relaxed, Ralph Batley was sitting smoking now, leaning well back in his chair, his gaze directed into the blaze. The expression on his face was a curious one, it wasn't only that he looked miles away; it was as if the essential part of him, the soul of him, was lost.

When Shane at last brought his tales to an end the boy had been sitting at his feet for some long time, and the old man looked down at him and said, 'Aye, Michael, if that mule hadn't gone lame on me and I'd reached that plot of land and staked my claim, I'd have been the richest man in the world this night, I would that. There now,' he leaned back in his chair, 'I've talked meself as dry as a fish . . . and just look at the clock.' He pointed. 'Time's up.'

'Is it bed?'

Although the boy did not speak with the Irish twang he used the same idiom as the old man and Shane laughed as he replied, 'Aye, bed it is, and that's where I'm going an' all, for me eyes are asleep in me sockets and if it wasn't that I knew me road I'd never find me way upstairs.' He slapped at the boy's cheek with a gentle slap, and as Linda looked at them a warmness enveloped her, there was something so endearing about them both.

'Wash your hands and face and have your milk.' Mrs Batley spoke to the boy while still prodding away at the mat and not until the child returned from the kitchen did she leave the frame. Then saying to him, 'Bid good night,' she walked slowly towards the staircase.

'Good night, Uncle.' Linda watched the boy support himself on the arm of the leather chair then reach up and plant a kiss on the side of Ralph Batley's cheek. The salutation was not returned but Ralph Batley's hand came on to his head and ruffled his hair as he said quietly, 'Good night, Michael.'

Now the child was standing in front of her, looking up at her from under his eyebrows in a manner she found characteristic of him. 'Good night, Miss,' he said shyly.

'Good night, Michael.'

From where she sat she watched him and his grandmother go up the stairs side by side, and her eyes followed them along the balcony until they were lost to her sight. She turned to find that Shane's eyes were on her, and his wrinkled lids blinked rapidly as he met her gaze. Pulling himself to his feet now he said, 'Well, I'll bid you good night an' all.'

'Good night, Mr MacNally.'

'Oh, bless us and save us, don't MacNally me, Shane is me name. If you want to give me a title then call me uncle.'

It was impossible not to be happy in this old man's company and she smiled widely and freely at him, saying again, 'Good night,' and adding now with a little stress, 'Uncle Shane.'

'That's more like it.' He jerked his head at her before turning towards the fireplace. 'Good night, boy.'

'Good night, Uncle.'

It seemed impossible that anyone could refer to the grim-faced man sitting deep in the big chair as a boy, yet perhaps only ten years or so ago he had been and looked a young man, a handsome young man that anyone could refer to as . . . boy, and not be so very far out.

When Shane reached the top of the stairs he met Mrs Batley and Linda heard their low exchange of 'Good nights', and on entering the hall again the older woman did not go to the mat frame but, turning towards the door that led to the kitchen, she said across the room, 'I'll make a drink.'

On this Ralph Batley rose heavily from his chair and, passing Linda without a glance, began taking

51

out the pegs that held the rug on the frame. Then he rolled it up and carried it across the hall to a cupboard under the stairs.

When he returned to the fireplace he did not resume his seat, but after knocking his pipe out, he kicked at the logs as he had done earlier in the evening, and stood, his back to her, staring down into the fire.

She sat waiting for him to speak; he must talk to her some time, talk about her appointment and tell her what was expected of her. Apart from the few remarks he had made to her in the byre and when she had first come into the room, he hadn't opened his mouth to her. Perhaps he was waiting for her to speak. She searched in her mind trying to make a choice of words with which to begin, but her mind seemed to have gone blank, and she was thankful when at this moment Mrs Batley returned to the room bearing a large brown jug in one hand and a tray in the other. When she had placed the jug on the hearth she said, 'Let it brew a while,' then she folded her hands one on top of the other on her stomach and for the first time that evening they became still, and looking at Linda she said, 'Well now, I'll bid you good night an' all. I'll give you a knock at seven. Good night then, and I hope you sleep sound.'

Linda rose to her feet, saying, 'Thank you, I'm sure I shall, Mrs Batley . . . good night.' She would have given anything to have added, 'I'm coming up, too,' but she knew they were being left together purposely to talk.

'Good night, son.'

Ralph Batley turned quickly now from the fire, his hand lifted in a protesting motion. Then as his mother turned away as if she had not noticed the gesture the hand dropped heavily to his side.

It was too much. He might be hating the situation but he needn't show it so plainly. Linda was turning from him when he said, 'Sit down.'

Reluctantly she faced him. He was pointing to her chair, and when she had seated herself again he took up his position, not in the seat close to the fire but in a chair to the left of her and slightly behind hers.

The fire crackled, the steam rose from the brown jug, and still neither of them spoke. How long the silence lasted she did not know, but her apprehension was overcome by a feeling of sudden and utter weariness helped considerably by the heat of the fire, and now, try as she might, she could not keep her eyes open. In this moment nothing seemed to matter very much. Even her employer temporarily lost his significance. Her lids had dropped and in another second she would have fallen fast asleep had not the peremptory question of 'Well?' brought her eyes straining wide.

As she turned her head and blinked at him she saw him rising from the chair and she said quickly, 'Oh, I'm sorry.'

'You're tired, we can talk in the morning.' His voice was neither concerned nor harsh, it was merely making a statement.

'No, no, I'm not really, it was just the fire.' She got to her feet.

'We go to bed early anyway.'

She made no move but stood looking at him, straight into his eyes, and he returned her look steadily for some seconds before he said, 'I don't think you'll like it here, the country is rough and the weather is vile, besides which the work is hard. I have only one man besides my uncle, and,' he paused before adding, 'as for entertainment, it's nil.'

She would not allow her eyes to waver from his and her voice was steady as she replied, 'I've worked long hours on my uncle's farm for a month at a time, and I don't mind isolation. As for entertainment, I manage a good deal of the time to entertain myself.' She knew that the last was not strictly true for if there was one thing she loved above all else it was to dance.

'You're very fortunate to be so easily satisfied. You must have acquired a great deal of wisdom in a short time.'

His tone was sarcastic and made her chin lift, and to hide her feelings and prevent her making a cutting retort in reply she was turning from him, when he said, 'I'm sorry. I also forgot to say that we're raw and uncultured up here.'

So quickly did she turn her head to look at him that she found him off his guard for a moment. His face had suddenly relaxed and there was a sadness about it that reminded her of the expression on Michael's face when his grannie had stopped him talking about his mother, and he had turned to the fire and cried silently in his loneliness. It came to her that this was the dominating factor she had found in the few hours she had been in this house – loneliness. The loneliness that was deep within Mrs Batley and would not allow her hands to be still for a moment, the loneliness of the boy who was forbidden to talk about his mother, the loneliness of Uncle Shane living on dreams, and the loneliness of the man before her. She had felt his loneliness from the first, although she had not been able to put a name on it right away.

She had an almost uncontrollable urge to put her hand out to him in comfort. Her voice was low when she said 'Good night' before turning quickly from him and going up the stairs.

As she reached the balcony and glanced sideways down into the hall, she saw that he was just moving away from the foot of the stairs. Parallel with her now, he walked towards the fireplace as she walked towards her room at the end of the balcony.

Once inside she did not immediately busy herself by getting ready for bed, nor yet by unpacking her luggage, but slowly she sat down on the rug before the fire, and staring into the dying mushed wood she asked herself what awful thing had happened between the two families she had met within the last few hours to create the hate that existed between them. Feuds weren't infrequent between farmers over land and rights of way, she knew. Also there could be jealousy over stock. But the feeling between the Cadwells and the occupants of this house was something different. It was something deep and menacing. The loneliness that she had sensed in each of the Batleys was not a separate thing, it was a rope binding them together, and in her mind's eye she saw the rope stretching across the cliffs and down the valley and into the heart of the Cadwells' house, the house that was almost a twin to this one, so much so that evidently it had sprung from the same idea, from the same plan. And people didn't build alike in hate. It was usually friendship, deep-linked friendship and admiration that brought about a similarity in dwellings, and only some deep wrong could have forced the houses and their occupants apart.

She did not know who was in the right and who was in the wrong, but already in her heart she knew where her sympathies lay . . .

2

It must have been around five-thirty in the morning that Linda awoke with the feeling that she was cold. When she had got into bed she had been as warm as toast, in fact she had felt there were far too many clothes on, but now she was so cold that she could well imagine that she was lying out on the hillside under canvas with only one blanket covering her. This then was what they meant by . . . weather . . . and weather. Sometimes the dawns in the south had been cold but nothing compared with this. She put her head under the bedclothes and curled herself into a ball. Almost immediately she heard the distinct sound of someone moving about outside and she lifted her head from under the clothes, struck a match and looked at her watch. It was only half-past five. He was certainly about early, perhaps something had gone wrong with the calf. As she thought of this she heard the creak of a door opening on the landing and then the padding of footsteps going down the stairs, accompanied by a soft cough. Surely that couldn't be Mrs Batley, not at half-past five in the morning!

She heard no more after this until a knock on

her door and a voice saying, 'Are you awake? It's seven,' brought her upright in bed.

She murmured, 'Yes, yes, I'm awake,' and realised with a start that she must have fallen into a deep sleep in spite of the cold.

The comfort that the room had held last night was gone. Her breath hung on the air, the water she washed in was icy cold and she guessed that she had never dressed so quickly in her life before. The whole proceedings from start to finish did not take more than ten minutes. At the speed she had dressed she made her bed and left the room tidy, and as she stepped out on to the landing the hands of the big old grandfather clock, which stood against the wall to the right, had not reached a quarter-past seven.

Although her only desire was to get near the fire she stopped at the head of the stairs and looked down into the hall. The fire was blazing, the black kettle was singing on the hob, the long refectory table was laid for breakfast, and in the far corner of the room Mrs Batley was on her hands and knees polishing vigorously at the floor.

The older woman looked up as Linda came down the stairs, and she paused in her rubbing for a moment to say, 'By, you're early down!'

'Early?' Linda, reaching the foot of the stairs, looked about her. 'I should say I was very late. You look as if you've got a day's work done already.'

'Well, not quite.' Mrs Batley was rubbing vigorously again. 'It being Sunday I don't rise until half-past five or thereabouts. Other mornings I'm up at five.'

'My goodness.' Linda's tone spoke her admiration.

But Mrs Batley thrust it aside saying, 'Oh, there's no merit in that, I can't sleep after five, I never have been able to, it's what you've been used to.' She paused, then added, 'But I meant you were quick down. Breakfast's not till half-past seven, but pour yourself some tea out if you want it.' The rubbing went on.

Then as Linda stood in front of the fire, thankful for the glowing warmth on her back and the hot tea sliding down inside her, Mrs Batley asked, 'You warm enough in the night?'

'I was until about dawn; it was rather chilly then.'

'Yes,' Mrs Batley nodded her confirmation, 'it gets nippy between four and five.'

It was just as Linda finished her tea that she heard the back door open and voices in the kitchen. Instantly she made out Shane's merry voice and the deep, restrained voice of her employer. But she was surprised to hear Michael's voice and she was thinking, 'Poor child, to be got up so early,' when Michael, running into the room, disabused her of the opinion that he had been made to rise with his elders, for he shouted excitedly to his grandmother, 'She's lovely, Gran, and walking about, and Uncle Ralph says I can give her a name.'

He was opposite the fire now and, becoming aware of Linda, he pulled up sharply. Turning his eyes full on her but looking not at her face but at her legs, he exclaimed in high pleasurable tones, 'What long legs you've got; they're just like the calf's.'

'Michael!'

Michael's voice was cut off abruptly and he looked towards his uncle. Ralph Batley was standing within the doorway and he added curtly, 'Sit up to the table.'

On this the boy's head drooped slightly and he turned about and took his place at the table, and as Linda looked at the pathetically narrow little back she felt a momentary anger against her employer. What right had he to squash the child like that; it had been the same last night. One couldn't say that the boy was afraid of his uncle, but he obeyed him mutely as if he was some kind of personal god.

For a moment she forgot her apprehension at the coming talk with her employer, a talk that was inevitable for she must know the extent of her duties on the farm, and she was filled with an urge to oppose him in defence of the boy and so she said, on a light note, 'Wait until you put on breeches, Michael, and you'll find your legs will grow three inches right away.'

Michael screwed quickly round on the chair and was about to speak again when Ralph Batley said, but quietly now, 'Go and help your grannie fetch in the plates.'

'Yes, Uncle.'

As the boy slid swiftly off his chair Shane came breezily into the hall exclaiming, 'Did I hear talk of breeches? Oh, hello there.' He beamed across the room towards Linda. 'Did you sleep well?'

'Yes, very well, thank you.' Linda returned his smile, and he went on, 'Did I hear you say that breeches make your legs longer? Well, I can vouch for that meself, I can indeed, for without me own here,' he slapped his thigh, 'it would look to all appearances as if I was hobbling about on me knees.'

Linda laughed outright and Shane laughed with her, and at the peak of his laughter he looked at her breeches much as Michael had and commented, 'I'd say you've got fine legs for a horse.' Then his head went further back and he cried, 'You know what I mean.'

'If we can stop discussing Miss Metcalfe's legs for a moment, Uncle Shane, I think we might start breakfast, the porridge is on the table.'

There was no anger in the words. It would have been better if there had been, the cut they made in Linda would have been less deep. She felt as if she was actually shrinking under her employer's gaze. His grey eyes looking at her now held that cold, impersonal look she remembered from last night, as if there was not an emotion yet created that could bring warmth into them. When his gaze dropped from her she did not go to the table and take her place, but she went into the kitchen to assist Mrs Batley and also to give herself time to regain her composure before sitting down to breakfast opposite to him.

The meal was passed almost in silence and, as last night, Linda was amazed at the amount of food that was consumed. The house itself might be without its luxuries and modern conveniences but the amenities of the table were certainly not neglected, in fact they were even lavish.

When the meal was over and she went to help clear the table Mrs Batley said quietly, 'That's all right . . . leave that to me . . . I would get out.'

Taking this broad hint she hurried upstairs and, snatching up her duffle coat, she was out on the landing within a matter of seconds. Undoubtedly it was her speed that brought her within hearing of the conversation, for Uncle Shane's low, rumbling murmur came to her from the hall saying, placatingly, 'Hold your hand a while, man. Think of the saying the iron fist in the velvet glove . . . although mind, I'll admit, when I saw her standing there with the firelight on her she looked for all the world like some picture in a magazine trying to entice you away to Switzerland for the winter sports.'

'Exactly.'

That one word brought Linda's hand tightly across her mouth. Exactly! It spoke volumes. There came back to her mind Mr Cadwell's words, 'He's wanting a cart-horse and he's getting a year-old filly.' But why couldn't he wait and judge her on her work and not go totally by appearances . . . Well, she would show him that she was no year-old filly.

Her attitude of mind was expressed in the squaring of her shoulders as she marched noisily to the top of the stairs, but as she descended them and watched the two men walking towards the kitchen door her courage wavered and slithered downwards and she warned herself: Go steady, go quiet, don't get off to a bad start.

When she reached the kitchen Shane was saying, 'I'll go off to the top and run another wire along them spiles.' He did not speak to her, but as he went out of the door he jerked his head sideways towards her, and even with such a mundane action he had the power to convey warmth, and this heartened her. Whoever was against her, Shane was for her.

'You'd better start by seeing the buildings.' Ralph Batley was buttoning up his coat and he did not look at her as he spoke, and knowing his feelings towards her, she found difficulty in even emitting the syllable 'Yes.'

The side door of the house led on to a paved square. It was bordered on two sides by a dry-stone wall but opened out on to grassland, and as she stepped from the shelter of the wall her eyes darted about her in amazement for she had the impression that she could see to the ends of the earth, so open was the land before her.

There, some distance to the left, she glimpsed the sea sparkling under the hard winter sun. But her employer had turned sharply to the right and she turned, too, keeping just slightly behind him. Now they were in the farmyard, and as her torch had indicated last night, she saw it was not only as clean as farmyards go, but scrupulously so.

'This is the main shed.' He opened the door and stood somewhat reluctantly aside to let her pass, and now he was behind her speaking in rasping, low, gruff tones as if determined to get it over and done with. 'We have eighteen milkers, all Ayrshires.'

She looked at the empty byres and asked in surprise, 'Are they out?'

'Yes, of course. They're hardy. They need to be up here.'

She closed her eyes for a second. Would he never stop emphasising that everything had to be hardy to exist on this farm?

She had seen the parlour system of milking and the latest modern machinery. Here nothing was modern, but even so she wanted to exclaim on the beautiful condition of the byres . . . they were spotless. She wanted to remark on the cards in their little slots attached to the posts, each bearing the name of a cow, but she couldn't bring herself to say a word.

He passed her now and walked down the length of the cowshed to enter the dairy. Here the cleanliness was almost of clinical standard. The urns were gleaming, the wooden table taking up one wall was the whitest she had ever seen. A marble slab along the farthest end of the dairy held an array of patters and wooden rollers all laid ready to hand. No attitude of his could stifle now her admiration and she exclaimed, 'Why, this is lovely.' And to her it was lovely, for such cleanliness touched her as poetry or music would touch another.

'My mother sees to this.' He was away ahead of her again, and as she followed him she thought, I might have known, yet she questioned: Where on earth does she find the time with all that housework and cooking to do?

She was now walking behind him through a narrow open passageway and into another yard, a stockyard. Here, hemmed in by three high walls, were about a dozen head of Galloway cattle, all, with the exception of two, very good specimens. These two had bare patches on their rumps which they were endeavouring to enlarge by rubbing their haunches against the corners of the hay feeder in the centre of the stockyard. The sight of them enjoying this recreation brought Ralph Batley striding towards them, and hitting out right and left with the flat of his hand, he thumped their rumps, crying, 'Away out of it! Away, Judy! You too, Beth.'

For the moment Linda entirely forgot her employer. Here were twelve Galloways, fine animals – they looked as good as any her uncle had charge of – and she was to work with them for the next year. Perhaps she would help to bring their calves into the world as she had helped with the one last night. She became lost in the happy thought, and she gave evidence of it when she spoke, for, quite unthinking, she voiced her opinion of the feeder by placing her hand on it and saying, 'They'll always rub on this kind. My uncle got rid of his. You wa . . . ant . . .' Her voice trailed off as she was suddenly made aware of what she was saying by Ralph Batley's narrow gaze fixed on her. And now she stammered in apology. 'What I meant was they're apt to rub against this.' Her fingers fluttered over the sharp corner of the feeder. And she went from bad to worse by quoting some information she had picked up from her uncle. 'I suppose it's because their skin gets irritable when they're fed too much pro . . . tein.' Again her voice trailed away. Her eyes dropped from his and miserably she was turning about when his voice held her.

'Do go on. I have the wrong type of feeder, I am feeding too much protein. . . Do go on, there's a lot I would like to learn about this type of cattle.'

Her body made a quick jerk and she was facing him, but she did not raise her eyes, nor even her head as she said stiffly, 'I'm sorry, it's not my intention to try to teach you anything, I've come here to learn. What . . . what I said was . . . not meant . . .' Her head was drooping lower again when his next remark, and the tone of his voice, whipped it upwards as he said, 'Well, I hope at this juncture we're not going to have any tears.'

Her teeth were clenched so hard that her jaw bones seemed locked as she stared back at him, glared back would be a more correct definition of the look which she now gave him, and her voice showed her anger as she said, 'I am not given to crying. You needn't be afraid, Mr Batley, you will not have to contend with tears in my case.'

Their eyes were hard held, nor did they speak for some seconds, and only her anger was sustaining her to look back unflinchingly at this man who she was telling herself at this moment was worse than a dozen Mr Cadwells rolled into one.

'I would not waste your energy in giving way to temper, Miss Metcalfe, you'll need it all for your work.' He swung away from her, and she drew in a deep breath and let out a long-drawn 'Ooh!' Last night she had had it in her to feel sorry for him. She felt then that he was lonely, sort of lost. But at this moment she wished she had never set eyes on him.

He was holding the gate open for her and she stalked past him.

To add to her discomfort, he said, 'We're not going that way.' He was standing at one end of the passage and she at the other. Again she drew in a deep breath. And now, when she saw that he was amused in a cynical kind of way, she felt really furious.

Through door after door she followed him, and she made no comment on anything he said until they came to a great barn. Garaged just within the entrance stood an old Jeep, and in a far corner, lying half-way in a straw-filled box, was a Collie dog. One back leg, Linda saw, was bandaged. But even with this handicap the dog tried to hobble towards its master as he moved forward. She watched Ralph Batley gently lead the sick animal back towards the kennel again, saying in much the same tone as he had used to the cow last night, 'There, there, now. Take it easy, Jess.'

For the moment forgetting her own feelings, Linda found herself kneeling down by the dog and asking, 'What happened?'

'A trap.'

'A trap?' she repeated. 'Oh, the poor thing.' She stroked the dog's head, and as she was licked vigorously in return she remembered that she had seen no other dogs about the place, which was odd, and this caused her to ask, 'Have you only the one?'

'Yes.' She felt him straighten up, and she was still looking at the dog when he said, 'We had another, it was poisoned a fortnight ago.'

'Oh no!' She turned her head slowly and looked up at him, and was not surprised now by the grimness she saw on his face.

In the stillness that followed, her mind swung to the Cadwells but she dismissed the thought. They didn't look the kind of people to stoop to petty cruelties like that, poisoning a dog and setting a trap. Likely it was someone after game of some kind . . . But you didn't lay poison to catch game. She shook her head at herself.

Ralph Batley was speaking now from where he was standing near the Jeep, and after giving the dog one last tender pat she got to her feet and went towards him.

'We fill up out of here every day or so.' He pointed to where the bales of hay were stacked deep in the barn, which she saw had two floors for at least half its length, the upper floor being accessible by means of an open ladder set against the right-hand wall. 'The feed goes into the corrugated hut at yon end of the main byre, it's easier to get at these dark mornings . . . Well,' he turned towards the entrance of the barn, adding, 'I think that's the sum total of the buildings. Now for the land.'

She was walking abreast of him now, and as they approached the end of the barn she noticed a flight of wooden steps going up to a door in a brick building. This building was attached to the end of the barn and as he had not taken her into this place she looked up and remarked casually, 'Is that the granary?'

He did not follow her look nor did his eyes turn from their forward gazing as he said, 'No, the grain is kept in an off-shoot of the house.'

'Oh.' She did not press the matter and say, 'Well, what do you keep up there?' Later on she would take a walk up the steps to the loft and find out for herself.

They were going in the direction of the house again when he stopped and said, 'There's the bull . . . And Sep Watson. You'd better meet them both.' He was talking over his shoulder to her as he continued, 'As for the bull, I'd give him a wide berth for the moment. Later on, when he gets used to you about the place . . .' His voice trailed off as he opened a gate, and she thought, Well, he does think there will be a later on, that's something.

When she first saw Sep Watson standing next to the bull within the strong-walled bull box she was immediately struck by the incongruous similarity between them, for the man had the same points as the Galloway, his body was heavy and his legs were short. His face, too, was short, in his case with a compressed look, and seemed to spread downwards into his thick powerful neck. And to make the similarity almost uncanny his ears were pointed sharply outwards. They were for all the world like 'cocky wee lugs' as the ears of a good Galloway were termed. But whereas these points might make a prize bull they, on the other hand, made for a repulsive man.

'This is Miss Metcalfe, Sep.' The introduction was made in a flat, almost inflectionless, voice.

The man left the animal which he was grooming and came slowly towards the iron barred gate. He did not open it but looked over it, and for no reason she could explain, for his tone was very civil as he said, 'How do?' she felt the blood rushing to her face.

'How d'you do?' She inclined her head stiffly.

'Miss Metcalfe will give you a hand with the milking this afternoon, Sep.'

'Aye, all right.' The man looked at Ralph Batley and nodded.

'You can show her the ropes.'

'Aye.' Sep Watson now turned his glance on Linda and added with a grin that showed a set of surprisingly large white teeth, 'Pleased to, Miss.'

'Thank you.'

There was nothing offensive in either the man's words or manner yet Linda was experiencing a feeling of panic, the thought of standing near this man somehow terrified her.

'Here Leader!' Ralph Batley called the bull towards him, and it came shambling heavily forward, pushing Sep Watson aside in the process, which only caused the man to laugh. 'Good fellow! There's a boy.' Ralph Batley fondled the animal's head and like some great dog its tongue came out and slobbered him. It was evident to Linda that her employer was very proud of this animal.

When with a final pat he turned away she followed him, and they continued as before in the direction of the house, but when they came to it he did not turn right or left but kept straight on, and it seemed to Linda as she walked rapidly by his side that their destination could be the horizon, for in front of them there lay nothing but the sea and the cliff edge, and Ralph Batley walked almost to the brink of it before he stopped. Looking down she saw that from his very toes started a line of steps. They were cut out of the solid rock and dropped steeply down the face of the cliff until they reached the cove below. And the sight of the crescent of dry sand, with the jagged walls of rock on each side stretching out into the water to form a sheltered harbòur, brought from her an involuntary exclamation of delight, for she could see herself in the late hot evenings of the coming summer plunging into the cool waters of the lovely little bay.

The exclamation or something in her face must have conveyed her thoughts to Ralph Batley, for immediately he said, 'Don't be misled with what you are seeing, that small stretch of sand down there is the only innocent thing connected with our cove.'

Refusing to have her dreams entirely shattered, she remarked somewhat dreamily, 'It looks beautiful to me.'

'It's the worst piece of coastline for miles; you'll see what I mean when the tide's out.'

'But the boats.' She pointed to where a sailing dinghy and a small cruiser were bobbing on the sunlit water some distance from the shore. 'How do they get in and out?'

'They don't – at least so little that it makes no odds. The dinghy we have to edge carefully between the rocks to get her through the gap out into the open sea. The cruiser can only get out through the gap at certain periods when the tide is coming in and the weather calm. But she's rotting now and hasn't been out for years.'

'What a shame.'

He passed no comment on her remark but said, 'Don't go down these steps when there's a wind of any kind, there's air currents sliding along the face of the cliff that will lift you up before you know where you are.'

She looked at the steps. It was likely quite true what he said, but she also felt he was exaggerating the danger. He was going to allow her no pleasure to look forward to. The weather here was tough . . . the life was tough . . . and now the scenery was not only tough but spelt danger. All of a sudden she found that she could laugh at his tactics, and this fact acted like a tonic. If she could laugh at him she would not fear him, and not being afraid of him her work would be much better. She had the inclination to whistle but checked it.

They had now turned from the cliff edge and were going, she realised, in the direction of Surfpoint Bay and the road she should have taken last night. But they had not gone more than half a mile along the cliff top when the open land suddenly ceased and she saw the barrier of wire fencing. It was topped with barbed wire similar to that she had noticed last night, beginning at the cliff edge. She just stopped herself in time from exclaiming, 'Is this the Cadwell boundary?'

Yet once again he seemed to read her thoughts, for without looking or indicating the fencing with even a motion of his hand, he said flatly, 'This is the extent of our land.'

The distance between the wire fencing and the edge of the cliff at this point was about thirty feet, but at the other end she knew that it was not more than fifteen feet and by the looks of things it would become narrower with each storm, for at the far point the cliff was evidently crumbling away. Instinctively she knew that the land here had not always been fenced in. At one point there had been a good road leading down into Surfpoint Bay. There must be virtually a right of way along the cliff top, and this had been left, but only barely. For the moment her curiosity got the better of her and she wanted to probe the reason why this should be and so she said, 'Wouldn't it be a quicker way to take the milk down if you could use this road?'

'I do use it.'

She looked at him, her eyes wide, and then she remembered the little girl down at Mrs Weir's being sent on to the cliff top to see if Mr Batley's car was coming. He was mad, he must be stark staring made to take the Jeep along this road . . . and the cliff crumbling. She shuddered, and then she asked quietly, 'What about the back road?'

She was daring his anger she knew in referring to her acquaintance with this road, for it would remind him of how she had come to the farm. But his voice was still impersonal as he replied, 'It's four miles or more that way and time counts.'

The subject was closed. He turned abruptly about, and now he led the way across fields that hadn't the appearance of fields to her mind for they were studded with crops of rock, and again fields that were but the steep sides of fells. Some of the sloping land was scree covered and showed the tracks of sheep. She was about to broach the subject of sheep when quite suddenly they came upon a valley. It was deep and wide and showed immediately to be good grass land, at least the best she had seen so far. When her eyes ranged down it to the left there was an unbroken vista right to the horizon . . . that meant the valley opened out on the cliff top . . . but when she turned her gaze upwards through the valley she saw the gleam of wire . . . the boundary again. Why was this valley, this pleasant, sheltered valley that was surely an asset to the Batley farm, cut off by a boundary running across what was apparently its middle – for far beyond the wire fence she could see the hills rising on either side.

She brought her gaze from the land and glanced at Ralph Batley, and although she was certain that his bitterness against the Cadwells was not primarily concerned with land, she could gauge his feelings about this particular matter from her own at the moment, for she felt incensed that the only decent pastureland she had so far come upon was mostly denied to the Batleys and evidently owned by the Cadwells when the location pointed the other way.

Beyond the valley the land rose steeply and the hills took on the appearance of small mountains, and whenever she reached the top of a rise there to the left lay the sea and the jagged coastline.

At one point they came upon a flock of sheep, well over a hundred she reckoned, all black-faced Cheviots. They were skirting the scampering animals when Ralph Batley, pulling up sharply, cried, 'No, no, not again!'

The words had a desperate sound, and she followed his gaze towards where a sheep was trotting on the outskirts of the flock. She knew very little about sheep but it did not require much knowledge for her to realise what it was he was dreading. Foot-rot, which showed itself first in lameness — and definitely that sheep was lame. Yet on this rough ground it could have got its hoof caught in a cleft.

He was hurrying on now, and she was surprised that he made no attempt to round up the lame sheep. She was behind him when they climbed yet another hill, and just as she reached the top she saw him cup his hands to his mouth and call, 'Shane! Uncle!'

There in the distance was the old man wiring staves together. He turned on the hail and waved his hand and, dropping the railing, came hurrying over the distance.

When they were still many yards apart Ralph Batley shouted, 'Do you know one's lame?'

Shane, stopping in his tracks, exclaimed, 'No, begod no! They were fine and well yesterday, I looked them over in the valley.'

'They're just beyond the rise and one of them's limping badly.'

Shane was now close to them and his old hairy face showed his concern as he said, 'In the name of God, man, how could they get it? The land's as clean as a new pin and we went over them foot by foot no more than two weeks ago.'

Linda watched Ralph Batley rubbing his hand roughly up and down his cheek. His gaze was now pointed away from the old man towards the sea, and she wondered if she was hearing aright when she thought he said, 'There are such things as wishing.' And she knew that she hadn't been mistaken when Shane turned on him with surprising roughness as he cried, 'Be your age, man. Who's talking like a mad Irishman now? I'm the one who thinks up spells and omens and witches' wishings. If it's only a witch doctor we have to contend with then we'll fix him, never fear.'

There was a moment's silence, then the old man gently put out his rough hand and, gripping his nephew by the arm, shook him almost playfully saying, 'Come on now, come on.'

Linda watched Ralph Batley turn his eyes slowly towards his uncle and she knew a moment's curiosity and surprise not unmixed with sympathy when she heard him say, 'They've only got wishing left, they've used up every other device.'

'Well, you're strong enough to stand up to that. Come on now, come on. If the worst comes to the worst we can round up the whole flock and dip 'em again.'

A short while later, walking with her silent employer back over the fells, Linda attempted to sort out her feelings. She realised that her main feeling at the moment was surprise and this was caused by the thought that this stern, taciturn man should need any reassurance whatsoever, for he seemed not only a law unto himself in his own domain, but over-brimful of self-confidence.

Then there was her curiosity; this, she knew, was a natural desire to get to the bottom of the reason for the feud that existed between the families of the Cadwells and the Batleys. And last, and she would have said least, the grudging feeling of sympathy this man evoked in her. On the face of it this last emotion was utterly absurd, for at the moment her employer looked and sounded as if he stood as little in need of sympathy as did his own bull.

Linda had not been working with Sep Watson for more than an hour before she discovered a number of things about him. Apart from the knowledge that he was a married man and had five children and lived in a cottage four miles across the fells in the direction of Longhorsley, she found that he was a talker. But in spite of this she realised he was also a very good worker. Although his movements were slow and heavy the work seemed to dissolve under his practised hands. But her main discovery was that Sep Watson did not like his employer.

The first indication she had of this was when she was standing looking at a particularly nice cow and Sep Watson's elbow gave her a quick dig in the back and his voice, issuing from the corner of his mouth, whispered, 'Look out, no standing around, here's God Almighty comin'.' When, in the next moment, Ralph Batley entered the cowshed and she heard Sep Watson's servile tone as he answered him, she thought to herself, He's a crawler.

When Ralph Batley had left the cowshed without even a glance in her direction, Sep Watson, busy again with the milking, turned his slanting glance on her and remarked, 'You don't want to let him get you down. Take my tip, "Yes sir" him and "No sir" him, and then go your own way. If you're cute you'll manage it.'

As Linda looked down into the horrible grinning face she realised that this man already accepted that she was on his side of the fence . . . she was a worker and so was naturally opposed to the boss. Then with his head pressed into the side of the cow and his face hidden from her he mumbled, 'He's always got my goat, right since he was a lad.'

'Have you worked here since you were a boy then?' Linda's repulsion was for the moment overcome by her curiosity.

'Aye, on and off, like. I take a spell away for two or three years some place else, but I always come back. I worked for his father. Oh, his father was

78

a lad. Huh!' He jerked his head upwards now on a laugh. 'By! he was. He could carry more drink than four dray horses. Aye, those were the days, things used to happen then. The old boss and Jack Cadwell – he's got Crag End Farm – they were up to all larks. They were pals . . . just like their fathers afore them that built the houses . . . but they were always fightin' and gamblin'.' His head went further back still and he gazed upwards towards the roof of the byre as he said, 'I'll never forget the day he gambled the south side away, right from the cliff top round to the valley.'

Linda's eyes were stretched wide as she repeated, 'He gambled the land away?'

'Well, sort of. Jack Cadwell had always wanted the valley stretch but Batley would never sell an inch of ground. But over the years he piled up a tidy sum to Jack Cadwell in borrowing, and one night they had a big drink up and they played cards for it. If Batley won he would be cleared of his debt and keep his land, if he lost the land would go to Cadwell to pay for the debt. It was as easy as that. You've only to look at the cliff top to know who won.'

'It's fantastic.'

Slowly Linda lifted the pail of milk from the man's side, and he repeated, 'Aye, it's fantastic, but that's nowt. Oh, my! if you knew the history of this family it would make the hair in your ears waggle. It would make a book, aye, it would that, but if anybody read it they wouldn't believe it. No, they wouldn't.'

Linda carried the milk into the dairy. So that was it. The fact that part of the land had been gambled away in a drunken orgy was enough to embitter anyone.

She could understand her employer's attitude a little more now. Yet, as Sep Watson suggested, it was far from being the real cause of the bitterness. She was filled with curiosity and wished that the cowman was other than he was and she could talk to him, even question him, but such was the effect the man had on her that she knew she would never be able to bring herself to question him with regards to her employer and his family. Yet she also knew she would be unable to close her ears to his prattle, for she might live in the Batley house for the next year and be no nearer to the deep sorrows that affected them . . . they were not the talking kind, even Uncle Shane with his kindliness would be restrained, she felt, in discussing the family's affairs.

It was just as they were about to finish for the night that the man supplied her with yet another bit of information. It concerned Michael. The child had been trailing her footsteps for most of the afternoon and he only left her side when his grannie's voice hailed him from the house. From just inside the door of the cowshed Sep Watson watched the boy running across the darkening yard and he remarked in an undertone, 'Taken to you, hasn't he?'

When Linda made no comment he went on, 'He wants a mother.' Then he laughed a deep, thick, quiet laugh, and his voice was quiet too as he continued, 'Not that you look the mother type to me. Well, you know what I mean. I can tell you I got a bit of a gliff when I saw you. You don't look cut out for this ramp, although mind, I'll say this, you're not dim.'

'Thank you.'

Linda's voice was small and cold and it brought another quiet, deep laugh from him. Then as he pulled on his coat he said. 'It's any port in a storm with Michael, and it's natural, I suppose, all bairns should have a mother. Like animals, they need a bit of snuffling now and again. But there, he wouldn't have got much snuffling from his own mother, she wasn't the type to snuffle.'

He turned and looked at her now, knowing that he had whetted her curiosity, and he stood waiting, and in spite of her feelings towards him and her intention of never questioning him about her employer or his family she could not restrain herself from asking, 'Is she dead?'

'Dead? No, she's very much alive. She was always alive, she took after her old man. She was his favourite and lad mad since she could walk. She hooked Lance Cadwell, he was the middle one of the three sons. Old Cadwell nearly went up the lum for he had somebody else cut out for Lance, somebody with money. The match was hopeless right from the start and within a year or so they were divorced. Young Patricia married again when the child was around six, but the new husband didn't take to the lad and he took bad . . . the kid, nerves, so he was packed off here.' He jerked his head upwards and exclaimed, 'Oh, you don't know the half of it.' Then putting his hand out swiftly and chucking her under the chin he said, 'You're interested, aren't you? You haven't been able to make the set-up out. I know. We'll have to get together one of these days and I'll tell you the whole history, eh?'

Linda had darted back from him, and on this his squat face seemed to expand further as he grinned and exclaimed softly, 'There's one thing I've found out about you . . .' he paused, holding her eyes for some moments before finishing . . . 'you've got a lot to learn . . . Good night.'

When he went through the door Linda leaned against the wall and closed her eyes. She was no fool. That last remark hadn't meant that she had a lot to learn about farming. She knew what he meant by it and the thought terrified her, the man terrified her. It was just the essence of bad luck that her co-worker had to be a man of Sep Watson's make-up and mentality.

'What's the matter?'

'Oh!' She nearly leapt from the wall.

'What is it, are you feeling ill?' Ralph Batley was standing close to her, his face not a foot from her own, and she had to take two great gulps of air before she could bring out, 'No, no. I'm not ill.'

'Then what is it?' He was looking at her with a slightly mystified look, and then she saw his eyes move swiftly in the direction of the door and it was some seconds before he spoke. 'Was it Watson?' he asked. 'Did he— ?'

'No. No, it wasn't. It's nothing.'

On no account must she say anything against the cowman. She knew within a little how much her employer relied on this man, for he was a very efficient worker, and should she infer anything there would undoubtedly be trouble. Yet, she told herself and rather ruefully now, the trouble wouldn't be for Sep Watson, but would more than likely descend on her own head. She knew that her employer, to use his own words, had never wanted a woman about the place, so it was natural that should any trouble ensue between her and the cowman he wouldn't get the blame. Yet as she raised her eyes to Ralph Batley's face there came a small doubt into her mind, for his expression for once had lost its hardness, and the curve of his mouth was softened as he said, 'Manners in general around here are apt to be rough, but should Watson at any time say anything to you that you don't like, come straight to me . . . you understand?'

She nodded slowly, then said, 'But he didn't – he . . .'

She was silenced by his uplifted hand and he accompanied this gesture with, 'All right, all right, we'll leave it at that.' Then after a moment he ended, 'Now go in and have something to eat. You can tell my mother that my uncle and I will not be in for some time and not to wait for us. You can also tell her it isn't rot . . . it was just one lame.'

'Oh, I'm glad.' She smiled at him, then quickly lifting her duffle coat from a hook, she put it on and pulling the hood about her head, she went out and across the yard and into the house.

It was close on seven o'clock before Ralph Batley and Shane came in, and at the sound of their approach Mrs Batley threw down the sock that she was mending and hurried towards the scullery. Linda, from where she sat to the side of the fire, listened to her voice talking low and rapidly. But two words only could she make out, and these were, 'Say nothing,' and as the words came to her she looked down on the boy lying sound asleep within the circle of her arms.

After tea the child had edged himself off the mat and to her feet, and brought with him his books and his engine. Next he had knelt at her side with his elbows resting on her knees. His following move was to sit on the edge of her chair and in such a position that it had been natural for her to put her arm about him. It was when his grannie was out of the room that he had sat on her knee. He had not looked at her as he took up this position but had talked rapidly, explaining the picture in the book he held close to his face.

On entering the hall Mrs Batley's step had been checked, and over the distance she had looked at them. Then without making any comment at all she resumed her seat and took up her darning, and in some subtle way Linda knew that the older woman was hurt at the sight of her grandchild being cradled by a stranger. It should be her daughter who was sitting here nursing the boy.

Shane was apparently obeying orders when he entered the room for he said nothing but, 'Ah, well, I'm glad that's over for I'm as hungry as ten bullocks.' Studiously he avoided even glancing in her direction. But when Ralph Batley entered the room he did look at her, yet she could gauge nothing at all from his expression, for his face was wearing the blank look which seemed to be habitual to it.

Michael stirred within her arms and snuggled closer to her, but Linda sat without moving. She was very much aware of the two men to the side of her eating their meal. She was also aware that although Ralph Batley from his position at the table had a view of her and the boy, he never once now looked in their direction.

Mrs Batley was at her darning again. After some time had elapsed and there came the sound of a chair scraping the floor as it was pushed back from the table, she said, without raising her eyes, 'Would you carry him up?'

When Ralph Batley's figure shut out the glow of the fire as he bent above her, Linda kept her eyes on the relaxed and sleeping face of the boy. Then as she gently passed the child over to him there was a moment of contact when their hands touched, but it was only a moment, for she felt his recoil as if he had been suddenly stung. The action was like a slap in the face and she found herself flushing as if with shame.

Mrs Batley followed her son upstairs and Linda sat stiffly in her chair, staring towards the fire and she did not raise her head to look at Shane when he came and stood by her side. One kind word and she would cry. She had emphatically denied earlier that she was given to tears, but it had been a long and trying day and she was very tired, and now, because a man had drawn his hand sharply from contact with hers, she was feeling hurt, as she had never been hurt in her life before.

Uncle Shane gave the kind word. With his hand gently patting her shoulder he said, 'The child's taken to you, it's a very good sign.' Then after a silence during which his hand became still he added, 'And he's not alone, no, not by a long chalk. In spite of what you might think, you've started well on your first day.' The fingers gave another gentle pat as he ended, 'Aye, you have that.'

It was too much. Linda with head bowed rose swiftly from the chair and under the pretence of clearing the table she hurried with some dishes towards the kitchen, and there, because the lump in her throat threatened to choke her she put her face under the cold tap. She had found in the past when her father's biting remarks had become unbearable, that cold water had a very steadying effect on keeping her tears at bay. Whatever happened, Ralph Batley must be given no opportunity for further comment on tears.

3

Following on a long and good night's rest, because she had retired early the previous evening, Linda found that the fears and hurts of yesterday had sunk into their right perspective and the day ahead even had a certain glow about it. This was brought into effect when Ralph Batley bade her good morning in a voice that was quite pleasant . . . and gave her, what with a little stretch of imagination could be termed, a smile. It was as if he were trying to make up for his involuntary action of last night.

She had not as yet let the thought of Sep Watson enter her mind, and when she reached the bacon-and-egg stage of the breakfast she was engulfed in a happy feeling, and it was at this point that the knock came on the back door.

That a knock on the door at this time of the morning was an unusual occurrence was made evident when she watched every head at the table move upwards. She knew that the cowman did not get here till eight o'clock; later, he had informed her, if the weather was bad. But as if her mind touching on him had conjured him out of thin air, there he was, his breadth actually filling the hall doorway. He looked agitated and his breathing spoke of his having run hard.

Both Ralph Batley and Mrs Batley had risen together and they were halfway across the hall towards him when he said, 'It's the sheep, they're out, some . . . some on Fenton Moor and t'others . . .' there was a pause in his speaking and he took a deep breath before bringing out, 't'others are in Cadwell's.'

The next few moments were uncanny, at least to Linda, for no-one, not even Michael, made any comment. Not a syllable was spoken as they all scrambled, one after the other, into the kitchen and flung on their coats.

Last night she had left her duffle coat among the others, and now she was thrusting her arms into it as she ran out into the cold, drizzle-filled morning, Mrs Batley at her side.

She had not gone far when the older woman's hand gripped her arm, pushing her forward as she said, 'You . . . you go ahead, lass, your legs can carry you.'

Without any comment Linda sprang forward. She was a good runner and she liked running, and in a short while she came up with Shane. He was gasping and panting and he pointed ahead to where Ralph Batley's bounding figure was disappearing down into the hollow, and yelled, 'Follow him. I'll make for the moor.'

Slithering and stumbling she dropped into the valley, then climbed the other side just in time to see Ralph Batley once again disappear from view. The direction he was taking was new to her, and soon she found herself on a narrow, winding path that seemed never ending. Suddenly she came upon outcrops of stone like miniature cliffs and for a moment she could imagine she was on the beach. Still running swiftly she rounded them, to pull up abruptly in startled surprise. She was close to a sunken main road and there, like a tableau before her, were three men – Ralph Batley and the two Cadwell men. Ralph Batley, with his back to her, his feet astride and his hands held stiffly by his side, gave some indication as to what his expression was like. Out beyond him, over the fence, in the roadway she could see the bouncing heads of two horses and the upper part of their riders. The two Cadwell men were vibrating with anger. Yet this word was not quite enough to express the older man's emotion, for his face was convulsed with a dark rage as he pointed to the Batley boundary and cried, 'Don't tell me that you know nothing about this! That wire's been cut, and in several places. It doesn't need a blind man to see that. Sheep don't bite through wire. Your bloody vermin have got the rot and you think to pass it on to mine. Nearly every blasted one of them's lame, look at that.' He pointed his crop down the road.

'That's not rot, that sheep's lame.' Ralph Batley's voice sounded unnaturally quiet as he went on, 'And if every one of them had rot their combined stink couldn't come from anything more putrid than what I'm looking at now.'

In a flash the horse's forelegs were brought from the ground and it was swung round to mount the bank. In another second, with his mouth spewing oaths and his crop raised to strike, the elder Cadwell man and the horse would have been upon Ralph Batley but for a voice screaming. 'Stay! Hold your hand there.'

Linda, who had been transfixed by the scene, had not noticed Mrs Batley's arrival. She watched her now advance to the side of her son and look down on the Cadwell man. The horse was standing in the ditch frothing and prancing and bouncing its rider, giving the impression that Mr Cadwell was boiling in his own rage. He was not looking at Ralph Batley now but at Mrs Batley, for she was speaking to him in what sounded to Linda under the present circumstances a very odd way. Her voice held neither fury nor anger, rather the tone seemed to imply despair. 'So you've started again,' she said.

'Has he ever stopped?' The words came grinding from between Ralph Batley's lips.

'No. Nor I won't until I finish you off, you bloody upstart.' Mr Cadwell turned his fiery gaze on to Ralph Batley again. 'Farmer. Huh!' His head went back on a mirthless laugh. 'Why don't you go back to your garret and play at making your dolls? Or have you decided to play with live ones now?' His eyes swung to where Linda stood at the other side of Mrs Batley, and after raking her for a second with his sneering gaze he ended, 'But mind she's not pinched from you an' all. That would be a laugh, wouldn't it?'

In the instant that Ralph Batley swung himself up and forward over the broken fence his mother threw herself on him, screaming, 'No! no! I tell you no.' Her hands breaking his spring brought him doubled up over the wires, and for a moment he could not extricate himself from the barbed thongs hooked in his clothes. As he hung there Mr Cadwell let out a bellow of a laugh and cried, 'That's just how I'll see you end up, like your old man, bent and broke.'

'Shut up! Shut up, will you! Shut that vile mouth of yours.' Mrs Batley was on the edge of the bank now, glaring down into the face of the Cadwell man.

Rouse Cadwell, who had so far not spoken, now brought his horse round to his father's side and said, 'Come on, that's enough.'

But Mr Cadwell was not to be led away so easily and he cried at his son, 'I'll go when I see their scum off me land.'

Mrs Batley, drawing in a shuddering breath, turned to her son and in a voice full of pleading she beseeched him as she stared up into his frozen countenance, 'Go on, lad, no more now. For God's sake, no more. Get them off . . . please.' She shook his arm as if bringing him out of a trance and ended softly, 'For my sake.'

With pity swamping her Linda watched her employer move away. It was as if he could not trust himself to go down the bank near the Cadwell men. Her eyes followed him as he jumped the fence further down, then cross the road and go through an open gate into the Cadwells' field to where, in the distance, she could see the broad bulk of Sep Watson rounding up the sheep.

When Mrs Batley spoke quietly to her, saying, 'Can you get those off the road?' she immediately slithered down the bank. She had to pass close to the horses but she looked at neither of the riders.

There were only two sheep in the roadway, but as sheep will, they proved difficult and were determined to go in any direction but the right one, and each on his own side of the road. When finally she got them together they would not be persuaded to return straight up the road but seemed bent on entering the field again through the wire fence.

When she saw the horse and rider coming towards her she thought, 'Oh, the devil, he's doing it on purpose to make things worse.' But when Rouse Cadwell, having passed her, brought his horse broadside to the road and the sheep scattered away before it, she turned and looked at him in surprise. His face was unsmiling but it no longer showed anger. She turned her gaze quickly from him, but as she scrambled out of the ditch and on to the road again, his voice brought her eyes back to him as he said quietly, 'Don't let this upset you, it's all part of a pattern.' Then bending forward and his voice dropping low, he added in an aside, 'Don't forget that torch.'

At the same moment that she turned away from the horse and rider she saw up on the far bank behind the fence the bristling figure of Ralph Batley. He paused for only a second, but it was long enough for him to look straight at her. His face was livid, and she wanted to call out, 'I wasn't talking to him.'

The sheep had now bounded away and being unable to get past the elder Cadwell man and his horse, they scrambled up the bank and through the torn wire and into their own domain, seemingly unnoticed by either Mr Cadwell or Mrs Batley, for when Linda reached them it would seem that they were aware of no-one but themselves. Mrs Batley was speaking in a quiet, intimate sort of way that puzzled Linda. She was saying, 'Jack Cadwell, you'll know no peace until you can forgive. You're so important to yourself you can't imagine you're not important to everybody else, too. Nobody must let you down or they'll suffer for it. Well, hasn't there been enough suffering all round? Aren't you satisfied?'

'I'll never be satisfied, Maggie Ramshaw, and you know that.'

He was calling Mrs Batley Maggie Ramshaw. Although Linda could not make head or tail of what was being said, she knew that the beginning of this conversation lay far back in the past.

Mr Cadwell now turned his horse about and joined his son, and they stood like two dark sentinels while Sep Watson and Ralph Batley drove the sheep out of the Cadwell land, on to the road and over the wire gap into their own field. And when this was accomplished Mr Cadwell, looking up to where Ralph Batley stood once more on his own land, cried, 'Let it happen again and I'll impound every damn one of them, or better still, I'll shoot your rottin' vermin.'

Ralph Batley made no reply, perhaps because his mother was holding tightly to his arm.

Not until the Cadwell men disappeared from view did Mrs Batley release her hold, and then with a great intake of breath and indicating the fence with a weary sweep of her arm she said, 'Now let's get this up.'

Ralph Batley did not immediately start on the repairs, but after looking at the fence he beckoned Sep Watson towards him and asked, 'How did you know they were out?'

'Well, it was like this,' Sep Watson looked from his employer towards Mrs Batley, 'you know old Badger Mullen? Well, he must have been on the prowl last night, he was passing our way around seven and he knocked and said there were sheep on the road and he fell into them in the dark.'

'How did you know they were ours?' Ralph Batley was looking intently at his man.

'Well, I didn't.' Sep Watson's tone was now slightly huffed. 'But I thought I'd better not leave anything to chance, knowin' how things are, so I got on me bike and away I came. It was gettin' light then I saw the gap, and when I rode over the moor I saw they had reached there an' all.'

'This was no break-through, that wire's been cut. And they would never have got into Cadwell's if the gate hadn't been open, it's got a slip catch on, it would have to be lifted. . . Was Badger Mullen drunk?'

'No, he daren't make the home brew now, not in any quantity anyway. He was as sober as me.'

Ralph Batley bit on his lip and turned his eyes away from the man and gazed thoughtfully for a long moment, and then he said, 'Well, you'd better go and see what Shane's up to.'

'Aye.'

'Come back here as soon as you get them in.'

'Aye.' Sep Watson's face looked dark as he passed Linda, and he muttered something to her which she could not catch.

Ralph Batley had his head bent and he was pulling at the twisted wire of the fencing as he spoke to her. 'Bring me a coil of wire and the cutters and as many staves as you can carry along with them. You'll find them all in the workshop. If you can find Michael he'll help you . . . and a hammer.'

She ran all the way back to the farm. When she had collected the required articles and there was no sign of Michael she set out laden like a donkey. But her load was so unwieldy that every now and again she had to stop and re-adjust it. When finally she returned Ralph Batley was alone, and as she dropped her burden, one piece after another, on to the ground he turned and looked at her. Then, making an impatient movement with his head, he exclaimed, 'I didn't mean you to bring all that amount.'

'Well, this is what you asked for and I couldn't find Michael.' Her own tone had a slight edge to it, and he glanced again at her sharply. 'You could have made two journeys,' he said.

'It's done now.'

For the next half-hour she worked with him, helping to repair the fence, and there was hardly a syllable exchanged between them except, 'The hammer there,' or 'I'll have that piece of wire.'

Next followed an inspection of the whole boundary line bordering the road and the moor, and it was well in the middle of the morning when they again returned to the farm.

Mrs Batley was standing at the kitchen doorway. 'Come in,' she said quietly, 'and have a drink, it's ready.'

They stood, each in his own way, before the fire in the hall, drinking the hot cocoa, and the scene raised the same uncanny feeling in Linda as had the one earlier when the news that the sheep were out was received without a word. No-one was making the slightest reference to what had transpired. If it wasn't for the grimness on Ralph Batley's face and the deepened sadness in his mother's eyes, Linda could have imagined that she had dreamt the whole thing.

If the Batley family as a whole chose to ignore the happenings of the morning, Sep Watson certainly made up for their reticence, for from the moment Linda joined him in the cowshed after lunch he talked of nothing else, and he vented spleen particularly on his master.

'Not a damned word of thanks. No "thank you, Sep, for racing your guts out and coming to tell me the sheep had broke through." Oh no, his lordship is not expected to do things like that . . . Did you hear him go at me as if I'd done it, as if I'd pushed the bloody things through to the Cadwells'.'

He stood confronting her, standing squarely before her in the gangway of the byre, an empty pail in each hand, and he did not wait for her to answer, but clashing the pails together with such a clang that she actually jumped aside, he continued, 'He'll go too far one of these days and I'll leave him on his backside. I've done it afore, and he can't get anybody up here for love or money . . . you're only here 'cause he couldn't get anybody else.' He bounced his head at her on this, then turned from her and into a byre.

Linda would have liked to take him up on this last, but she warned herself, 'Say nothing, let him go on.'

And he went on for most of the afternoon and without interruption, for Ralph Batley did not put in an appearance. Linda surmised he must be doing the circuit of the rest of the boundary fencing, making sure there were no weak spots. Yet if this morning the wire had been cut it could be cut again.

On one of her journeys from the dairy to the byre with the pails, Sep Watson stopped milking for a moment and, turning his great flat face upwards to her, he asked, 'What did Cadwell say to the missis?'

Linda remembered every word, every pregnant word that she heard pass between Mr Cadwell and Mrs Batley, but she was certainly not telling this creature what she had overheard, so she replied tartly, 'I didn't hear anything. I was on the road busy getting the sheep in most of the time.'

'By! I'd like to have been there when they were at it, it would've been worth hearin'.' He pursed his thick lips and jerked his head. 'That's the first time they've been face to face for nearly three years to my knowledge. Every time they meet he pays her back, knocks a bit off, so to speak.'

'Pays her back? What are you talking about?'

'Love's young dream, of course. You wouldn't think as things are now that Jack Cadwell and the missis . . .' he jerked his head in the direction of the house . . . 'were thick at one time, would you?'

Linda's face showed her distaste for the man and disbelief of his words. Recognising this, he straightened up his short body and said, 'You don't believe me, do you? Well, it's true. She ran the hills with him when she was young. You wouldn't think to look at her now that she was a spritely piece and a looker in her way, but she was . . . and she had money. Aye,' he rubbed the bottom of his nose with the back of his hand and gave his characteristic thick laugh as he went on, 'it was bad enough to lose her, but to lose her money an' all and to his own pal, Peter Batley, well, it was more than his stomach could stand. But they did it quick like, away to a registry office one morning and he could do nowt about it, not on the surface he couldn't. But he's paid her back ever since.'

Linda was staring down into the cowman's face, but she wasn't seeing it, she was seeing Mrs Batley's

98

pain-filled eyes, her work-stained, restless hands, her face that rarely smiled. The Batley history that had baffled her from the moment she stepped into the house was taking shape. At least she had its beginnings – Mrs Batley, Maggie Ramshaw the girl that was, had thrown over Mr Cadwell for his friend, Peter Batley. Whether her choice had been for the best Linda could only judge of what she knew of Mr Cadwell. Peter Batley had evidently been a heavy drinker; very likely, too, a weak character, but whatever he had been, Linda felt glad that the girl Maggie Ramshaw had chosen him rather than Jack Cadwell.

Sep Watson was still talking as he worked away at the milking. 'She had a tidy sum. Her father and mother died one after the other and left her with Brookside. It was a farm bigger than this 'un, and she sold it, and there she was with a nice packet that Jack Cadwell was just waiting to spend. And then, bang! . . . she's Mrs Peter Batley. Oh, boy, I remember how the countryside rang that day. There was bets laid on as to how long Cadwell would take to finish Batley off, with the fists, that was. But nobody thought he would do it the clever way, make him drink himself to death. . . Here, where you goin'?'

'I'm going to take the feed over.'

'What about the milk?'

'That's the last, surely you can take that in yourself.'

'He said you had to help me, he said you had to stay here and help me.'

Linda stopped on her way to the door, and although she couldn't see the man she called back to him, 'Then you can tell him that I haven't done my job properly, can't you?'

She received no answer to this, but when she heard the scuffling of his feet as he rose from the stool, she turned about and hurried out and towards the big barn. At the moment she could stand no more of Sep Watson's prattle. Her mind was repeating over and over again, Poor Mrs Batley, poor woman. Because she jilted him, if jilted was the word, that Cadwell man had tortured her for years. Sep Watson had said yesterday that Mr Cadwell was furious when his son had married the Batley girl. Under the circumstances she could imagine his fury. To be baulked of money coming into his family for the second time, and from the same source, would be more than just a blow to his pride. But the business of Patricia Batley marrying Lance Cadwell must have happened more than eight years ago, for Michael was turned seven, yet Sep Watson said the last time Mrs Batley and Mr Cadwell had met was three years ago. What had happened then? In her mind's eye she saw the face of Ralph Batley and she sensed that whatever clash had flared up again between the two houses was in some way directly concerned with him. There returned to her mind, as it had done a number of times today, the enigmatic sentence that Mr Cadwell had thrown at Ralph Batley. 'Why don't you go back to your garret and play at making your dolls?' And he had referred to herself as a live doll. Whatever the meaning of it, it had filled Ralph Batley with fury.

When she reached the barn she saw that she would have to get the hay from the upper storey, and this was going to be no easy task on her own. But knowing that she would have to accomplish it herself, for she had no intention of going and asking Sep Watson's aid, she pushed a hand trailer close to the ladder, her intention being to topple the bales of straw from the edge of the platform above down on to it. When she had climbed the ladder and reached the floor on the upper storey, she gazed around her with interest. It covered a very large space, and not having the height of the ground floor, it had the appearance of being twice its size. She saw immediately that there wasn't only hay stored here but a number of other things, boxes and crates, all empty as far as she could gather. She walked down a gangway between the hay and the crates, and when she reached its end she found that although the bales of hay were stacked to the end of the barn, there was a passageway between the last crates and the wall. The light was dim up here, but through a chink between two warped boards just below where the side of the barn joined the roof, she saw what appeared to be a door. On closer inspection she found that it was a door. She was thinking that it was a funny place to have a door when she remembered the outside brick building attached to the end of the barn. Of course, this door, too, would lead into it. She hadn't yet had time to investigate it from the outside, and so she turned the handle, but the door did not open. Thinking it might be stiff she put her shoulder to it and pressed forward, but she could make no impression on it. And then she realised that the door was locked. Why? Oh, well, perhaps the outside door would be open. When she had finished loading up she would run up the steps and try it. Likely it was some sort of a storeroom, she was thinking, when a voice from behind her seemed to hit her in the neck and knock her forward.

'Interested?'

She placed her two hands flat against the door for a moment before swinging round, and she could almost have cried with relief so see that the man facing her was Sep Watson and not her employer. As much as she disliked this man she almost welcomed him at this moment.

'Oh,' she laughed shakily, 'you gave me a start.'

'Aye, I seemed to . . . You trying to get in there?'

'Yes, I wondered if it was another storeroom.'

'No, it's not another storeroom and it's locked.' He pointed to the keyhole. 'It's always kept locked; nobody's been in there for three years.'

Three years again. She looked at him, waiting for him to go on. He didn't go on immediately but stood looking at her, a smile on his flat face, and she knew he was savouring the power of his knowledge, keeping her on tenterhooks. Although she wanted to know, and badly, why that door was kept locked, she had no intention of asking him or even waiting until he decided to tell her, and she was moving away from the door, keeping close to the wall of straw so as not to come in contact with him, when he said, 'Bet you'll never guess what that place was?'

In spite of her good intention she stopped and looked at the man as he leant forward, his face now one oily grin. 'Boss's love nest.'

Although she did not move she felt her whole body swiftly recoil. And he felt this too for, the smile wiped from his face now, he said sullenly, 'You don't believe me, do you? You're a disbelieving little puss, you are. But that's what it was. Him and his lady love spent days in there, and not another soul near them. She had her own key and I've seen me bump into her first thing in the morning, aye, around seven in the summer time when I come early. Mind you, I didn't blame him for that for she was a luscious piece. He used to keep on an extra man in those days so's he could have more time for his larking.'

Linda felt as though she was going to be sick, literally sick. She must get away from this man and his evil chatter. She pressed past him and was at the beginning of the alleyway between the hay and the crates when she was brought to a sudden breath-checking halt, for there, just stepping off the top of the ladder at the other end of the barn, was Ralph Batley. His step was slow and measured as he walked towards her, but before he had covered half the distance Sep Watson had pushed past her and hurried to meet him, and he began immediately to talk, his voice so low that she could only catch a word here and there. But the fragments of two disjointed sentences coming to her brought a sharp exclamation of denial from her. 'You're lying,' she said. 'I wasn't sneaking about.'

'You were.' The cowman turned towards her as she came up with them. 'I followed you up; you were trying to open the door.'

She glared back at him for a moment then switched her eyes to Ralph Batley's face. 'I did try to open the door, but I wasn't sneaking. I came up here to get the hay, and saw the door. I thought it was a storehouse or something.'

'Or something!' Sep Watson's chin jerked upwards, and he turned from her and addressed his employer again in the oily tones that he kept especially for him. 'She's done nowt but question me since she come. She's as nosey as you make 'em.'

'Oh, you . . . you lying beast. I've never asked you a single question. Oh!—'

'No? What about yesterday in the byres? Couldn't get the pails back quick enough before you started.'

'That's enough!' With a movement of his head Ralph Batley indicated that the cowman should get going, and not until he had watched his lumbering figure descend the ladder and disappear through the barn door did he turn towards Linda.

Again sustained by her righteous indignation she had no fear of him, and she spoke rapidly in her own defence, unintimidated by his steely gaze. 'I don't care whether you believe me or not, but I've never questioned him, so there.'

'I believe you.'

She was not only taken aback by this statement but by the quality of his voice. For it was quiet; she could even think it was kind and reassuring, and belied the look in his eyes.

'Talking is Watson's mania, if he hasn't anyone to talk to he talks to himself.' There could even be the suspicion of a smile on his lips, and as she looked at them her breathing became steadier and on a great intake of breath she dropped her eyes from his face and said, 'Thank you.'

She was moving away when his hand came out but did not touch her, and he said, 'You would like to know what I keep in the room at the end of the barn?'

She felt the blood rushing not only over her face but over her whole body. It was as if she had been caught red-handed in a misdemeanour and she stammered, 'It . . . it doesn't matter, I'm not interested. It was only that I thought it was a store-room, as I told you.' She had an impelling desire at this moment to get away from him. She did not want to hear his translation of . . . a love nest.

'Oh, I can tell you what it is.' His voice now had an airy note. 'I haven't got a dead body stored away there or anything like that. It's a studio. Before I was a farmer I was a sculptor.'

A sculptor. She found herself looking at his hands, and to her further embarrassment he made a strange, disparaging sound in his throat, then placing his hands together he examined them as if he hadn't seen them for some time. Having turned them first one way then another, he said, 'I suppose I was born a farmer and sculpturing was only a dream that interrupted it.' It was for the moment as if he was thinking aloud. Then flinging his hands quickly downwards as if throwing off the dream, he looked at her and said rapidly, but still in a quiet tone, 'I want you to promise me one thing. Should Watson molest you in any way, you will come and tell me. Don't be put off by thinking you will be depriving me of a good man. They're never so good but there are better. He's likely told you already that he can't be replaced. Don't believe him. . . You promise me?'

'Yes.' She inclined her head slowly with the affirmative. They looked at each other for a moment longer, then the strange interview was over. She turned from him and went towards the ladder, and as she descended the first rung she saw that he hadn't moved from where she had left him.

It was only as she reached the barn floor that she remembered the reason why she had gone up to the loft: it was to get the feed. She was looking at the trailer that she had placed ready to take the bales when Ralph Batley descended the ladder. He passed her without any further word, but even when he had left the barn she did not immediately get on with the job. A sculptor, and that was his studio. But why was it locked? He had evidently worked there at one time. She remembered Mr Cadwell's strange words that morning about Ralph Batley living in a garret and playing with dolls. It was evident that he had been away from the farm at one time for a period of years, but when he had returned he had still kept up his work, for there was the studio. But why had it been locked for three years, and what had happened to the girl? She found her mind dwelling on the girl. What had she been like? Luscious, Sep Watson had said. What had gone wrong? She couldn't guess, and she would likely never know, for she would hear no more chatter from Sep Watson. Her mind coming to Sep Watson she felt a thread of fear spiralling through her. Ralph Batley had said that should the cowman offend her she should go and report him. There was never a good but there was a better, he had said. That had only been to reassure her, for good farmhands were difficult to come by and a man would think twice before taking a post on this bleak hillside. It would have simplified matters if there had been accommodation for a worker and his family, but there was none. But she knew if she was not to report the cowman she must avoid him at all costs, and this was going to be difficult to say the least.

She sighed somewhat wearily. Worrying wouldn't get the work done, and she could see no further use in speculation. She began loading the trailer with the bales of hay. Because of their size and the weight of the trailer she could not trundle more than two at a time across the yard to the storeroom, and it was when she was making her fourth journey in the growing dusk that Shane came on the scene. Back bent, putting all her weight into the job, she did not see him until his voice crying,

'Hold your hand a minute, what're you up to, pushing that load? Where's Watson?' brought her up straight and she smiled at the old man. 'Oh, I can manage quite well, Uncle Shane. They're not very heavy, just awkward,' she said.

'Awkward, be damned! That's no job for you.' She could see that he was angry. 'Leave them where they are this minute and go an' tell Sep Watson to come out here.'

'No, no. Please.' Her voice was urgent. 'I can manage quite well. He . . . he would have helped, but I didn't ask him. And please, please, Uncle Shane,' she put her hand on his arm, 'don't say anything to him . . . don't go for him, it isn't his fault.'

He stared at her intently for a moment, then pushing her almost roughly aside he took up the handles of the trailer and, saying, 'Go and give Sarah her feed, I was just on me way to her,' he thrust the trailer ahead.

She lingered rather longer than was necessary in the byre with Sarah and her calf. It was warm in the byre and quiet, and the sight of the little Galloway mother and her spritely baby was comforting somehow. Sarah seemed to have taken a liking to her; perhaps she remembered that the hand that was stroking her back now had gentled her head a couple of nights ago. Anyway, it was a nice thought, and Linda stayed on talking softly to the animal.

When at last she dragged herself away from Sarah and was on the point of opening the door to leave the byre, it was pushed roughly in, knocking her backwards against the wall, and there in the dim light stood the menacing figure of Sep Watson, dressed ready for his homeward journey. He did not attempt to enter the byre, but with the door gripped in his huge fist, his eyes narrowed and his lower jaw jutting outwards, he growled at her, 'Think ye're smart, don't you, well, let me tell you: you watch your step, missie, or you won't reign long here. And it's me that's warning you, mind you that.' He banged the heavy door back on her and she only just warded off its impact by thrusting out her hands.

He was gone and she was left standing trembling from head to foot. Ralph Batley had said: 'If he molests you in any way let me know.' At this moment she wanted to fly to him and cry, 'I'm scared, I'm frightened of that man.'

She stood for a moment longer until she had steadied herself, then went out and across the yard towards the house, and as she neared the back door Michael came running after her, crying, 'Wait! wait!' then hanging on to her hand he looked up into her face as he said, 'Guess where I've been?'

She shook her head.

'Down to the Bay with the milk. Uncle let me drive. Well . . . well, I had my hand on the wheel, anyway . . . Oh, I'm hungry, starving! Gran's baking.' He dashed ahead of her now and burst open the back door, shouting, 'Gran! Gran! I drove the car.'

When she entered the kitchen she could hear his voice chattering away to his grandmother. There was a smell of baking bread all about her, the air was warm and pungent, and as she let the hood of her duffle coat drop from her head and was about to loosen the button at her neck she blinked rapidly, then went swiftly forward and placed her hands flat on the white wooden table near the stove. A feeling of faintness had swept over her and she felt for a moment that she was going to fall. Her head drooped lower. She didn't know how long she stood like this before she heard Mrs Batley's voice at her side saying kindly, 'What is it, girl?'

She shook her head slowly from side to side, then Mrs Batley, turning her about and looking into her face, said, 'Are you feeling faint like?' But she did not wait for an answer, instead she unbuttoned the duffle coat and, pulling it off Linda, murmured kindly, 'Come away in and sit down, it's the heat, it often has that effect on you when you come out of the cold . . . Out of the way now.' She brushed her grandson aside as she brought Linda across the hall to the fireplace. And when she had seated her in an armchair, she said, 'The tea's just mashed, have a good strong cup and you'll feel better.' Then turning to her grandson, who was standing at Linda's side peering sharply into her face, she said, 'You go, Michael, and rake up your uncles. Tell them tea's on the table . . . Away now.'

Reluctantly, Michael went to do his grandmother's bidding, and she brought the tea to

Linda and said, 'Here, drink this up, you've had a heavy day.'

'No, no, it was just the cold, as you said.' Linda sipped hurriedly at the tea.

Mrs Batley had turned away and was arranging the plates on the table. With her back still turned, she said quietly, 'My son told me about Sep Watson.'

Linda, in the act of taking another drink from the cup, stopped and looked towards the older woman. 'I don't want to cause trouble, Mrs Batley.' Her voice was anxious.

'I know that, girl.' Mrs Batley was still moving the plates. 'Sep's a good worker, he knows his job, none better, but he's ugly inside and out. He's always been the same. And you must do as my son says – if he annoys you in any way you must tell us. He can be a nasty customer, Sep Watson. He's just had it hot and heavy and gone home with his tail between his legs.'

So that was it. Ralph Batley must have gone for the cowman, that was the reason for him threatening her.

Mrs Batley moved towards the fire now and, picking up the kettle, said, 'I understand he's been talking, and he'll go on talking. Some of what he says will be the truth and some will be his idea of it.' She bent forward and screwed the black kettle into the heart of the fire as she asked quietly, 'Did he say anything about my son today?'

Although Mrs Batley's back was towards Linda, it was as if she was being confronted with the older woman's honest round eyes, for she dropped her head forward as she murmured softly, 'Yes.' She could not lie to this woman, nor did she think there was any need.

'What did he say?'

'I can't . . .' Linda shook her head . . . 'I mean I can't repeat . . .' Nor was it in her to repeat what the cowman had said, and she ended lamely, 'It was just about the studio.'

'Oh, the studio.' Mrs Batley repeated her words. 'Did he tell you why it was locked?'

'No.'

'No? Then he was keeping it for another time likely.' Of a sudden Mrs Batley was standing before Linda and looking hard at her. Without taking her eyes from her she pulled a chair forward and sat down and began talking rapidly in a voice little above a whisper. 'There's not much time, they'll all be in in a minute. Whatever Watson said it would be something nasty, so I'll tell you the truth and it'll keep things straight in your mind . . . My son should have been a sculptor, not a farmer. He was a sculptor, a real sculptor, but when his Dad died the farm was in − in a pretty bad state.' Linda watched the older woman close her eyes as if on a bitter memory before going on rapidly, 'He came home and tried to work at both. There was a girl, from the other valley. She was of some consequence in the district and had been on friendly terms with the Cadwell boys, especially the eldest, Bruce, but as soon as she sees my son she goes all out for him.' Mrs Batley's eyes dropped from Linda's now as she added more slowly, 'And he for her. The feeling between the Cadwells and us was bad even then, for you see my daughter, Michael's mother, had married the second son, Lance.' Linda gave no indication that she already knew this, but continued to look with pity on this woman. 'Bruce Cadwell wanted this girl. You see, her people were important, not so much with money as with position, and it would be a feather in his cap if he got her . . . the Cadwells are like that, they like feathers.' This was the only vindictive note that Linda had heard from Mrs Batley, who went on, 'And because of this girl the fire that had smouldered between our two houses for years burst into flames. It had just been waiting for a match, and it was struck when Ralph and her became engaged.'

She spoke her son's name softly, Linda noticed, but never put a name to the girl. Mrs Batley now drew in a deep breath that lifted her chest upwards, and as she let it out she said, 'Then ten days before the wedding she ran off with Bruce Cadwell.' It was odd, Linda thought, but did she detect relief in this statement?

Whatever exclamation Linda was about to make was stilled now by the voice and racing steps of Michael coming through the kitchen. Mrs Batley, holding Linda's gaze for a second longer, patted her knee in silence, then quickly getting to her feet she went towards the table, calling to Michael as he now ran towards her, 'What have I told you about those wellingtons, get back and take them off.'

'They're coming, Gran.'

'All right . . . do as you're bid.'

Linda was still sitting in the chair when Ralph
Batley and Shane entered the room. Mrs Batley had
talked about her son and the hurt he had received.
She had not spoken of her own hurt that went back
deep into the years. But one thing Linda gauged
from what she had just been told. Although Ralph
Batley had become an embittered man because of
being jilted by this girl, the break had brought
nothing but relief to his mother and, in a way, she
was suffering from a feeling of guilt because of it.

Linda raised her eyes and looked towards the tall,
spare arresting figure of her employer approaching
the hearth and thought, and very much in the
idiom of Uncle Shane, 'Why, the girl must have
been daft,' and on this the colour rushed back into
her face . . .

No-one would have guessed during the evening
that followed that the day had been full of turmoil
right from its beginning, for at times the hall was
filled with laughter. Shane had brought out two
packs of cards and had invited Linda to join in
a game of snap with Michael and himself on
the hearthrug. Forgetting everything and letting
herself go, she lost herself in the fun. On her
knees, her head close to those of Shane and the
boy, she waited her chance and did her share of
yelling, until Michael, turning on the old man,
cried playfully, 'Oh, Uncle Shane, you're cheating,
that wasn't yours, it was . . . was . . .' He turned
his eyes upwards to Linda and in the quiet that had

settled on the room for a second he said, 'What's your name? What can I call you?'

'Call me Linda.' Linda was smiling warmly down on him and he repeated, 'Linda,' and then childishly bit on his lower lip and wagged his head.

'Linda,' Shane was nodding at her now, 'it's a lilting name . . . And are we all to call you Linda, eh?'

'Yes. Yes, please.'

'D'you hear that?' Shane sat back on his hunkers and looked towards Mrs Batley and his nephew. Mrs Batley smiled and nodded back to him, but Ralph Batley was not looking at Linda, his eyes were fixed on the fire. It was as if he had not heard Shane's remark. But in the next moment he was forced to turn his attention to the group, for Michael, bobbing up and down on his knees, cried, 'Oh, that's what I'll call the calf . . . Linda. Can I?' The boy looked first at Linda and then towards his uncle. Linda had said nothing, and now she waited to hear Ralph Batley's comment. He was not looking at her but at the boy, and he seemed to give the question some thought before he replied, 'Miss Metcalfe might not like the suggestion.'

He could not have made it more clear that he, at least, was not going to use her Christian name. As last night, when his hand had jumped from contact with her own, the hurt feeling returned but not in its intensity. Last night she had felt hurt and repulsed because she thought that his rejection was personal, but from what she had heard of him today she now surmised that his attitude was more of an armour against all things feminine, and so she was able to answer quite brightly, 'Oh, I don't mind in the least. In fact, I shall feel honoured to have the calf named after me.' She turned her soft, warm gaze down on Michael, and in an instant the boy threw himself across her lap, wound his arms tightly about her waist and buried his face in her breast. His action left no-one in the room untouched. Mrs Batley, in an assumed leisurely fashion, rose from her chair and, laying down the mending she had been busy with, said, 'Well, come along now, time's up.'

'Aye, the evening's fled . . . go on now.' Shane hoisted the boy from Linda's lap with one hand on his bottom, and he smacked at him playfully as he pushed him towards his grandmother. And when, a few minutes later, having given the boy his wash and his milk, Mrs Batley escorted her grandson up to bed, Shane rose to his feet and saying to no-one in particular, 'I'll go and have a look round,' he left the room.

Linda was still sitting on the hearthrug, her legs tucked under her. Ralph Batley was still sitting in his chair, his gaze once more directed towards the fire, and in each silence-filled moment that followed Linda became more and more aware of his presence, and, strangely, she sensed that he too, although he did not move a muscle, was very much aware of her for, and her heart sank at the thought, she embarrassed him. She felt his aloofness, forged by his experience, had built itself a steel armour about him, making it impossible for him now to break through. Then, as if to give the lie to her thoughts, his voice asked quietly, 'Do you think you're going to like it here?'

She wanted to turn round with almost girlish effusion and cry, 'Yes, oh yes, I'm going to love it,' but she forced herself to keep her gaze steadily turned towards the fire and answer in a calm voice, 'Yes, I'm sure I shall like it . . . that is if I can satisfy you.'

This was a statement that could be answered or side-tracked without giving offence. He side-tracked it by saying, 'I understand you are very interested in Galloways.'

'Yes.' She looked at him now. 'Yes, I am, very.'

'They are breeding them quite a bit in the south.'

'Yes, but just certain farmers. It's an expensive business, breeding.' She nipped at her lower lip wondering if once again she had trodden on soft ground, but he immediately confirmed her statement by saying, 'Yes, you're right, it is. You've got to have a side line to keep going. Have you been to any of the big shows?'

'I went to the Royal Counties Show at Portsmouth in June.'

'Mm! did you? I read about that. I hope to show next year at Castle Douglas. I'm taking Great Leader up and a couple of heifers.'

She had screwed round on the hearthrug and was facing him now, her hands clasping her knees. She could not see the expression on his face, it was lost in the heavy shadow of the winged chair. But they were talking, really talking, for the first time since her arrival.

'There's a cattle market in Morpeth . . . perhaps you know?'

'Yes, I had heard there was one.'

'It's held on Wednesday. I'll be going in but I won't be taking any stock.' He did not add, 'Would you like to come?' but now fell silent, and for no reason she could understand she felt his sudden withdrawal. It was as if he had said his piece and now it was over, and that was that.

Yet Linda was not depressed by his retreat into silence again. Turning to the fire she sat gazing into it once more. He had talked to her in an ordinary way and he had asked her if she was going to like staying here. She felt warm and strangely content. Sep Watson was once again forgotten. She lifted her arm on to the seat of the chair near her and rested her head upon it . . .

How long she had been asleep she did not know, but she woke with a start when she heard Shane's voice whispering softly, saying, 'She'll be cramped to death lying like that.'

'Oh!' She blinked and stretched one arm outwards. 'Oh, I'm sorry, I must have fallen asleep.' Then as she tried to move she groaned aloud and laughed as she groaned.

As Shane's arm assisted her to her feet she became aware that her hair had become unpinned. It was lying dishevelled on her shoulders, the grips sticking out of it at angles. As she smoothed it back from her face she glanced towards the winged chair. It was empty and there was no sign of Ralph Batley in the room. She smiled at Shane and said, 'Thanks,' then looking to where Mrs Batley was stripping the loose covers from the cushions of the big couch, she asked, 'How long have I been asleep?'

'Over an hour, I should say.'

'I think I'll go to bed.'

'Yes, I would.' Mrs Batley turned and gave her a quiet smile.

'Good night, Mrs Batley.'

'Good night.'

She did not say Linda, perhaps the use of Christian names did not come easy to her. But not with Uncle Shane, for when she turned to him saying, 'Good night, Uncle Shane,' he nodded his kind, hairy face at her as he quietly said, 'Good night, Linda girl, good night.'

If during the next few days Linda could have discounted the personal tragedies of the occupants of Fowler Hall, she would have said there was an ordered harmonious peace pervading the farm, but knowing something about the lives of the people in the house she had to confess that this feeling was perhaps only within herself. Perhaps it was because of the knowledge that her employer had accepted her that she was feeling as she did. Whatever it was, even the presence of Sep Watson could not impinge upon her present feelings. In any case, the telling off seemed to have had a salutary effect upon him, for he kept his distance, and when he did come in contact with her he was civil, oily civil.

Moreover, she had been heartened by a reply to her first letter home. Her mother said she was relieved and delighted that she liked her work and was settling down . . . and Daddy sent her his love. Linda could even believe this letter, for now he had her mother to himself he could be generous. Uncle Chris, too, had written, he said he knew of course that she would like the job. Mr Ainslie thought very highly of Mr Batley, that was why he recommended her to him, and she must work hard – she laughed at that. Uncle Chris thought he worked hard but the northern work, like the northern weather, was different, harder, harsher . . . different.

And then came market day.

Long afterwards she remembered how she had woken on this particular morning with a bubbling feeling surging through her. Last evening, right out of the blue, Ralph Batley had said to her, 'Would you care to come in tomorrow? I don't think it wise for my mother to come with the cold she has on her. I have to go to the bank and also see my solicitor. You could get the shopping if you wouldn't mind doing that.'

Mind doing that? She felt like a child going on a school outing, happy, excited, expectant . . . Of what? Like a child, she did not question.

About fifteen minutes before they were due to leave at half-past ten, she dashed into the house, changed into her ordinary clothes, quickly made up her face, and was on the point of leaving the room when she remembered the torch, Rouse Cadwell's torch. She hesitated a moment before going to the chest-of-drawers. She had no wish to see or speak with Rouse Cadwell or any of the Cadwells, she was firmly and wholeheartedly on her employer's side, but she had borrowed his torch and he had reminded her of it only a few days ago. If she were to run into him then she could give it to him; if she didn't see him she would post it to him from the post office in Morpeth, and that would be over and done with. Quickly she opened the drawer and slipped the torch into her handbag, then ran downstairs.

As on that first evening she had descended the stairs into the hall and brought all their eyes upon her, now the procedure was being repeated. There they all stood as she moved down the staircase, Shane, Michael, Mrs Batley and Ralph Batley, and under their concerted gaze she gave a self-conscious little laugh and on reaching the last step she smoothed down the front of her coat as she said, 'It seems odd getting into these clothes again, I feel I've been wearing breeches for months.'

But no-one seemed to have any comment to make on this. Ralph Batley turned towards the kitchen door, and his mother, after a long look at Linda, followed him. Michael was hanging on to her arm now, his face very aggrieved as he said, 'I wish I could come.'

Then Shane, putting his hand on the boy's head

but looking at Linda as he did so, said, 'You're a bonnie sight, Linda. I wish I had me years afore me again.'

'Oh, Uncle Shane.' Linda laughed softly at him. Then leaning forward she whispered teasingly, 'If you had I would fall for you right away.'

'Away with you!' His tone held mock sternness and he flapped his hand at her. 'Laughing at a man because he's up in years. Away with you!'

She went away with Michael clinging to her arm. But at the back door the child was restrained by his grandmother saying, 'Leave go and behave yourself, boy, you'll rumple her.'

Ralph Batley was already at the wheel of the Jeep, and as she climbed up beside him he slipped in the gears and she turned and waved to the group standing in the yard. The Sunday School treat feeling was very much to the fore at this moment.

The journey to Morpeth was uneventful except for one thing. Ralph Batley had taken the main road through Widdrington that led straight to Ashington, and it was in this last town, while held up in a traffic jam, that a voice from a station wagon to the left of Linda said, 'Hullo, there, Ralph man.' The speaker was evidently a farmer, somewhat older than her employer, and although he was leaning across the wheel looking in the direction of Ralph Batley, Linda knew his eyes were taking her in.

'Hullo, there.' Ralph Batley's returned salutation did not sound over friendly.

The man was grinning widely as he said, 'Having a day off?'

'Not more than usual.'

The remarks flowing back and forward in front of Linda sounded ordinary, but their implications, she knew, were far from ordinary, and later she was to think that this meeting had a great bearing on what followed, for after parking the Jeep near the market-place, Ralph Batley turned to her and with a curtness that had faded slightly from his manner during the last few days said, 'You have the order, you'll find the three shops over there . . .' he pointed . . . 'I'll be back here round about two.'

She knew a dampening of her spirits as she answered, 'Very well.' Then as she turned from him he spoke again. 'About lunch,' he said. His voice sounded slightly hesitant now as he ended, 'The Earl Grey does a very good lunch.' He did not say where she would find the Earl Grey or add, 'Would you like to meet me there?' Perhaps if it hadn't been for the traffic jam and the man with his wide grin he might have said that, but she would never know.

'Very well, I'll try it. Two o'clock, you said?' She tried to keep the disappointment out of her voice. 'Good-bye.' The next moment she was walking briskly away from him into the throng of people. It did not matter to him that she did not know the town. All that mattered was that since the farmer had chipped him he was not going to lay himself open to the same thing happening again.

It did not take long to give in the orders, the arrangement being that the goods would be packed and ready for her to pick up later. Mrs Batley's personal requirements at the chemist and the hardware store took a little longer. Her own shopping amounted to buying a box of sweets for Michael and a copy of the *Farmers' Weekly*. And when all this was accomplished the time was not yet twelve o'clock. But there was much to see, and she had not yet been round the market.

It was, she found, the usual type of cattle market, with its pens full of animals and its farmers prodding and pressing the beasts. Leaning over a sheep pen she saw two girls dressed in breeches. They were about her own age and definitely attached to farms. Had she been so dressed she might, through the camaraderie of the attire, have approached them, but she knew that in her present attire, there was nothing to associate her with a farm and she felt somewhat shy of joining them. She became aware that she herself was drawing curious glances.

At one stage when she handled the haunches of a young heifer there was laughter from behind her, and she turned to find two men greatly amused at her action. The look that she levelled on them sobered them somewhat, and as one made a crude remark on how a heifer should not be judged, she was reminded forcibly of Mr Cadwell comparing her with a year-old filly.

As she moved away a man, detaching himself from another group, exclaimed, 'Why, hullo there,' and in the next moment she was face to face with Rouse Cadwell.

'Oh, hullo.' She smiled. 'I was hoping I would see you.'

That was not what she had meant to say at all, but she was flustered, for the eyes of the two men were covertly watching her and their grins were in evidence again.

'Now that is nice.'

Linda's face became straight, and her voice was flat and emphatic as she said, 'Please don't mis-understand me. You asked for your torch, I've brought it.' She opened her bag and handed him the torch, and as he took it into his hands he patted it and said jovially, 'Nice torch, good torch for bringing her to market.' It was as if he was talking to a dog. Then dropping his jocular tone he asked quietly, 'Are you on your own?'

'Mr Batley is with me.'

'Oh.' His lip pursed and his head bounced gently. Then he said, 'You'd be going straight back?' This seemed to indicate his knowledge of Ralph Batley's movements on market-day and suggested that her employer stayed no longer in the town than was necessary. But she did not think of this as she replied, 'No, I'm having lunch first.'

'Alone?'

'Yes . . . no.'

'Well now,' his lips were twisted into a little smile, 'make up your mind. But I can tell you what you're doing, you're lunching alone, aren't you? You haven't been invited to have it . . . with

125

your master.' He stressed the last three words with a deep intonation. 'But you shan't have it alone,' he went on. 'Will you have it with me?'

'No, thank you.' Her voice was stiff.

He looked at her in amused silence for a moment, before saying quietly, 'Now let's get this straight. You're not a Batley . . . what's happened between them and us has nothing whatever to do with you. Right?'

She did not answer, only looked squarely into his dark, narrow, handsome face as he went on, 'You've come to market, you're off duty, you've got to eat, so why not eat with me?'

She paused for a moment before answering in a level tone, 'Ask yourself, if you were in his place how would you like your employee to take lunch with a member of the opposite camp, for you are in the opposite camp, aren't you?'

He was looking at her with his head on one side. 'You are a very nice girl, you know, besides being a very beautiful one,' he said. 'Why didn't we think of taking a student?'

'There's no reason why you shouldn't.'

'No, I suppose not. But you wouldn't happen twice, would you? You wouldn't like to change over?'

'Don't be silly.' Linda's tone was sharp. She pulled the large collar of her coat up around her neck and was in the act of turning away when his hand came out and touched her lightly as he said seriously, 'I'm sorry, I was only joking. But do come and have lunch with me . . . Please. If you

126

don't want to run into Batley we can go some place away from the centre of the town. I can understand your feelings about the matter, honestly I can.'

He could be nice, even charming, this Rouse Cadwell. Under other circumstances she might have accepted his invitation and thoroughly enjoyed herself, but not now, not for the world would she do anything that would annoy the Batleys, mother or son. Now her tone was much softer as she said, 'Thank you all the same, but I'm sure you understand that it would be better not to. Good-bye.'

'Good-bye.' Although he held her glance as long as he could he made no effort to detain her, and she walked swiftly away from the market.

The encounter with Rouse Cadwell had shaken her somewhat, for all the time she had been on tenterhooks in case Ralph Batley should appear. She decided to have her lunch straight away, then return to the shops and collect the orders. This would fill in the time until two o'clock. Strangely now she wanted to be away from Morpeth and back on the cliff top, on the wind-strewn farm.

She was approaching the Earl Grey Hotel when she saw a modern Rover car pull up outside. The door was pushed open and Mrs Cadwell alighted. She was dressed in a gun-metal-coloured coat with a large opossum collar. On her black hair was perched a small hat made up of glistening green feathers and small pieces of fur. She looked statuesque, expensive, and not at all like the usual conception of a farmer's wife. She was the antithesis of Mrs Batley. Why Mr Cadwell had married this woman Linda didn't know; perhaps she had money. By what she had learned of him he laid great stock by money. Well, whatever the reason, she had not been able to eliminate his first love from his mind.

Without seeing her Mrs Cadwell cut across Linda's path and walked into the hotel, and Linda found herself not following her but walking straight ahead. She could not go into the hotel and risk being seated near to the Cadwells, for likely Mr Cadwell would join his wife for lunch.

She walked on for some way, then up a side street she saw a sign hanging over a small window, advertising lunches and grills. The small window, she found on entering the restaurant, was deceptive. The place was of considerable size and contained a number of rooms, all busily attended by efficient-looking waiters. From the hallway she saw that one room was entirely taken up by men. The one next to it seemed to be given over to families, and into this she went and found a seat in a far corner.

The lunch was good but expensive, as much she guessed as she would have paid at the hotel, perhaps more.

She took the meal leisurely, then went up to the ladies' room. It was as she descended the stairs to the small foyer again that she saw Rouse Cadwell for the second time. He was taking up his coat from the hallstand and as he turned and thrust his arms into it they came face to face.

'Well, don't tell me you've been lunching here.'
His voice held amused surprise.

'Yes . . . yes, I have.'

'Now isn't that silly? You in one room and me in another! Don't you think it is?'

'No, I can't say I do.'

'Oh, well, have it your own way. Did you have a good lunch?'

'Yes, a very good lunch.'

'They are noted here for their steaks . . . did you try the steak?'

'No, chicken.'

'Oh, I never have their chicken, they buy the old birds from us and they're tough.' He was laughing, and she could not help but smile back at him.

He was opening the door for her as he spoke and she had just passed him and was stepping into the street when she wished with all her heart that the earth would open and swallow her whole, for there, about to enter the restaurant, was Ralph Batley.

Even the night she had first made his acquaintance and the name of Cadwell had brought a look of mad hatred into his face, was nothing compared to his expression at this moment. His ice-grey glance moved once between them before settling on Rouse Cadwell, and, strangely, it was Rouse Cadwell who spoke, and even placatingly as he said, 'Now look here, Batley, it isn't—'

Ralph Batley cut him short with words that seemed to be wrenched from some black depth within him: 'You try anything on and I'll kill you.'

'Listen . . . but—' As Linda put her hand out protestingly towards her employer she felt herself almost lifted off the ground. It was as if he was taking a child by the arm and sweeping it along. She almost cried out at the pain of his fierce grip and she protested weakly as he hurried her away. 'You must listen . . . I wasn't . . . Please . . . please, you're hurting me.'

'Shut up.'

When he turned into a side lane that was practically deserted Linda cried, 'Stop it. Stop it, will you?' She dug her heels into the rough road and dragged on him, and this action seemed to bring him to his senses, for he released her and so quickly that she almost fell. Rubbing her arm now with her hand she muttered, almost on the verge of tears, 'I can explain.'

She saw that his face was contorted with his anger, and he growled at her, 'Don't talk! Shut up!'

He now turned and went hurriedly forward again. After a moment she followed him, but at a distance. The lane brought her into the street where the Jeep was parked, and as she approached it he swung away across the road towards the shops. She made no effort to follow him to help carry the parcels, but climbing into her seat, she sat with her head forward, rubbing gently at her arm.

What she had tried so hard to avoid had happened. He had found her with Rouse Cadwell and had immediately jumped to the conclusion the meeting had been pre-arranged.

Although she did not raise her head she was aware of him making several journeys between the Jeep and the shops. She could not help but be aware of this, for the boxes of stores hit the floor of the Jeep behind her as if they had been dropped from the cliff top.

When at last he took his seat beside her the Jeep seemed to become filled with his fury. The gears were rammed in and the Jeep leaped away. It was as well it was a slack time in the town otherwise they would surely have run into something.

The journey was almost half over when she made a decision. She must, no matter how he reacted, explain the situation. She must make him listen, for once they got back on the farm he would avoid her so skilfully that to talk to him would become almost an impossibility.

They were not returning by the main road but by a narrow, winding side road that was little better than a track. At one time, when they were bumping across an open stretch of moor, she thought they had left the road altogether. It was at this point that she spoke. Turning her face full towards his iron-stiff profile she said loudly, for it was impossible to speak softly against the noise of the Jeep, 'Will you stop a moment and listen?'

The Jeep bumped and jolted but went on.

'Please.'

Still there was no response. She turned her head to the front and it drooped as she clamped her teeth hard down on her lower lip. The next second she had swung round and was yelling at him, 'Stop, will you! Stop and let me speak.'

The Jeep stopped so suddenly that she was flung forward, her brow hitting the windscreen. She dropped back into her seat, dazed for a moment, then turned to him to find him looking at her as if he loathed the sight of her. His face held so much bitterness that she cried out immediately, 'Don't look at me like that. I haven't done anything that I'm ashamed of.'

'No, of course you haven't.' His voice had the terrifying quiet quality about it. 'Duplicity isn't anything you would be ashamed of. Why should I blame you for acting according to your lights? You have no standards.'

'I did not meet Mr Cadwell by arrangement.' Her voice was high as she cut in on him. 'You can say what you like about standards, it doesn't hurt me. But what I'm telling you is the truth.'

'You just ran into him by accident and had lunch together, that was how it happened, wasn't it?'

'No, it wasn't. I did run into him by accident but I didn't have lunch with him.'

'Don't lie to me.' He was yelling now. 'I saw you in the market . . . you were arranging where you would meet, weren't you? And then you come out of Sprigley's together, and you have the nerve to sit there and tell me you didn't have lunch with him?'

'Yes, I have.' She was spitting the words now.

'Oh, don't be such a stupid little fool!'

'How dare you!'

Their eyes were blazing each into the other's, and when he now spoke his lips moved with a curl back from his teeth as he said slowly, 'And what about in the lane the other morning when he was whispering to you? Are you going to tell me that a man whispers when he has nothing to say, nothing that the rest of the world might not hear? It all fits in.'

'I had borrowed his torch; he was asking for it back.'

'Oh,' his head went up and he let out a cruel laugh, 'oh, this is the limit. Rouse Cadwell is short of a torch!' Now his head was forward again and his face was not more than six inches from her as he said, 'What d'you take me for, a damn fool? And don't play the naïve stuff to death. If you can't think up a better lie than that, then I advise you to keep quiet.'

'I tell you I'm not lying.'

'Shut up.'

'I won't shut up, and don't speak to me like that.' Now justifiable anger rising swiftly in her, she cried at him, 'I have told you the truth. Who do you think you are, anyway, talking to me in this manner. You don't own me . . . why, you would think I had committed a crime. When I come to think of it, I'm a fool. Why should I try to convince you that I wasn't having lunch with Mr Cadwell. Why? I'm unmarried and I'm free and I can have lunch with whoever I like, and what's more I'm going to. The next time you accuse me of having lunch with Mr Cadwell there will be more than a grain of truth in it, it will be a fact, I can promise you that.'

They were caught up now in a silence. It settled on the Jeep like a weighted blanket. His face had a death-like whiteness about it while hers was suffused with the heat of her anger. Then with the shattering brittleness of cracking ice he said, 'I won't avail myself of that opportunity, Miss Metcalfe. I will release you from your agreement and you can leave at the end of the week.'

Ignoring the stab that seemed to pierce her clean through her breast, she cried back at him, 'I won't wait until the end of the week, Mr Batley, I'll leave at the earliest opportunity, tomorrow morning.'

'Suit yourself.'

The gears were rammed in again, the Jeep bounded forward, and in spite of the jolting Linda sat as stiff as a ramrod. She was raging inside. She seemed to have been impregnated with Ralph Batley's own fury; she could not find words within herself to describe him; she only knew that she hated him; she wished she had never met him . . . she couldn't wait until tomorrow morning when she would have seen the last of him.

When after what seemed a never-ending journey the Jeep bounced from a narrow side lane and on to a main road, she realised that it was the same road that led down to Surfpoint Bay and a curious question, one that she could not voice, cried in her head. Why is he going this way? Then within a few minutes she had the answer, for the Jeep turned sharply off to the right and into nothing more than a lane, then right again, and now she found herself being whisked and jolted through the narrow rock passage which led to the cliff path. Her anger was suddenly shot through with fear. Why had he come this way? In his present mood he seemed capable of anything.

As the Jeep came out of the narrow gorge and to where the road divided, the right one leading to the Cadwells' house and the other along the cliff top to the farm, she could not prevent herself from crying out, 'Stop! Stop! do you hear? I'm going to walk.'

He took not the slightest notice of her and the Jeep swung sharply to the left. For a moment she gazed straight ahead, then, as if drawn by a magnet, her eyes slewed towards the cliff edge, not more than four feet away. As she cast one terrified glance far below her to the beach her stomach seemed to heave upwards. She closed her eyes, and when a few seconds later she opened them the distance to the cliff edge had widened. When they flew past the end of the boundary of the Cadwells' land and on to the open cliff top, her whole body seemed to crumple and she slumped back for a moment against the seat. But it was only for a moment, for this last action of his which seemed to her to speak of unnecessary cruelty brought her rage bubbling upwards again, and when the Jeep came at last to a jolting stop in the yard opposite the kitchen door, she turned on her employer a look that was more than a reflection of his own. Then flinging open the door she jumped out, to be confronted almost immediately by Mrs Batley.

The older woman was standing in the kitchen doorway and she exclaimed in some surprise, 'You're back early . . . is anything . . .? Her mouth hung open on the words that did not come, and as Linda hurried past her without a word she grasped her arm and asked rapidly, 'What is it? What's happened?'

'I'm leaving.' Linda was so angry at this moment that her pity and affection – for she had found herself becoming very fond of Mrs Batley – in no way helped to soften her attitude.

With her hand still on Linda's arm and holding it tightly, Mrs Batley turned to her son as he came towards the door now carrying a box of groceries in his arms.

'What's all this? What's happened?'

He did not pause in his step as he said, 'Miss Metcalfe has told you. She's leaving, and don't try to stop her. I want her to go and she wants to go. It's mutual.'

Mrs Batley turned her eyes on Linda again, and slowly relaxing her grip, she allowed her to move away.

Linda, almost running, went across the hall and up the stairs and into her room, and dropping down on to the side of the bed she sat rubbing at her arm. He was nothing but a wild, rough brute. Oh, if only she could get her things down to the Bay she would leave this minute, this instant. She turned and buried her face in the pillow, but only for a second. Springing up she walked to the window. She wouldn't cry, no, she wouldn't. He was a beast, a beast, she wouldn't cry because of him.

There to the right of her lay the farmyard. She could see Shane coming towards the house with Michael at his heels. She turned her eyes quickly from them both, she wanted no softening effects. She looked away to her left and over the open ground to the cliff top and down to the sea, where she could just see the far end of the Bay with the ugly, dangerous rocks dotted about it. Well, they could be as dangerous as they liked, they wouldn't affect her, she wouldn't be here in the summer, and thank goodness for that.

The murmur of voices from the hall now penetrated the room, Shane's raised above the rest. Would Shane believe that she'd had lunch with Rouse Cadwell? Well, it wouldn't matter if he believed it or not, she didn't care. The voices died away and she still stood at the window. Then asking herself angrily what she was standing there for when she should be packing, she turned about and went to the wardrobe and began pulling down her clothes . . .

It must have been an hour later when her trunk and two suitcases were packed that the knock came on the door, and she turned her head sharply towards it before saying, 'Yes, come in.'

Quietly as if she was a stranger in her own house, Mrs Batley entered the room, and closing the door softly behind her, she looked not at Linda but at the luggage lying at the foot of the bed. Then coming slowly forward she stood before Linda, and with the sadness in her voice matching that on her face, she said, 'I'm sorry about this, heart sorry.'

Linda could not bear to face the older woman's eyes, and she turned her head away until Mrs Batley said, 'I'm going to ask you something point-blank. Your answer cannot make any difference now, but I know you'll tell me the truth . . . Did you go and have lunch with Rouse Cadwell?'

Linda was now looking directly at Mrs Batley and she could not keep the bitterness from her tone as she replied, 'No matter what I say, you'd still believe your son, it's only natural.'

'That I won't.'

A weighty silence hung between them and then Linda, with a heavy sigh, sat slowly down on the bed again, and after closing her eyes wearily for a moment, she said, 'Well, it was like this, Mrs Batley . . .' and she went on to tell the older woman exactly how her meeting with Rouse Cadwell had come about, right from the night of her arrival when he had lent her the torch, even the whispered words as he bent from his horse in the lane, and then the happenings in the town today.

When Linda had finished speaking Mrs Batley, after staring down on her for a moment, put out her hand and patted her arm as she said softly, 'There's one thing I'm glad about, I wasn't mistaken about you. But there, nothing can be done now; you're going, and as I've said I'm heart sorry.' When the hand slid down her arm and the rough, worn fingers pressed the back of her hand as she ended, 'I had taken to you, girl,' Linda's defence was almost broken.

The next minute Mrs Batley was moving towards the door, but before leaving the room and without turning, she said quietly, 'He's out and won't be in for some time . . . come down and have a bite of tea.'

'No, thanks.'

'Please.' Mrs Batley still had her back towards Linda, and looking at the drooped shoulders Linda was forced to say, 'Very well, then.'

Some minutes later, when she descended the stairs and saw below her the big room with the table set as usual for tea, and the fire glowing and the air of homely comfort pervading the whole atmosphere, she felt a wave of regret that this was to be the last evening she would spend in this house, and she knew that she would always remember this hall-cum-living-room with a feeling of home-sickness.

Shane and Michael were already at the table and they both looked at her but did not speak. The expression on Michael's face was one of hurt bewilderment, whereas Shane's expression was so grim that she could hardly recognise him as the kindly old man she knew, for at this moment he looked a reflection of his nephew. She had not been seated at the table for more than a few minutes when Shane got up hurriedly, almost toppling his chair backwards in the process, and as he made for the kitchen door Mrs Batley, who was coming into the room, said to him, 'What's the matter? Aren't you having your tea?'

'No . . . no, Maggie, I have no taste for it. I'll go and have a look round.'

Linda saw Mrs Batley watch him for a moment before coming to the table, and then taking her seat she looked to where Linda sat with an empty plate before her, and she said, 'Eat, my dear. Have a little something.' She pushed a laden plate towards her and when Linda shook her head she said, 'All right then, Michael will put a fire on in your room, won't you, Michael?'

Staring at Linda, the boy nodded. And when Mrs Batley ended with, 'I'll bring you something up on a tray later,' Linda thrust her hand across her eyes and beseeched her, 'Oh! Mrs Batley, don't . . . don't.'

She could call up anger to fight anger but before this kindness she was melting into her natural self again. And she knew she mustn't do this, her indignation must sustain her until tomorrow when she would be gone from this house. With a muttered 'Excuse me' she rose from the table and went swiftly up the stairs again.

Once more in her room Linda could no longer restrain her tears, and she gave way to a passion of weeping that seemed to rend her apart. She had been in this house just over a week, yet during that time she seemed to have experienced every emotion in life, and now her anger was being washed away in the storm of her weeping.

She had to fight for control when a gentle tap came on the door and Michael's voice said, 'I've brought the sticks.'

Keeping her face averted from him she went towards the window under the pretext of drawing the curtains, then she busied herself with her dressing-case while he slowly laid the sticks on the paper and then the coal, and finally put a match to the fire. His work done, he did not immediately leave the room, and Linda was forced to turn towards him to see him staring at her. There was a lost look in his eyes, it seemed to envelop the whole of his small body, but the lost look was not alone, the childish gaze that was on her was also accusing and he gave proof of this when he said, 'My mummy went away, too.'

That was all. He turned about and left the room.

The child's few words spoke plainly of the misery that had taken its toll of his nervous system, and Linda felt as though she were sinking down into a well of guilt. His mother had let him down, now she had let him down. She wanted to run after him and say, 'Listen, Michael, it wasn't my fault.' But did it matter to him whose fault it was . . . she was leaving and that was final. Ralph Batley had said, 'She wants to go and I want her to.' There was no more to be said.

She heard Mrs Batley's voice now; it was coming from outside, from somewhere below her window, and she was calling across the yard, 'Have you seen your uncle?' Linda did not hear the reply, but after a while she heard Mrs Batley's voice again and in the distance now calling, 'Shane! Are you there, Shane?' And again, 'Shane! Are you there?' and as Linda listened the guilty feeling became more acute . . .

The fire was crackling brightly and Linda, sitting hunched up before it, was now thinking dully about what she was going to do. It wasn't that she was afraid of not being able to get another position, but she was wondering if she should go home until she got fixed up somewhere or stay in the north and seek another post here. She remembered the *Farmers' Weekly* she had bought only a few hours ago. But she had, in her temper, left it in the Jeep, and she wasn't going to venture out of this room any more tonight . . . she couldn't bear the thought of running into Ralph Batley before tomorrow morning, when it would be impossible to avoid him then, for he would have to take her and her luggage down to the Bay. She shuddered at the thought.

Mrs Batley's voice broke in on her thoughts again. It was coming from the landing this time, and she seemed to be calling down into the hall. 'He's not up here, I knew he couldn't be up here.'

Linda rose to her feet. Were they looking for Michael? Had something happened to the child? She remembered the look on his face, and she had opened the bedroom door and was on the point of stepping on to the landing when her employer's voice checked her. It was coming from the direction of the stairs, and she heard him ask, 'How long is it since he went out?'

'About an hour or an hour and a half,' came Mrs Batley's reply.

On this Linda realised they were not talking of Michael but of Shane. Then Mrs Batley's voice, holding a desperate note, said, 'Oh, don't say he's gone down to the Bay. But I'd like to bet anything that's where he is at this minute . . . Oh, after all this time to start again . . . I should have realised it, the way he left the house, there was that look on his face.'

'And you're blaming me.' The words that Ralph Batley spoke were low and bitter.

'No, I'm not, son, only I'm worried. If he gets bottled up he'll never make his way along that cliff path, you know how he goes on, dancing and acting the goat . . . it's a black, dark night. I'm worried, Ralph.'

Linda heard no more but she seemed to see the mother and son looking at each other. Then came the sound of Ralph Batley's steps running down the stairs, and a few minutes later the back door banging told her that he was on his way to Surfpoint Bay and The Wild Duck.

Softly she closed the door, and with her back to it she waited. When she heard the Jeep start up she could not help but hold her breath. Would he take the cliff path in the dark? When the throb of the Jeep did not become louder but faded into the distance, she knew that he was going by the back road and she closed her eyes and sighed.

Some time later, hearing the chink of crockery from down below, and remembering Mrs Batley's promise to bring her up a tray, she got to her feet instantly. She couldn't let the older woman wait on her, she had enough to do. Anyway, she didn't want anything to eat at all.

As there was no fear of running into Ralph Batley now, she went hastily from the room and down the stairs and straight to Mrs Batley's side, and looking from her to the tray she said, 'It's very kind of you, Mrs Batley, but I really don't want anything to eat.'

'We've all got to eat, girl.'

'But really I couldn't.' She put her hand out tentatively and touched Mrs Batley's arm.

'All right, as you say.' The older woman looked wearily ahead for a moment, then turning her eyes towards the large curtained window which faced the sea, she changed the conversation entirely by saying, 'The wind's getting up. It's going to be a rough night.'

'Yes. Yes, I think it is.'

After this attempt at small talk they both stood, uncertain what to say or do next, and as if by common consent they sat down.

The minutes passed. Then, as the noise of the wind dropped for a moment, there came into the room a strange sound: it was of distant hilarious singing. And when there followed the sound of the Jeep stopping in the yard Linda knew that Uncle Shane had arrived. Glancing swiftly towards Mrs Batley she saw that her face had a grey ashen look, and she was surprised when she did not immediately make for the kitchen, but rising went to the fireplace, and with one hand pressed against her side and the other stretched upwards on to the mantelpiece she stood with unusual stillness gazing down into the fire.

Quickly Linda turned away. She must get upstairs before Ralph Batley entered the house. And what was more, she couldn't bear to see Uncle Shane drunk. As she hurried across the hall she heard Shane's thick voice crying from the kitchen, 'Leave be! Leave be!' and she had her foot on the first step of the stairs when he came with a shambling run into the room crying, 'I'll not be baulked, nor preached at. I'm a man, amn't I?'

If Shane saw Mrs Batley he took no notice of her, but seeing Linda about to ascend the stairs he came at her with a rollicking rush, crying thickly, 'Aw! me darlin', there you are. There's me bonny lass. Come away. Come away. Come on, let's have a dance, a farewell dance.' He had pulled her down from the third step when Mrs Batley's hands came upon him, dragging him away. But he would not release his hold on Linda and she found herself once more in the middle of the room. She had a glimpse of Ralph Batley standing in the doorway. But even as she saw him he disappeared back into the kitchen again, and Mrs Batley cried, 'Sit down, Shane. Sit down! Do you hear?'

'Aw! Maggie, give over, will you, you're always worryin'. Let's have a sing-song, eh?' His voice breaking into song, he yelled, 'To the toot of the flute and the twiddle of the fiddle-o, Hoppin' up and down like a herrin' on a griddle-o.'

It should have been laughable but it wasn't. Linda was filled with a deep sadness as she looked down on the old man. He was sitting now, but he still held tightly to her arm, and when Mrs Batley struck at his hand, crying, 'Leave go!' he said to her in a hiccupping whisper, 'Whi . . . sht, Maggie! Linda here and me are goin' to have a party . . . a farewell party.'

'Leave go of her, Shane, do you hear? Leave go this minute.'

'Don't be vexed with me Maggie. Don't be vexed with old Shane . . . a man's got to do somethin' when he sees his world going wrong and he cannot put it to rights. Well, a man's got to do somethin', so he closes his eyes . . . I've closed me eyes, Maggie.'

'Leave go of her, will you?'

'Aw! she doesn't mind old Shane, she doesn't.' The old man was looking up into Linda's face now, his voice low, thick and sad. 'She's a girl after me own heart for she's got spunk. Aye, she has that, for all her gentle ways she's got spunk, and I'm going to tell her why I've got drunk this night, I am, I am. And she'll listen to old Shane, won't you, me dear?'

'Yes, yes, of course, Uncle Shane.' Linda's voice was scarcely above a whisper. She was cut to the heart at the sight of the old man. For all his jovial ways he'd had a bearing, a dignified bearing; there had been about him a suggestion that he had not always spent his days doing odd jobs on a farm. But now all dignity was stripped from him and it hurt her deeply to see him only as an object of pity.

She was not aware for the moment that Mrs Batley had left their side until she heard her voice speaking urgently in the kitchen, and the next moment Ralph Batley was in the room. He was standing opposite to her at the other side of Shane. Putting his hand under his uncle's armpit he gave a hoist as he said curtly, 'Come along.'

But Uncle Shane was not to be moved so easily, for looking up at his nephew, he laughed as he cried, 'Oh, there you are. There you are again, my pig-headed paddy. Aw! . . . aw! . . .' He pushed roughly at Ralph Batley's chest. 'Leave me be, will you? I'll go when I'm ready. Don't annoy me, for you know,' he wagged a solemn finger now up into his nephew's face, 'I'm agen you this night, aye, I am that. Not that I don't love you, I love you like a son, an' always have done, and I've bled for you, aye, I have. When that loose slut got her claws into you I bled for you . . . and I got drunk that night, didn't I? . . . paralytic. Now, now! Leave go of me, I won't rise until I'm ready.' He thrust Ralph Batley off while he still retained hold of Linda's sleeve, and he cried at him now, 'Every man gets a second chance, and you got yours, and what did you do? You closed your eyes, like me the night, only with a difference.'

'Are you coming or have I to make you?' Ralph Batley's voice was quiet, so quiet that Shane, pretending that he didn't hear him, turned towards Linda and, blinking his heavy eyelids and smiling widely up at her, said, 'Oh, me darlin', when I first saw you kneelin' near that wee cow when her labour was on her, I thought of the mother of God, I did that. For your beauty is like gold

. . . leave me be!' He tried to thrust off Ralph Batley's hand again as he cried, 'I'm not going up, I want to talk to her . . . for isn't she off in the mornin'?'

With a jerk Shane was brought to his feet and Linda found herself free. Ralph Batley was now propelling the old man forcibly from behind towards the stairs, and Shane, making one last effort, hung on to the knob of the balustrade until his fingers were forced off by Mrs Batley, and he was borne up the stairs like a child, his arms flailing wildly, his voice still yelling. Helpless in his nephew's grip, he made the undignified journey across the landing, and when his bedroom door banged on them his voice was heard for a moment or so longer, and then there was silence.

The silence descended on the whole house, and it seemed to Linda that it would go on forever when a small voice from the balcony said, 'Gran, Gran.'

Slowly Mrs Batley raised her head and looked upwards to where Michael was standing in his pyjamas, peering through the banisters, and she said wearily, 'It's all right. Go back to bed, it's all right.'

Linda watched the small figure turn reluctantly about and disappear from view, and then she looked towards Mrs Batley, whose face was now greyer than ever. And when the older woman, catching her glance, said, 'I'm sorry you've been subjected to this,' she could say nothing, for she was being weighed down with the sense of guilt again and the feeling that Uncle Shane's lapse lay at her door. She wanted to say something comforting but she couldn't. The silence swallowed them and became unbearable and so, saying quickly now, 'Good night, Mrs Batley,' she turned and went upstairs.

Poor Uncle Shane . . . the pity of it. But she wasn't to blame. How could she be? She had known him only a matter of days. She endeavoured to recall now some of the things he had said, but checked her thinking by saying to herself, 'He was drunk, things a man says when he's drunk don't make sense.'

Slowly she undressed for bed, and when she had turned out the light and got between the sheets she lay stiffly on her back with no idea of sleep in her mind. To sleep one must relax, and her body felt as stiff as if it had been set in cement. Then with surprising suddenness she flung round on to her face and once again she was lost in a storm of silent weeping . . .

At what time she fell asleep she didn't know, but she knew that she was dreaming, she told herself that she was dreaming. It was a habit she had acquired years ago. When in dreams she was being chased by weird animals and her legs suddenly refused to move, she would comfort herself by shouting, 'It's only a dream! it's only a dream!' This was likely an echo of her mother's voice when she would wake her from the nightmares and would say, 'It's only a dream, darling. There, there, it's only a dream.'

The dream that she was now in had taken on the form of a never-ending nightmare. Sometimes it was Great Leader who was chasing her, and just as the bull's hooves were about to come down on her she would regain the use of her legs, and then once more she was running, bounding into the air. Now it was Sep Watson chasing her, and just as he was clutching at her flying hair, Ralph Batley's hands came out of the air and flung him towards the sea and she watched him toppling over and over down the cliff. And then again she was running, from Ralph Batley this time, and she heard his steps sometimes pounding just behind her, sometimes in the distance, coming and going, coming and going. He wasn't trying to catch her, but like a sheep dog he was pressing her forward to the cliff path. Whichever way she darted there were the footsteps to the right, to the left and behind her. And now she was on the actual cliff path, racing towards its narrow end, knowing that when she reached it she would jump from the cliff to escape her pursuer. It's only a dream . . . it's only a dream! But still she ran, on and on, her heart pounding against her ribs as if it was going to burst. The steps were nearer now, close behind her, and then his hand came on her shoulders and she let out a great cry, yelling, 'No! no!'

As the cry escaped her lips she woke to reality more terrifying than the dream for a hand was on her shoulder and, there above her, his face alone looking so gigantic that it seemed to fill the room was Ralph Batley. As she shrank downwards into the bed in terror he said quietly, 'Don't be afraid, wake up.'

She remained still, staring at him, her eyes fixed wide.

'Are you awake?' He gave a gentle shake to her shoulders.

She blinked now and gasped as she said, 'Yes, yes, I'm awake.'

'There's nothing to be afraid of.' He had straightened up and she saw that he was dressed only in his breeches and his shirt, and this was unbuttoned down the front. 'My . . . my mother is ill, I need help. Will you come down?'

'Ill?' She was sitting up now, the covers gathered under her chin. 'Yes, I'll come down immediately.'

The minute the door had closed on him she sprang out of bed. She was still half-dazed with sleep and the terror of the nightmare, and she groped around for a few minutes before she could find her dressing-gown, but by the time she reached the landing she was wide awake.

Hearing her employer's voice speaking softly in the hall, she ran to the head of the stairs and from there she saw him bending over the couch.

When Linda stood by the couch and looked down at Mrs Batley she was amazed at the change she saw. Her face was the colour of lint and her eyes seemed to have dropped back into their sockets, in fact there seemed to be no eyes at all behind the closed lids. She seemed to have put on twenty years in a few hours.

Glancing up into Ralph Batley's face, Linda saw no semblance of the man she remembered from yesterday, and when he beckoned her aside from the couch she moved quietly with him into the kitchen and there, turning slightly towards her but keeping his eyes averted, he said, 'I've phoned the doctor. He won't bring his car across the fields, I'll have to go and meet him.' Wetting his lips he added, 'I'm very sorry I've had to get you up.'

'Under the circumstances I don't expect an apology.' Her tone was sharp. Then as she watched him pull his duffle coat from the back of the door she asked more softly, 'What is the matter with her?'

She saw him give a little shake of his head and pause for a second with his arm half into his coat as he said, 'I don't know.' His voice had a frightened note, which sounded odd coming from him. Then he went quickly out into the night, and after looking towards the door for a moment, she returned to the room and to Mrs Batley's side.

The older woman hadn't moved, and if it hadn't been for a slight, slow rise of the blankets that covered her Linda would have imagined that she had already died.

The collar of her blouse hanging over the edge of the blanket showed her to be still dressed, and this made Linda question the time. She couldn't have gone to bed, and it must be the middle of the night, three o'clock at least!

The grandfather clock on the landing began to strike at that moment and Linda, to her

152

amazement, counted twelve strokes. Only twelve o'clock. She felt as if she had been asleep and in that nightmare for hours and hours.

Mrs Batley made an almost imperceptible movement and opened her eyes. Slowly she turned her weary gaze towards Linda. 'Ralph?' the name was just a faint whisper, and Linda, taking her hand and stroking it gently, said softly, 'He won't be a minute, Mrs Batley, he's just gone to meet the doctor. Lie quiet.'

'Girl.'

Catching the whisper, Linda bent over Mrs Batley and said, 'Yes, Mrs Batley, what is it?'

Mrs Batley stared up into her face for a moment and her lips formed words, but no sound came. She was trying to say something but the effort was too great, and Linda said softly, 'Don't worry, just lie quiet. Don't try to talk.'

Mrs Batley's lids slowly closed again and as Linda sat looking at her she thought, Oh, be quick, be quick. He's surely had enough time to get to the road and back again. The doctor mustn't have arrived yet. As the minutes wore on she found herself praying rapidly, beseechingly. Then the back door opened and the next minute Ralph Batley came into the room accompanied by a man who in age and build was not unlike Uncle Shane except that he was clean-shaven.

He gave Linda one searching glance as he came towards the couch, then as he stood gazing down on Mrs Batley he divested himself of his coat and, throwing it with bad aim towards a chair, he lowered himself slowly on to the side of the couch and, taking up the bloodless-looking hand, he said, 'Hello there, Maggie.'

Mrs Batley opened her eyes and looked at the doctor, then slowly she closed them again.

After a moment of staring down on her the doctor rose to his feet. He took Ralph Batley by the arm and drew him away from the couch and said quietly, 'Can you get her bed downstairs? That room of hers is too far away, she won't stay in it, but if she's down here there's more likelihood of keeping her in bed.' He paused, then turned his eyes towards the couch. 'And she's going to be in bed for some time, I'm afraid,' he ended.

'What is it?'

'I'll tell you better when I've examined her, although I've a good idea already. You can't work an engine night and day, it's got to stop sometime.'

Ralph Batley's expression remained the same. The only indication that he was deeply affected was given by his hands. Linda watched as he dug into the cushion of one thumb with the fingers of the other hand.

'Shall I bring it down into the hall?' he asked quietly, referring to the bed.

The doctor glanced round for a moment, then said, 'No. No, she'd be in the thick of it here, you wouldn't be able to keep her down. What about the front room? Can you get that warmed up within the next hour or so?'

'Yes, yes, I'll see to that.'

'All right then, go on about it and leave her to me.'

When he reached Mrs Batley's side again Linda moved away, he did not seem to require her. Ralph Batley had gone into a room across the hall, it was the sitting-room and had not been used during her stay in the house. He would be lighting the fire, so she must get the bedding down. On this she ran upstairs and into Mrs Batley's room where the bed was still undisturbed, and stripping it she carried as much of the bedclothes downstairs as her arms could hold . . .

An hour later a fire was burning brightly in the sitting-room, and not far from it Mrs Batley was lying in bed, looking worse, if it were possible, than she had done as she lay on the couch. They had transferred her with the least possible fuss, and she still remained in her clothes.

Linda was in the hall when the doctor and Ralph Batley came out of the room, and the doctor was saying quietly, 'Well, Ralph, this is no surprise to me, I've been expecting it for the last two years.'

Linda saw Ralph Batley rub his lips one over the other before he asked, 'But what is it?'

'A number of things. Sheer exhaustion for one thing, a tired heart, a very tired heart. She'll have to be careful . . .' He came towards the hearth and, taking up his stand with his back to the fire and looking about the room, he said, 'It's going to put you in a fix for there's no need for me to tell you she's been doing the work of three women for years. But that's past, you'll have to make other arrangements . . .'

'I . . . I'll see to that.' Ralph Batley broke in, speaking hastily. 'But . . . but can you tell me if there is any danger?'

'No, not if she remains quiet and isn't troubled in any way. She's had all the worry she can stand. Anyway, there's one thing you can be thankful for at the moment, you've got help.' He glanced towards Linda and gave her a quiet smile. 'But I'm afraid that, however willing, one person won't be able to do all she did. But then she wanted it that way, she was always a worker . . . oh, yes.' And now he added something that brought the colour, not only to Linda's face but also to Ralph Batley's, for addressing her pointedly he said, 'She can give you her orders from the bed and teach you to cook . . . you're not old enough yet to be up to her standard.' He paused, staring at her, then added, 'Well now, I must be off. I've got two babies just waiting to yell at any minute.' He nodded to Ralph Batley as he finished with a laugh. 'Shouldn't be surprised if there's a message awaiting me when I get back.'

Ralph Batley made no comment on this, he was leading the way towards the kitchen door and it was from there that the doctor turned and said quietly to Linda, 'Good night.'

'Good night, Doctor.'

As she walked towards the sitting-room, her face still hot, she repeated to herself, 'She will teach you to cook.' In the room she looked at Mrs Batley. The sleeping tablet was having its effect, her breathing was easier and her face was more relaxed and a little less grey.

The room was lit by a central light and the shade was too bright, it needed something to soften the glare. She remembered she had a green silk headscarf upstairs but it was packed in the trunk. In a matter of minutes she was in her room. Scattering her neatly folded clothes from the trunk she retrieved the scarf and ran downstairs again. After pinning it round the light she brought two cushions from the settee and arranged them in the stiff-backed armchair before settling herself quietly by the fire.

After a while a slight movement in the hall told her Ralph Batley had returned. As he came into the room he glanced at the shaded light before going to the bed and looking at his mother. As if compelled against his will, he turned now towards Linda and beckoned her out of the room.

Rising slowly from the chair she followed him, and when they were a short distance from the sitting-room door he said, 'I can manage, you must go to bed.'

'I'm not going to bed.' Her voice was level. 'I can sleep all tomorrow if I want to,' she laid slight stress on these words before adding, 'whereas you will have to work.'

There was a conflict raging within her as she stared into his face. Some part of her was still angry with him, but a greater part, a part that was attempting to envelop her mind, urged, Tell him you'll stay, at least for a time. He looks at his wits' end. But the angry section thrusting its way forward said, And be snubbed for your pains.

'That will be my worry.'

There, she said to herself, what did I say?

'I'm sorry.' His eyes dropped from hers. 'You have been very kind, but . . . but I must stay up tonight in case she wakes and needs me.' He turned from her towards the fire, adding under his breath, 'If you care, you could sleep on the couch.'

'Very well, I'll do that.' Her own voice was soft now. 'Can I get you anything?'

'No. No, thanks.'

A few minutes later she was lying on the couch staring across the space towards the fire. She had not bothered to go upstairs and get a blanket for the room was warm, and so she was surprised in more ways than one when he stood before the couch with a travelling rug in his hands.

'It will get very cold towards dawn in spite of the fire.' It seemed for a moment that he was just going to hand the rug to her, and then he shook it out and dropped it gently over her. He did not touch her but he looked at her and she at him, and during the space of time their eyes held, something leaped the bridge between them. She felt it in the trembling of her hands and the throbbing of her throat, it was as if a live thing had entered her being. And did she imagine in this instant that his eyes were no longer cold, steel grey, but that there was a deep depth of warmth in them, or was it a trick of the firelight?

He moved away and she pulled the rug close about her and lay staring towards the fire.

158

Although she lay with her eyes closed she did not sleep, there were so many things to think about, so many things. She heard two o'clock strike, then half-past. It must have been near three o'clock when the sullen glow of the fire that was resting on her closed lids was replaced by darkness, and without opening her eyes she knew that Ralph Batley was at the fireplace making up the fire. She heard the hiss and spit of fresh wood on the embers, then, although she had heard no movement whatever, she felt that he was standing by the side of the couch looking down at her. When after a few seconds there was still no movement, she had a strong desire to open her eyes but repressed it . . . he thought she was asleep, otherwise he wouldn't be standing there. Then she had startling proof of his presence for she heard his breathing distinctly and realised with an inward tremor that his face could not be far from her own. The urge to open her eyes wide and surprise him was overpowering . . . she had never yet seen him at a disadvantage, this would be the moment . . . but she did not move. And then her heart seemed to give a loud bounce which reverberated through her body for he was whispering. Very, very softly, he was saying two words and he repeated them. It was only with the greatest possible effort that she went on feigning sleep, for she wanted to reach out her hands to him and give him an answer to his words, she wanted to say, 'It's all right, I won't.' A few seconds more and she knew she was alone again and she turned her face into the cushions and in a very short time she was asleep . . .

It was Shane's agonised voice that woke her. He was saying, 'God in heaven! what have I done? She looks like death.'

'It wasn't anything to do with you, take a hold of yourself.' Ralph Batley's voice was low and harsh. 'If there's anyone to blame it's me.'

'Oh, boy, what have you done, you've done nothing but work and work.'

'That's just it, I couldn't see anything else but work, I couldn't see that she was ill. Doc Morgan says that he's been expecting it for the last two years and there was I, letting her get on with it. Working from Monday morning till Saturday night.'

The voices were coming nearer the couch now, making their way towards the fire, and Shane's voice had a tremor in it as he said, 'But Maggie's always worked, not just this last year or so.'

'Yes, and that's the trouble. But I could have made things easier. I should have made her have that washing-machine and floor-polisher last year when we talked about it.'

'Aw, boy, it would have been as she said, they would have been a nice couple of ornaments decorating the kitchen, for she wouldn't have used them.'

'That was just bluff, she didn't want me to spend the money on them.'

There followed a silence before Shane said, 'Aye . . . aye, well, there might have been some-thing in that. Her main idea was that you should

160

plough every penny back. But what's goin' to happen now? How are we goin' to manage without Maggie?'

Again there was a silence. Then Shane's voice whispered, 'There's only Peggy Johnstone who would come up this far, and she's expecting a child any minute now. If only the young girl here . . .'

'Ssh!'

Linda knew that the eyes of the two men were on her and it was quite some time before Shane's whisper came again, 'She's still asleep.' And then, 'Would you have it in your heart to ask her to stay a while?'

There was another space before the answer came. 'She wouldn't, not after the way I went for her yesterday, hell for leather.'

'But why did you?'

'Oh, I don't know . . . Seeing her with a Cadwell, it looked for the moment like the old pattern over again. She must have thought I was mad, and I was for a time. She would never understand the feeling between the Cadwells and us.'

'What if I were to ask her?'

'No, I did the damage, the rest is up to me. But look, go and get a wash and I'll see about breakfast.'

When they moved away into the kitchen she lay for a moment longer savouring a feeling of power, sweet power. She had not dreamed the two words she had heard in the night. She said them to herself, 'Don't go, don't go.' But could he, the master of the house, the god of this domain, bring himself openly to apologise to her and ask her to stay? Before she had sat upright on the couch rubbing the sleep from her eyes, she knew that she would not put him to any test . . . enough it was for her to know that she was needed.

Before going upstairs she crept towards the sitting-room door. Mrs Batley was still asleep. She seemed to have sunk deeply into the bed and her face once more was ashen and old looking.

Then she went swiftly to the kitchen. Ralph Batley was at the stove. He had the pan in his hand and his back towards her, and without any preliminaries she said to him quickly, 'Leave that, I'll see to the breakfast in a few minutes, I'm just going to change.'

He had only time to turn towards her before she hurried from the room.

She stopped for a moment at the head of the stairs and looked at the clock. It said ten past five. So early! She felt as refreshed as if she had been asleep all night.

It was nine o'clock in the morning. Mrs Batley had been washed and was now attired in her nightdress, and with Linda supporting her head had just finished drinking a cup of tea. And now, lying back on her pillows, she lifted a hand and clutched weakly at Linda as she moved away from the bed. 'I . . . I want . . . will you . . . ?' The words were brought out with a painful effort, and Linda, stroking her hand, said reassuringly, 'I know what you want to say. But don't worry, I'm not going

162

to leave you, I'm going to stay on and look after you.' And then with a smile she stroked the older woman's hair back from her brow and finished, 'The doctor said you've got to teach me to cook and do it from here.' She now patted the bed and her smile broadened as she saw the look of utter relief come into Mrs Batley's face. But when painful tears welled from the corners of the older woman's eyes she said hastily, 'Oh, don't cry, Mrs Batley, everything's going to be all right.'

'What's the matter, is she——?' Ralph Batley's voice came from behind her, and without turning Linda said, 'She's all right, I was just telling her that I had asked you if I could stay on.' She straightened the sheet under Mrs Batley's chin, then turning to the side table she picked up the cup and saucer and left the room.

She was in the kitchen at the sink when Ralph Batley passed through on his way outside and she did not turn her head in his direction until he spoke to her.

'Thank you,' he said.

She looked across the table towards him but could find nothing to say, but the colour swept up to her forehead when he came slowly towards her. In this moment he looked different, entirely different from the man she knew as Ralph Batley. Not only his eyes but his whole face had softened, and it was not hard to imagine that at one time here had been a strikingly handsome man. She could almost see what the face had been like before the flesh had left it to its bony contours. There was

163

even a suspicion of a smile on his face as he said, 'That is what is known as heaping coals of fire.'

'I did not intend it should be.' Her eyes dropped from his and he said quickly, 'I know that, and I want to say now that I'm very grateful to you. Also I'm very sorry for my behaviour yesterday.'

Her eyes came up to his and she let her smile envelop him as she said, 'Mine wasn't very exemplary either.' Then a wonderful thing happened. They laughed together, quietly they laughed together, and when their laughter subsided they were still looking at each other. Slowly she turned to the sink and he to the door.

Through the window she watched him as he strode down the yard and disappeared round the dry-stone wall. Outside the sea fret had soaked the land and darkened the sky, but somehow the morning was very bright.

4

Although Linda's first day as a substitute for Mrs Batley had been filled with every kind of household chore, plus nursing, there was only one duty of which she would have been pleased to be relieved, it was making Sep Watson's break tea. He had come into the kitchen around ten o'clock and, looking at her closely, he had said, 'Sad thing about the missus, ain't it? Worked to death I would say. I've thought it for years.'

'Do you want something?' Linda had asked him.

'Aye, me tea.' He had given her a twisted grin, and as she put the kettle on the stove he went on as if nothing had interrupted him, saying, 'Nobody but a fool would take on running this house on their own, no matter what the bribe.'

On this she swung round on him, but with an effort she refrained from making any comment. That's what he wanted, that she should talk to him, argue with him, discuss the family with him – well, she wasn't going to be drawn. So she remained with her gaze fixed on the kettle willing it to boil. And then he said softly, 'Hear you had an up and downer with the boss in Morpeth yesterday.'

She was round at him before she could stop

herself, demanding, 'How do you know what happened yesterday?'

'Ah, things get around in these parts. Perhaps it's them seagulls that carries the messages, eh?' He gave his thick laugh, and then he said, 'Suits you, the blush. You could do with a bit of colour, among other things.' He cast his eyes swiftly over her slim figure.

For a moment she was not afraid of him and she faced him squarely, saying, 'If I hear any more of that kind of talk from you I'll report you to Mr Batley. You know what happened last time.'

'What kind of talk? What're you gettin' at? I haven't said nowt, nowt out of the way.'

At that moment the back door opened and Shane came in. His glance darting between them, he asked, 'Anything wrong?'

'No, nothing.' The kettle was boiling and she mashed the tea, and when she pushed the jug across the table towards Sep Watson he looked at her and said with quiet civility, 'The missus usually gives me a slice of something.'

Going to the pantry Linda cut a slice of meat pie and, putting it none too gently on a plate, she handed it to him.

When the door had closed on the cowman Shane said quietly, 'Tell me, what was he saying?'

'Oh, it was nothing, just some silly remark.' And then her tone changing, she turned to the old man and said quickly, 'I don't like him, Uncle Shane.'

'You're not the only one, girl. I wouldn't trust him as far as I could toss him. Be careful of him is my advice to you.' He was half-turned from her when he said softly, 'Before the subject is closed finally let me say that I'm glad to the heart that you're staying with us. God works in very strange ways. He let me get drunk to act as the last straw to break Maggie's back. Don't you think His ways are strange?' His head was dropped to the side now, and he was looking at her with a side-long glance. And for reply she said, 'I'm glad to be staying, Uncle Shane.'

By the end of the first week Mrs Batley was showing signs of improvement and the house had fallen into a new routine, a routine that filled every second of Linda's day. But although her hours were long those of Ralph Batley seemed to be longer, for when she rose at six in the morning he was already up, and when she went to bed towards ten at night he was still busy.

As Mrs Batley began to recover there came a slight feeling of gaiety over the house. The hall had on more than one occasion been filled with high laughter. That the laughter was against her, Linda did not mind in the least. Her first efforts at baking the bread had not been the roaring success that she had imagined it would be. Following Mrs Batley's instructions it had sounded easy. But the reason why her loaves refused to rise became evident when Ralph Batley picked up a basin from a side table in the kitchen and, after smelling it, he looked over the rim of the basin at her and said softly, 'This is the yeast. I think it should have gone in the dough.' That was one of the occasions when they had laughed, and Linda thought that the wasted batch of bread was a small payment for the look on Ralph Batley's face, for his laughter seemed to transform him.

There was only one incident that brought a sad note to the new atmosphere. Jess had died and Michael had cried bitterly. Not even the knowledge that another sheep dog, and a retriever pup, were to become members of the farm as soon as his uncle could drive over to Elsdom Farm, which lay beyond Morpeth, seemed to bring him any consolation.

That Linda had not been out of the house for a week did not trouble her. The weather had been vile, squalls of rain and winds that could cut through you weren't any inducement to be about the farm. But the weather today, like a capricious woman, was showing its other side. The sun was bright, even warm where it came through the kitchen window, and Linda had a sudden longing to take a walk just along the cliff.

The sun must have stimulated the same idea in the minds of Mrs Batley and her son, for some time during the morning Mrs Batley, looking anxiously at Linda when she brought her a drink, said, 'You look peaked, girl, you've lost your colour. Look, the sun's shining, go out for a while, just a walk round.'

'This morning?' Linda looked at her in much amazement. 'And the dinner to see to? Would you have taken a walk round in the middle of the morning?'

Mrs Batley shook her head slowly. 'No, lass, but I can see now things would have been better if I had done. I should have let up a bit.'

'Well, things will be different when you get up, you can rest assured of that.' Linda bounced her head towards her.

'I feel sometimes that I'll never get up again. It's a dreadful feeling.'

'Oh, of course you will, you're much better, so much better.'

'I feel so weak' – Mrs Batley shook her head slowly – 'like a child. I wouldn't have believed that I could have lost my strength like this.' Then looking towards Linda she said, 'What I would have done without you, girl, I just don't know. What would have happened to them?'

'Something would have turned up, it always does. There now, drink your milk.'

As Linda was moving from the room Mrs Batley called after her, 'But you must get out, I'll see Ralph.'

Linda turned quickly to her. 'No, no. Please don't say anything to him. I'll go out if I want to, never worry.'

But before Mrs Batley could see her son, he, too, spoke to Linda on the same matter. She was setting the table for lunch when he passed through the hall on his way to see his mother, and he stopped and looked at her before saying, 'Shane's going to stay in for a couple of hours this afternoon so that you can take a walk.'

'But I don't want to walk.' And now that she was

being pressed she felt that she didn't.

'You've never been across the door this week and we won't get many more days like this. I think you should. I'm merely being selfish as always. If anything should happen to you I'd be sunk.'

The look on his face did not match the self-centredness of his words, and Linda, dropping her gaze from him as she moved round the table setting out the cutlery, said, 'Very well, I'll go out for a little while.'

He stood for a moment longer, his eyes hard on her, before going towards the sitting-room and his mother, and he left her feeling strangely happy.

Although the day was one the northern winter has rarely to offer, with the atmosphere perfectly clear and the air as bracing as spring water, although the view from the cliff path was magnificent, the coastline could be seen for miles winding away in a rugged curve, Linda was finding no joy in it. To the right of her lay the moors, great stretches of land with touches of brown that spoke of past glories of heather. She had passed the Batley boundary some time ago and had been walking for at least an hour, yet had seen no-one, not even in the distance. The scenery was grand and rugged, but it was lonely. You needed someone with you to enjoy it, someone to combat the solitariness that cried aloud up here. She had a sudden longing to be back in the warm atmosphere of the farm kitchen, and immediately she began to retrace her steps, taking now a left-hand path which shut out the lonely grandeur of the coastline.

The path led further inland than she had imagined, and when she came in sight of the boundary wires she realised that she wasn't far from the road. It was as she was passing the crop of rock near where the sheep had broken through the wire, which was the only part of this side of the Batley boundary open to the road, that she heard the sound of horses' hooves. The rider, she thought, could be anyone from around here, but it could also be one of the Cadwell men, perhaps Rouse Cadwell. She stopped for a moment and remained in the shelter of the rocky hillock. The sound of the hooves came nearer, but slower now. When the rider came into view and she saw the head and shoulders of the elder Cadwell man, she was more than thankful she had kept out of sight. She pressed herself against the rock and from her slanted vision she could see his head. He was looking up and down the road. Then she saw him bend forward towards the high bank as if he were going to pick something up, or put something down. A minute later he galloped off.

When the sound of the hooves had faded away Linda went tentatively towards the bank. She did not trust the Cadwell man, she never had. Above the spot where she had seen him lean forward she examined the wire. It was only a few yards from where Ralph Batley had fixed the new strands, but there was no sign of a break in the wire now.

Why had he stopped here at this spot, and what was he picking up from the bank? She leant well over the wire, looking up and down the grassy slope but all she saw, that was not of nature, was a crumpled piece of paper. It was as if someone had thrown it away, but the fact that it was wedged in a small hole at the back of a root of hawthorn she found rather curious. Lying flat now along the bank, she put her arm under the wire and found she could just reach the hole. When she withdrew her hand she was staring in amazement at a crumpled five-pound note. Her eyes moved in the direction the rider had taken. Five-pound notes didn't wedge themselves in holes. Her mind began to race. If what she was thinking was right, this money would be collected later this evening around quarter-past five. But no, Sep Watson couldn't be as vile as that, working for the Cadwells against a family who had employed him for most of his life. But her instinct told her that the cowman could be as vile as that, and she remembered back to the morning when, practically on this very spot, Ralph Batley had questioned the man as to how he had known the sheep were out. She remembered that his answers had made her uneasy then, but she had taken the matter no further in her mind.

Gone now was the idea of sauntering back to the farm. She set off at a run and didn't stop until she came within sight of the farm buildings. But it wasn't these that brought her running to a walk, it was the sight of a burly figure filling the archway in the high brick wall. Although she could not see his face she knew that the man was Sep Watson, and although she had just caught sight of him she knew, too, he could have been watching her for some time, for from where he was standing he could see the hills beyond the valley. She told herself quickly that he could gauge nothing from her running, but even as she thought this she was reminded of his cunning. He might be dull-witted but he was like a fox, wary, and nothing escaped him. She did not go towards the archway but walked now with seeming casualness towards the front of the house and knew a great measure of relief when she saw the Jeep in the yard. This meant Ralph Batley had returned from taking the milk down to the Bay. Yet, as far as she could see, there was no sign of him about the buildings. But as she made her way up the yard to the farm kitchen she heard his voice, and the high laugh of Michael.

As she opened the kitchen door Michael ran to her with a cry, saying, 'Oh! you're back. Uncle was saying he was going to send a search party for you, it's getting dark.'

Ralph Batley had his back towards her and he didn't turn and chide his nephew for chattering. He went on pouring the boiling water into the teapot. It could have been that she had never entered the kitchen.

'Can I speak with you a minute?'

He turned his head quickly in her direction. His face had a quiet look – she nearly put the word contented to it. Yet no, that didn't suit his expression. He looked now at the boy and said, 'Go and fetch Uncle Shane, he'll be in the shed.'

Michael hesitated for a second, and then his desire to be with Linda dared him to make a protest in the form of saying, 'But Uncle Shane's just gone out.'

To save the boy from the sharp reprimand that was coming to him, Linda said quickly, 'I won't be a minute, I just want to have a word with your uncle. There's a good boy, go on.' She opened the door and pressed him outside, and when she closed it again and turned to her employer he was standing at the far side of the table, waiting for her to speak. And she did so rapidly, as if she was still running. Without any lead-up she said, 'I've seen something. It's very odd, but near the wire where it was cut the other day, where the sheep got through, I saw . . .' She now paused and lowered her gaze from him for a second before continuing quickly, 'Mr Cadwell. He was riding by and stopped near the bank. I was curious. I saw him bend down as if he was picking something up, and when he was gone I looked at the bank and I saw something in a hole, a piece of paper. It was—' she paused again, 'it was a five-pound note.'

Although her employer was looking straight at her Linda knew he wasn't seeing her, and she closed her eyes for a moment to shut out the changed countenance of the man before her, for it was the face she had seen as he stood on the bank a few mornings ago ready to spring on the elder Cadwell man. She saw his Adam's apple move rapidly twice, and then he said, 'You're sure of this?'

'Sure? Of course I am. I had it in my hand, a five-pound note.'

'What did you do with it?'

'I put it back. I feel . . . I feel . . .' She turned her head to the side. She thought that she knew how her employer regarded his cowhand, and yet, what if she were wrong?

'What do you feel?' His voice was hard, as if she was in some way to blame for what she was telling him.

Her head came round. 'I feel it will be collected . . . and soon.'

'Yes. How soon?'

'About quarter-past five.'

He stared hard at her for a moment before swinging away from the table. 'My God! He's been in our employ for years. He's a funny customer, I know, but not that bad. And yet.' He turned and faced her again, saying slowly now, a puzzled note in his voice, 'It would all add up . . . Everything. But why should he do it?'

'I don't know. Money, I should think, and spite.'

'Yes, and spite. It's odd, but for some reason I haven't got to the bottom of, he's always hated me.'

She watched him draw in a long deep breath. Then looking quickly at his watch, he said, 'You say it's near the wire?'

'Yes.'

'Where were you?'

'Behind that crop of rocks.'

He nodded, then said, 'Look, carry on as if nothing had happened. Go for the milk. Could you keep him occupied until I get out, just for a few minutes, he mustn't see me. I've got to get to the bottom of this, and if I do I may get to the bottom of everything that has happened to this farm for years. Everything. I may catch the servant of the jinx, and my God, if I do he'll need someone to pray for him.' His voice held a deep, threatening quality, his face was dark with passionate anger. And now he added rapidly, 'Don't tell my mother anything of this.'

'No, no, of course not.'

'Go on then. Take the can for the milk, it will be nothing unusual at this time. Try to keep him occupied for a moment or two until I get along the top. Will you do that?'

The last was a question, a little softer now, and it conveyed that he knew how distasteful to her the request was.

For answer she picked up the big shining can from the dresser and went out.

When she entered the dairy there was no sign of Sep Watson, for from the side door she could see the full length of the cowshed. What should she do now? Michael . . . she would pretend she was going in search of Michael. Yet how would she keep the man in conversation? She had never spoken voluntarily to him from the first day she had been here. Wood . . . Yes, wood. She would ask him if he would bring a load of wood to the house before he left off work, and that should be any minute now. She hurried out into the yard again and towards the byre where Sarah and her calf were housed. But there was still no sign of the cowman or Michael.

It was Michael's voice that at last indicated where Sep Watson was, and she was led towards the big barn. As she stood in the doorway she saw Michael standing in front of the cowman. The cowman was looking down on him, but as Linda came in through the open doorway they both turned towards her. Linda spoke to the boy first as if she hadn't seen him for some time. 'I've been looking for you, Michael,' she said, 'your tea's ready. Did you find Uncle Shane?'

'No, no.' Michael's voice was high and excited. 'I'm looking now. I was . . . I was asking Sep.'

Sep Watson was now looking towards Linda, and not taking his eyes from her, he spoke to the boy. His voice was quiet and ordinary sounding and did not match the look on his face. 'Your Uncle Shane was in the store the last time I saw him.' Before the cowman had finished speaking Michael had darted away out into the yard and Linda was left alone facing the man.

As he stood staring at her, not speaking, Linda told herself not to be afraid, there was nothing he could do. Ralph Batley had asked her to play for time and that's what she must do. She said, 'We're down on wood. I wonder if you'd bring a load in?'

Slowly he stepped towards her until there was not more than two feet between them, and then he repeated her words. 'You want me to bring some wood in?'

Linda swallowed and put her hand gropingly behind her and touched the wall of the barn for support, and she endeavoured to bring a coolness into her tone as she said, 'Yes, that's what I said. Bring some wood in.'

'Why d'you want me to bring wood in? You've never asked me afore.'

'Well, I'm asking you now.'

'Aye, you are, and why are you asking me? If I didn't know I'd be puzzled. I'd say to meself, "Why is this hoity-toity madam stooping to speak to me?" That's what I would say to meself, there must be a reason for it. But I've got no need to ask you, I know the reason.' As his lips closed on the last word his great hands shot out and gripped her shoulders, bringing an involuntary scream from her lips. 'Go on, have a damn good scream, nobody'll hear you. You've settled your own hash. Old Shane went off to the north side after a heifer not ten minutes gone, and you, you know what you've done? You've got rid of your protector. Aye! Aye!' His voice was high in his head, soft and high and terrifying. Linda's eyes were fixed on him with the hypnotic stare of a trapped rabbit. Her limbs seemed paralysed, even the terror that was filling her now could not galvanise her into any action. 'He's running hell for leather up to the road to catch somebody out, isn't he? You must have seen something that wasn't meant for you to see this afternoon. You came running like a scalded cat over the hills, I watched you. I wondered at the time and then the bairn's just told me the reason. Aye, the bairn was listening in. Bairns are funny things, aren't they? You generally get the truth out of bairns. Michael's just told me his uncle's gone up to the top boundary to catch a man who's going to get some money that's been left there. Bairns cause a lot of trouble, don't they? You!' The cowman's voice suddenly turned to a deep growl. 'You sneaking little heifer! For two pins I'd throttle you.' His hands were round her throat, she couldn't have screamed now if she had wanted to. His body was pressed against her, his hot, smelling breath was over her face, his squat nose was almost touching hers and his eyes, like pinpoints of fire, were boring through her head. And he hissed at her now, 'I'm finished here. I've known it was comin' anyway. It makes no difference, I can get a job anywhere, but I like doin' things in my own way. I don't take to being stumped by a long-legged bitch like you. An' I'm tellin' you now, you're a goner be sorry afore you're very much older that you crossed me. By God! you are. When I'm finished with you, me dear, you'll wish you had kept on the right side of Sep Watson. Come here!' As one arm went round her his other hand clapped over her mouth, and she felt herself lifted bodily from her feet. And at this moment she came to life – struggling, kicking, shrieking life. But the shrieks could not get past the grip of his hand. She fought and kicked as he carried her up the length of the barn and round behind the end bales, and there with a jerk of his arm as if he was throwing a bullock off its feet, he flipped her flat on her back. For a moment she was sickened and stunned by the fall, then in a frenzy of terror she was fighting him, kicking, rearing, struggling. When for a second his hand was pulled from her mouth the compressed screams that were filling her body escaped, but only for a moment for his hand now gripped her face as if he meant to crush the bones. And a wild terror enveloped her when the wind was knocked clean out of her body with the weight that fell upon it, and for a second everything went black about her. The next moment a light that seemed as bright as the sun pierced the darkness and the weight was lifted from her, and she lay dizzy and sick, conscious only of a struggle and gasping breaths at her side. A volley of curses in a terrible Irish voice told her now that it was Uncle Shane who was fighting like a madman with the cowman. She turned off her back on to her side and was attempting to rise when she was knocked flying across the floor into a bale of straw. And she knew that it was Uncle Shane's body that had been hurled against her. She was lying on her face now, and as she felt the old man struggling gallantly to his feet amid a flood of oaths Sep Watson's voice came to her again, but now it was directed towards the old man.

'Stay where you are, if you get off your knees I'll knock you flat. I'm tellin' you mind.' There was a scrambling sound by her side and then Sep Watson's voice crying, 'Well, you asked for it.'

Drawing her head into her shoulders she waited,

expecting the old man to come thundering to the ground, but instead her dazed mind became aware of a new sound, a strange sound, as of feet dancing on the wooden floor of the barn. This was followed by the thick sound of blows, of deep gasping breaths. Uncle Shane couldn't be standing up to Sep Watson like that, couldn't be pounding him like that. She turned slowly on to her side again and then, in the weird light of the lantern that Uncle Shane had stood near the wall of the barn, she saw, with overwhelming relief, the figure of Ralph Batley. He looked gigantic and even terrible as his fists pistoned in and out as they contacted the cowman. Sep Watson, she saw, was returning blow for blow. It seemed that the cowman did not feel the hammering fists. The weirdness of the scene was increased by the silence of the combat, only the sound of the blows and the quick intake of breaths filled the barn. She was aware now of Uncle Shane standing near her, he had pulled himself up and was resting with his back against the bale of hay, blood running from the corner of his mouth. Linda now put her hand to her face as she saw Ralph Batley stagger backwards and almost fall as the ox-like arms flailed about him. As she covered her eyes there came the sound of a blow as if a piece of wood had suddenly split. When fearfully she opened her eyes again, it was to see Sep Watson lying on the ground.

Like a boxer trying to recover, the cowman got to his hands and knees and shook his head, and then slowly pulled himself to his feet again. But he did not put up his fists; instead, with lowered head, he looked upwards at his master and said thickly, 'I'll hev you for this, you'll see.'

'Get out while you're whole . . . Go on, get!' Ralph Batley spoke to the man as he would not have done to an animal, and as the cowman stumbled towards the door of the barn he added, 'If I see you on my land again . . .' He didn't finish but turned swiftly now towards his uncle and Linda.

'You all right, Uncle?'

'Yes, yes, I'm all right. Just a split lip. Nothing, nothing. Here a minute, here a minute.' The old man pulled his nephew aside and said something to him in an undertone.

Linda was now sitting with her back towards the bales. She felt, as she put it to herself, slightly odd. All the strength had gone out of her body; she had a great desire to cry. When her employer's hands came down to her she put hers into them, but was unable to pull herself from the ground. She knew she was beginning to tremble, and again she wanted to cry. Her head drooped forward and when his hands came under her arms and raised her gently to her feet, she said, 'It's all right, it's all right.' And then she knew it wasn't all right, her legs were going to give way, and she added hastily, 'I must sit, I must sit down.' But there was nowhere to sit and she hung on to his arm.

'Are you . . . are you hurt?' His voice was quiet.

She did not answer for a moment, she felt sore and bruised all over, and she dare not trust herself to speak. Her one desire at the moment was to cry, cry with relief at the escape she had had.

'Look at me.' His voice was soft, even gentle. 'Linda, look at me. Did he . . .? Uncle Shane said . . . Tell me what happened.'

He had called her Linda, but she did not even comment to herself about it. At the moment it had no effect on her, she only wanted to cry and he didn't like crying. She managed to gasp, 'No, no,' before the storm of tears overwhelmed her. She was hardly aware that she was being held in his arms, her head pressed into his shoulder, or that his voice was saying in the endearing terms he had used to Sarah, 'My dear, my dear.' She was only aware that she was crying as she had never cried in her life before, and she felt she would never stop.

She knew he was carrying her across the yard, but she felt no wonder in it. And then she was sitting in a chair by the kitchen table, and she didn't seem to care at the moment what happened for she dropped her head on to the table and sobbed into the crook of her arm.

'Drink this. Come along, stop crying. Now stop crying. Do you hear? You'll make yourself ill.'

Her head was brought up from the table by his sharp tone, but she did not look at him, nor attempt to take the glass from his hand.

'Drink it up, all of it.' He put the brandy to her mouth, and at the first swallow she coughed and spluttered over his hand. It was the spluttering that pulled her to herself – she was being stupid, she must pull herself together. She drew in slow, deep breaths of air, then she lifted her head and murmured, 'I'm all right now.'

When his hand came out towards her and smoothed the rumpled hair from her forehead she became quiet inside. It was a quiet laced with a single thread, a thread of wonder, a thread that she recognised must have very gentle handling or it would snap. She tried to clear her mind, to deal with a new situation. She managed to put matters on to a commonplace footing by asking, 'How . . . did you get back so soon? Did you—?'

It was now Ralph Batley's turn to avoid her eyes, and he turned from her as he did so, saying, 'I'll never really know. It's strange, but I thought I heard the conch shell.'

'The conch shell?' She was looking enquiringly at his back.

'It's a superstition attached to the house. It goes that danger is imminent to one of the family if they hear the sound of the conch shell. Isn't that so, Shane?'

Shane was at the sink dabbing his mouth with a damp cloth, and he nodded towards Linda, saying, 'Yes, that's so.' Then looking at his nephew, he asked, 'You heard it, boy, you sure you heard it?'

'Well, I came back. I was on my way to trap Watson.'

'To trap Watson? What about?'

Ralph Batley, speaking tersely and somewhat wearily, went on to explain to Shane what had occurred, and ended, 'I think we'd better get cleaned up.' He looked down at the tear in his coat, and touched his jaw bone tenderly before adding, 'And remember, not a word to my mother.' He cast a look between Linda and his uncle, and bringing everything back to normal with a bump, he now said, 'We'll have to get out a new schedule, it's going to be time and a half for all of us.'

'Yes, aye, it will be that. Well, I'd better go in to Maggie and tell her I fell over me own feet and greeted a wall.' Shane smiled wryly. 'I'll have to tell her something to account for this.' As he was about to leave the kitchen he turned to his nephew and asked quietly, 'Is there anything left in that bottle, Ralph?'

'Help yourself, Uncle.' Ralph Batley's voice was quiet and his uncle's reply had a grateful note as he said, 'Thanks boy, thanks boy.'

They were alone together in the kitchen now and it seemed to Linda that they both were uneasily aware of the other. She shivered just the slightest when he came and stood in front of her.

'It was strange about the conch shell, wasn't it?'

Her heart began to pound. 'Yes, yes it was strange.'

They were looking at each other. She had her head tilted slightly back when his hand once again touched her brow and smoothed her hair. The shiver became a tremble when he lifted a strand of hair behind her ear.

'Sit still while I get the tea.'

She sat quite still when he turned away. Even if she had felt like helping him, which she didn't, she would still have obeyed him. The effect of Sep Watson's attack had taken all her strength from her, and now she seemed weakened still further by this feeling. It was as if the thread of wonder had begun to restrict the beating of her heart.

5

It was at the skin-shivering hour of five o'clock the following morning, in obedience to the sound of an alarm clock, that Linda pulled herself out of bed. It was the same clock that had for years aroused Mrs Batley. With half-closed eyes and chattering teeth she dressed herself, finding as she did so the soreness in her back and her right hip where she had hit the ground when Uncle Shane had been hurled against her.

Although she had still been somewhat unnerved when she came to bed, she had worked out what was to be her routine. She would rise early as Mrs Batley had done, get through the household chores, then go to the dairy and try her hand at making the butter, and also help in any way she could with the outside work, because she realised that until they got another hand it would be almost a round-the-clock job for Ralph Batley and Uncle Shane. But when, a short time later, she descended the stairs and saw the lamp turned up and a fire blazing high, she blinked her eyes questioningly – she had heard no movement in the house.

When she entered the kitchen Ralph Batley turned from a stooped position over the stove and asked somewhat sharply, 'Why are you up at this time?'

She watched him jerk his hand away from the spluttering steam of the kettle, which he lifted on to the hob of the fireplace, before she answered him, and then it was with a question, 'Have you been up all night?'

'No, of course not.' He put the teapot on the table.

'How is your mother?'

'Oh.' He paused as he pulled the cups towards him. 'Still asking questions. She doesn't believe Uncle hit a brick wall, or that I tore my knuckles on the barbed wire, nor yet that you came back from your walk suffering from a bilious attack. You can hardly expect her to. The fact that something was amiss was clinched in her mind when she saw that Michael had been crying.'

He handed Linda her cup, and as they drank their tea there was quiet between them. Mrs Batley, Linda knew, was no fool. She herself had thought it would have been wiser to tell her the truth, for she would only question Michael later, and he was bound to confess to her his part in the affair of yesterday, as he had done to his uncle last night. The boy had apparently witnessed the fight in the barn and in some vague way had felt himself responsible for it. This had caused him to hide in the byre with Sarah. When Ralph Batley had found him there, it hadn't taken much questioning to make him reveal that he had listened to what Linda had been saying and had run to tell the cowman the exciting news.

Linda was only half-way through her cup of tea

when her employer thrust his arms into his coat preparatory to going out. He had his back to her and she expected him as was usual to leave the kitchen without any formal word of farewell, this was five o'clock in the morning, yet she wasn't surprised when he turned towards her. Not only turned, but came towards her, until he was not more than a bent arm's distance from her. Then he said quietly, 'I never asked how you were.'

'I'm feeling all right, just a bit stiff in the hip.'

His hands were hanging by his sides, he was looking straight at her and the expression in his eyes was familiar, she had seen it in those of Michael. He said now very quietly, 'You must try to take it easy today.'

'Yes . . . yes, I will.'

They were still looking at each other, then so quick was the movement that she almost jumped back in fright for his arms seemed to spring upwards, and the next minute she was enfolded in them, pressed close to him, hard against him, painfully hard, with her face against the coarse fibre of his coat. If she had wanted to return the embrace she would have found it impossible, for her arms were pinioned. She had no time to think or react for within a second she was back as she was. He had released her as quickly as he had taken her to him, and when she found herself standing alone in the kitchen she put one hand to her throat and with the other supported herself against the edge of the table. Her heart seemed to be bounding painfully and joyfully upwards, she could feel it under her hand as she gripped her throat. It was as if it was trying to escape, bound out into freedom. Minutes passed while her mind went galloping into the future, until with a quick movement of her head and a lifting of her shoulders she pushed the joy down, saying 'Don't be silly,' and she remembered, as she spoke to herself, the look on his face that was similar to Michael's. Michael's face expressed loneliness, deep loneliness, and his uncle was lonely too. That was it. With a sudden tired movement she sat down in the chair near the table and, looking towards the fire, she asked herself, Would she pander to his loneliness? She remembered last night he had said, 'My dear . . . my dear,' and he had also called her Linda. But she also remembered that he had talked like that to the cow. 'My dear . . . my dear,' he had said to Sarah. Could she take these endearments as a sign of love? She had last night because she wasn't herself, but in her right mind she was no stupid, fanciful girl. A man, and a man of Ralph Batley's calibre, did not love lightly. She had seen his face black with passionate rage, she knew that he could hate, and she felt that his love would be of equal intensity. So, because a few moments ago he had held her in his arms, she would not allow herself to imagine that this was the beginning of a passionate love for her. No, like Michael he was lonely and lost and she was the only young female thing near. She thought of the upper barn, the locked door, the love-nest as Sep Watson had called it, and she rose to her feet. If the loss of his loved one still had the power to embitter him so much, she couldn't see that he would be able to gather even a sediment to offer to anyone else. She looked towards the fire. She liked playing mother to Michael, would she like playing mother to Ralph Batley? If it was to be that or nothing, what would she do? She bit on her lip but did not give herself an answer; instead she started on the chores of the house. There was work to be done, lots of it, and such things would have to wait until she had time to give them thought. At least, so she told herself at this unromantic hour of the morning.

It was five hours and a lot of work later that Linda, pausing to take a breath, said to herself, 'Well now, that's all done, the dinner's all ready and every-thing, I'll just take Mrs Batley her milk in and then I'll go.' Go, in this case, meant to the dairy. She took up the tray and went swiftly across the hall and into the front room, and an exclamation escaped her on the sight of Mrs Batley sitting up on the side of the bed, her dressing-gown pulled round her.

'Oh, Mrs Batley, you're not to get up.'

'Now girl, say nothing. I'm up and I'm going to stay up. You fetch me me clothes, you know me skirt and blouse, you know me everyday things.'

'No, Mrs Batley, I'm going to do no such thing.' Linda put the tray down. 'If you don't get back into bed I'll go for—' she almost said Ralph, but ended with 'Mr Batley.'

'It's no good, I'm going to stay up. Things are not right, I know they're not right.'

'Everything's going smoothly, Mrs Batley. Please go back to bed.'

Mrs Batley did not answer, and Linda saw by the expression on her face that she was determined to have her way. She also saw that she looked more ill than she had done yesterday. Leaving the room without another word, she ran across the hall through the kitchen and out into the yard and into the cow byres.

'Mr Batley! Mr Batley!' There was no answer to her call. She came into the yard again and called, 'Uncle Shane!' But there was no answer to this either. Uncle Shane would be up in the top field. Where Michael was she did not know . . . likely following his uncle. Perhaps Ralph Batley had gone up to the top boundary to test the wire. After last night's business anything could happen. She felt that Sep Watson would stop at nothing in the way of spiteful revenge. She ran towards the high stone wall and the archway, and she had no sooner come through the archway than she saw the figure of a man crossing the field from the main road. But it was neither Ralph Batley, Uncle Shane nor yet Sep Watson. It was with a thrill almost of horror that she recognised the man coming towards her as Rouse Cadwell. Her instinct was to turn and run, but she couldn't, he had seen her, he had even lifted up his hand in salute. She looked behind her into the yard again. This was awful. On top of all that had taken place, if Ralph Batley was confronted with a Cadwell again there would be trouble. It was this thought that drove her towards him. But whatever approach she had expected him to make, jocular or otherwise, she was surprised by the abruptness of his voice when he said immediately, 'Where is he . . . Batley?'

She was nonplussed as she stood looking at him and stammered in her reply. 'Mr B – B – Batley? I don't know. I was looking for him myself. He's not about.'

She moved her head in the direction of the farmyard but did not take her eyes off him.

'Haven't you any idea? Is he down in the Bay?'

'No, no, he can't be down in the Bay, he's likely on the land somewhere.'

He looked behind him towards the valley, and as he did so she moved a step nearer and appealed to him beseechingly as if the Batley family were her own kin and, as such, their concerns dear to her heart. 'What is it? What's happened? Mrs Batley's ill, there's been enough trouble. Is it about Sep Watson?'

He brought his head sharply to her. 'Sep Watson?' It was a question and she knew he had been surprised by the name. 'What about Sep Watson?' She shook her head and said, 'Oh! I thought that was why you had come.'

'No, I haven't come about Sep Watson. You wouldn't understand, but I must see Batley. By the way, where's old Shane?'

'I don't know, I can't find him either.'

He made a tut-tutting sound, then added, 'Well, I'd better go and look for one of them.'

She was about to say, 'No, please, please wait,' when her head was jerked round in the direction of

193

the fells to the left, and there coming over the brow of the last hill was her employer. She saw him stop, stop dead. She could not see his face but her imagination gave her a good idea of what its expression would be like, and she almost groaned to herself.

Rouse Cadwell had also seen Ralph Batley but he did not now move towards him, he simply stood waiting for the other man to come up.

In the comparatively short time that Linda had been at Fowler Hall she had seen a variety of emotions expressed in her employer's countenance, mostly strong, tearing, unhappy emotions, but she had never seen such a look as was on his face now. It was so cold, so full of what could only be described as hate, that she turned her eyes away from him, for although his gaze was now directed at Rouse Cadwell it had been full on her for the space of ten strides, and she was shivering as if from the impact of a blow.

It was Rouse Cadwell who spoke first. His voice was harsh and yet there could be detected a placating note in it as he said, 'Don't start, I just want a minute with you. I want to talk to you.'

'What can you talk to me about that I don't already know?'

Rouse Cadwell looked at Ralph Batley for a moment and his lips took a rather scornful lift as he said, 'You don't let up on yourself or anybody else, do you, ever? There are some things that you don't know and that's why I'm here.' He now looked towards Linda, then turning his gaze back to Ralph Batley he said quietly, 'I'd better speak with you alone.'

Linda watched her employer's eyes lift towards her and the bitterness in his voice hurt her as he said, 'Let her stay, by all means let her stay.'

Now Rouse Cadwell gave a short laugh as he answered 'You're on the wrong tack as always, Batley, but since you don't mind who hears my news, here it is . . . Our Bruce is home and he's in a dangerous mood, he's looking for Edith.'

The look of amazement that swept over Ralph Batley's face seemed to wipe out the dark suspicious blackness for a moment. She saw him mouth a word, perhaps it was the name Edith, but no sound came from his lips.

'Is she here?'

'What!' The word had a cracking sound as if a whip had been flicked.

'Well, she disappeared a week ago. He found out she came north, this way in fact.' Rouse Cadwell paused, then went on with harsh quietness, 'If you're shielding her, Batley, you'd better think again. Get rid of her if you don't want murder done, for I'm telling you he'll come up . . .'

'And I'm telling you' – Ralph Batley's voice was thundering now – 'let him put a step inside my boundary and there'll be murder done. You tell him that, d'you hear?'

'I came in good faith, I thought you'd better be warned.'

'Good faith!' Ralph Batley almost spat in the younger man's face. 'Could ever a Cadwell keep good faith? Five-pound bribes left in holes for Watson. Well, you can tell your father he'll have to find other means with which to do me down, for his henchman's gone.'

'What are you talking about? The old man may have his faults but he wouldn't pay Watson to do his dirty work.'

'No? Ask him then. There was a five-pound note stuffed in a hole in my boundary bank last night, it isn't there this morning . . . Now get going.'

In this moment Linda felt sorry for Rouse Cadwell, she felt he had come as a friend. She watched his jaw tighten, she watched him bite down on the retort he was about to make, she watched him turn swiftly away and stride towards the gate. When she looked back at her employer his eyes were on her but they were no longer accusing – at least he knew that she hadn't come out to meet Rouse Cadwell – but his face was wearing the tight-closed look she had seen on it the first time she met him. She said quietly, 'I was looking for you. Your mother's up, she insists on staying up, she doesn't look well. I thought I'd better find you.'

He blinked and jerked his head once as if to bring his thoughts back from a far place, and he repeated, 'Up?' Then he strode towards the archway and Linda followed him, her eyes on his back . . .

An hour later Mrs Batley was sitting propped up in a big chair to the side of the fireplace in the hall, and Linda was once more along with her employer in the kitchen, but the atmosphere, unlike what it had been at five o'clock this morning, was tense and strained. The kitchen door was closed and he was speaking in a low voice, 'You'll say nothing about this; you'll give her no hint of what Rouse Cadwell said.'

'Of course not, why should I?' Her voice was cool and impersonal.

'I'm asking you because if she gets wind of this matter she'll become greatly upset.' He paused. 'You understand?'

She had her eyes on him as she inclined her head slowly downwards. 'I understand.' There was a sick feeling in her chest, she felt weary, tired. Early this morning, even with a heavy day's work in front of her, she had felt fit to cope, but now all she wanted to do was sit down, sit down and think. Her mind at this point said, Think that he meant something when he took you in his arms? Don't forget you told yourself then that you knew it meant nothing, he was just lonely. Well, nothing has changed, he's still lonely and he's still in love. Get that into your head, he's still in love with that woman, that Edith, and from what Rouse Cadwell says, she's back. She turned from him saying, 'You needn't worry, I'll say nothing to distress your mother. I think you should realise that.'

'I do, I do.' His voice was now deep and unsteady. 'But you don't know what it could mean to her if she . . .' The words trailed off and she turned and looked at him again, saying quickly now, 'Your mother won't hear of anything through me that might hurt her, you can rest assured on that point. If that's all you've got to worry about then your mind can be at rest.' She knew that her tone was curt, she meant it to be curt. She turned from his troubled gaze and went out of the kitchen and into the hall, thinking that it was a great pity Mrs Batley had taken ill when she did. If that hadn't happened she would have been gone from this place and would have been saved a heartbreak that was only at its beginning.

The storm came up about teatime, preceded as storms usually are by a stillness and heavy sky, and it was not long before every person in Fowler Hall knew that they were in for a night of it. By eight o'clock the rain was hitting the windows with the force of machine-gun bullets, and the wind screaming round the house seemed bent on tearing it from its very foundations. Uncle Shane, coming into the kitchen on a blast of wind, forced the door closed and stood with his shoulder to it as he pushed home the bolt. Linda, turning from the stove where she had been stirring a pan of broth, looked towards the old man, and it did not need any close scrutiny on her part to see that he was very tired, almost exhausted.

'Do . . . do you think you could come and brave it and give us a hand, Linda?' The old man's voice sounded hoarse and cracked. 'The cattle are uneasy. One of us has got to stay with Sarah, we've had to put her calf in a separate box, just in case she might hurt her in her trampling. She never liked storms and now you can hear her almost above the wind. Would you mind very much staying with her for a while, there's a light there. We've got our work cut out in the big byre. It isn't the cattle there, it's the roof, although they are kicking up enough shindy.'

'Yes, yes, of course, Uncle Shane. Look, have a cup of soup before you go out and I'll just tell Mrs Batley. There' – she scooped a bowl of broth from the pan – 'you can give yourself a minute to have that.' As she left the kitchen she added, 'Michael needn't go to bed for a time yet, he's frightened anyway, he'll be much better staying with his grandmother.'

Linda was gone from the kitchen for a matter of minutes. When she returned Shane was no longer there, but the soup bowl was empty. Swiftly she got into her duffle coat. Once outside she thrust a piece of wood through the handle of the door to keep it from being blown open. It was when she left the shelter of the wall that divided the house yard from the farmyard proper that the real force of the gale caught her, and she was almost lifted from her feet. The only way she could cross the yard was to turn and, walking backwards, press against the wind.

As she passed the big barn a section of her mind told her that she should have brought Ralph Batley a can of soup, but this was dismissed as she realised it would have been ripped from her hand before she was half-way across the yard. By the time she had struggled towards the door of Sarah's byre she realised that she was more than a little frightened by the ferocity of the storm. She had witnessed storms before but nothing like this. Mr Cadwell, on that night of her first coming to this part of the country, had sneered at her when she had said she was used to rough weather. There was weather and weather, he had said, and this was what he had meant.

At last she was in the small byre and the sound that greeted her was, to say the least, weird. Coupled with the noise of the storm, it did not tend to calm her nerves. But so agitated were the animals and so pathetic the crying of the little calf that soon her own fears were in the background. She went between the two of them, talking to and soothing them, until at last, like weary children, they settled down . . .

It must have been about an hour later when Linda, sitting on the box with her back leaning against the stanchion of the byre, felt herself being lulled into sleep by sheer weariness. The thunder of the storm was so persistent that it seemed as if it would go on forever and life would have to be adjusted to it. The byre had a sweet, warm smell, the whole atmosphere, engulfed as it was in the noise from outside, acted as a drug. Not that Linda needed much of a drug to put her to sleep for she had been on her feet since five that morning, and when she felt her head and lids drooping she did nothing to resist the blissful oblivion about to overtake her.

Whether she was asleep and dreaming, or awake and seeing aright she didn't really know, but before her mind's eyes there flashed a picture. It was of the door of the cowshed being thrust open and a dishevelled, wild-looking woman standing framed for a second in the dim light of the lantern.

Then Linda was on her feet, and when wisps of straw began to whirl in the atmosphere around her and the wind, forcing itself up to the roof, threatened to lift it off, she ran towards the open door and forced it shut. She had seen a woman standing here, she hadn't been dreaming, dreams didn't open doors. She had seen a woman. Pulling the hood of her coat over her head and buttoning it under her chin she snatched the lantern from the hook and went out into the yard. Standing with her back to the cowshed wall and lifting the lantern above her head, she peered round the farmyard, and for one fleeting second she saw the figure again. It was just a distorted bulk, a wind-contorted shadow, but Linda knew it was the woman who had opened the cowshed door and that she was now going into the big barn.

She hesitated a moment, her eyes turning in the direction of the main cowshed where Ralph Batley was, and then she was looking towards the big barn and within a second she was making for it. Hugging the walls as far as she could, and then once again pressing her back to the wind as she reached the opening. And there, lifting the lantern above her head, she looked about her. There was no-one to be seen. Her eyes lifted to the ladder leading to the upper floor, and as she walked slowly towards it she imagined that above the turmoil of the storm she heard a thud that had no connection with the elements outside. Slowly she mounted the ladder, feeling as she did so that all this had been gone through before. Perhaps in that fleeting second when in half-dream, half-reality, she had looked towards the wild-looking figure standing in the doorway of the cowshed she had known what was to follow.

As she reached the upper storey of the barn and moved slowly towards its end she knew whom she would find there, she knew whom she would see when she turned right to the door of the studio – to the door of the love-nest. Not only her heart but her whole body and mind felt heavy, dull, and sick at what this meant.

She came to where the packing-cases were stacked, and turned right. And now she could see the door, and it was closed. Then she drew in her breath sharply as she saw the prostrate figure lying across the threshold of the studio.

As, with the lantern in her hand, she stood stiffly looking down at the figure at her feet, a feeling of revulsion came over her. She didn't want to touch the woman. And then, the lantern standing on the floor, she was bending over the huddled form and lifting the rain-drenched face. It was a white, dead-looking face, a frighteningly dead-looking face, but a startlingly beautiful one.

Leaving the lantern where it was she turned and groped her way along the loft and scrambled down the ladder. She was out in the yard once again, running now with the wind towards the byre. She unlatched the door, and when it was almost wrenched from her grasp she forced it closed and stood with her back to it gasping. And then she called twice, 'Mr Batley! Mr Batley!' There was a movement from somewhere high up in the roof. When she saw her employer sitting astride a beam, his hands reaching towards the rafters, she called again, 'Mr Batley!'

His body was twisted round and his face was looking towards her. 'What is it?'

'It's . . . it's . . .' She could have said, 'It's Edith.' So sure was she of the woman's identity, so sure was she of the pattern that life was now about to take, she almost said, 'Your Edith. It's your Edith, she's come back.'

'What is it, girl? Is it Maggie? You look like a ghost. Is it Maggie?' This was Shane speaking.

'No! no!' She shook her head, aware now that Ralph Batley was scrambling down the ladder near the beam. When he stood before her he, too, said, 'What is it?' and then asked, 'My mother . . . she's all right?'

'Yes, yes, she's all right. It's . . . There was a woman, she came to the shed. I was sitting with Sarah. I thought I was dreaming, and then I saw her going into the barn. She's there now, upstairs. She's – she's unconscious.' She stared at her employer. Did he know without being told who the woman was?

'A woman? What woman?' Shane's voice came in between them. Neither Ralph Batley nor Linda answered the old man, but something equivalent to the tight grip of a fist closed round her chest as she watched him swing round and run towards the door without even thinking of donning his coat.

'Saints alive! What woman would be out on a night like this? Are you sure, girl?'

'Of course I'm sure, Uncle Shane.' Linda's voice was strangely level now. 'I know who she is.'

'You know who she is? What d'you mean, child?'

'Did Mr Batley tell you that young Mr Cadwell called here this morning?'

There was a flicker in Shane's eyes before he replied, 'Yes, yes. Name of God! You don't mean . . .' He, too, was out of the door, and Linda now followed him, but more slowly. She went across the yard, walking backwards once more, and when she reached the barn and went up the ladder her legs felt strangely heavy. As she turned the corner near the boxes she saw that the door to the studio was open. The lantern was standing on the table and on a couch near the wall lay the woman. Both Uncle Shane and Ralph Batley were standing looking down at the inert figure, and as Linda neared the door Shane's voice came to her in an almost fear-filled whisper, saying, 'In the name of God! What a predicament. You'll have to get her out of here, boy, and lose no time at all. You understand that, don't you?'

'Where is she to go?'

'Phone them.'

'I doubt if she'll thank me for that. We must wait until she comes round, she'll know what she wants to do.'

'But Ralph man, think. Think!'

'We can't do anything until she comes round.'

Linda hearing the almost level tones of her employer, thought with painful clarity, He wants her to come round, he couldn't possibly let her go without her coming round. She met his eyes as he turned from the couch and for a moment she imagined that he looked ashamed; and she thought, He is ashamed, ashamed of still being in love with this woman who had been stolen from him. Or did she leave him willingly for another man? And in this moment, too, she thought, Thank God I didn't let this thing get a hold of me. Thank God I realised that it was loneliness, not love. But the thought, like most reasonable thoughts, was devoid of comfort.

Shane was now hanging on to his nephew's arm, gripping it tightly, and his voice held a stern, almost angry note as he said, 'Have you thought about your mother? Have you thought about Maggie? This will drive her mad. She's in no state to have any more worry. Look, I'm telling you, boy, phone them, they'll come and take her.'

'Perhaps she doesn't want to be taken. Don't you see?'

The old man stared at his nephew for a moment before saying, 'Well, if she wants to or not, that's beside the point. Do you want all hell to be let loose? I'm thinking of nobody but Maggie at this moment. She's had enough, she's had enough, boy.'

'I know, I know, and so have I, Uncle Shane. I've had enough, too, don't you realise that? D'you think I asked for this?' His voice was hard and bitter. 'D'you think I'd have laid myself open to this? But I can't tell them she's here until she comes round. It'll be up to her. If she's running away, who am I to stop her?'

As the grip loosened on his arm Ralph Batley turned to Linda and in his eyes there was a look of appeal, but she was soon made to realise for what the appeal was meant. 'She will need some dry clothes, and blankets and a water bottle. Do you think . . .?'

She did not let him finish but turned hastily away, yet she had not reached the end of the passageway between the crates and the wall before she was pulled to a stop, and in the dim light from the lantern standing in the room behind them they peered at each other. His hand was holding her shoulder as he began rapidly, 'She's ill, more ill than Uncle Shane realises. Her pulse is very low, I may have to get a doctor. This is all very painful to me, you can't understand, you don't know what it means. I knew her years ago, she was a . . . a close—'

'A close friend of yours. Yes, I understand, Mr Batley, there's no need to explain.' Her voice was cool and level, even to herself it sounded indifferent. When his hand dropped from her shoulder and he said in a flat-sounding tone, 'Well, that's all right then,' she looked at him a moment longer before turning from him.

As she walked in the darkness towards the end of the loft she warned herself to be careful in case she went over the edge. When a desperate voice deep within her said, 'Oh, what would it matter, even if I were to go over the edge of the cliff,' she chided it saying, 'Don't be a fool, don't let it get you down.'

Again she had to force her way across the yard. The rain had stopped now but the wind was still tearing and screeching, still clawing at the buildings as if bent on uprooting them.

When she looked into Mrs Batley's room she was thankful to find that the older woman was asleep and that Michael, curled up in a chair before the fire, was also asleep. She decided to leave him there until she had taken the things to the loft.

Quickly now she ran upstairs. Taking a warm dress from the cupboard and her dressing-gown from the back of the door, she went to the linen cupboard in the bathroom and gathered some blankets in her arms before again making her way downstairs. In the kitchen she filled a hot-water bottle, and as she hesitated on the thought of filling a can of soup the door opened and Shane came in.

Never had she seen the old man's countenance look so thunderous. Without any preamble he said, 'We only needed this. Do you know what this means, girl? All the old business over again. He'll go mad again, stark staring mad . . . she bewitched him. I thought when you came . . .' His head dropped and he swung it from side to side in a desperate movement. 'Why has God to inflict people with such troubles, people that's done Him no harm? I tell you, there'll be trouble.' She did not remind him that he believed that God worked in strange and wonderful ways, but she watched him pull off his cap and scratch his head violently before she said, 'Help me over with these things, Uncle Shane, please.'

His tone was one of defeat as he replied, 'Leave the blankets, I'll be over after you in a minute.'

'Do you think you could manage to bring a can of soup?'

'I'd like to bring a can of poison if I had my way.'

Sadly she turned from him and went out into the night once more.

The door to the studio was closed and she didn't knock but pushed it open and went straight in, some part of her was hoping, she knew, to surprise him. This part of her should not have been disappointed because there he was, on his knees by the low couch, and the woman had her eyes open and was looking at him. Yet he seemed strangely unperturbed as he rose to his feet and came towards Linda, saying quietly, 'Do you think you could help her off with her things?'

She made no answer to this but walked towards the couch and placed the dressing-gown and the dress across the foot of it before turning and looking at the woman.

The eyes that looked back out of the white face were soft, brown, melting eyes, they were frightened eyes, but behind the fear was a quality to which Linda, for the moment, could not put a name. She did not know this woman, only of her, and she was prepared to hate her, but the eyes looking up at her reminded her of Sarah's eyes, they were beseeching and asking dumbly for kindness. She was surprised at the warmth of her own voice as she said, 'You must get these wet things off. I've brought you a dress and a dressing-gown. Do you think you could sit up?' When she went round to the other side of the couch to help raise the woman up she found they had the studio to themselves. The woman could barely assist herself, and she did not speak as Linda, with gentle dexterity, stripped her of her wet clothing. But when finally she was arrayed in the dress and dressing-gown, she whispered in a voice that for all its faintness held a warm charm, 'Thank you. Oh, thank you.'

Linda went to the door now and opened it. Outside, standing with unusual patience, his face almost as white as that of the woman she had just undressed, was Ralph Batley. He was holding the blankets and the can of soup, but Uncle Shane was not to be seen. He came in, and going to the couch, he opened the blankets one by one and put them over the woman. When this was done he poured some soup into the lid of the can. Kneeling once again, he put his arm underneath her shoulders and said quietly, 'Come, drink this.'

The couch was low and Linda told herself that he would have to kneel. As she stood looking at them she was torn by conflicting desires. One was to run out of the room, the other to stay and witness this scene and what would follow. She saw the woman's hand come up and touch the lid of the can and also the fingers that held it. The moment of contact seemed to act as a spring releasing her emotions, for Linda watched her push the can away and turn on her side and bury her face in the crook of Ralph Batley's arm. As she listened to the shuddering sobs and watched their effect on her employer she told herself to get away, out of the studio, away from the self-inflicting pain, but she didn't move. Then the woman, between her sobs, began to talk disjointedly. 'Oh, Ralph, Ralph. Oh, what have I done? Oh, Ralph, Ralph. I can't go back, I can't. Don't send me back, he'll kill me. I was mad, Ralph, I was mad.'

'Keep quiet, keep quiet. Don't excite yourself. Try to rest.'

'But, Ralph.' Linda watched the slim hand groping up towards Ralph Batley's face. When she saw him disengage himself and get to his feet she felt no relief, he was only embarrassed because she was witnessing the scene.

'Don't leave me, Ralph, don't leave me, please, please.' The hand was outstretched to him and Linda saw the muscles of the right side of his face work like pistons under the skin. She waited for him to turn towards her and he did, and she

210

was in no way surprised by his words. 'Go and get some rest. Tell Uncle Shane I want him when he has a minute.'

She gave him a long, straight look and turned towards the door. When she reached it he was behind her, and when she went out into the loft he was still with her. And now he spoke rapidly and quietly. 'Michael mustn't know of this, you understand. He'd blurt it to my mother. Can you keep him with you in the morning?' He paused and swallowed. 'She'll be gone tomorrow, some time tomorrow.'

'I'll do my best.'

'Linda.' His hands were lifting to her but the almost imperceptible recoil that she made from them was sensed by him, and they dropped to his sides before the gesture had hardly commenced. As he swung round from her and went into the studio again she closed her eyes for a moment before once again groping her way along the loft.

It did not need an alarm to get Linda out of bed the following morning. Last night she had been so tired that she could have fallen asleep on her feet, that was up until she had seen the woman framed in the doorway of Sarah's byre. If she had slept at all it had been in fitful, troubled doses. She had been so wakeful that she knew the exact time the storm had died away.

It was just on five o'clock when she descended the stairs, but no bright fire greeted her this morning, no shining lamp or spluttering kettle on the kitchen hob. As she set herself the task of rectifying these omissions she could not overthrow the resentful feeling that was enveloping her, nor yet erase from her mind's eye the face of the woman who had haunted her all night. It was almost with unseemly haste that she prepared a jug of tea, and when she stepped out into the calm but biting dawn it did not affect her, as did the feeling of apprehension that swept over her when she came within sight of the studio door.

Afraid of what she might see by an unannounced entrance, she knocked on the door, and when after a moment there was no reply she turned the handle. There before her, fast asleep on the couch, lay the woman, Edith Cadwell. She could not think of her as Edith, only as the woman, or that woman. And there, not an arm's length from her, stretched out in the big, old, dilapidated chair, was Ralph Batley. They were both in deep sleep. Their hands hanging, hers over the side of the couch and his over the arm of the chair, seemed to suggest that they had been locked together before sleep had relaxed them. The scene was painfully intimate, it had a nakedness about it that stabbed so deeply into Linda that she was forced to say to herself roughly, 'Well, what did you expect?' The lantern she saw was burning low and in a short while would be out if not refuelled. She went and stood by her employer, reluctant to touch him. She did not touch him, but said sharply, 'Mr Batley!'

He stirred, shook his head and opened his eyes, then closed them again before stretching them wide.

'I've brought some tea.'

'What?'

It was evident to her that for a moment he did not know where he was, but only for a moment. Then he said, 'Oh! Thanks, thanks.'

'The lamp needs oil, it'll soon be out.'

'Yes.' He stood up and stretched himself; then said again, 'Yes.' Without looking at her he took a mug of tea from her hand and having drunk it he asked her quietly, 'Will you stay here until I come back? I'll get the oil first, then do a round, I'll be as quick as I can.'

She did not look at him as she answered, 'Don't forget there is your mother to be seen to, and Michael.'

He did not answer her immediately and she knew he was angered by her words. 'I won't forget. I'm sorry I have to ask you to do this, but if she wakes up and finds herself alone she may be—' He paused, then added, 'She's in a high state of nerves – very frightened.'

The only reply she made to this was to raise her eyebrows slightly and go and take his place in the chair.

When he had gone she looked round the room. It was something, she thought, that one would see in a ghost picture. Cobwebs were hanging from the rafters. On the bench running along the length of one wall there were what she judged to be three heads. They were covered with sheets, and these, too, were joined together by cobwebs. The floor was covered with a fine dust. The only other article of furniture besides the couch, the chair and the bench was a bookcase, and this was draped with the clothes she had taken off the woman last night, and in the far corner, piled one against the other, were chunks of wood, pieces of stone, and canvases, and all covered with the netting of cobwebs.

She had hardly made her survey of the room when Ralph Batley returned with the oil, and when he had refilled the lantern the bright glow showed up the dirt in the studio still more. He directed neither look nor word to her before leaving the room again, but the glance he cast swiftly towards the woman on the bed was not lost on Linda.

She had thought of this stranger as a woman, yet looking at her now, at the pale, beautiful face, she knew that here was still a girl, and her intuition told her also that here was a person who could have the word enchanting attached to her. This thought made her vividly conscious of her breeches and rough coat, made her feel gawkish, without confidence. It was at this moment that the brown eyes opened and looked at her, and they remained wide.

'I've . . . I've seen you before.' The voice was very low and soft. Like the eyes, it had a far-away, dream-like quality.

'Yes. You saw me last night.' Linda made her tone ordinary.

The head turned slowly on the pillow. 'I feel very tired – so tired.' The eyes were turned on Linda again. 'Ralph . . . where is Ralph?'

'He is on the farm seeing to things.'

'What is your name?'

'Linda, Linda Metcalfe.'

'You . . . you are—' She took in a slow, long breath and eased herself up on the couch and lay for a moment before continuing, 'You are staying on holiday?'

'No. I work here. I'm a student, an agricultural student.'

The bloodless lips formed the words agricultural student but there was no sound from them. She turned her cheek to the side of the couch and, looking at Linda, she asked slowly, 'Do you know who I am?'

'Yes. Yes, I know who you are.'

'Oh!' The eyes widened still further, then they were lifted from Linda and she watched them moving around the studio, and when the girl said softly, 'I used to know this room very well,' she stiffened inside.

'Oh, if only we could see ahead, if only we knew.' The great brown eyes were on Linda again and they rested on her face for a while. 'You are young, very young,' the girl said, in a soft, appraising tone.

'I don't think I'm much younger than you.'

'I'll never be young again, I'm old, old, old.' As she repeated the word for the third time she put her hand towards her hair, and then added wearily, 'I must look a terrible sight. I think I had a bag with me. I'm not sure.'

'There's a bag here.' Linda walked towards the bench and picked up a leather bag and brought it to the girl on the couch. She watched her open it and take out a comb, but when she attempted to put it through her hair it appeared too much for her, and she lay back against the head of the couch, her long hands lying limp before her on the blanket.

'I'm weaker than I thought. It's just tiredness, it'll pass.'

'Let me have the comb.'

When Linda stood behind the couch and combed the tangled hair, she told herself she would do this for anybody who was sick. She was combing the last strand of the thick auburn hair down to the shoulders where it turned naturally inwards, when the door was pushed open and Ralph Batley entered, carrying a laden tray. On the sight of this a feeling of resentment welled up in Linda. He had asked her to stay until he had done a round, but he had spent the time preparing a dainty breakfast for the newcomer, for she saw at a glance there was little difference in the setting of the tray from what she herself would have prepared.

She handed the comb to Edith Cadwell.

'Thank you. That was sweet of you.'

Linda made no rejoinder to this but, picking up her coat, went out of the room. But she had not reached the end of the packing-cases when she heard her name called. She paused but did not turn.

When Ralph Batley was standing confronting her he spoke in an undertone but briskly, saying, 'I want to talk with you, not now, later. I must explain.'

'There's no need, there's no need to explain anything to me, but I should have thought that you'll find it difficult to keep this matter a secret from Michael if you are going to carry trays up here.'

'Trays?' He screwed his eyes up at her. 'There'll only be this one. And Michael isn't up yet.'

She raised her brows and jerked her head slightly to the side but kept her eyes fixed on him as she repeated. 'Only this one? You think there will be only this one?'

When his gaze moved from hers and she saw his teeth clamp down on to his lip she walked away. She could not trust herself to look at him any longer.

The farmyard was still in darkness but the sky was high and star-filled, and she stood for a moment looking up into it before turning aside and running towards the small byre. It was black dark inside the byre, and although she did not speak to Sarah or the calf they made no uneasy movements. Groping her way to the post between the two pens she stood with her head against it and her hands gripping it. Her throat was tight and her eyes stinging with tears, and she had to let them flow to relieve the awful pressure that threatened to choke her. Her crying was quiet, and when it ceased she felt her way to the box and sat down, and in the darkness enveloped by the warmth and familiar smells of the animals, she faced the fact that she loved Ralph Batley, she loved this man who, because of his passionate overwhelming love for a woman who rejected him, had become a different being. Over the last few days she had glimpsed what she thought should be the real character of her employer, a character that was not without tenderness. When this woman had thrown him over the tenderness had turned into hatred. Now she had returned. She had sought him out, she had come to him in need, and the tenderness had returned too. She felt that from the moment he had looked down on the prostrate figure he had become the old Ralph Batley, a man who would be like putty in the hands of anyone so charming as the woman who was now lying in the studio. The fact that she herself had been held in his arms for a brief second yesterday morning, the fact that he had called her Linda at least three times since then were as nothing. These facts now took on the appearance of tiny, unimportant incidents, driftwood on the crest of a mighty wave, swept away on the return of an old love, an only love – men like Ralph Batley didn't love lightly.

She rose from the box, wiped her face with her handkerchief, straightened her shoulders, closed her eyes for a moment and said a little prayer, the substance of which was that she wouldn't make a fool of herself. On this foundation she went out and towards the house to start the business of a strange day.

6

It was forty-eight hours later and the studio was still occupied. The repercussions to this were many, and they all held the one element – tension. It filled the house until the atmosphere was almost unbearable to Linda.

Short-handed as they already were, the work was getting more and more behind. Open conflict had sprung up between Shane and his nephew, who, in turn, was treating Michael with unjustified harshness, curtailing the child's movements at almost every step. Mrs Batley too, sensing the troubles that enshrouded her loved ones, was not only asking, but demanding, explanations. Her strength of will was aiding her to sit up in the chair by the hall fire, and Linda knew that it was only fear of collapsing that stopped the older woman from leaving the house. And then there was the cause of the tension, the visitor in the studio.

Why hadn't Edith Cadwell gone by now? Was it because of Ralph Batley's desire to keep her? This question kept hammering at Linda every hour of the day. She had paid three visits to the studio yesterday, each time carrying a meal, at the request of her employer – he had not talked to her as he had promised but had merely asked her if she would try to get some food to Mrs Cadwell. He called her Mrs Cadwell, and as far as she could see the hated name had now no effect on him. Each time she had gone to the studio she had found it empty except for the woman on the couch. Mrs Cadwell had remained on the couch all day yesterday, and all day today.

Although, naturally, she hadn't seen her employer entering the barn she was aware that he must have visited the studio frequently, and if she had needed proof of this she had had it only a few minutes ago. When, after some manoeuvring, she had managed to evade Michael and take a meal up to the studio, it was to find Edith Cadwell in a state of agitation. She had clutched at her hand and implored her. 'Please! please! don't let Ralph send for a doctor. I'm all right, I only want another day. If he sends for Doctor Morgan he is sure to tell them. He would persuade Ralph to tell them and then my husband . . . he'd kill me if he were to find me here. I must go, I know I must go, but at the moment I don't feel able.' She had released the grip on Linda's hands and, lying back and looking about the studio, she added, 'It's so peaceful here. Oh, you don't know, you can't understand. I've dreamed of the peace of this room. It looks neglected now, but it wasn't always like this.' The brown eyes were full on Linda, the soft, melting gaze was, in spite of herself, drawing on her sympathy.

'You are a kind person, aren't you?'

'Not more than anyone else.'

'Oh, yes you are. You don't want me here. Now don't look like that, it's only natural, but you're still kind.'

Linda had found herself taken completely off her guard. She realised as she looked back into the brown eyes that there was an astute brain working behind the soft, melting glance. Edith Cadwell's next words confirmed this.

'You know at one time Ralph and I were very close. We – we were to be married.'

'Yes, I know.' Linda's voice sounded even and flat and without interest.

'You know? Who told you?'

'Oh, things get about – where there's no other form of entertainment people talk.'

Apparently this answer did not please Edith Cadwell, and for the first time Linda saw a look of sharp annoyance on the white, thin features, and she knew that the annoyance had gone deep when Edith Cadwell allowed her to leave the studio without further words.

And now Linda was standing at the kitchen table preparing the supper, she was so tired and weary that she felt she could have fallen asleep where she stood. She was telling herself that no matter what happened, as soon as she had washed-up she was going straight to bed. She couldn't keep her head up another hour. And her thoughts were finishing philosophically: Anyway, I can do nothing, what has to happen, will happen, when she heard Uncle Shane's raised voice coming from the yard, calling 'Ralph! Ralph!' The next minute the kitchen door burst open and the old man stood gasping as he looked towards Linda. 'Where is he?' he cried. 'Have you seen him?'

'Yes. He went in to Mrs Batley not more than a minute ago.'

Uncle Shane was supporting himself with his two hands on the table now, and he said between gasps, 'Go and get him for me. Make some excuse, say you thought you heard me call.' He nodded sharply. 'That's the truth, anyway. Go on now, quickly.'

Bemused, Linda went out of the kitchen across the hall and to the front room, and she looked to where Ralph Batley was standing near his mother's bed. Going no further than the door she said, 'Uncle Shane's needing you a moment, Mr Batley. I think it's one of the cows.'

A few minutes later when he came into the kitchen Ralph Batley looked in surprise from his uncle to Linda, but as he was about to speak Shane cut him short, saying 'There's someone about the place, I saw him at the bottom of the studio staircase. Did you know the light was coming from under the door there? I thought for a moment it was yourself, and when I crossed towards you I knew my mistake, for whoever it was scuttled away. I thought he went into the barn but didn't go after him, I hadn't a light with me, and anyway, I didn't want a clunk on the head from behind. You'd better come, and come quick. What did I tell you? I can't help saying it, I told you this would happen.'

Linda looked at Ralph Batley's face. It had turned a dirty grey colour and his eyes had darkened considerably. When he made a sharp movement towards the cupboard in the corner of the kitchen, Uncle Shane's hand came out as his voice rapped, 'No! no! boy, no guns.'

Linda watched her employer hesitate for a moment before swinging through the door, the old man at his heels.

She stood staring at the closed door. Uncle Shane was right, of course he was right. But what if the other man had a gun on him? What if he shot . . .? Her harassed thoughts at this moment were interrupted by a tinkle coming from the vicinity of the hall, it was the recognisable tinkle of a telephone bell, but it was the first time she had heard the telephone ring since she had come to this house. Taking into account that it had been out of order for the first three days after her arrival, to her knowledge it hadn't rung since. She went quickly into the hall and towards a dark little cubby-hole of a room under the stairs that Ralph Batley used as an office. The bell ringing again directed her to the instrument, but when she picked it up and said 'Hullo' no answering voice came to her. She was repeating the word when she heard what could have been a quick intake of breath on the wire, and then a voice said, 'I want to speak to Mr Batley.' It was a woman's voice and she recognised it.

'I'm afraid . . . he's not in.'

'Is he on the farm?'

'Yes . . . yes, he's just gone out into the yard.'

224

'Will you take a message?' The voice paused. 'It is important. Will you tell him to phone me . . . Mrs Cadwell?'

'Yes, yes, I'll tell him that, Mrs Cadwell.'

'You'll find him as soon as you can?'

'Yes, yes, I'll go right now.'

'Thank you.' There was the click of the receiver being replaced and then Linda slowly put down the phone.

When she entered the hall again it was to see Michael running out of his granny's room, and he cried to her, 'Who was on the phone? Granny says, who's on the phone?'

'It was a wrong number. Someone . . . someone thought this was a school . . . a boys' school in Morpeth.' The glibness of her reply had a somewhat disturbing effect on her – the situation in this house was such that she always had to be thinking a step ahead to soothe Mrs Batley's fears, or, to be more correct, to hoodwink her and the boy. The thought wasn't pleasing, and as Michael ran from her again to give the news to his grandmother she went hastily into the kitchen. She had no desire to go outside, no desire to meet whoever it was prowling about the buildings. Her encounter with Sep Watson the other evening had frightened her and she felt that if she met up with him again the effect would be more than unnerving. But as she stood hesitating, she knew that Mrs Cadwell hadn't had Sep Watson in mind when she came on the phone to the Batleys. It was her son she had had in mind. She herself could almost tell her employer the message Mrs Cadwell was going to give him, that her son was looking for his wife and he was coming to find her in Fowler Hall. With a gesture that was a mixture of impatience, weariness, and desperation, she pulled her coat from the door and, thrusting her arms into it, went out.

From the main yard she saw the light from a swinging lantern. It was near the barn and, going towards it, she called, 'Mr Batley! Mr Batley!'

It seemed that Ralph Batley leapt towards her, so quick was he at her side, and before she could speak he said, 'Yes? What is it? What's the matter? Have you—'

'I've just come to tell you,' she broke in on him, 'there's been a phone message. It's from Mrs Cadwell, she wishes you to phone her immediately.' She could not see what effect this had on him as his face was in shadow, but he was some time in answering her, and then he said rapidly, 'Will you go up to the studio and stay for a while.' He paused. But when she made no answer he added, 'It'll just be for a short while. And you need have no fear, we've been all round up there, there's no-one about, only . . .' He left the name unsaid. 'Will you . . . please?' His tone was hurried and urgent, yet he was speaking as if asking a favour of her, and she felt that much as she had tried to hide her reluctance to visit the woman in the studio, he was aware of it.

'Very well.'

'Here, take this light.' He thrust the lantern into her hand and for a moment their fingers came in contact. His felt cold and hard.

She was shaking slightly as she entered the big barn, she did not deny to herself that she was afraid, and although she had the light with her and swung it backwards and forwards, she expected at any moment to feel herself thrown to the ground. On the upper floor she walked quietly and cautiously towards the end of the barn, and it was as she turned right to go towards the studio door that she halted. She had imagined for a moment that she had heard a voice, a male voice, and it brought her to petrified stillness. After some seconds while she held her breath she swung the light along the passage towards the closed door of the studio. Then it came to her again, a thick murmur that could only mean a man's voice. She had the desire to turn and flee back down the barn. Ralph Batley had said he had searched up here. He knew his own barn, and there would not be a corner he had left untouched . . . and would he have missed out the studio? No. Of course not. It would have been the first place he would have made for. And yet she could hear a man's voice coming from there. No-one could have entered the studio by the staircase door, that was locked, and to her own knowledge there was no key in the lock. Anyway, it would have to be opened from the inside to allow someone to enter.

Her curiosity and a form of high indignation set her moving towards the door. The murmur was still going on, yet not audible. It wasn't until she stood to the side of the door, her ear pressed against the lintel, that she could make out any words at all, and these were disjointed. 'One good turn . . .' These were followed by a mumble, and then after some more murmurings, 'I'm as good as me word—'

She now heard the soft, rapid tones of Edith Cadwell's voice, but so low was it that she could make out none of the words. And then again she heard the man's voice, saying this time on a low, surly note, 'OK' and again the soft tones of Edith Cadwell's voice. There followed a longish silence which was broken by the man saying, 'I'm no hand with a pen.'

Linda knew that voice, and she felt that she could endorse that its owner would be no hand with a pen.

Although she strained her ears now no further sound came through the door. She told herself that she should thrust it open and surprise Sep Watson, but her common sense warned her that her efforts would be useless. She was checked by the thought, too, that perhaps Edith Cadwell was trying to save Ralph Batley from an underhand attack by the Cadwells. No, no, her mind rejected this. There was something fishy here to say the least. Why had Ralph Batley not been able to find the cowman when he searched this place a few minutes ago? Should she go for him now and tell him Sep Watson was in the studio, talking to Edith Cadwell, an evidently unafraid Edith Cadwell? But what good would that do? By the time he could reach here the bird, in the shape of Sep Watson, would have flown. What she could do would be to thrust open this door

and scream her loudest. Both Ralph Batley and
Uncle Shane would be about the buildings, they
were bound to hear her. This was an idea that if
dwelt upon would have to draw on courage for
its action. She knew she was very low in courage
at this moment, and it could only be done if she
didn't stop to think. She turned from the wall and,
grabbing the handle, thrust at the door. When it
merely shuddered under her impact, she felt the
amazement covering her face. It was locked.

'Who's that?'

It was some seconds before she could find her
voice to answer.

'Me, Linda Metcalfe.'

It seemed a long time before the door was
opened, and Linda found herself standing on the
threshold stock-still, looking at the pale, haggard
face of the girl. Neither of them spoke, but after a
moment Edith Cadwell, her steps almost tottering,
made her way back to the couch, and the voice
Linda now heard bore no resemblance to the crisp
whispering she had listened to a few minutes
earlier.

'I was so afraid when Ralph told me about
Watson being on the prowl I . . . I felt I must
lock the door.'

Linda came slowly into the studio; there was
no place for anyone to hide except . . . her eyes
moved down to the couch, low as it was a man
could hide under that. The blankets were trailing
on to the floor covering the front. She went slowly
towards the couch, trembling now from head to

foot. Bending down she lifted the blankets from the dusty floor and put them further over Edith Cadwell's legs. She looked at the girl as she did this, but there was no protest from her, no quick movement of the hand to stop her, and when she stepped back from the couch she could see for quite a way under it. There was no-one there. She asked herself, had she been dreaming or was she a little mad? But no, she had heard Sep Watson's voice coming from this room. And now she looked towards the door that was never opened, the door that led to the outside staircase, and from it to Edith Cadwell again. She was lying with her eyes closed and she asked in a weary voice, 'Have they found him? Has Ralph found him?'

Linda forced herself to answer calmly, 'No, not yet.' Then she added, 'Did he say it was Watson he was looking for?'

'Yes. Yes, I suppose so, or how would I have known? He . . . he told me there had been trouble with him. Anyway, I . . . I do hope it is Watson, if it isn't it could be . . .' She broke off and closed her eyes, and Linda, after gazing at her steadily for a moment, moved away. She walked round the head of the couch towards the door, but it wasn't at the lock she looked but at the floor. The room was still dusty, the floor very dusty, no attempt had been made to clean it up, there had been no time. There were footmarks about two feet from the door, and the light grey dust, mostly seepings from the barn, should have remained intact to the skirting board or to the bottom of the door, but it wasn't intact.

The door fitted flush to the floor and there were tracks where it had scraped the surface. The door that always remained locked had been opened, but there was no key in the lock. To make sure that her surmise was correct she looked along the floor to each side of the door. The dust here for some way from the skirting board was quite undisturbed.

When she turned from the door to go back to the couch it was to find Edith Cadwell's eyes on her. She was twisted round and looking over the head of the couch, and her eyes were no longer brown and soft, they were black and almost fierce.

'What's the matter, what're you looking for?'

'Nothing. I was just wondering if anybody could get in this way.'

'No, they couldn't, that door's locked; it's always locked.'

Linda came to the foot of the couch again and stared at the pale face. She wanted to say, 'You're lying, you've just let him out through that door. You've got a key to that door. You must have kept it all those years. You've got keys to both these doors, duplicate keys.' And she might have said it if she hadn't, at that moment, heard the quick step of her employer coming along the barn. She turned hastily away from the staring eyes and went out, for she couldn't trust herself to witness the play-acting that would take place when Ralph Batley came into the room.

She was halfway along the passage when they met, and to his quick enquiry, 'Everything all right?' she could only incline her head before moving on. But she had hardly turned the corner near the boxes when the rapid, quick-firing sound of his voice drew her to a halt. He must have cut short some words of Edith Cadwell's for he was saying, 'Now, you listen to me, Edith, this can't go on. It's got to end and right now for everybody's sake. I'm taking you in to Morpeth to a hotel – you'd better get . . .'

'What! You can't, you can't. Oh, Ralph, I'm not well enough to go, you know I'm not. Give me until tomorrow morning, please. Please, Ralph.'

'Now, Edith, don't get het up like that, it's no good. I've just had a phone message – from . . . from Mrs Cadwell, she's in a dreadful state. She says that . . . that he's been out walking the countryside for the last two days because he feels that you're here, he knows that you're here. He's given you until tomorrow morning to go back. All right, all right' – the words were sharp – 'I know you're not going back, I know you can't go back. But you can't stay here. Edith, I've told you, anything more to upset my mother and I dread to think of the consequences. Doctor Morgan warned me . . .'

'Oh, your mother, your mother, always your mother. Don't you realise that all that's happened and what's happening now is because of your mother? Don't you realise that? Don't you know that it was because of her that I did what I did? I felt that I couldn't stand her for another day, and the thought of spending a life-time in this place with her was too much. Just waiting for her to die.'

'Be quiet, Edith! How dare you say such things.' His voice came as a growl to Linda.

'I dare because they are true, and you know they are true.'

'You went with Cadwell because you thought he could give you more than I could. Not in money, oh no, you had plenty of that, but you thought he would lavish on you the whole of his time to the exclusion of everyone, and everything. You thought that he would profess his love for you every hour of the twenty-four, and he didn't and you found he was just a man and took you for granted. That's the truth and you know it. My mother had nothing to do with it.'

'It isn't. You are changed . . . cruel. But it doesn't matter, nothing matters except one thing and you know what that is, Ralph.' There came a pause now and Linda waited for the next words. They came, soft and clear. 'I still love you, Ralph. I've never stopped loving you. I knew I'd made a fool of myself the first night. Come here, Ralph.'

'No, Edith, you made your choice three years ago, you'll have to stand by it, and him. I've had to stand by it. You affected a number of people's lives when you took Cadwell and what is done is done.'

There was a silence now in the whole of the barn and Linda could imagine that it was empty of human beings until Edith Cadwell's voice came again. Her tone was quiet and flat, but her words were startling. 'You think you're in love with that girl, don't you?'

'Be quiet, Edith, I'm not discussing any—'

'You think you're in love with her,' the flat tone persisted, 'but you're not. You can't be in love with any other woman, Ralph, there's been too much between us. Anyway' – there came a light touch into her voice – 'you'll never really be a farmer, there's just a tiny fraction of you a farmer, and I can't see the sculptor in you ever going over the brink for anyone like her. She's pretty and healthy and she appeals to the farmer side of you – the cow girl, a female Sep Watson.'

By this time Linda was standing clutching the front of her coat, her head bowed down, and her heart jumped under her hand as Ralph Batley barked, 'Be quiet! Do you hear? If you dare make such comparisons . . .'

The barn was once again lying under a silence. It went on and on until suddenly it was broken by a low moan, followed by the faint sound of weeping, painful weeping.

When Linda heard the dull thud which meant that the studio door had been pushed to, she raised her head. He had not denied Edith Cadwell's accusation, nor had he admitted it. But a cow girl, a female Sep Watson. If he hadn't seen her in this light before, the picture Edith Cadwell had painted was too vivid for him not to see it now. And the door of the studio was closed and Edith Cadwell was crying.

Slowly Linda made her way to the end of the barn. She had been jealous of Edith Cadwell, yet she had seen that one could like the woman, more than like her. At least these were her feelings up to a moment ago, now she felt she hated her. That anyone could liken her to Sep Watson . . . Sep Watson, the name brought her to a halt at the top of the barn steps. She could go back now and accuse her of hiding Sep Watson and letting him out the side door, of having a key to the side door. She could say to her, 'You were talking to him, planning something,' but where would it get her? She had no proof. Ralph Batley had searched this barn only minutes before she herself had entered the studio, and there was no place in the studio for anyone to hide but under the couch. Should she accuse Edith Cadwell of hiding the cowman under her couch? Even if she did, she couldn't see Ralph Batley believing that. The question would be, for what purpose. There seemed no purpose.

As she reached the floor of the main barn Uncle Shane came from the yard saying, 'Is that you, girl?'

'Yes, Uncle Shane.'

He came close to her and, lifting the lantern, looked into her face. 'You sound tired. You are tired, go on to the house. Go on now and get yourself to bed, and don't worry. Whoever was here has made off. We've combed the buildings. Away to the house now, and I won't be long after you, I'm dropping with sleep meself. Where is he now?' He did not leave Linda time to answer but added, 'Is he up there?'

'Yes.'

'God in heaven! there'll be trouble, there'll be trouble. I can smell it. Ah well, we can do no more, only pray, eh? Go along now, go along. There's a good girl.' He patted her shoulder as he shoved her forward, and Linda went, across the yard and into the house where slowly she finished setting the supper.

When she went to see to Mrs Batley the older woman was strangely quiet, asking none of the usual questions about the house or its running, or yet the farm, but after a while she looked at Linda closely and said, 'Don't bother about anything more, I'm all right. And I'm quite able to get up and get what I want. Go on now, get yourself to bed, you look dead beat. It's too much for you . . . Now don't say anything' – she lifted her hand – 'we'll talk about this tomorrow. Good night and God bless you, girl.'

Her tone was such that Linda found herself crossing the hall blindly. As she passed the big couch near the fire she felt she would have liked to throw herself full length on it and give way to the pressure round her heart.

She was surprised in the act of drying her eyes by the kitchen door opening, and more surprised still to see the form of Ralph Batley standing there. She had expected Uncle Shane to come in long before her employer. She turned her back on him and went to the cupboard, but before her hand had turned the latch he was confronting her. His hands on her shoulders, he pulled her round to face him, and the tenderness in his tone threatened to bring the tears to her eyes again. She did not look at him as he said, 'Mrs Cadwell is leaving in the morning. When she is gone I want to talk to you, you understand?'

She wanted to lift her eyes to his and say, 'Yes, yes, I understand,' but with the picture in her mind of the studio, and the sound of weeping behind the closed door, she said, 'You're always asking me to understand.'

There was a pause before he spoke again. 'Yes, yes, I suppose I am, and I want you to go on understanding until tomorrow.'

She felt his fingers moving gently in the flesh of her shoulder. From her downcast eyes she saw him come nearer and she felt that in the next moment she was going to rest against him, but he released her. When she raised her head he was standing near the door, taking off his coat, and from over his shoulder he said, 'Go to bed now. I'm going too, and Uncle, we'll all have an early night.'

It was out before she could check it: 'What about—?'

'She's well enough to be left. I've locked the door, no-one can get in.'

She looked at him and, as she thought, 'No-one can get in, but someone can get out,' she had the desire to tell him all she knew. But would he like her any the more for blackening Edith Cadwell further? And apart from the disturbed dust on the floor, what could she prove? Wearily now she said, 'I've seen to Mrs Batley, and Michael is in bed. There is a hot dish in the oven if you want it. Good night.'

'Good night . . . Linda.'

As she went out of the kitchen and into the hall her body felt warm. She knew that he was standing looking at her. As she ascended the stairs she saw him come from the kitchen, and as his eyes lifted to hers their gaze held for a moment. Then she was in her room, leaning with her back against the door, her eyes closed, until she chided herself harshly, saying, 'Get yourself into bed, before you freeze or drop.'

At some point in her dreaming Linda heard a bell ringing. It went on and on until she got the idea of lifting her hand and stopping it. Then she went into a deep, quiet sleep again.

'Linda! Linda! Wake up.'

'What? What is it?' She was leaning on her elbow looking into Michael's smiling face.

'It's time to get up, it's seven o'clock.'

'Seven o'clock!' She was sitting bolt upright now. 'But the alarm?' She looked to where the clock lay on its face and she remembered faintly putting out her hand and switching off the bell. 'Oh, Michael. All right, go on, I'll be down in a minute. Is everybody up?'

'Yes.'

'Oh dear. Not your grandmother?'

'No, she's still in bed. She said you hadn't to be wakened but Uncle Shane sent me.'

'All right, I'll be with you in a minute . . . Dear, dear, dear.' All the time she was dressing she kept repeating, 'Dear, dear, dear. Fancy, oversleeping like this.' She was still in a daze and talking to herself as if it had been her habit to rise at five o'clock every morning.

When she reached the hall Michael was trotting back and forth between the kitchen and the table. The breakfast she saw was set after a fashion, and the boy called to her, 'I've set the table and washed-up the supper things. I'm going to the top field with Uncle Shane and if the mist clears when the tide goes out, he says I can go down to the boat. Are we going to have bacon?'

Linda realised that Shane was doing his utmost to keep the boy away from the buildings.

'Yes,' she said, 'yes, we'll have bacon. Thanks for setting the table, I'll see to the rest. Where's your uncle, your Uncle Ralph?'

'I don't know, about somewhere. I haven't seen him since I got up.'

Linda did not see Ralph Batley until half an hour later. When he came into the kitchen his face was stiff, and he did not address her with any preliminaries but said immediately, 'Things never go according to plan, do they? I've got to make a decision, I've to send for either Doctor Morgan or the Cadwells.'

'Why the doctor?' Linda's voice was low.

'She's running a temperature, well over a hundred, she's feverish.'

She wanted to say, 'I'd phone the Cadwells,' but she didn't. Instead she said, 'Have you talked it over with Uncle Shane?'

'No. Is he in?'

'Not yet.'

They were seated at breakfast when Shane came in. The old man had no light patter these days and he had just taken his seat at the table when his head, in fact all their heads, were turned in the direction of the front door. During the time Linda had been in this house she had never heard the front-door bell ring. Since she herself had come in the front door on the night of her arrival she couldn't remember seeing it being opened.

'Will I go?'

Ralph Batley, rising from the table but looking towards the door, answered Linda, saying, 'No, no, I'll see to it.' They all watched him open the glass door, then go into the porch. They listened to the sound of the bolts being drawn and the chain being lifted, then there was nothing more until he opened the glass door again and, holding it back, allowed the regal figure of Mrs Cadwell to step through into the hall.

As Shane got sharply to his feet, Ralph Batley, stepping aside from his visitor, went softly to his mother's door and closed it. Taking no heed of the sharp enquiry that came from within the room, he now approached Mrs Cadwell again and said quietly, 'Take a seat.' As he turned the chair round for her, the tall, grey-faced woman shook her head and looked straight into his face. 'I am looking for my son, Ralph.'

Linda watched her employer's eyes flick downwards for a moment before coming to meet Mrs Cadwell's piercing glance again.

'Have you seen him?'

'No, Mrs Cadwell, I haven't seen him.'

'He was coming here last night.'

'I didn't see him.'

'But he didn't come back. He was in a state when he went out. We waited up and when he didn't come back his father went out looking for him. He and Rouse have been out most of the night. If you know anything, for God's sake, Ralph, tell me. He wasn't himself, he was near mad because of—'

'What's this?'

They all turned towards the voice of Mrs Batley. She was standing in the doorway of her room, her dressing gown hugged about her, and now she walked slowly towards Mrs Cadwell and again she said, 'What's this?'

'Hullo, Maggie. I'm . . .' Mrs Cadwell's voice was very low, 'I'm sorry to find you ill. I . . . I came about Bruce.'

'Bruce?' Mrs Batley flashed a look of enquiry towards her son, then bringing her small, bright eyes back on to the tall woman she demanded, 'What about Bruce? Why have you come here?'

'Sit down. Sit down, Mother.' Ralph Batley had taken his mother's arm with the intention of leading her to a chair, but she shook it off, saying almost roughly, 'Leave be. I knew there was something going on, I want to know what it is.'

'Just this, Maggie.' Shane spoke for the first time. 'Bruce Cadwell is looking for his wife, he thought to find her here.'

As Mrs Batley exclaimed, 'God in heaven!' Ralph Batley's head lifted sharply, and his eyes flashed a warning towards his uncle, and the old man stopped and turned himself about and went towards the fireplace.

'Have you known of this?' Mrs Batley was now looking towards her son and he hesitated before answering her. 'Yes. Rouse came the other day and told me, and Mrs Cadwell' – he inclined his head towards the visitor – 'phoned me last night. But I haven't seen . . . Bruce.' He seemed to have difficulty in speaking the name and Linda wondered if Mrs Batley's next question would be 'But have you seen her?' But it was Mrs Cadwell's remark that caught the attention of the occupants of the room when she said, 'He went out without a coat. It was when he got the letter, it was put through the door late on, I . . . I thought it was from you.' She was looking again at Ralph Batley, and now he answered her sharply, 'A letter from me? To . . . to Bruce? I've written him no letter. If I had anything to say to him it would be face to face. Why did you think it was from me?'

Mrs Cadwell remained silent for a moment then she answered hastily, 'I don't care who it was from, I only want to find him. He has been distraught for days. He had quarrelled with . . . with Edith. They were always quarrelling but they made it up again. He followed her here from London – he knew she was here, she got off the bus in the Bay. Mrs Weir saw her, spoke to her. She came this way all right, there's no doubt about it.'

'Mrs Cadwell.' Ralph Batley was speaking again, his voice deep in his throat now. 'I want you to believe me, Bruce and I have not met, you can rest your mind on that. It's the truth.'

Mrs Cadwell's head was bent. 'Very well,' she said. Slowly she raised her eyes and looked towards Mrs Batley and her voice was sad. There was a painful, lost sound about it as she said, 'I'm sorry, Maggie. I'll go now. They are still looking, I've got a dread about me, you know, Maggie.'

Now Mrs Batley answered and her tone, too, was soft and quiet. 'I know, Beatrice. Try not to worry. You'll find him, he's likely just walking.'

Ralph Batley led the visitor across the hall and they all listened as they had done a few minutes ago to the front door being opened and closed again. When he returned Linda waited for Mrs Batley to start firing questions at him, but she didn't, and Linda realised that so deep was the understanding of this woman for her son that she could restrain her own feelings in consideration for him. She sat quietly in her chair for some moments, and then it was Michael she spoke to.

'Will you bring some wood in, Michael, the fire's going down, I see.'

'Yes, Gran.'

As Michael reluctantly left the room Linda made to follow him, but Mrs Batley's voice checked her, saying, 'Stay.' And when the kitchen door had closed on the boy she looked at Linda and said, 'I feel you know all about it, whatever there is to know. Your face is too frank and open to hold dark secrets.' Now she turned and looked towards the stiff, dark countenance of her son and she spoke one word and that quietly, 'Well?' she said.

'I haven't seen Bruce Cadwell.'

'I believe you . . . but have you seen her?'

Linda could not bear to look at her employer's face.

'Now, Maggie, don't worry yourself, he's told you.' It was Shane speaking.

'He hasn't answered my question, Shane. Ralph, look at me.'

Ralph Batley looked at his mother and Linda felt something twist inside of her when he said, 'I haven't see her, Mother.'

She watched the mother and son stare at each other for a long moment, then Mrs Batley's eyes dropped to her hands, and Ralph Batley turned sharply about and went out of the hall.

When the sound of the outside door banging shook the house, Mrs Batley, looking towards Shane, said quietly, 'I don't believe him, Shane, and you won't tell me the truth either, will you?'

'Now, Maggie.'

'All right, all right, say no more, don't sin your soul.'

'Aw, woman.' Shane could find nothing to add to this and with a jerk of his head he lumbered away. And Linda was left alone with Mrs Batley, who sat in silence now gazing down at her hands as if to probe from them the extent of the trouble weighing on the house.

As she was about to lift the laden tray and go into the kitchen Mrs Batley said, 'Why are men such fools?' Linda cast her eyes swiftly towards the old woman and Mrs Batley, raising her head, added, 'You wouldn't know, not yet, but they are fools. Come here, girl.'

When Linda was standing in front of her, Mrs Batley, looking up into her face and shaking her head slowly, said, 'And you're so bonny.'

'Oh, Mrs Batley.' It was with some difficulty that Linda kept her voice steady.

'You are, you are a bonny girl. But away and above that, and what is more important, you are a nice girl.' The worn hands came out and caught Linda's and there was unusual strength in the bony fingers. 'Beauty without a kind heart is worthless. There, there—' she patted Linda's hand gently now, adding softly, 'don't upset yourself, what has to be will be.'

Linda put the tray down on the kitchen table, and she closed her eyes for a moment as she repeated to herself Mrs Batley's words, 'Don't upset yourself.' She was so caught up in the emotions of this house that even without the feeling she had for its master she wouldn't have been able to remain untouched by the hate and love that threaded the Batleys together. She glanced at the clock, it was just turned eight, the routine of the day had hardly begun and yet she felt weary already, and as she stood for a moment looking out of the kitchen window a most oppressive feeling of dread enveloped her. It was like a premonition of evil, and she tried to shake it off by saying, 'Don't be silly, don't go looking for trouble.' But fifteen minutes later when she had apparently thrown off the feeling, it returned with startling intensity.

She was at the sink when she saw Uncle Shane, he came at a staggering run across the yard. She saw him halt for a moment and look towards the farm buildings before making his way towards the kitchen door, but she was out in the yard before he reached it.

'What is it, Uncle Shane? What's happened?'

The old man's face was blanched and his eyes staring wide as he gripped hold of her arm to support himself. 'Is he . . . is he indoors?'

'No, Uncle Shane, he's about the farm somewhere.'

The old man was about to speak again when he turned quickly aside and to Linda's astonishment vomited in the yard.

'Oh! Uncle Shane, Uncle Shane, what is it?' She went to support his head but he thrust her roughly away with his hand and stumbled into the kitchen. Grabbing a towel from the rail he sat down by the table and wiped at his mouth as he gasped, 'Find him. Find him quickly.'

Linda stared for a second at the old man before turning and dashing out of the room. As she ran across the yard calling, 'Mr Batley! Mr Batley!' she thought that she had done nothing in the last three days but run here and there calling 'Mr Batley, Mr Batley.' At any other time she would have given a wry smile to this thought, but not now. Whatever had frightened Uncle Shane was something that was going to frighten the other occupants of the house.

It was Michael who shouted to her, 'Uncle's in the bull pen.'

When she got round the corner of the buildings it was to see Ralph Batley coming out of the pen, and without any preliminaries she shouted to him, 'Will you come? Something's happened to Uncle Shane, he looks dreadful. He's in the kitchen.' Before she had even finished speaking she turned round and was making her way back to the house with Ralph Batley hurrying at her side.

'What's the matter with him'

'I don't know, he looks dreadful. Something awful must have happened, he was sick in the yard.'

He now sprinted ahead of her, and when a minute later she entered the kitchen he was holding his uncle by the shoulders and the old man was looking up into his face and saying pitifully, 'It was up at the end of the valley, just inside where the gate used to be leading into the Cadwells'. I saw it lying in the ditch, the dark thing, and I went and looked. He was face downwards, the back of his head was all blood and the back of his coat, too, was soaked in blood. He was dead cold, he must have been lying there all night. Oh, my God! What does this mean? Tell me, boy, what does this mean?'

Linda saw her employer slowly raise himself up now, his face the colour of a piece of lint, dirty lint. He did not answer his uncle but stared over his head and said softly, 'God Almighty!'

'You know what this means, boy, don't you?'

'What?' The word was muttered dazedly as if he was emerging from a drugged sleep.

'I said, you know what this means, don't you?'

'Uncle' – his gaze fell heavily on the old man – 'I didn't kill Bruce Cadwell. Could I have faced his mother this morning if I had?'

As Uncle Shane's head drooped and he made no reply, Ralph Batley suddenly cracked at him, 'I tell you I didn't do it.'

'Ralph!' Mrs Batley's voice came calling from the hall and the sound of it startled her son. Looking down at his uncle again, he whispered, 'Come on.'

'Ralph!' The voice was coming near, but before Mrs Batley reached the kitchen her son was well out into the yard. But the old man was not so quick, and Mrs Batley's voice halted him as he was going through the door.

'What is it, Shane?'

When he turned his white, shaggy, whiskered face to her and didn't speak, she said, 'Oh, what is it? Tell me, man, what is it?'

Shane did not answer, he simply turned from her and walked drunkenly after his nephew.

'What has happened?' Mrs Batley was leaning against the table looking towards Linda now, but Linda did not answer her either. She, too, felt that any moment, like Uncle Shane, she could be sick.

'It's Bruce Cadwell, isn't it?'

248

Linda turned her back on the older woman and Mrs Batley said quietly and fearfully, 'They've found him . . . is he dead?'

Linda bit into her lip and lowered her head, and after what seemed a long time, Mrs Batley spoke again. 'I knew it,' she said. 'I've been waiting for it for a long time, years in fact . . . And the things they dreaded came upon them.'

When Linda heard the soft shuffle of Mrs Batley's slippers she turned slowly about. She was in the kitchen alone now. Groping her way towards a chair she sat down, and putting her elbows on the table she pressed her face into her hands, her eyes dry and burning. There were some tragedies that went beyond tears. In the picture behind her closed lids she saw Ralph Batley going towards the gun cupboard last night. He hadn't taken the gun then, had he taken it later? He had said he hadn't killed Bruce Cadwell, and she knew that every farmer in the vicinity carried a gun, but she felt sure that there was only one farmer who hated Bruce Cadwell enough to shoot him.

7

It was lunch time for other people, but not for the Batleys, nor yet the Cadwells. Linda was standing in the hall facing the police inspector and for the third time he asked her the same question in a different way. 'You have seen no-one suspicious about the farm?'

'No, no. I told you.' How could she mention Edith Cadwell? How could she mention Sep Watson without incriminating her employer, and what was more, making him out a liar? She knew that everyone, without exception, suspected Ralph Batley to some extent, and some, the Cadwells primarily, were adamant as to his guilt.

Questions had arisen at the beginning of the enquiry concerning the whereabouts of Mrs Bruce Cadwell. Politely and tentatively the inspector had asked Ralph Batley if he had come across Mrs Cadwell of late, and the reply he had received had been a curt no.

Everyone in the room, with one exception, had their eyes on Linda. – Mrs Batley, Uncle Shane, the two policemen and the inspector, all but Ralph Batley were looking at her, but she knew that not one of them was waiting for her answers with the trepidation that he was. As she lied to the inspector, the very core of her being was bruised with the knowledge that her employer would swear his life away, and let her do the same, to shield Edith Cadwell. If that wasn't love, what was?

The inspector had finished with her for the moment and was again addressing Ralph Batley. In a polite quite impersonal tone, he asked. 'There is no place anyone could hide around the farm buildings, Mr Batley?'

'No, none that I don't know of.'

'But it wouldn't be impossible for someone to hide here?'

'I suppose not, but there's only the big barn.'

'You wouldn't object to us looking around?'

'No, not at all.'

Linda put her hand to her throat and she could not help staring at her employer, but he did not meet her eyes. His answer to the inspector told her plainly that Edith Cadwell was no longer in the studio. But hadn't he said she was ill and had a temperature? Where was she? She couldn't be roaming the countryside, she would soon be recognised. He must have worked fast between the time they came and took the body of Bruce Cadwell from the ditch and an hour ago when the inspector arrived from Morpeth.

'That'll be all for the present. Thank you . . . Thank you.' The inspector nodded to one after the other. His voice was such that he could have been a friend who had dropped in and was now taking his leave. As he made to move out of the room he turned to Ralph Batley, saying pleasantly, 'Don't bother to come, we'll find our way around. By the way' – he had reached the door leading into the kitchen now and he turned once more to him, saying casually this time – 'you said you only have the two guns, the twelve-bore and the four-hundred and ten?'

'Yes. Yes, those are all I have.'

'And you said you dismissed your man a few days ago. Did he have a gun?'

'Not to my knowledge.'

'Very good. Thank you.' The inspector smiled and went out.

Linda looked at Mrs Batley now, and Mrs Batley was looking at her son and in a voice edged with trembling was asking him, 'Do they know what gun it was?'

'It was a twelve-bore.' Ralph Batley's voice was thick and it deepened as he added, 'But I didn't use it. I didn't do it, Mother.'

'No, son, I know you didn't do it. At first I thought you might have, but you'd shoot no man in the back, not twice in the back. I know you didn't do it. But what I feel strongly' – now her voice rose to a trembling pitch – 'is that you know who did do it.'

'How should I know who did it?' They were confronting each other.

'Is she about the place? I'm asking you: Is she about the place?'

'If she's about the place they'll find her, won't

they? If I were hiding her here would I let them search?'

'You wouldn't be able to stop them.'

'No, I don't suppose I would, but I'd be worried wouldn't I?'

Mrs Batley's eyes were the first to drop away.

'Maggie . . . Maggie' – Shane's voice came at her now, like a thin reed pipe – 'have you a drop of anything by you?'

'You are having no drops today, Shane. There are enough troubles on the house, God knows, without you going mad. Have a strong cup of coffee.' She looked towards Linda. 'Would you mind making a pot of coffee, Linda, please?'

Compassionately Linda glanced at Uncle Shane's bent head. If she had her own way she would have given Uncle Shane a bottle of spirits at this moment, for the old man was in deep distress. But Mrs Batley knew best.

She kept her eyes averted from the master of the house as she made her way into the kitchen, but it was only a short time later as she was putting the coffee pot and cups on to the tray that he came in and stood by the table.

'Do you believe I've done this?' His voice was deep, almost guttural.

She answered him after a perceivable hesitation. 'No, not now.' Then her eyes flicked away. 'I did at first, before I· knew he had been shot in the back. I . . . I think like your mother on that point.'

'Thank you.' Across the table they stared at each other for the space of seconds. 'I'm in trouble, Linda.' His voice was still deep and thick but now gave evidence of the riot of emotions he was clamping down on. 'They think I did this, they're out to prove I did it. The Cadwells will help them every step of the way, naturally.'

Linda did not answer this confidence with any sympathetic words, instead she asked a question. 'Where is she?' she said.

'Up in the rafters.'

'The rafters?'

'There's a ledge where the big beams meet at the side opposite the studio. It's high up and doesn't look broad enough to hold anyone, they'll never look for her there.'

'I thought she was ill.'

'She is. In many ways she's a very sick woman.'

'Does she know what's happened?'

'Yes. I had to tell her. She became terrified; she thinks' – he paused, and his eyes were veiled from Linda's gaze – 'she thinks they might blame her.'

'Mr Batley' – she was leaning across the table towards him – she had wanted to say 'Ralph' but she couldn't – 'Mr Batley, I think you should know that she has a key to the staircase door, or . . . or is that no news to you?'

His eyes were on hers now, hard and penetrating. 'It is news. What more do you know?'

She swallowed. 'I should have told you this before . . . Sep Watson was about the place last night. When I went up to the studio after meeting you, and you said you couldn't find anyone, I heard his voice. It was – he was – he was in the studio talking to Mrs Cadwell.'

She watched his lower jaw slowly sink downwards, then snap closed.

'You're sure of this?'

'Yes, I heard them. I heard them talking. I – I meant to surprise them but the door was locked, and when she opened it there was no-one but herself there. Then I saw that the staircase door had been opened, the dirt on the floor was scraped where it had been pulled back. She knew that I knew.'

'Is – is that all you know?' He was still looking intently at her.

'Yes.'

'Are you sure?'

'Yes, yes, if I knew anything more I would tell you.'

When he swung round from her and went towards the door she said quickly, 'You can't go to her now, they're still about the place.'

He paused. 'I'm not going to her, I'm going to see if I can find Watson. If they ask where I am, say I've gone to see to the sheep near the top boundary.'

'Yes, all right, I'll do that.' She stared at the closed door for some time before lifting up the tray and going into the hall. And it was as she stood pouring out the coffee before the still-bowed head of Shane and the silent, gravely troubled woman that Michael came dashing into the hall crying, 'Gran! Gran! Grandfather Cadwell is coming along the cliff path, he's very angry. He pushed Grandma Cadwell away, and she fell down and she's limping.'

Both Shane and Mrs Batley rose to their feet together, and Mrs Batley, in a low tone, said, 'Now, Michael, listen to me. I want you to go and stay with Sarah and the calf, stay there until Linda comes for you. Go now.'

'But, Gran . . .'

'Go, Michael, do as I bid you. And don't come back until I tell you.'

'Yes, Gran.'

The boy went slowly out of the room, and Mrs Batley, turning to Linda, said quickly, 'Where is he . . . Ralph?'

'I think he has gone to look for Sep Watson.'

'Sep Watson? Why Sep Watson?'

'He was about the place last night, I heard him, Mrs Batley.'

'You heard him?' This was Shane speaking now. 'Why didn't you say so afore?'

'Well, I . . .'

'It doesn't matter, it doesn't matter. Ralph's out of the way and thank God for it. Go and open the front door, Linda. Quickly now, for they may get round into the yard and meet up with the inspector and the others.'

'That's the best thing that could happen in my opinion.'

'Quiet, Shane! I'll deal with John Cadwell.'

Linda almost ran to the front door but her fingers fumbled at the bolt and chain and when she had the door open there was no sign of Mr Cadwell outside. Then she almost left the ground as his voice came from behind her in the hall crying, 'Where is he? It's no use, Maggie Batley, you won't be able to hide him under your skirts any longer.'

She was on the point of closing the door when she caught sight of Mrs Cadwell coming from the cliff path and approaching the end of the house, and the change, even over the distance, in the smart, austere woman drew her immediately outside and towards her.

'Are you hurt, Mrs Cadwell?'

'I – I've hurt my knee. Is my husband . . .?'

'Yes, yes. Let me help you.' She took Mrs Cadwell's arm and helped her towards the front door and in through the lobby. Then they were in the hall under the thunder of Mr Cadwell's voice.

'He'll hang, Maggie Batley. I'll not rest easy until he's got his deserts. If I don't get him, they will, and when they have him if they don't finish him off I'll wait until my last day, but I'll get him.'

'Stop bawling, John Cadwell, I don't want to fight with you. You're in trouble, deep trouble. Whether you believe it or not, my heart bleeds for you at this moment, but my son isn't the cause of that trouble, he didn't kill Bruce. You've never liked Ralph, John, but in your heart you know he's not the type of man to crawl up behind another and shoot him in the back. You'd know that if you'd stop to think. There are others who wanted Bruce out of the way, I don't need to name them, and you'll likely find out soon enough who shot your son.'

And now with a composure that simply amazed her Linda watched Mrs Batley turn towards Mrs Cadwell and say, 'Sit down, Beatrice. Get off your legs. Are you hurt much?'

Mrs Cadwell did not answer but slowly tried to lower herself into a chair, groaning as she did so with the pain of her knee, and Mr Cadwell's voice came at them all again crying, 'You can talk until you're black in the face, Maggie Batley, I know your whelp.'

'Don't call my son a whelp. And you don't know him.' Mrs Batley was facing him again. 'You've always thought what you wanted to think, not only about him but everybody else. Now you listen to me' – she raised her hand at him – 'stop waving that gun about, hasn't there been enough gun play? All right, all right, I know what you're going to say, but think man, think. If Ralph had wanted to kill Bruce he would have done it three years ago, he knew where they both were at the time and his blood was hot against them. He's had time to cool down quite a bit in three years, don't you think?'

'No, I don't. He still wanted Edith. You can't tell me that a man who is deprived of a woman ever forgets her. Love might cease but hate takes its place, and in hate, or love, he would have her if he got the—'

'Shut your mouth, John Cadwell.'

As Mrs Batley rapped out this command Linda's eyes were drawn towards Mrs Cadwell. She was sitting with her hands clasped tightly on her knees and her head bowed, and Linda's sympathy and understanding went out to this woman, for hadn't her husband just said that he had never forgotten Maggie Batley, or Maggie Ramshaw, that was. Whether in hate, or love, it would be hard for anyone to decide at this stage, but Mrs Cadwell's drooping attitude seemed to point to a certain knowledge. Linda had thought of Mrs Cadwell as a dignified, rather haughty individual, now she saw her as just another woman, hiding behind a façade.

'Go home, John Cadwell, and wait, and I have a feeling it won't be long before you know the truth of the matter. But I tell you here and now, you are barking up the wrong tree when you are hunting my Ralph. And finally, listen to me, John.' She did not add Cadwell this time, and it was as if she and the tormented man before her were in the room alone, for she said, quietly now, 'If you do Ralph an injury in any way you'll have me to deal with, whatever you do to him I'll do to you, that is a promise, John.'

Not only the tone but Mrs Batley's whole attitude made Linda shudder. She was amazed at the strength of this sick woman. She turned her face away and looked at Uncle Shane. He had his head bowed as if the scene was too painful for him.

'Could I ask you to phone, Maggie, and get them to bring the car?'

All their eyes were turned now towards Mrs Cadwell, and Mrs Batley, her attitude changing again, answered quietly, 'Yes, Beatrice, yes.'

'I'll do it.' Linda hurried away to the room under the stairs, glad to escape for a moment from the terrible raw emotions.

When she got through to the Cadwell house it was Rouse Cadwell's voice that answered.

'Mr Cadwell, this is Linda Metcalfe. Will you please bring the car? Your mother is here and has hurt her knee.'

'What . . . what's happened? Is my father there? Has he . . .?'

Linda answered the racing questions briefly and calmly, saying, 'Yes, he's here.'

'Has he . . . is Batley . . .?'

'Mr Batley is away in the top field. Your father hasn't met him.'

'Thank God for that.' There came a sigh on the wire, then Rouse Cadwell's voice, changing suddenly, said, 'But why I should thank God for his safety I don't know, because if I meet him myself I won't be accountable for what might happen.'

'You'd be wrong, Mr Cadwell. Mr Batley didn't do this thing . . . I know he didn't.'

'Personal opinions won't help much in this matter. My brother is dead, and the police are not

260

fools, they'll find the proof they're after. Anyway, I'll bring the car over at once. If Mother can't walk I'd better bring it along the cliff road.'

'Yes. I'll tell them.'

When Linda re-entered the hall she was surprised and apprehensive to find that Mr Cadwell had already gone and Shane was helping Mrs Cadwell towards the glass door. Mrs Batley was standing in the middle of the room looking after them. When Linda came up to her she did not look at her, but taking hold of her arm held it firmly until Shane had pulled the door closed, then she turned to her. 'You said he went to find Sep Watson. Did he go to the house?' Her words were running one into the other.

'I don't know, Mrs Batley.'

'Do you know where Sep Watson lives?'

'No.'

'You know the place where the sheep got out? Take that road. It's a little cottage standing back on the right, you can't miss it, it's the only one thereabouts. Tell him that Mr Cadwell has been here. Tell him to be careful and not run across him if he can help it.' Mrs Batley now looked downwards as she said, 'I thought I could manage John Cadwell but this is beyond me. He's beside himself, and he won't rest until he meets up with Ralph . . . Go! Go and warn him. Hurry now.'

Linda ran out of the hall and through the kitchen, whipping her coat from the back of the door as she did so, but she had the sense to draw to a walk until she had left the farm buildings. Now, taking the cliff path, she ran swiftly until she came to the valley, then down it and up the other side and through the narrow, winding path to the outcrop of rocks that were near the boundary. She was passing the largest of these when a soft hissing of her name brought her to a dead stop, and there, standing well within the shelter of a rock and almost hidden by scrub, was Ralph Batley. Silently he beckoned her towards him, and when she came up he cautioned her to silence. As she looked at him enquiringly he bent his head and whispered, 'Watson, he's down on the road. Twice he's got under the wire, then gone back again. I don't know what his game is, but wait.'

As they stood tense and close together, his face only inches away from her own, she could not but comment to herself on the almost drastic change in his appearance. It was, she thought, as if she were looking at a different man, an elder brother to the man she knew. True, most of the time his countenance had been stiff and forbidding, but now his face looked so much older. He looked weary, and his eyes had a sad, defeated look. Compassion for him rose in her. She had the strong urge to put her arms about him and comfort him. Even the knowledge that he might love another woman didn't matter at this moment, all she wanted to do was to give him some measure of comfort. But as she couldn't bring herself to do this she delivered to him the message that had brought her here. 'Your mother sent me.' She had her lips near his ear. 'Mr

Cadwell has been to the house. He had his gun with him and was very threatening. Your mother begs you to be on the look-out and take care.'

He turned his head and looked at her, but what reply he was going to make was checked. With the quick pressure of his hand on her arm he warned her to silence. She watched him now look cautiously round the rock, then stretching quickly upwards he gripped a jutting piece of stone with his hands and, finding a foothold about three feet from the ground, he hoisted himself up over the edge of the rock. He stayed in this position for only a few seconds, before dropping to the ground again. 'He's gone, that was his bike I heard.' He moved further into the open now and it was with his back to her that he gave her an answer to the warning. 'I'm not afraid of meeting up with Cadwell,' he said. 'He's a rough, uncouth swine, and he's not above hiring others to do his dirty work. I know where I stand with him. At a pinch he'd fight it out, clean, according to his lights.'

'He didn't talk so generously of you.'

'No. Well, that's beside the point, but if I'd only him to fear at the moment, I wouldn't worry, but I'm up against someone more dangerous than Cadwell. At one time I thought there couldn't be anyone worse than he is, but you live and learn . . . Come on, we'd better be getting back.'

There was now no chance to keep up a conversation, for he did not suit his steps to hers. She had almost to trot to keep pace with him. But just before they came in sight of the farm buildings he slowed his walk, and turning to her, he said quietly, 'If they've gone, I want you to help me . . . will you?'

'I'll do whatever I can.'

'Have you a spare breeches and jacket?'

'Breeches and jacket?' She screwed her eyes up at him. 'Yes.'

'Good. Can you get them out, do you think, without being noticed? Wear two pairs at once, or something like that.' He shook his head. 'It's this way, I've got to get her out . . . Edith. She must get away, and if she was wearing your things, and that scarf you sometimes have over your head, she could go in the Jeep with me, as if we were going to the Bay with the milk. I must get her as far as Morpeth, once there she can look after herself.'

'But I thought you said she was ill, she had a temperature. You were going to get the doctor.'

'I know, I know what I said.' His voice was terse. 'She was feverish, and she is ill, but now, ill or well, she must get away. Do you *mind* giving her your clothes?' He paused. 'I'll see that you don't lose by it.'

'That won't be necessary,' she said sharply. Then went on, 'I keep a spare coat hanging in Sarah's barn. I doubt if I could get another pair of breeches over these, but there's a pair I put out for cleaning. They're in the bottom of the cupboard in the kitchen.'

'Good. You can easily get them from there, but whatever you do don't let my mother see you. You'd better go now, round the front way. I'll go through the arch. I expect the police will have gone by now. But if by any chance they've gone back into the house do nothing for the moment. Wait.' His hand went out as she turned away – his fingers were touching lightly on her shoulders – 'I want you to know how grateful I am.'

'That's all right, it's nothing. Anything I can do to help, you know I will.'

'Yes. Yes, I know that. You're so good.'

Their eyes held, then almost simultaneously they turned from each other . . .

When ten minutes later Linda entered the big barn, Ralph Batley was waiting for her, but he was not standing idle, he was hosing out the pens. And she knew as she watched his quick, nervous movements that this too must be a worry to him, for the work schedule had gone completely adrift.

'I've got the things.'

He turned off the tap and hung up the hose before speaking. 'There's nobody about the yards, how about the house?'

'They're gone, your mother says they left about ten minutes ago. She said the inspector wanted to see you again, he's going to ring and tell you what time he's coming out.'

'Is he?' He made a deep obeisance with his head. 'Well, I hope he finds me at home.'

She could make very little out of this remark. She followed him now towards the big barn and watched him pick up a ladder from the floor and hoist it up on to the first storey. When she herself had ascended the steps he was at the far end of the barn, and when she reached the line of boxes he had already set the ladder up against the beams. She watched him mount upwards and heard him say softly, 'Edith . . . Edith.'

When the white thin face appeared like a blur over the side of the beam the effect was eerie to say the least. It looked, Linda thought, like a disembodied thing floating near the roof.

'Come down.'

'Have they gone?'

'Yes. Can you manage? Here, take my hand.'

'I'm all right, I'm all right.'

It was with amazing alacrity that Edith Cadwell descended the ladder, and when a moment later she stood in the passageway Linda could not help commenting to herself that there wasn't much sign of illness about her now. Fear, yes, because the girl's face was almost livid with fear.

'Linda has brought some of her clothes for you, I want you to get into them. You won't be noticed dressed like this in the Jeep. I'm taking you to Morpeth.' He did not look at her as he spoke but pulled the ladder from the beams and laid it on the floor.

'No. No, Ralph, I'm not going, I'm safer here. They won't come back.'

'They will come back, Edith.' He was facing her now and his voice sounded strangely flat to Linda, weary and flat, as if he hadn't just made this statement but had been pressing it home for some time.

'I'm not going, I tell you I'm not going, Ralph.

266

What would I do? Where would I go?' There
was a note of panic in her voice.

'You said last night you had friends in Morpeth
and you would go there today, that you'd be safe
there . . .' He paused here for a long moment
before adding, 'He wouldn't find you there, you
said. Well, there's no need to worry now, is there,
Edith?'

Her lips were trembling and the muscles of her
face twitching. 'I'm not going, Ralph.'

They were both quiet, staring at each other,
their wills warring.

'This is the last place they would think of
looking for me.' Her voice was low now. 'Anyway,
why should they bother, it was only . . . only Bruce
that was out to find me, not anyone else?'

There followed a silence while the eyes of each
probed the other. So lost in their searching did
they become that it was borne home painfully to
Linda that they were momentarily oblivious of her
presence.

Then Ralph Batley's voice cut into the spell,
saying, 'They will want to question you, they
will want to know where you have spent your
time during the last few days . . . There are a lot
of things they'll want to know, Edith.'

'Ralph! Ralph!' On a sudden she flung herself
against him, her arms round his neck, her composure broken, pleading now like a child. 'Ralph,
don't send me away. Please! Please! you can't send
me away. Please, let me stay here, I feel safe with
you. I always felt safe with you. This will pass over,

they will forget all about me. I don't mind your mother, I don't, I don't. I'm sorry I said the things I did. I'll put up with anything . . . Oh! I didn't mean that, I only meant . . .' Her head sank on to his shoulder. 'Don't send me away, Ralph.'

Linda turned away. She felt that both of them had entirely forgotten her existence, but in this she was wrong, for she hadn't taken more than a couple of steps when Ralph Batley's abrupt tones stopped her, saying, 'Let me have those things.'

As she picked up her coat and breeches from where she had placed them across one of the empty packing-cases and handed them to him, Edith Cadwell moved swiftly forward. Her voice a faint hissing whisper now, she said, 'I won't put them on, I won't. I'm not going, I tell you I'm not going.'

'Listen to me, Edith' – he rounded on her quickly – 'if you were yourself you would know that this has got to come to a head some time. You have either got to get right away or face up to the Cadwells. What is it going to be? I can't keep you here any longer.'

'Face up to the Cadwells? Why should I face up to the Cadwells? I have nothing to do with the Cadwells any more. I am free! Ralph, I'm free, don't you realise that . . . free.'

Gently he removed her clawing hands from his coat, but he held them within his grip as, continuing to look at her, he said, softly but insistently, 'Edith . . . Edith, get this into your head, if you don't get away now you'll *have* to face the Cadwells. And what is more . . . the inspector.'

'The inspector?' Her mouth hung open for a moment before her whole body jerked and she tried to pull her hands from his. 'I know nothing, what could the inspector have to ask me?'

'Don't get excited. Now don't get excited, Edith. Edith, listen to me.' He shook her. 'Everybody is under suspicion until this matter is cleared up, everybody. Me, you, everyone. But most of all me . . . and you. Don't you understand? It's for your own good, your own good, I want you away.'

Linda now watched the great brown eyes slowly turn on her, and something in their depths startled her, and for the first time she thought that what Ralph Batley had said about this girl was true – she was ill and not just physically ill.

The next second the eyes were jerked away from her and all three of them had turned their gaze towards the end of the barn, and the sound of footsteps.

'Are you there, Batley?' The voice, unmistakably that of Rouse Cadwell, brought their eyes together. Ralph Batley now using both hands simultaneously pushed Linda forward while at the same time he thrust Edith Cadwell back in the direction of the studio.

When Linda reached the edge of the upper floor and looked down she could not help an exclamation escaping her, for there below her was not only Rouse Cadwell but with him was Sep Watson.

There was no exclamation of surprise from Ralph Batley when in the next second he came to her side, but Linda, glancing quickly at him, guessed that he was momentarily taken off his guard by the sight of the cowman, yet his voice gave no indication of his feelings as he asked gruffly, 'Well, what d'you want?'

The question could have applied to either of the men standing below, but it was Rouse Cadwell who replied, 'I want to talk to you, it's important.'

After a moment of staring at them Ralph Batley turned round and descended the ladder. When Linda, following him, reached the foot he was saying menacingly to Sep Watson, 'I told you what would happen if I found you on my place again, didn't I?'

'It's that very threat that kept him away' – it was Rouse Cadwell speaking – 'so he came to me. He has something to tell you. Do you want to hear it?'

'That will depend, won't it?' Ralph Batley was staring at the cowman when Rouse Cadwell said, 'It might mean the saving of your neck.'

This statement seemed to make no impact on him but, still looking at Sep Watson, Ralph said, 'Well go on, I'm waiting.'

Linda would have said that no circumstances could have changed Sep Watson, but the man standing before his old employer did not look the thick-set, dull-witted, gossiping bully that she remembered. It seemed to her that the wave of fear that enveloped the farm had reached him, for his face was drawn and his voice when he spoke was neither bumptious nor whining, but the voice of a man in trouble.

'I . . . I came round last night.' His eyes dropped away from Ralph Batley's at the next words. 'I was after gettin' my own back, I came to do you a mischief. Well . . . not you yourself, your things. I meant to get one of the cattle, say Sarah, or set this here alight.' He now lifted his head and moved it in a wide circular movement above his thick shoulders. 'I saw a chink of light coming from the studio door, the outside door, and it set me wonderin' as I knew you didn't use it no more. It was when I was goin' up the stairs that old Shane came on the scene and I bolted. I made for up there.' His head jerked towards the upper platform of the barn. 'I knew it wasn't you in there 'cos I'd seen you go into the house, but I thought it might be . . .' He paused and once again his eyes dropped, and Linda shivered, knowing that it was herself he had imagined would be in the studio.

'Go on, we know who you thought was there. Go on.' Ralph Batley's voice had a rasping sound.

'Well, I pushed the door open and then I got the gliff of me life when I saw it was Mrs Cadwell. She was frightened for a minute, and then when she heard you comin' she acted funny like. She told me to get under the couch and keep mum, an' I did. And then you came in and she played on that there'd been nobody near her, and when you was gone she said a funny thing. She said . . . well, that I was the answer to her prayers and would I take a note to her husband? Then she said she had no paper, there was plenty of pencils 'bout the place but no paper, an' would I just write and say would he meet her at the gate in the valley? I told her I wasn't much hand with a pen but I'd do it . . . I thought it was one way of getting me own back. Then she let me out of the top door, she had a key. And it wasn't until I was half-way 'cross the first field that it dawned on me I hadn't me gun, she had taken if off me when I got under the couch.'

Again the cowman's eyes flickered downwards and Ralph Batley said, 'I didn't know you had a gun, Watson. You always professed to have no use for them.'

'Aye. Well, that's what I told you. But I've always had a gun. I did a bit of poaching on the side.'

'What is it?'

'It's a twelve-bore.' Now the cowman's eyes were looking straight into Ralph Batley's and his voice took on an agitated earnestness. 'I went home and scribbled out the note and took it up to the Cadwells' – he motioned to where Rouse Cadwell was standing silently listening to the story he already knew – 'and then I came on back here. I went up to the studio again. It was round about midnight, and I tapped on both doors but couldn't get an answer. I kept at it for a while but couldn't make her hear. Then I decided to give it up and come back the night. And then . . . well . . . and then I heard the news, the news that Mr Cadwell had been shot in the back, twice, and that it was a twelve-bore that done it. And I knew if they found the gun . . . well, they only had to take finger-prints and they'd know it was mine. You see . . . you see' – he turned his head away now and looked towards the wide opening of the main barn, as he went on – 'that couple of years I was away just after the war I was doing a stretch. I broke into a shop and was caught and beat the bloke up afore they got me.' Now his head jerked towards Ralph Batley again as he gabbled, 'But I didn't do this, I'm no murderer. Not that many a time I didn't feel like conking you off 'cos of your high and mighty airs and graces, but I'd never have been able to bring meself to do it. Set the barn alight, aye, or put a bullet into a beast, aye, or lay poison an' do the dogs in, but not murder. I tried to come this mornin' when I heard, but knew what kind of reception I'd get. So I went to Mr Cadwell here, for I'm not takin' the rap for nobody, her or nobody else. When she took that gun off me she held it gingerly, as if she was frightened of it, and I remembered after, she had her hanky in her hand when she pushed it behind her on the couch. She must have known what she was goner do then, for she wasn't frightened of any gun, she was a good shot, you know she was.'

The truth seemed terrible to Linda, staggering, yet she felt she had known it all the time. But she had to admit she had only surmised it. Nevertheless, someone else had been aware of it, vitally aware of it, and this was proved true when Rouse Cadwell said in a quiet tone, 'You knew this all along, didn't you, Ralph?' The very fact that he hadn't added Batley, or just used her employer's surname, spoke volumes for his changed opinion.

Ralph Batley did not answer, but he turned slowly about and looked up the ladder towards the studio door. Then without looking back he said to no-one in particular, 'Wait here.' Slowly he ascended the ladder, and when he disappeared from view Linda continued to listen to each heavy lagging step he made towards Edith Cadwell, and she wondered what he was thinking, what agony of mind he was enduring. Some seconds later his voice came faintly to her, calling, 'Edith! Edith!' then louder, 'Edith! Edith!' She heard him running the width of the barn. She was with him in her mind as he looked here and there between the bales and she knew the exact moment he would make his reappearance at the edge of the upper loft.

'She's gone. There's no sign of her.' He scrambled down the ladder, and before any of them had reached the opening of the barn he was past them, but when his eyes turned towards the staircase leading from the studio her eyes were on it too, and the open door.

'She's desperate, and ill.' He was speaking to Rouse Cadwell. 'The cliffs, she'll likely make for the cliffs.' Like missiles from a catapult the two men covered the yard, then Linda was running, racing after them towards the cliffs, and the oddness of the situation could not help but penetrate her thoughts, for here she was running almost side by side with Sep Watson.

'There she is.' Ralph Batley's shout came back to her, and the next instant her heart missed a beat as she saw Edith Cadwell seeming to leap into the air from the cliff edge. Then noting the point at which she had disappeared she knew that Edith had not jumped over the cliff but was descending to the beach by the steps.

Linda was away ahead of Sep Watson now, and just behind the two men when they reached the cliff top and there, looking down through the veil of sea fret she saw the ghostly outline of Edith Cadwell walking into the water.

'My God, she's taking the boat out.' Ralph Batley followed this by a yell, 'Edith! Edith! That's no good, wait a minute. Do you hear? Wait a minute!'

She watched him now as he sprang down the cliff steps, expecting him at any moment to lose his balance. On his heels went Rouse Cadwell. Her own descent had to be more cautious. She remembered that Ralph Batley had told her to be very careful if she ever descended to the beach this way. It was strange but this was the first time she had used these steps, and as she tried to move more swiftly down their slippery surface she realised that his warning hadn't been unnecessary. As she stepped on to the beach Rouse Cadwell's voice came to her now, shouting, 'Edith! Don't be a fool, Edith! You'll never make it, the tide's going out, you'll be swept through the gap.'

When, panting, Linda reached the water's edge it was to see Ralph Batley tearing off his coat and kicking off his shoes. He was already in the water when he discarded his trousers. Rouse Cadwell too was standing in the water, and he appealed to Ralph, shouting at him, 'It's no use, you'll never do it, you'll be carried out by the current. She must take her chance, man, don't be a fool.' And he put out his two hands to restrain his one-time enemy, but at that moment Linda saw her employer drop into the shivering-cold water and she shut her eyes tightly.

The trembling that now filled her body was a mixture of fear and shock from the cold water, for she was standing beside Rouse Cadwell, and they both gazed helplessly to where the two objects were being swept towards the narrow gap. Ahead was the slim little sailing dinghy, without sails now and being tossed like a cork on the turbulent, churning water as it rushed on its way back to the open sea.

'He'll never make it, he'll never reach her, he's mad.'

Linda's mind echoed Rouse Cadwell's words as she watched the threshing arms now hardly perceivable against the white froth of the water.

'My God! She's . . . she's over, she's over . . . Oh, Edith!'

Linda herself was speechless. She could voice no

cry, utter no words. She could just make out the dim black outline of the upturned bottom of the boat, and it said to her, what chance has a man in those waters if a boat could be heeled over like a matchstick? Her heart was like lead within her when Rouse shouted, 'He's got her, he's got her!'

'Where?' She strained her eyes through the fret, trying to pick out the figures that evidently Rouse was seeing.

'He has, he has, he's got her. Look there! If he can only make those rocks, the tide's going down. If only he can reach them he could hang on.'

'But for how long?' Linda was asking the question of herself, because even with the tide out these rocks would still be surrounded by deep water.

'Yes, look! He's made them. Oh, thank God! Now if he can only hold on.'

Linda found that she was clinging to Rouse Cadwell and he to her, but when in the next moment he thrust her away she had her work cut out to retain her balance. When she saw him run towards the cruiser at the end of the bay she yelled, 'You can't use that, the engine's broken.' For answer she got a backward wave of his hand which drew her swiftly out of the water and along the beach. He was tearing at the rope attached to the mooring stage when she reached him, and again she cried, 'The engine's gone, Uncle Shane . . .'

'There's a quant pole, I've quanted this across the bay dozens of times. Where's Watson?' They looked along the beach but could see no sign of the cowman. Linda was raising her eyes to the top of

277

the cliff when Rouse Cadwell said sharply, 'Come with me, I might need a hand.'

'Yes, yes.' She was already lumbering her way through the water, and as she pulled herself up the three steps attached to the stern of the little cruiser, she wondered vaguely for a moment if she was in the middle of a nightmare and would soon happily wake up. But when Rouse Cadwell hoisted himself aboard and, grabbing the quant pole from its rest on the top of the cabin, thrust it into the water, she knew this was no dream nightmare, but a terrifying live one.

'Go to the bows, yell if you can see them.'

Hanging on to the cabin rail she went round the narrow deck. When she reached the bows she could see the two figures clinging to the rocks and she shouted back, 'They're holding on, he's . . . trying to pull her up.' She gazed towards the rock and the two bobbing heads, but one minute they were in front of her, the next they seemed to be swept away, but this she knew was the erratic movement of the boat as Rouse Cadwell wielded the pole.

The tide was carrying the cruiser as it had carried the sailing dinghy, rapidly towards the gap leading to the sea, and she wondered nervously, what if Rouse Cadwell couldn't control the boat and the current actually took them through the gap, what would happen to them?

The bobbing heads were now in front of her, and she called anxiously back over the cabin top, 'More that way,' gesticulating wildly with her arm. 'Hurry! He's having to hold her up. Hurry!' It was just as she made this second demand that she was almost knocked over the bows and their progress stopped abruptly.

'What . . . what is it?' She went halfway along the deck hanging on to the cabin rail and looking to where Rouse Cadwell was pushing madly at the pole. 'We've struck a sandbank . . . good God! She's heeling. Look out! Here' – he turned and made a grab at Linda – 'come up this way, on to the top.'

When she clutched at his hand she saw with amazement that he was up above her and the cabin top looked like a sloping roof. As he pulled her to his side it was with horror that she realised that the boat was heeled right over.

'Her bottom's like mush. Must have hit a rock. Look, can you swim?' He had to shout above the noise of the rushing water.

'Yes, yes, I can swim.'

'Go back to the beach then, I'll go on to them.'

'No, no, I'll come with you, I'm a good swimmer, a strong swimmer.'

'Have it your own way, there's no time to argue.' He was throwing off his things and Linda did the same, and as she dropped into the water a second after him she felt she would die with shock, so cold was it. She had said she was a strong swimmer, but she had judged her ability by calm waters and the public baths. Here the fight was not to swim but to resist being carried away on the outgoing tide.

The crawl was her best and strongest stroke and at one stage, as she lifted her head for air, she glimpsed to her intense relief that the two figures were now lying prone on the rocks ahead. He had made it, he was safe. Thank God for that.

As she felt the tug of the current she had to urge herself on to greater efforts. Then never again in her life was she to experience greater joy as when she lifted her head upwards and saw stretched downwards to her, the beloved face of Ralph Batley.

With a heave and the agonising feel of the skin being ripped off her knees, she was pulled up on to the rock where she lay for a moment coughing and spitting out the sea water. She wondered rather dazedly why his hand had released her so suddenly and why he had said no word to her. She turned slowly on to her side – pressing the salt water from her eyes, and the explanation was given to her and she cried out against it. 'Oh, no! oh, no!' When she saw him slip into the water again she had no need to ask what was the matter now.

The way Rouse Cadwell had asked her, 'Can you swim?' seemed to point to himself being an excellent swimmer, but it had been proved to her only a minute ago that you could not judge your prowess against such a current. To her horror now she saw that Rouse himself was in difficulty, grave difficulty, for he wasn't swimming, just keeping himself afloat and being swept with the current towards the gap. She saw, too, that it was a tired swimmer that was going to his rescue, for there was no fight now in the flailing arms of Ralph Batley. After long agonising moments she saw the two men meet, crash together would be a better description. Their arms were about each other and they seemed to be whirling in a mad dance. It was agonising minutes later that she realised they were not struggling to return to her and Edith Cadwell, but were swimming towards a sharp black point away from her, and then she saw the reason for this. They were making for the calmer water, away from this rock which was in the main stream of the current. When at last she saw them both clinging to the black point she took in a great intake of breath, yet at the same time she asked the question, how long could they hope to hang on there? But anyway, they were out of the pull of the current. Her mind, released for the moment from the anxiety concerning them, turned to the inert figure at her side, and she bent over the twisted form of the woman who was the cause of their present plight, the woman who had killed her husband and might yet be the means of destroying two other men. Her heart was bitter against this woman until the moment when her fingers touched the sodden face and turned it towards her. Her hand came slowly off the cold flesh and her head turned from the wide staring eyes, larger now and more deeply brown than ever. She thought of artificial respiration, but she had never given artificial respiration. Yet she knew that had she been most proficient in this matter it would have been of little use. She shuddered violently and looked desperately towards the two men again, and she saw now that Rouse Cadwell was no longer clinging to the rock, and Ralph Batley was hanging on to it with one hand only, using his other arm to hold Rouse Cadwell to him.

She was on her feet now. Should she swim to them? It was evident that something was wrong with Rouse Cadwell and that Ralph Batley was very tired. Desperately she looked towards the shore where she could just make out the figures of Mrs Batley, Uncle Shane and Michael, and two other figures, male figures, whom she didn't recognise, for neither of them had the bulk of Sep Watson.

It was as she thought frantically, I must go to them, perhaps between us we can get Rouse Cadwell to the beach, that the faint chunk-chunk-chunk sound came to her, and it brought her eyes swiftly to the gap . . . The coastguard? No . . . A lifeboat could never get through that narrow gap. The little cruiser that was now lying half submerged might have made it in its heyday with its engine full throttle, but anything the size of a lifeboat could never get through that slit in the rocks. But there it was again, the chunk-chunk-chunking, coming nearer and nearer. She could hear it clearly now above the surge and gurgle of the water . . . When the little red object shot through the gap in the rocks and forged its way steadily into the bay she found she was laughing, yet her face was wet, and not with the salt water, and she chided herself saying, 'Stop it, pull yourself together.'

Linda was past feeling surprise when she saw that the man at the tiller of the little outboard motor dinghy was Mr Cadwell himself. As he came nearer she saw him glance first towards the men and then towards her, but before she could shout anything to him he had made his way towards the point of black rock.

As she watched the precarious business of hoisting Rouse Cadwell into the little boat she realised what the trouble was with him . . . cramp. And she shuddered at the thought of what might have happened had not Ralph Batley acted when he did.

As the boat and its three occupants came towards her Linda thought how strange life was. Only that morning Mr Cadwell had threatened to kill Ralph Batley, yet here he was rescuing him. But Ralph Batley had saved him from losing another son, that was certain.

There was no talking when the craft reached the rocks. Linda bent down and held it steady while Ralph Batley and Mr Cadwell got out. The older man stood for a short time looking down at his daughter-in-law. Linda could not see his face so she could not gauge his feelings, but whatever he was thinking his hands were gentle as he lifted her with the help of Ralph Batley into the dinghy.

The boat was now very low in the water and Mr Cadwell, looking up at Linda, said gruffly but apologetically, 'It won't take us all.'

Before she could say, 'It's all right, go ahead,'

Ralph Batley had pulled himself back up on to the rock again and, looking at his old enemy, said quietly, 'She's overloaded as it is, we'll wait.'

Mr Cadwell, his face grey and harrowed looking, with none of his usual bumptiousness evident, inclined his head. Then dragging off his coat, he threw it up towards Linda before starting up the engine again.

As she watched the boat move away from the rock Linda wondered how this miracle had come about, for it was nothing short of a miracle that Ralph Batley and Rouse Cadwell had been saved. And then she remembered that there had been one figure missing from those on the beach. If Sep Watson had been there his bulk would have identified him. It must have been he who had informed Mrs Batley and Shane, then run to the Cadwells for help. Perhaps his knowledge of Mr Cadwell telling him that word of mouth would be more effective in this case than a plea over the phone. Anyway, however Mr Cadwell had been urged to take out the dinghy in this fast-running sea was no matter. The wonder of it was he had done it.

Thankfully she pulled her knees up into the warmth of the coat.

'You're cold.'

'Ye—es.' Her teeth were chattering but she looked up at him with a wry smile as she said, 'You don't look very warm yourself.'

Slowly he lowered himself down beside her. His face looked tired and sad but in a way relaxed, like a man who had come through a severe operation.

'You've been very brave.' He was looking at her and she said on a cracked note, 'Me? What have I done?'

'What have you done? Well' – he shook his head slowly – 'the time isn't now, but later I'd like to tell you, when this business is all over . . . You understand?'

'Yes, yes, I do, Ra–Ralph.' There, she had spoken his name for the first time and had to stammer it.

'You're very cold.'

'No, no, I'm not really.' And she wasn't, for through her shivering body was coursing a warm, comforting glow. She knew as he did, that it wasn't the moment for expressing joy, but she could not stem this radiance that was flooding her as swiftly as the tide was running out to the sea.

His arm was about her, holding her tightly as they sat side by side looking towards the bay. They watched the figure of Edith Cadwell being lifted from the craft, they watched Rouse Cadwell being assisted on to the beach, and then Mr Cadwell was heading towards them again. As the dinghy chunked nearer, the pressure of Ralph's arm about her tightened and his large hand covering hers brought her fingers slowly and unobtrusively towards his lips. As the kiss spread across her fingers she did not look at him but towards the shore, and the oncoming boat, and her heart became strangely quiet. He had said, 'The time isn't now,' but he had given her all she required at the moment, other things could wait. There was a lifetime stretching before her at Fowler Hall and it would be filled with . . . the other things. The tender embraces, the passionate embraces, the giving . . . the taking. Laughter around the fire in the hall when the day was done, when the work was done, for there would be work, endless work. But it would be all part of living . . . living to the full. No, the time was not now, but it would come, she could wait.

Slowly she relaxed against him, and she had the idea that she was being drawn into his body, held fast within the portals of strength, tenderness and yes . . . arrogance, that went to make up this man. She was no longer Linda Metcalfe, she was already Linda Batley, and the joy of it was almost pain.

THE END

The Fen Tiger

Catherine Cookson

CORGI BOOKS

1

Rosamund Morley was dreaming; she was dreaming that she was putting her signature to the bottom of a document and this document concerned Heron Mill. She was not buying the mill – it was being made over to her as a deed of gift, and the donor on this particular occasion was her uncle. Sometimes, when she dreamed this dream, it was her cousin Clifford who would be the donor, and not only would she be getting the house but him too, not as a deed of gift but as a husband, and she looked forward to this part of the dream.

This dream was as familiar to Rosamund as was the room in which she slept. It usually occurred during the early part of her sleep, and had she wakened one morning and told herself she'd never had her dream she would have been surprised and perhaps a little apprehensive – she always had her dream.

Tonight the pattern of the dream was as usual – at least up to a point. She signed the document, she kissed her uncle (it was her uncle who was bestowing the gift tonight), then, turning from him, she ran out of the sitting-room, through the low hall and to the top step leading down from the front door. There, below her, lay the garden that separated the house from the river bank. The river was narrow at this point, being merely a cut meandering off Brandon Creek, but it still needed a ferry to cross it. She could not see the little red boat below the bank, but the sunlight glinting on the chain picked out its moorings on both sides of the river. The dream was still keeping to pattern: one minute she was standing on the steps of the house, the next she was climbing the wheel-house inside the old draining mill itself. When she reached the top she ran out on to the rickety balcony, and, standing within an arm's length of the decaying wooden slats of one of the sails, she threw her head back and laughed with pure joy. From this point she could see the world – her world. Except for the little wood across the river on the Thornby land the earth was flat as far as the eye could see. There were great tracts of yellow, and red, and brown, and patches of black, such black that no artist could have captured the depth, and intersecting the colours ran silver ribbons – the rivers. Far to the left of her the silver ribbon was broken by the high banks of weeds, that was Brandon Creek. To the right of her, away, away right, the silver was very faint, for the banks of the River Wissey were high, even wooded in parts. Then right opposite to her was the Great Ouse. Two hours run down the Brandon, but only six miles as the eye went over the top of Thornby House, the main river ran towards the sea, delayed only by Denver Sluice itself.

At this point in her dream she would drag her eyes from the landscape and call out. Whether she saw him or not she would call out, 'Hello, Andrew,' and on her shout Andrew would appear. He would be sitting on his tractor in the middle of one of his fields and would shout back 'Hello there, Rosie.'

Although the nearest Andrew Gordon's land approached the mill was a mile away where it met the boundary of the Thornby land, Andrew and the tractor would appear in the dream to be just down below her. She would lean now through the decaying struts in the old mill wheel and laugh down on Andrew, but at this point he would not be alone, for her sister Jennifer would be sitting perched up high beside him. She would wave to them both before turning and running down the rickety stairs again, filled with such happiness that the feeling was almost unbearable, even in a dream. Jennifer had Andrew, and she had Heron Mill.

When she reached the foot of the winding stairs she knew she would be greeted by her father and that she would wave the deed of gift gaily above his head. True to pattern, she was greeted by her father, but the dream from this point changed. Instead of having the document in her hand, she saw it was in her father's hand and he had set a match to the corner of it, and as the thick dry paper crackled, the smoke obliterated him from her sight and she heard herself screaming, 'Don't! Oh, Father, don't! Don't! You don't know what you're doing.' And then her hands were on him and she was struggling with him to retrieve the remnants of the paper.

'Rosie! Rosie! Wake up, do you hear?'

She was sitting up in bed, being gripped by Jennifer's hands while she herself had hold of her sister's shoulders.

'What . . . what's the matter?'

'Wake up! Get up! Oh, Rosie, wake up! The house will be in flames in a minute.'

Rosamund was on her feet. 'Where . . . where is it?'

'Father – his bed's smouldering. I tried to wake him – I nearly choked – I couldn't get him off.'

Rosamund, ahead of Jennifer and on the landing now, was met by a wave of smoke coming along the passage from the open door at the end.

Just as a few minutes earlier in her dream she had groped towards him, now, in reality, she was doing the same.

'Father! Father! Wake up. Wake . . .' She coughed and spluttered as she swallowed deeply of the smoke. Then, motioning to Jennifer, she gasped, 'Pull him off.'

Together they pulled the heavy inert form on

to the floor, then, backing towards the door, they dragged him on to the landing.

Kneeling by his side and holding the tousled grey head between her hands, Rosamund pleaded as she looked down into the white face, 'Oh, wake up! Father! Father! Wake up!' She looked quickly at her sister. 'He's breathing all right . . . Look!' She cast her eye along the passage. 'Shut that door a minute. No, wait!' She laid her father's head gently on the floor. 'We'll have to throw it out – the mattress.'

As they heaved the smouldering mattress from the bed and struggled with it towards the window, Rosamund could not help being amazed at the fact that the whole thing wasn't in flames, for it was burning to the touch. The window was narrow, and, although the mattress was only a single one, they had a job to get it through, and an exclamation of horror was dragged from them both as, with the first draught of air, it burst into flames.

'Oh God! It might have . . .' Rosamund closed her eyes for a moment before turning swiftly towards the landing again.

Henry Morley was still lying in the same position and the two girls stood looking down at him helplessly.

'He could die like this,' Jennifer said.

'Oh, be quiet!' Rosamund's voice was curt.

'Well, what are we going to do? We can't lift him.'

'We'll have to try. You take his legs.'

As Rosamund put her arms under her father's shoulders and attempted to heave him upwards, and Jennifer raised his legs slightly from the ground, it was evident to them both that they could do nothing but drag him.

'It's no good.'

No, it was no good. As Rosamund lowered her father to the floor again she said, 'Well, something's got to be done. I'd better go for Andrew. I'll phone for the doctor from there. Andrew will come back with me. That's if he has returned from the show. Oh, I hope he has.'

'Blast this leg!'

This remark seemed irrelevant to the situation, but Jennifer always used it, in times of crisis, and Rosamund said sharply now, 'Stop that!' She was speaking as if she were the elder of the two, whereas she was two years younger than her sister. But it was she who had for many years taken the lead in the small family. She knew too at this moment that if Jennifer had not been handicapped with her limp, an almost imperceptible limp it must be admitted, she would have had no taste for running across the fens at night, even with the moon full. And so she said quickly now, 'Get some blankets out of the cupboard; it's warm, but you never know. I'll take the Tilley.' She turned to where a Tilley lantern was glowing on a little table near the wall. They had made a practice of always keeping the lantern alight for just such an emergency as had occurred. At times Rosamund had been very tempted to save on the oil, but she was glad now that economy had not driven her to this false move.

She ran into her room, and, not stopping to take off her pyjamas, she dragged over them a pair of slacks and pulled on her shoes. Then, rushing on to the landing again, she was about to pick up the lantern, when she realised that in taking it she would leave Jennifer in the dark. And to be left alone in the dark would be as frightening to Jennifer as running across the fens. There was no time to stop and light another lamp, so she said quickly, 'I won't bother with the lantern, it's practically broad daylight.'

Jennifer's relief came over in her voice as she said, 'I'll have the lamps lit by the time you get back. Hurry, Rosie; please hurry.'

Rosamund said no more but ran down the stairs and into the dark hall. Groping knowingly past the table on which there were a number of brass ornaments, she opened a cupboard door and pulled out a short coat, and she was thrusting one arm into it as she unlatched the front door.

The bright moonlight illuminating the much-loved scene from the front steps did not touch her at this moment, for suddenly she was overcome with irritation and was thinking along the lines that Jennifer so often voiced. What was rural beauty if you couldn't have a telephone or electric light, or electric appliances of any kind? And what was rural beauty without mains water? To have to draw your drinking water from a well that had a suspiciously river flavour, and hump your bath water by buckets from the river to the old sedge-roofed washhouse at the back of the house . . . she was right, Jennifer was right.

She stepped into the little ferry and began to pull frantically on the chain. The water felt cool, and there intruded into her irritation the thought that it would be nice to have a swim. By the time she had reached the other side and scrambled up the path through the tall reeds on the bank she was almost back to her normal way of thinking and she chided herself by saying, Now stop it and thank God for what you've got . . . for what we've all got . . . Oh, she did, she did. She did thank God every day of her life for Heron Mill. Her only fear was that one day they would have to leave it. The fear rose in her now and almost checked her running. That day could be imminent. If anything happened to her father, that would be the finish. If he died, Heron Mill would die too, and they would have no home, with or without electricity. But Jennifer could have a home. Yes, that would be the one thing that would make Jennifer take Andrew. And when that happened she herself would have to do what she had always planned to do in such an emergency: take a job as a domestic – she was better at that than at anything else.

She was sprinting at an even greater pace now, thinking as she ran, Oh, dear God, don't let him die . . . Like a child, her prayer was two-fold, for there was a great deal of personal benefit to be derived from its being answered. Much as she loved her father – and she did love him, not as a daughter loves a father but rather as a mother a wayward child – she loved the mill house equally, because in Heron Mill she had come to know her only home, she had come to feel a sense of security never experienced before. Almost every day during the last six years she had told herself that all she wanted out of life was a home and security.

As she raced over the field towards the little wood she thought, I'll make for the top end and jump the dyke there. But as soon as the word dyke came on to the surface of her mind she shrank inwardly away from it and told herself, Don't take any chances. Go over the bridge at the Goose Pond – it'll only take you a few minutes more.

She might love the fen-land and the rivers with an almost passionate feeling, but she would never be able to bring herself even to look on the dykes with a favourable eye. These deep silt-filled slits in the black bog-like earth, which were as necessary to this underwater land as veins are to the body, had always filled her with a strange fear. Even in the daylight, when she forced herself to look down to the bottom of one she would shudder and imagine herself falling in and then trying to get out. An ordinary ditch had sloping sides, but those of most of the dykes were vertical. The thought of what would be the impossible task of trying to claw one's way up those soft silted banks always filled her with horror.

She was in the wood now and, her thoughts directing her route, she took the path to the left which would bring her to the Goose Pond, a name given to a broadening of the cut that was more in the nature of a miniature lake than a pond. The far side of the pond formed part of the boundary between Willow Wold Farm, Andrew's place, and the grounds of Thornby House, as also did the old, almost rotten wooden bridge that spanned the cut just beyond the pond.

For years now they had used the path through the woods in the Thornby grounds as a short-cut to Andrew's farm, for to go along the river bank on their own side, even as far as the Goose Pond, would have taken nearly three times as long owing to the winding nature of the river.

It was not really dark in the wood, not at this end anyway, for the trees were tall and well spaced. Towards the river, however, where the sapling willows made a denser undergrowth, it would be much darker. But as she knew the wood almost as well as she did every inch of the mill, the darkness presented no problem, and certainly no fear. For mile on top of mile in the fens it was possible to walk and not meet a soul. A chance encounter would nearly always be with someone known. Even in the holiday season, the hirers of the motor cruisers rarely ventured into the fens proper.

So the encounter was all the more startling when it took place.

She was nearing the edge of the wood and was a little out of breath. She also had a stitch in her side, when the thing loomed up in front of her. For a split second she imagined it was one of the cattle that had strayed from Andrew's land. This happened sometimes in spite of all the precautions Andrew took. But when she found herself pinioned in a grip as tight as a river grab, she let out a blood-curdling scream, at the same time lifting her foot and using it on her assailant. That her foot had found its aim on the man's shin became evident, for, emitting what sounded like a curse, he jerked his leg backwards.

'What the devil! What're you up to, eh?' She felt herself shaken like a rat. 'Answer me! What've you been up to?'

'Take . . . take your hands off me.'

There was a moment's silence, a moment during which she stopped struggling and the man's hands slackened their steely grip without actually releasing her. She could not see his face, she was held so close to him, but she knew that his jacket was of a rough tweed, also that he had been smoking, for she recognised the particular brand of tobacco – it was the same as her father used. Strangely, this last thought seemed to calm her, and she was just going to demand, 'Who are you?' for she was sure he was no-one who lived within a wide radius of the fens, when she was dragged forward by the shoulder, and before she could protest effectively they were beyond the perimeter of the wood and in open land. And there for a long moment they both stood surveying each other.

The man before her was broadly built, thick-set she would have said if it had not been for his height, but it was his breadth that gave him the massive look, for he was under six foot. He was bare-headed and all his features stood out clearly in the moonlight. His cheek-bones were high, his nose thin, as were his lips. His chin was squarish and looked bony. In contrast to the blackness of his hair, his eyebrows were light and not bushy as one would have expected with the quantity of hair on his head and the bristle on his cheeks. They were narrow and finely curved and gave to the face a delicacy that every other feature on it contradicted bluntly. She could not see his eyes, for, although the eyebrows did nothing to shield them, the bone formation formed a deep cavity in which they now lay peering through narrowed slits at her.

Although she could not see his expression, her valuation of herself gave her his summing-up: a slip of a thing, of no height at all, with an oval-shaped face and a mouth much too big for it, a nice-ish enough nose, copper-coloured hair, too long to be smart and not long enough to be attractive, and eyes . . . Like his own eyes, hers were screwed up and he would not be able to see them. Anyway, they changed from hazel to grey according to moods, and sometimes even to a dark sea green when she was angry. They could be that at this moment. She guessed the surprise on his face was caused by her sex, and this was proved when in the next moment he said, 'What are you up to, running mad like that? I thought you were . . . Who are you?'

Who was she? Who was he? was the question that should be asked. 'What business is that of yours?' Her voice was high and still held a tremble of fear in it in spite of her outraged feelings.

'You're trespassing on my land. I think that should give me the right to call this incident my business.'

'Your land?' She felt her eyes opening wide and her mouth following the same pattern. Then she brought it closed on a gulp and began, 'You're. . .?'

'Yes, I am.'

'Mr Bradshaw?'

'Yes, that's correct.'

'Well, I thought . . . I didn't know you were back . . . you've been coming back for . . . for years and never have.'

'I've been in residence for three days.'

The 'in residence' sounded stuffy and on another occasion she would have laughed, but all she could think now was, Three days and we didn't know.

Then, she rarely went up that way near the house. Still, Andrew would have known. But Andrew had been away for the last three days at the cattle show.

She said, lamely now, 'Oh, I'm sorry! I would have called if I had known.'

'I don't expect visitors.'

'Oh.' She was slightly nonplussed, but too bewildered now to be annoyed, at his tone. 'Very well.' She nodded her head once before turning away.

'Wait. Who are you?'

'I'm Rosamund Morley from Heron's Mill.'

She had merely hesitated in her walk and she was conscious now that he was following her.

'Where are you going at this time of night?'

'I'm going to Willow Wold Farm, Mr Gordon's farm. I've got to get a doctor.'

'Someone ill?' He was by her side now.

She kept her gaze directed ahead as she replied, 'My father. He was smoking in bed and set the mattress alight.'

'Is he badly burned?'

'He's not burned at all as far as I could see; the mattress didn't catch alight until we threw it out of the window . . . my sister and I. But he's overcome by smoke, we can't get him round.'

'Wait.' His hand came out and pulled her to a stop, and although she shrugged away from it she stopped and faced him.

'If the road to that particular farm is no better than it was twelve years ago and the doctor's got to find his way along here' – he stretched his hand downwards indicating the path – 'it would be an hour, very likely two, before he gets here. Your . . . your father should have that smoke out of his lungs as soon as possible, if it hasn't already done the trick.'

She shivered at the crudeness of his words.

'Where have you left him? In the air?'

'No. No, he's a big man, we couldn't move him. He's on the landing. I was going to get Andrew . . . Andrew Gordon to give us a hand.'

'Come on.' His voice sounded quiet now, ordinary, and as she looked at his retreating figure going back into the wood she called to him, 'Are you a doctor?'

Now the voice changed again and the answer was flung back to her, 'No, I'm not a doctor.'

She hesitated, her hands moving tremulously near her mouth. Andrew wasn't a doctor either, he would have done no more than lift her father on to a bed; but had she reached Andrew's place she would have phoned for a doctor. What was more, she didn't like this man. Yet, nevertheless, if he could do anything for her father . . .

He was well ahead of her now and his voice

sounded indifferent, even as it said, 'Well, anyway, I'll go and have a look at him.'

Pulling herself as if out of a daze, she muttered aloud, 'But I still must get the doctor.' And she had turned about and taken half a dozen paces, when she was brought to a stop in her tracks. The next instant she was running frantically after the man. If he barged into the house – and barge he would, for that seemed to be part of his nature – Jennifer would have a fit, literally. She could almost hear her screaming. Jennifer had not the trust in the fens or its people that she herself had, that was why the doors had to be bolted at night, even although at times they never saw anyone for weeks on end, with the exception of Andrew and workers in the distant fields. At one time, when the Cut was kept clear, dinghies used to come up from the pleasure cruisers berthed on Brandon Creek, but not now, for the great clump of reeds breaking away from the bank had formed thick barriers here and there right up past the mill.

'Wait . . . wait a minute!' She was gasping hard as she came up to his side. 'My . . . my sister would be taken by surprise if you went in . . . if you went in on your own. I must go with you, but . . . but I still must get the doctor.'

'How long have you lived at the mill?'

She was trotting behind him now. 'Six years.'

'What became of the Talfords?'

'I don't really know. My uncle bought the place from an old couple – that's all I know.'

'What do you do? Farm?'

'No, we haven't any land, just about an acre. Mr Brown, he lives at yon side, he bought the land right up to the back of us. We . . . we make jewellery.'

'What?' He paused in his walk and turned his head towards her.

She said with dignity now, 'My father was a silversmith . . . still is.'

'Oh . . . odd pursuit for this part of the globe.'

'I don't see why it should appear so.' Her voice was slightly huffy.

'I thought that kind of thing would have done better in a town.'

'Whatever is sold in the shops has to be made . . . we make the jewellery.' We did, she added ruefully to herself at this point.

They were out of the wood now and could see the gleam of the river. When they came to the ferry he looked down on the little red boat with scorn.

'Huh!' The sound was deprecating in itself, and the words that followed more so. 'A new innovation. What's happened to the old punt?'

'How should I know?' She was snapping and hating herself for doing so, but this man's tone got her on the raw.

'It's likely lying somewhere upstream with its bottom out.'

'Yes, that's exactly what happened to it.'

'I thought you said you didn't know.'

'I didn't know it had been used as the ferry; there's an old punt lying round the bend there, if that's what you mean.'

'That would have lasted another thirty years with a bit of care. It was a fine-built punt; I used to see to it when I was a boy.'

She did not ask, 'Did you live here as a boy?' She knew from the little gossip she had heard about the owner of Thornbury House that he had been born here and had not left it until about twelve years ago.

When they reached the little boat landing he did not offer to help her out but climbed the bank and stood looking towards the mill. But when she reached his side he said, 'It'll soon need stilts. The land must have sunk a foot since I saw it last. Have you had another step put on?'

'No.' She walked past him. 'The steps are the same as when we came. I'd better go in first and tell my sister.' She ran up the five steps and into the hall, calling softly, 'Jennifer! Jennifer!'

'Yes?' Jennifer came out of the room with the lamp in her hand. 'You've never been there in this time. What . . .'

'Listen, I can't explain now. I've met Mr

Bradshaw from the House. He's back, he's coming to have a look at Dad.'

'Mr . . . But where?'

'Ssh! I'll tell you later.'

As she turned the man stepped into the hall – just one step, for there he stopped. He was looking over her head, and she smiled a little cynically to herself. She knew what had halted him: Jennifer, with her flaxen hair hanging over her shoulders, her frilly nightdress gushing out from beneath her three-quarter-length dressing-gown, and then her face, touchingly feminine in all its features. The wide blue eyes, the curved lips, the slightly uptilted nose and the thick creamy skin, and all this enhanced by lamplight. Definitely the Lady with the Lamp, Rosamund thought without any malice, for in spite of being the antithesis of her sister she loved her, and at this moment she was rather proud of her, for she was indeed having an effect on this brusque-mannered individual.

'This is Mr Bradshaw . . . My sister.' The introduction was accompanied by rather an impatient movement of her hand, and then she asked, 'Has he come round?'

'No.'

Jennifer was still staring at the man as he followed Rosamund up the stairs.

As she crouched down beside her father, Rosamund looked across to where the visitor was kneeling on the other side, and she said, 'He

309

seems better now; he's breathing more deeply.'
She watched the man lift her father's lids, then
put his ear to his chest. Afterwards he raised his
head slowly and stared into the older man's face.

'Is he . . . is he all right?'

'Yes, yes, I would say he's all right. At least, he
will be after this sleep. Let me get him up.' His
voice had the effect of pushing her aside, and she
got to her feet as he stooped with bended knees
and, to her amazement, lifted the heavy form
from the ground with no more effort than if it
had been herself he was carrying.

'Show me his room.'

'In here.'

Rosamund snatched up the Tilley lantern from
the table as she hastily made her way to her
bedroom. Placing the lantern on the top of the
chest, she flung back the rumpled bedclothes,
then stood aside to make way for the man as he
lowered her father on to the bed.

'He'll be all right. Cover him up.'

Rosamund didn't like his tone at all. It was as
if he were dismissing the whole thing as of little
or no importance.

'I'm still going for the doctor.'

'It will be a wasted journey and the doctor
won't thank you.'

'What d'you mean?' This question came from
Jennifer, who was standing just inside the doorway
now.

Mr Bradshaw turned and surveyed her for a moment before answering, but her beauty apparently did not affect him enough to soften the brutality of his reply.

'Your father is in a drunken stupor.'

Jennifer stared at him – too taken aback to make any denial. But Rosamund did. She said harshly, 'No! He can't be.'

'I'm afraid he can be, and is.' He glanced over his shoulder at her.

'It was the smoke – he's not drunk.'

The man now turned his look full on her where she stood by the head of the bed.

'Have it your own way, but he's not going to die from suffocation. He might have been a little affected by the smoke.' He raised his finely arched brows now. 'You seem surprised . . . don't you know whisky when you smell it?'

Did she know whisky when she smelt it? As far as she could remember back she had hated the smell of whisky. Yes, she knew whisky when she smelt it all right, for were they not imprisoned – Jennifer's word – in the mill on the fens because of precisely that . . . whisky. But she hadn't smelt any whisky from her father when they dragged him from his bed. For three months now he had never touched a drop, he hadn't been away from the place until yesterday . . . Yesterday? But either she or Jennifer had been with him every minute they spent in Ely – he couldn't have got any yesterday. But he had. As much as she disliked the man standing opposite to her, she knew now that he was speaking the truth. His sense of smell was apparently more acute than her own, but, not only that, there were other signs that had told him that her father was in a drunken stupor. She had seen her father in stupors before, and she would have recognised the reason for this one immediately had it not been for the panic occasioned by the smoking bed. It had never struck her for a moment that he was drunk. As if the shame were her own, her head was bowing. Then, checking its downward movement, she jerked it upwards and, looking at the man before her, said, somewhat primly, 'Thank you very much for your help.'

As he stood returning her gaze without speaking she thought, He must think me an absolute fool, racing madly across the fens at midnight in search of a doctor for a drinking bout. At this moment she could have flayed herself for her stupidity in not realising what the trouble was . . . what the stupor was.

The man turned from her and left the room without another word, and she felt as if she had been pushed back against the wall, not by his hand but by his look, which said, 'You little fool.'

She looked now at Jennifer. Her sister was staring at her, her fingers stretched tightly over her cheek. She didn't speak until the front door banged, then the sound seemed to jerk the words from her mouth. 'Oh, how awful, how humiliating. What possessed you to bring him here? If it had been Andrew it wouldn't have mattered . . . Anyway, I don't believe him, I don't believe him. Father couldn't have got anything yesterday. Did you leave him?'

'Leave *him*?' Rosamund shook her head. 'Do you think I would? I could ask you the same question. Did you?'

'No. No, of course I didn't. Only . . .'

'Only what?'

'He left me for a few minutes, in that café, when you went out to get the solder and things. He went to the cloakroom . . . You know . . . you remember, it was round by that partition just near the door where we came in. Oh!' She put her hand over her mouth. 'He must have slipped out. I remember now that shop next door. Groceries and wine-merchants. It would only take him a minute . . . Oh, Rosie!'

'Well, it's done now. But why didn't we smell it? He did.' She nodded as if the man was still in the room.

Rosamund now looked down on her father. He was breathing heavily and his face was flushed. Oh, why hadn't she guessed. She went slowly out of the room and across the landing to his room, and there, going down on to her hands and knees, she looked under the bed. But there was no sign of a bottle. Next she searched the wardrobe. Again no sign of a bottle of any kind. While she was doing this Jennifer was going through the chest-of-drawers.

'There's nothing here. Somehow I just can't believe it.'

'Look, Rosie, he mightn't have gone to the shop, I'm just surmising that. Likely that man is just surmising what he said as well.'

'He wasn't surmising, he knew all right. And so do we.' Rosamund's tone was flat. 'I would have had the gumption to realise it if it hadn't been for the panic over the fire. Well . . . there's nothing here, but he's hidden it somewhere. Wait!' She got a chair and, reaching to the top of the tallboy, she lifted the lid of what was used as a linen chest. Groping inside, she found what she was looking for, and not only one but four of them, four flat quarter-size whisky bottles.

'Four of them!' Jennifer looked at the bottles in disgust. 'And he promised. Oh, what's the use?'

'Well, it's no use going on. As you say, what's the use?'

'But he promised.'

'You should know by now that he's promised before. Come on, let's go downstairs and make a drink.'

'I don't know how you can take it like that, so flatly, so calmly.' Jennifer was talking at Rosamund as they went downstairs. 'And then tomorrow morning he'll be full of remorse, disgusting remorse.'

'And we'll forgive him as we've done before.'

'I won't — I told him last time — I won't.'

'Well, you'll have to marry Andrew and get out of it.'

'Don't be flippant, Rosie.'

Rosamund was entering the kitchen now and she turned almost fiercely on her sister. 'Flippant? Flippant about this?'

'I'm sorry, but it was the way you were taking it.'

'How do you want me to take it, tear my hair? I stopped tearing my hair years ago.'

Rosamund sounded almost sixty-two, not twenty-two, as she made this statement, and at this moment she felt that she wasn't a girl, she had never been a girl, she had always been a woman who had carried the burden of a weak, charming, drunken man. She went slowly towards the open fire that was still smouldering and threw on some pieces of wood. Then, going to the oil stove, she lit it, and when the flame was clear she put on the kettle . . .

Jennifer was sitting at the table, her chin cupped in one hand, and Rosamund was sitting in the armchair to the side of the fireplace. Neither of them had spoken for some time. They were one with the silence of the house, the silence that these incidents created over the years. Always there came a time when, discussing their father, it was impossible to say anything more, the feeling was too intense. Rosamund remembered the first time this silence had fallen on them. Her mother was alive then. She had been nine and Jennifer eleven and her father was . . . off-colour. Her mother had said, 'No, dear, don't go in to Daddy; he's got a very bad head, he's a bit off-colour.' Jennifer had just returned from a dancing lesson and she had swung out of the room, banging the door, her ballet shoes in her hand. When Rosamund had gone after her into their bedroom to tell her what a pig she was, banging the door when Daddy had a headache, Jennifer had hissed at her, 'Now don't you start else I'll slap your face. I'm sick of it, do you hear? Off-colour! I'm sick of the pretence. Off-colour! Why does Mammy keep on pretending? He's drunk, that's his off-colour, he's drunk.'

'Oh, you're horrible. Oh, you're horrible, our Jennifer. Daddy isn't drunk.'

'Don't be stupid.' The tone was different now – quiet, hopeless.

She had sat down on the bed beside Jennifer and the silence had fallen upon them. She knew that Jennifer was right, there had been something funny about Daddy's headaches and . . . off-colours. Lots of things became clear in that moment, the main one being the reason why her mother's people would have nothing to do with them. Her mother was a Monkton; even her father would say at times, 'Never forget your mother is a Monkton . . . a somebody.' The off-colour episodes too seemed in some way to be associated with this statement — 'Your mother is a Monkton . . . a somebody.' It was some years later before she realised why her father talked like this. He was not so much telling her that her mother was a well-born woman as blaming her mother for this fact. And yet he had loved her mother, who, in turn, had loved him. In spite of the 'off-colour' there had remained between them a warm passion until the day her mother died. There had been rows, heart-breaking rows, which would nearly always be followed by a move to another town where her father was going to work for someone who would appreciate him. He was going to begin again and everything was going to be fine. And it should have been, for Henry Morley was a craftsman in silver. He had gone to work for the Monktons as a boy and trained under one of their finest craftsmen. Monktons was a renowned firm of jewellers and they were very good to the men who worked for them, the right men, and they realised that Henry Morley was a right man. He had the fingers for a setting, he had an eye for line and design. He was thirty and very young to put in charge of a new workshop, but the Monktons thought he was the man for the job; and with just the right amount of condescension Arnold Monkton, the head of the firm, told him about this decision.

Three days later, when he was still walking on air, Henry Morley met Arnold Monkton's only daughter Jennifer for the first time – that is, to speak to. He had seen her from afar, but never had their glances met or their hands touched. When this did happen the impact on them both was like lightning and the outcome was as disastrous as if it had struck them, for Arnold Monkton did not play the forgiving father but let his daughter decide finally between himself and the upstart Morley.

The upstart Morley set out to show the old man, but soon he was to find that the task was greater than he had anticipated in the first bright glow of love and ambition. He could find work, but only as a man in a workshop. Men who had worked up to high positions in this particular line kept their positions and did not favour anyone under them who thought they knew better than themselves. After five years working for three different firms, and striving to show them his worth, Henry Morley felt he needed fortifying. He had liked a drop now and again when he could afford it, and whisky was his drink.

In the sixth year of their marriage Jennifer presented him with a daughter. They called her after her mother. Two years later another girl was born. They called her Rosamund.

That night, long ago, when the silence had ended and she had sat on the bed and watched Jennifer almost tearing her ballet shoes to shreds because she would not need them any more, and listening to her talking, Rosamund was amazed to learn that they had lived in seven towns since she was born. She was also horrified to learn that that very day her father had again lost his job, and so for a time there would be no more ballet lessons. She had watched Jennifer throwing the torn shoe into the corner of the room before, in turn, flinging herself on to the bed and bursting into tears.

Perhaps it was at that precise moment that she had taken charge of the household, for she even imagined that she actually felt herself growing up, and she must have been right, for how else would she have decided there and then not to let her mother know that she was wise to the real nature of 'off-colour'.

When she was fourteen her mother died, and this disaster seemed to break up Henry Morley completely. Jennifer, who was sixteen at the time and left school, decided that she would go in for 'rep', and she went in for it. At least she went after a job. It was as she was returning, full of the news that she had been accepted, that she was knocked down by a bus – entirely her own fault as it turned out. The joy at the prospect of being an actress must have blinded her, for she had walked straight under the on-coming vehicle. It was fortunate that she hadn't lost her leg, but she had lain in hospital for many months after the accident.

Henry Morley at this time became both a

pitiable and despicable figure; it all depended on which of his two children was viewing him. To Rosamund he was pitiable, and to Jennifer he was despicable, and not without reason, for when she came out of hospital, able to walk only with the aid of sticks, it was to find that they had moved, yet once again, this time into two dingy basement rooms.

The crisis came the week that Rosamund herself left school. She had been three days in her first job helping in a day-nursery when Henry Morley went down with a cold that developed into double pneumonia. Added to this, Jennifer's handicap with her lame leg and the nervous state her condition had evoked made her useless in looking after anyone, even herself.

Such was the situation of the little family flitting from one town to another that they were virtually without friends. The doctor who was attending her father might have done something. He suggested the patient should go to the hospital, but Henry Morley's grandiose attitude, which he sustained even with a temperature of one hundred and three, convinced him that the daughters were very capable of nursing him and running the house. The doctor was not to know that there was only a matter of three pounds at that time in the house, and no prospect of that sum being added to in any way.

It was at two o'clock in the morning, while

sitting by her father's bedside, that Rosamund wrote the letter to her uncle. She had only seen her mother's brother once and she was very small at the time. Her mother had dressed her and Jennifer in their best and taken them in a train right the way to London. They had gone into a big hotel and there she had met a man who looked surprisingly like her mother, and who had told her he was her Uncle Edward. She remembered him making her mother promise to keep in touch, and her mother saying that she would. But she hadn't. She had never heard her father speak of her Uncle Edward even when he was – off-colour. Yet at these times he would upbraid her grandfather, Arnold Monkton. She knew a lot about Arnold Monkton although she had never met him. And she came to realise that her father talked about her grandfather because he hated him, but he had not the same feelings towards her uncle. She sent the letter to the firm in London, and printed in a large girlish hand in the top left-hand corner of the envelope she wrote the word 'Private'. On the fifth day, the postman having passed the door yet once again and filled her with despair, she received an answer to the letter in person. Her mother's brother walked into the dingy, cold room, and from that day to this she always associated her Uncle Edward with God.

When her father was able to be moved he transported them all to decent rooms. Then one day he had asked her – not her father, nor her elder sister, but her – how she would like to live in a mill in the Fenlands of Cambridge. It appeared he had taken an old house with the idea of turning it into a week-end cottage for his family. How would she like it? Even without seeing it the mill on the fens took on a semblance of paradise.

But things did not go smoothly with regard to their taking up life in the mill, because Uncle Edward had a wife. Rosamund could never call her Aunt Anna, she thought of her as Uncle Edward's wife. On a visit, and unaccompanied by her husband, Anna Monkton intimated that it was a bit of a nuisance their going to live in the mill, for she had already gone to a great deal of trouble to furnish it, and a good many of her choicest pieces were there, and as there was virtually no road to the mill it had taken some time and not a little expense for the house to be furnished at all. She had also intimated that they could not possibly exist there without a boat on the main river.

Neither Rosamund nor Jennifer had liked their Uncle Edward's wife, nor she them, and Rosamund particularly feared her influence. This influence was made clear when her uncle, rather shame-facedly, told her that he would draw up a statement which would allow them to occupy the mill during their father's life-time. He had laughingly added that neither she nor Jennifer would find this any hindrance, for doubtless they would soon be marrying. Rosamund could almost hear his wife saying, 'We're not providing those two madams with a free gift.'

What Rosamund was sure that her aunt didn't know was that her Uncle Edward made her an allowance of twenty pounds a month. The money was always sent to her by registered letter. Twenty pounds a month meant that they would be fed, and the mill would house them.

Henry Morley at this time was in no position, or state, to make any protest, and he fell in with the arrangement with the acceptance of a child, yet beneath this acceptance Rosamund was always aware of a war raging, a private war, in which humiliation played a big part. For there were weeks on end when he never earned a penny.

When they had finally come to the mill, Henry Morley had been fired once again with the urge to . . . show them. There was plenty of room here for him to have his own workshop. He would start on a paying game, making imitation jewellery. All he wanted was a bench, a furnace, a few tools, and the basic materials with which to begin. By the time he had got these latter his enthusiasm had worn thin, but nevertheless he did begin, and as time went on turned out some very presentable pieces.

But, as Rosamund found, it was one thing to make the jewellery and quite another thing to sell it. After a great deal of correspondence the only reliable opening for sales was with a shop in Cambridge. The location was fortunate but the demand was small. As the owner of the shop flatly stated, he could get machine-cut bangles and brooches that looked exactly like the pieces that had taken hours of painstaking eye-straining work to achieve and for half the price. Unfortunately, Rosamund knew that neither she herself nor Jennifer could ever hope to have the skill that was their father's natural gift, but Jennifer was better at it than herself. Nevertheless this did not prevent Jennifer from hating it, as she did the isolation in which she lived. Yet, as Rosamund sometimes thought when her patience was tried to breaking point, Jennifer knew the remedy. She could either marry Andrew or she could leave the mill tomorrow and get a job – if, metaphorically speaking, she would forget about her leg and stand on her own two feet. With her father it was different; physically he was incapable of manual work, and he was of an age now when it was too late for him to attempt anything else. There was, Rosamund knew, a strong link of weakness between father and daughter, and as long as they had her to depend on they would foster it, and because she loved them she rarely protested.

'I wonder why we didn't smell it?'

'What?' Rosamund turned towards Jennifer. 'What did you say?'

'I said, why didn't we smell it?'

'Yes, why didn't we?'

'I've made the tea. You look miles away – what have you been thinking? Oh, Rosie . . .' Jennifer suddenly jerked her chair towards Rosamund's, and, gripping her hand, she begged, 'Think up something to get us away from here. I'll go mad if I stay here much longer.'

'Now listen, don't start that again.' Rosamund gave an impatient shake of her head. 'You know you can get away from here tomorrow. Andrew's just waiting.'

'That isn't getting away, and you know what I mean, I'd only be moving a mile and a half across the fens if I married Andrew.'

'He loves you; it would be different living like that.'

'Well, I don't love him, not that way. I like him, I like him a lot. I even think I could love him and would marry him if he would get a job in the town.'

Rosamund, rising impatiently to her feet and almost over-balancing Jennifer as she did so, cried, 'Don't be so stupid, Jennifer. Andrew's a farmer, that's his livelihood and you should be jolly thankful he is offering you such a home. And look, I'm warning you, don't try him too far. He's quiet, but just you remember: still waters, you know.'

'Rosie.' Jennifer was leaning forward, hanging on to Rosamund's hand now, and her voice was low and entreating as she said, 'If we could only get away for a while, just a while, say a month somewhere, abroad. Rosie . . . write to Uncle Edward and ask him – he'll do anything for you. And . . .'

The jerking of Rosamund's hand out of Jennifer's grasp stopped her flow of pleading. 'I'll do no such thing – I couldn't.'

'Very well.' Jennifer pulled herself to her feet. 'When Clifford comes next week I'll ask him myself.'

'Jennifer, you won't. Don't spoil . . .'

'All right, all right, I won't. But, Rosie, I tell you I'll go mad if I have much more of this . . . this . . .' She spread her arms wide, and they not only encompassed the room but the whole wide stretch of fenland by which the mill was surrounded.

'Things will pan out.'

'You're always saying that . . . Rosie . . .' Jennifer was standing in front of Rosamund now and her head was bowed as she said, 'If you marry Clifford you won't leave me here with father, will you?'

'Now, Jennifer, look.' Rosamund swallowed. 'There's no talk of Clifford and me. Look, don't get ideas into your head. Clifford comes here for two reasons: it's a place to make for upriver, and he knows we're lonely. He's . . . he's very like Uncle Edward; he's kind, but there's nothing . . . he's never . . .'

'You don't have to protest so much; he may never have said anything, but he's got the same look in his eyes as Andrew. He's in love with

326

you . . . Rosie, you . . . you won't be a fool and refuse him. You have no fixations about cousins marrying, have you?'

'Oh, Jennifer, don't take things so far. Please . . . Come on to bed, I'm tired . . . we're both tired. It's been quite a night; we'll talk about this some other time.'

As she made to pass Jennifer she was pulled to a halt. 'But if he should, just say if he should, you'd do something about getting us away from here.'

Rosamund gave a deep sigh. 'Yes, yes, of course I would. Under these circumstances I would never leave you here, but I'm telling you they won't arise. Come on.'

When they reached the landing Jennifer said, 'But where are you going to sleep?'

'I'll take the couch in the attic.'

'No, come in with me, there's plenty of room.'

Rosamund, now looking up at Jennifer, smiled and put out her hand and patted her sister's arm affectionately as she said, 'You know you hate us sleeping together; you love to sprawl, and I love the attic. Good night, I'll see you in the morning. I'll take the lantern. Good night.'

'Good night, Rosie.'

Before Rosamund took the narrow steep stairs to the attic she went into her father's room, and there she went systematically through his pockets. In a few minutes she had found what she was looking for – two pound notes and a quantity of silver. The whisky she guessed would have cost over two pounds, that would make up the five pounds he must have taken from the envelope a week ago. The five pounds was accompanying an order to Barratt & Company for a quantity of materials. Any letters to be posted were taken to the box that was nailed to a post on the bridge, three-quarters of a mile distance from the mill. The postman, when delivering the mail, picked up its counterpart. Her father had said to her casually that morning, 'I feel like a stroll, I'll pick up the letters on my way. Is there anything to go?' He had known quite well there was something to go, as he also knew that yesterday they would be going into Ely. The craving for drink had made him as wily as a fox, but more stupid, or he would have considered the fact that he would be found out. But apparently to satisfy his craving he was willing to risk that. Sufficient unto the day was the evil thereof.

She replaced the money in his pocket, and as she threw the coat over the chair the sound of something hard striking the wood caused her to pick up the coat again, and when she drew forth a tin of lozenges she was given the reason why they hadn't smelt the whisky from his breath. The directions on the box: 'Guaranteed to eradicate foul breath . . . plus the smell of spirits or beer. She returned the box to the pocket and went out of the room and up the ladder to the attic.

The attic was filled with a lot of old junk, which, silhouetted in the moonlight, gave a weird appearance to the room. That the faded couch against the window was often used as a bed was evident from the blankets folded neatly at its foot. Rosamund did not undress, nor sit on the couch, but she went to the window that reached from the sloping roof to the floor, and, curling her legs under her, she sat close to it, her head leaning against the framework, and as she looked out across the beloved land, across the river and the small wood, right to Thornby House, she did not think of the strange encounter with its master which had been the highlight of the last two hours; she thought of something that was of more importance to her, someone who was of more importance to her, and she sent her whisper out into the night towards the face of a young man which was now encompassing all the land, and she whispered to it, 'Oh, Cliff, Cliff, ask me to marry you, please. Please, Cliff.'

2

The antique grandfather clock with the painted dial that stood on the landing struck seven as Rosamund descended the ladder from the attic the following morning. She tiptoed quietly over the polished floor and down the bare oak staircase, for she did not want to waken either Jennifer or her father. She would light the fire, set the breakfast, then go for a swim. She always felt better after a swim in the morning, and on this particular morning she felt badly in need of a refresher. But when she opened the kitchen door she stopped in amazement, for there at the sink stood Jennifer.

'Surprised?'

'Surprised, baffled and bewildered.' Rosamund looked at the table set for breakfast, at the fire burning brightly, at the kettle boiling on the hob, then, turning her eyes on her sister, she asked, with a twist to her lips, 'You all right?'

'I couldn't sleep.'

'That's not new, but it doesn't get you up at this time.'

'Here, drink this cup of tea.' As Jennifer handed Rosamund the tea they exchanged broad grins.

Then as Rosamund seated herself at the table, Jennifer, going to the sink again and with her face completely turned away, said, 'I did a lot of thinking when I went to bed last night, with the result that today I'm going hunting.'

Rosamund slowly put her cup down on the table, and she screwed her eyes up as she repeated, 'Hunting? What d'you mean?'

'Just that. Do you know who we had in the house last night?'

'In the house?'

'Oh, don't be so dim, Rosie.' Jennifer had swung round now and was facing her.

'You mean Mr Bradshaw?'

'I mean Mr Bradshaw . . . Mr Michael Bradshaw.'

'How do you know his Christian name?'

'Oh, don't ask such inane questions. What you should be asking me now is why I'm going hunting?'

'Well, why are you? Oh, no! Oh, Jennifer, not that – really!'

'Why not?'

'Why not, indeed. He was most rude, uncouth; bullish, like a fen tiger. I would say he is the father of all fen tigers.'

'But an attractive one, you must admit.'

'Don't be silly. He may be married, you know nothing about the man.'

'Oh yes I do.' Jennifer laughingly threw her

head upwards, then, bending towards Rosamund, said, 'You know, what bores me with Andrew is really his farm talk. He prattles on and on talking his particular kind of shop, and quite a bit of his prattling came back to me as I was thinking in the night. He's always kept on about the Thornby land not being cultivated, and the weed seeds flying over on to his celery fields. Mr Brown and Arnold Partridge, from the Beck Farm, they keep on about it too. Andrew said they meant to do something, for there was valuable land lying waste, and if the owner wasn't going to make use of it, then he should sell it. Arnold Partridge even went as far as to make enquiries, and from information he gathered he found that our . . . Fen Tiger was a sort of rolling stone. He has been rolling ever since he left here when his father died. Andrew himself remembers the father. He says he was as mean as dirt and that the two were always at each other's throats. And I remember now that Andrew had the impression that our Mr Michael was going in for medicine.'

'That's not right. I asked him last night if he was a doctor and he said he wasn't. But all this doesn't prove that he isn't married.'

'I somehow think he isn't.'

'Don't be silly. Just thinking he's not married is nothing to go on, merely wishful thinking.'

'Is it? I remember the way he looked at me.'

'Oh, Jennifer!' Rosamund put her hand to her

head with an exaggerated gesture. 'Don't be so childish. Honestly, you would think you were ten years younger than me instead of two years older. You of all people should know by now that the more married they are the more they look like that. The wolf glare becomes intensified when they're married.' Rosamund suddenly threw her head back and let out a high laugh. 'We've already stamped him Fen Tiger, bull, and wolf, and you are going hunting. Oh, Jennifer, stop being funny.'

'I'm not being funny, I mean it. I'm going to pay him a visit today – quite casual like, as they say.'

'I think you're brazen. Anyway, what can he offer you that Andrew can't in the way of material things? Whatever he does with his land will be in the nature of farming, you would still be stuck on the fens.'

'Not with a man like that.' Jennifer turned and looked out of the kitchen window. 'That fellow wouldn't stay put; he'd want to travel, far, far, away. You know, Rosie, he seems like an answer to my prayer.'

'All I can say is that you're talking as if you had a touch of the sun. And—' Rosamund was turning away in disgust from Jennifer when she swung round to her again and, stretching out her arm, wagged her finger at her, saying, 'And don't forget that when you're making plans there are others who may be doing the same. What about our elegant Miss Janice Cooper? Their place is as near to him on the far side as we are. And she has one advantage over you. Besides being elegant, she knows how to farm. And then there's Doris . . .'

'Oh, shut up, Rosie. I wish I hadn't opened my mouth and just gone ahead and done what I want. At least, I thought you would see the funny side of it and not try to damp me down.'

'I'm not trying to dampen you down, I'm not, and you know that.' Rosamund's voice was now soft, even tender, and it sunk to a lower tone still as she ended, 'But all of a sudden I feel afraid somehow.'

'Afraid? What is there to be . . . ?' Jennifer stopped talking at this point, and, turning her head quickly, she listened. Then with an impatient movement she said, 'It's Father. Good Lord! Coming down at this time. Now for the remorse – I'm getting out.'

'No, no; please, Jennifer, stay. Don't make him feel any worse than he is. You needn't speak to him, but don't walk out on him.'

The next minute the door opened and Henry Morley entered.

He was a tall man and heavily built, with grey hair and a face that had at one time been handsome but which was now lined and sallow. One feature still remained to prove his past attraction: the eyes. They were a deep blue with a touch of humour in their depths. It was even evident at this moment, but of a slightly derisive quality.

He did not look at Jennifer, who was standing near the window again, but towards Rosamund, and he asked, pointedly, 'What happened? How did I come to be in your room?'

'Have a cup of tea first.'

'Is it as bad as that?'

Rosamund returned her father's glance and she watched him rubbing the side of his face slowly with one hand. 'You nearly set the house on fire.'

'I nearly set . . . What d'you mean?'

'You must have dropped off to sleep when you were smoking. Jennifer luckily smelt the smoke in time.'

'Oh Lor–r–d.' The last word was dragged out. 'But how did you get me into the other bed, I can't remember a thing.'

Rosamund turned towards the fire and pressed the kettle into the red embers as she said, 'We dragged you on to the landing, and as we couldn't get you round I went for Andrew.' She paused here, and just as her father was about to speak again she put in quickly, 'I ran into Mr Bradshaw when I was going through the woods. He came back with me.' Her voice was very low and her father's was even lower when he repeated, 'Mr Bradshaw? Who's Mr Bradshaw?'

'Thornby House . . . the owner . . . he's back.'

'And he came here and . . . and put me in your room?'

335

'Yes.' Rosamund was passing him now, the tea-pot in her hand, going towards the table, and she went on, 'You were suffering from the effects of the smoke and might have suffocated. That's why we had to get someone quick.'

'But you weren't suffering from the effects of the smoke, you were drunk.' Jennifer had swung round from the window and flung the bitter words at her father; and as they looked at each other she continued, 'We never guessed, not this time, but he had to tell us. He had to tell us you were in a drunken stupor.'

Rosamund wanted to turn on her sister and cry, 'Shut up!' but she knew it would be of no use. If Jennifer didn't have her say now she would later – that was Jennifer's way. Rosamund, her eyes laden with compassion, were fixed on the man standing to the side of her. She watched him close his eyes, then slowly droop his head and cover his face with one hand as he murmured, 'Oh no, no.'

'Oh yes, yes.'

At this Rosamund did go for her sister. 'That's enough. You've said it, and once will do.' She turned now and took her father's arm, and, pressing him into a seat, she said softly, 'Come on, come on. It's no use taking it like that – it's done.'

'I'll never be able to look the man in the face.'

'No, but you can look us in the face after sneaking off and getting that stuff from Pratt's.'

'Jennifer! Will you be quiet! If you don't I'll walk out and I'll stay out all day.'

This threat, simple as it sounded, had the desired effect on Jennifer, for after tightly clamping her mouth she flung round and went out of the kitchen.

Henry Morley was now sitting with his elbow on his knee supporting his head in his hand, and blindly he groped out and caught Rosamund's arm as he muttered, 'You know what I did?'

'Yes. Yes, I know. I would have found out sooner or later when the stuff didn't come, but I went through your pockets.'

'I'm a swine.'

'Yes, I know you are.' She was standing close to him now, and as she put out her hand to him he clutched at it and pressed it against his cheek.

'God! What would I do without you, Rosie? No recriminations, no nagging . . . It's been hell this last couple of weeks, Rosie. I planned it all, the day I took the letter to the post.'

'Yes, I guessed you did. Well, it's done; don't let's talk about it any more.' Her voice sounded matter-of-fact now. 'But I won't be able to send for the stuff until next week. We've got to eat and the money isn't due until the twelfth, you know that.'

'What can I cay?'

'Nothing; don't say any more.' She disengaged herself from his hand, and as she went to the table she said, 'As we cannot get on in the workshop until we get the stuff you'd better do a turn in the garden.'

'Yes, Rosie. Yes I'll do that.'

Rosamund closed her eyes for a moment. His patheticness, his utter humility, cut her to the heart. She sometimes wished he would bluster, fight, even damn her to hell's flames for her interference, but he never did. Also, apart from anything else, she hated these occasions when she had to play the part of the stern mother, for it made her feel old, old inside. There had been times when she had cried out against it, saying, 'It isn't fair, it isn't fair. Going on like this I'll be old before my time. Why can't Jennifer take the responsibility?' But that was before Clifford had started to come up the river every now and again in the boat. A look from Clifford told her that she was still young, merely twenty-two and . . . falling in love.

'What's he like, Rosie?'

'Who?'

'The fellow Bradshaw.'

'Oh . . . bumptious, the great I am, lord of all I survey. HE-MAN, and detestable. The lot, I should say.'

'He sounds pleasant.'

'I shouldn't worry about him. I don't suppose for a minute you'll meet him. When I said I would have called if I had known the house was occupied, he told me quite bluntly that he didn't want visitors.'

'He did?'

'Yes, he did.'

'Well, in that case he'll keep his distance.'

'Yes, I suppose so.'

It came to Rosamund as she said this that if Jennifer carried out her threat he might be persuaded to lessen the distance between the houses. Jennifer was beautiful, and her limp, which she used as a whipping block on herself, might have a claim on the man's pity; it had on Andrew's. But then Michael Bradshaw was no Andrew. He was as different from Andrew as a tiger from a deer. There she was again thinking of him, likening him to a fen tiger.

When she had first heard the term 'fen tiger', she had really believed it was some form of animal until Andrew explained it was the name given to a type of fen man, now almost extinct, but not quite, for here and there a descendant of the type of man who had lived deep in the trackless, treacherous fenland, and who fought against the land being drained with cunning, craftiness, and even murder, were still to be found. They were independent, often surly, and could at times call up the fierceness of their forebears, those raw, dark vicious men who fought the Dutch workmen of Cornelius Vermuyden who had come to reclaim the land from the water-logged wastes. The fenlands had at one time been so wild that the inhabitants had only made their appearances in the towns on festive occasions, perhaps merely once a year, when trouble nearly always ensued. Even in this day there were isolated incidents that made people say, 'Oh, a fen tiger at it.' And when this was said a picture was conjured up of a rough, crude individual with barely a skin covering the elemental urges that had at one time been allowed full sway. For many long years the people of the fens had been looked upon by the townsfolk as uncivilised – and not without reason, it must be admitted.

But all this talk of fen tigers had only succeeded in enhancing the charm of the flatland for Rosamund. That was until last night. But now she thought that if Michael Bradshaw was an example of a fen tiger there couldn't be a wide enough distance between the houses to suit her.

Yet her fragile, delicate-looking sister was set on hunting the tiger . . .

3

It was half-past two when Jennifer, dressed in a cream linen dress that caught up the silvery gold of her hair where it hung from below the large brown straw hat, stepped into the ferry and pulled herself across the river. Rosamund, from the bank, watched her drying her hands carefully on an old towel she had taken with her, then hang it on the post of the landing. She watched her incline her head in a deep exaggeratedly gracious bow before taking the path through the fields that would, in about twenty minutes' time, bring her to Thornby House. When she disappeared from view around the fringe of the wood Rosamund turned slowly and walked across the bank and up the garden, mounted the steps and went into the house.

It was cool inside the house, dark, shining and cool. The curtains were drawn in the living-room. Rosamund always saw to it that the strong glare of the sun did not harm the patina of the furniture. She loved and cared for the furniture as if it was her own, and there was always with her a little dread of the day when she would, perhaps, have to leave these beautiful pieces.

The Georgian desk with its gilt tooled moroccan top. Nearly all the furniture in this room was of the Georgian period. The bow-front chest, the chiffonier with raised back. Only the two splat-backed armchairs were Chippendale. She used to wonder why her aunt had brought these lovely pieces to this out-of-the-way place, until her father enlightened her. Anna Monkton apparently had been an auctioneer's daughter before she married Edward Monkton, and now, having almost unlimited cash at her disposal, she indulged in what was almost a mania with her, buying antique furniture and old china. Her father had added, and somewhat bitterly, that the pieces that filled this house were likely throw-outs compared to those she would have in her own home.

Rosamund could not see any of the pieces as throw-outs, and she guessed that neither did Anna Monkton. The mill had been intended as a week-end cottage, and she felt that her aunt had seen herself entertaining here in quiet and elegant style.

She now went to the desk standing to the side of the window, and, taking from one of its drawers an old notebook, she sat down and began to flick its pages. She had first started to scribble at the age of ten. When she was deeply troubled, or ecstatically happy, she experienced a driving desire to capture an impression of the emotion, and the only way to do this was to translate it into words. Her efforts at first were crude, and even now, twelve years later, she still looked upon them as frittling. She read the last piece she had written.

River reed-pipe,
Soft lined for water notes,
Play the murmur of ripplets lapping the stalk
Sent from the moorhen, as she floats,
And the night-moth, as he alights to walk.
River reed, play your music to the wind's
  time,
And bend and sway in the dance,
Nodding your head to the moon
And stilling all river things in trance.

She had been lying on the bank in the shadow of the reeds above the Goose Pond when she had written that. The moon had turned the pond into a magic world. Beyond the pond the sedge looked like a forest of trees, and the patches of meadowsweet like spilt milk. Purple feathery fronds of tall grass patted her cheek, and she had felt happy. Clifford had been earlier in the day, and she had walked with him to the end of Heron Cut, where the boat was moored, and seen him sail away down the Brandon Creek.

The poem had seemed good in the eerie magic of the fen night, but not now – it needed altering, polishing. She suddenly closed the book with a small sharp thud and pushed it back into the drawer. She felt unsettled, nervous, as if something was going to happen. She wished Jennifer was back, she wished she had never gone; she was crazy. She stood in the hall and looked out through the open front door towards the river. Its appearance had changed completely in the last few minutes. The sun had disappeared and the sky was grey. The whole of the flatland before her was covered with a dull blue haze out of which the wood reared up black and stiff. It looked like a storm. Oh, she wished Jennifer was back. Still, she would be there by now and the storm would likely give her the opportunity she was seeking: further acquaintance with the fen tiger. It was odd, but she was thinking of the man under that name now.

She stood, uncertain what to do. She turned her gaze towards a narrow passage leading off to the right of the stairs. At the far end a door led into the room which they used as a work-room. Her father was in there now, trying to make atonement by doing new designs, work which he had promised 'to get down to' as soon as possible. This meant, of course, when she had the money to send for the materials.

She looked out through the doorway again and asked herself what she would do. There were so many things she could do. There were the bedrooms, hers and Jennifer's – she had seen to her father's this morning. She could finish the curtains she had started last week. She could make some

jam – she had picked enough currants yesterday –
or do a bit of baking. It was rather hot for baking.
She shook her head, but nevertheless went into the
kitchen and commenced this last chore.

Her father liked blackcurrant tart; Jennifer liked
sultana scones. She would make them both.

The rain started as she began to gather the cooking materials together. It came in large slow drops
at first, then turned quickly into an obliterating
sheet. A flash of lightning lit up the kitchen and
a few seconds later Henry Morley opened the
kitchen door.

'You all right?'

'Yes. Yes, of course. It's not forgetting to come
down, is it?'

'Where's . . . where's Jennifer?'

'She . . . she went over to Andrew's'

'Oh, she'll be all right then. Nice smell.' He
smiled, and she returned his smile.

'Blackcurrant tart. As soon as it's done I'll bring
you a slice.'

'Good. Good.' He nodded his head like a boy
filled with anticipation of a beano, and when the
door had closed on him Rosamund stood for a
moment, her body quite still as she looked down
at the table, and the pity and love in her cried,
Poor soul, poor soul. He was, she knew, craving
for a drink, yet, aiming to please her, he pretended
he was dying for a piece of blackcurrant tart. If
it had been in her nature to feel resentment

on account of last night's business, his contrition would have melted it away.

It was as she was taking the tart out of the oven that she heard the scurrying in the hall, and as she opened the kitchen door she was nearly knocked backwards by Jennifer's entry.

'Good gracious! You're drenched! Why . . .'

'Help me off with these things – I'm shivering.'

Rosamund saw that Jennifer actually was shivering but as much with fury as with cold. 'Wait, I'll get your dressing-gown.' She dashed out of the kitchen and was back within a minute or so, and as she helped to pull the soaked petticoat over Jennifer's head she didn't say, 'What happened?' but 'Why didn't you take shelter?'

'Where?' Jennifer turned her head and fixed her with angry eyes.

'Didn't you see him?'

'Yes, I saw him . . . Oh yes, I saw him.'

Again Rosamund refrained from putting a question, but said, 'I'll get you a hot drink. Sit down.'

It wasn't until Jennifer had finished her second cup of tea that she began to talk, and then only in short explosive bursts. 'Of all the bumptious, self-satisfied, uncouth individuals. Who does he think he is, anyway? The Lord Almighty? . . . Back on the fens five minutes and acting as if he owned them . . . As if he had drained them.'

This unconscious touch of humour spurting from her sister's fury caused Rosamund to bite on her lip to prevent her from laughing outright. She asked quietly, 'What did he do?'

'Nothing.' Jennifer cast her eyes up to Rosamund, and repeated, 'Nothing, just that . . . nothing.'

'Nothing? Then what are you on about?'

Jennifer drew in a gulp of air, then let it out on a deep sigh, and this seemed to relax her somewhat, for her tone changed. Leaning back and looking up at Rosamund, she said, 'When I tell you you'll see nothing in it, it won't sound the same. You had to be there and see his face and . . . and his attitude.'

'What kind of an attitude? What d'you mean?' Even as Rosamund asked the question she knew quite well what kind of attitude Mr Michael Bradshaw had taken.

'Well. . .' Jennifer threw out her two hands palm upwards as she said. 'When I got to the house there wasn't a soul to be seen. I went along the side past the big drawing-room window – you know – I didn't intend to look, but when I realised there were no curtains up and that the room was empty, I did look, not only through the window but round about. The whole place looked as deserted as it always has done. I may as well admit that before I knocked at the door I had cold feet, I nearly turned and bolted, but when I heard someone inside I pulled the bell before thinking any further. The sound of it alone nearly scared me out of my

wits – you've never heard anything like it, Rosie.'
She shook her head, before going on, 'Then the
door opened and there he was. He was in shirt-
sleeves and was wearing breeches and wellington
boots. They were thick with mud and him inside
the house. Honestly, I didn't know what to say.
I felt a bit of a fool and I stammered something
about coming to thank him for his kindness last
night . . . Kindness, huh! He kept staring at
me, staring and staring and not saying a word.
Then just as he was going to speak something
distracted his attention. It must have been a dog
or something because he almost closed the door,
but he kept saying, 'Go to Maggie. Go to Maggie.
Go on now, go to Maggie.' Then the dog started to
whine, not a doggy whine at all, as if it were in pain
or something. It was really weird. And then he was
bellowing at the top of his voice, 'Maggie! Maggie!'
I heard someone scurrying across the hall and
caught a fleeting glimpse of a fat old woman and a
few seconds later he pulled the door open again.'

'Did he apologise or explain or anything?'

'Apologise or explain! No, not him. He came
outside and closed the door behind him and pro-
ceeded purposely to make me feel like a worm.'
She imitated his voice '"There's no need for
thanks, Miss Morley. Apart from lifting your father
on to a bed I did nothing, except distress you and
your sister."'

'Well, he was quite right, you know.'

'Yes, he might have been, but it was the way he said it, Rosie. He stood looking at me as if he knew everything I had been thinking since I met him last night. I . . . I felt as if I was practically naked. You've got no idea the effect he had on me.'

'Well, it's your own fault, you can't say it isn't. It was you who decided to go hunting.'

'Yes, I know, but don't rub it in . . . Really, I must have been barmy to think I could fall for anyone like that. Give me Andrew any day in the week, at least he's human.'

'Cheers. It's done some good, anyway.'

'Oh, be quiet, Rosie, and stop laughing. You wouldn't have laughed if you had been there, I can tell you that. He hadn't been outside the door a couple of minutes before it started to rain, great drops, and naturally I thought he would ask me in. But oh no! He walked away from me along the drive and I could do nothing but follow him, and when we came to the gate that's half hanging off – you know the one – he lifted it aside and said, "I'm afraid you're going to get wet if you don't hurry . . ."'

'And then?'

'That's all – there was no "and then" about it. I walked away like a little spanked child. I was furious and my leg stiffened and I knew that my limp was getting more pronounced with every step, and before I had gone many yards it began to pour, and the infuriating thing was I knew he was still standing watching me. I tell you, Rosie, he's an absolute beast. Fen tiger's right – he's uncivilised.'

'He evidently doesn't want visitors. He told me straight out last night.'

'But why? Anyway, when it was pouring like that he could have let me take shelter until it was over.'

'Yes, he could have done that.'

'Well, anyway, I hope he rots in his mansion. And he certainly will, for I can't see any of the men around here putting up with that attitude.' She twisted round in her seat now and demanded once again of Rosamund, '*Who* does he think he is, anyway?'

'The master of Thornby House evidently . . . feudal lord. Come on, drink your tea up and forget about it, and if it fairs up this evening we'll saunter across to Andrew's.'

Rosamund sighed again, and then she said, 'It's funny he hasn't been over; he would be back early last evening.'

'He runs a farm, don't forget.'

'Yes, I know, but . . .'

'Here, butter that scone while it's hot.' Rosamund handed her a plate, and Jennifer, getting to her feet and going to a cupboard near the window, took out the butter.

She was splitting the scone on the table before the window when her head came up with a quick jerk, and she put her face closer to the pane and peered through the rain. She had thought for a moment that she was seeing a little figure standing on the far bank of the river. She blinked her eyes, rubbed at the steam on the window and peered still more. Then excitedly she said, 'Rosie! Rosie! Here a minute. Am I seeing things? Look over there on the far bank.'

'What is it?' Rosamund pressed her nose to the pane, screwed up her eyes, and after a short silence she exclaimed, 'It's a child.'

'A child? There are no children about here, not that size. The Browns are all over fourteen.'

'It's a child, anyway.' Rosamund was speaking as she turned hastily from the window.

When she opened the front door and stood on the top step she could see more clearly. It was a child . . . yet. She did not continue with her thinking but spoke over her shoulder to Jennifer. 'Look! Hand me my coat.' She kept her eyes on the child who was now pulling on the ferry chain.

'What are you going to do? Bring her across? There may be someone with her – perhaps some fisherman has come up this way.'

'It doesn't look as if there's anyone with her, and there's no fishing up this cut, as you know.'

As Jennifer helped Rosamund into her coat she asked, 'Well, what are you going to do with her?'

'See where she's from first, or where she's going. She looks lost. And there's something . . .'

Again Rosamund checked her thinking. Instead

she darted down the steps and across the garden, and slithered over the wet bank to the landing.

The boat had more than a few inches of water in the bottom, but she did not stop to bale out, and as she pulled on the chain and the craft came nearer to the far bank she cried to herself, Dear, dear God, poor little soul! And when she stepped up on to the landing and looked down on the pulpy, almost formless, rain-drenched Mongol child, her heart was filled with compassion. The tightly drawn lids from which peered the little eyes were blinking rapidly. The mouth hung open and formed a misshapen 'o'. The thick stubby tongue was lying on the bottom teeth; the fair, sparse hair, plastered to the skull, gave the head almost a bald appearance. The shoulders were humped, and the legs sticking out from beneath the short dress were like two pudding stumps. The child looked about nine, but it was difficult to tell its correct age.

Bending slightly forward, Rosamund said softly, 'Are you lost?'

There was no answer, but the child continued to peer up through the narrow slits of her lids.

'Where is your mammy . . . or your daddy? Are they fishing?'

Still there was no answer, but the child, turning from Rosamund now, moved towards the boat and attempted to put her foot into it.

'Wait. Wait a minute.' Rosamund peered about

her through the rain, but there was no-one to be seen. Well, she couldn't leave the child out in this, she'd better take her indoors. She lowered herself into the boat and, putting her hand out to the child, said, 'Come on, careful now.'

Cautiously the child stepped into the boat, and as she sat down on the wet seat she lifted her streaming face up to Rosamund and smiled. The effort succeeded in contorting the face still further and made Rosamund cry out desperately inside, the question that thousands of parents had asked before her: Why did God allow one of his creatures to be born like this?

When they reached the other side she lifted the child out of the boat, and, taking her by the hand, ran her gently towards the house. She came without protest as far as the top of the steps, but there she stopped. Tugging now at Rosamund, she released her hand and stood leaning half in and half out of the doorway, staring at Jennifer where she stood just inside the hall, her face expressing her feelings.

'Oh! Oh, Rosie, whose is she? Did you have to bring her in? What about her people?'

'You know as much as I do, and don't use that tone.' Rosamund was muttering under her breath. Now she addressed herself to the child again, her voice calm and soft, saying, 'Come in, dear, out of the rain. You can wait in here for Mammy.'

She put out her hand towards the child, but it shrank away now without looking at her, for its eyes were still fixed on Jennifer.

'Can't she talk?'

'I don't know.' Rosamund straightened up, and, walking with a casual movement past Jennifer further into the hall, she murmured, 'Take no notice, she'll come in on her own. You can bring me a piece of cake and some tea and perhaps I'll get her to . . .'

Rosamund's voice was cut off by a high weird scream and she turned in time to see the child flinging herself on Jennifer, hands clawing at her dressing-gown and her feet kicking at her legs. Jennifer, taken by surprise, had staggered back in fright, and now as Rosamund gripped the child around the body in an endeavour to pull her away, Jennifer too screamed. 'Get her off me! Take her away! She's horrible! Dreadful! Look! Look at my hand – look what she's done.'

At this moment the door from the studio opened and Henry Morley came hurrying in. 'What is it? What's the matter?' He stopped dead at the sight of Rosamund kneeling on the floor holding a struggling misshapen child in her arms. 'What on earth . . . who is she?'

'Look, look what she's done.' Jennifer, now nearing hysteria, held out her bleeding hand,

'She did that?' Henry looked at Rosamund, and for a reply she said, 'Take Jennifer into the sitting-room, Father. Anywhere. Leave me alone for a while, please.'

'She'll do the same to you. You should never have brought her in . . . the frightful creature . . .'

'That frightful creature happens to be my daughter.'

As if they had all been jerked by an electric shock they swung round to the doorway where stood Michael Bradshaw. At the sight of him the child gave a cry that was half grunt, half gurgle, and with a shambling gait ran to him. In one movement he had picked her up, and the child, with her arms tightly round his neck, straddling his hip in a way that spoke of long practice. Neither Henry Morley, Jennifer nor Rosamund spoke. There was nothing that any of them could find to say. To Rosamund it was as if he had dropped out of the sky like an avenging angel. Why hadn't they heard him pulling the ferry over? Likely because of their concentration on the child. This then was Jennifer's dog, this poor, poor child. She could still think of her as a poor, poor child although she had viciously attacked Jennifer, and at this moment her pity was not only for the child but for the father, this arrogant bombastic individual. No wonder he didn't want visitors, and no wonder, too, that he carried his pride high and used it as a shield.

Oddly enough it was Jennifer who was the first to recover, and in a shaking voice she protested as she held out her bleeding hand. 'Well, look what she's done.'

'That is entirely your own fault. My daughter happened to see you when you decided to visit us a short while ago, and apparently she didn't like what she saw and she must have come to tell you so.'

'Now, now, look here, sir.' As Henry Morley moved angrily forward Rosamund thrust out her hand and gripped his arm. After one long look at the older man Michael Bradshaw turned about and walked steadily down the steps to the river, the child bouncing on his hip as he went.

'But that's no way to go on. What's the matter with the man, anyway?'

Rosamund, pulling at her father's arm, said softly, 'Look.' She pointed to where Jennifer was going into the kitchen crying bitterly now. 'Go and see to her, I'll be there in a minute. Go on, see to her.'

As her father reluctantly turned away to do her bidding Rosamund made swiftly for the front door, and, hesitating for only a second, she ran down the steps towards the boat.

Michael Bradshaw had placed the child on the seat and had the chain in his hand ready to push off when she reached the landing. Without any preamble she knelt down on the soaked wood so that her face was almost level with his own and began rapidly: 'I'm sorry; oh I am, I am. And please don't think it was meant. Jennifer . . . my sister . . . she was frightened for a moment. She . . . she hasn't been well lately. But we understand, we do, and we meant no . . .'

'Save your breath, I know what you meant. Just let me repeat what I said last night: I want no visitors. And pass that on to your sister, will you?'

It was hard to believe that under this still steely countenance the man was feeling anything but bitterness and hurt pride. Yet she reasoned that were there nothing in him but pride the child would not have run to him so eagerly, nor been enveloped in his arms so tenderly. She hadn't liked this man last night, she didn't like him much more now, and yet, of a sudden, she was deeply sorry for him.

She stood up and turned away and walked stiffly through the rain. When she reached the hall door again she heard the rattle of the chain that told her they had reached the other bank, but she did not look round.

As she went into the kitchen Jennifer greeted her wildly with, 'That's what it was. I thought it was a dog, or an animal, but it was her; it was . . . that!'

'Jennifer!' Rosamund's voice was like a sharp rap. 'Don't call it "that". It's a child, a little girl. She can't help being as she is. And if you had a child like her, and you never know . . . no, you never know . . . how would you like someone to call it "that dreadful creature"?'

Both her father and Jennifer were staring fixedly at her, and to her own dismay Rosamund knew that she was going to cry. She turned swiftly about and left the kitchen. Running up the stairs, she went into her own room and sat by her window, biting hard on her lip to prevent the tears coming.

The rain was easing off now and the sun was breaking through. Soon the whole of the fenlands would be a moving picture of sunlight, vapour steam, and glowing colour. This was the time she liked, sunlight after rain, the time that would bring a sense of peace weaving through her; but as she looked out over the fens now, she had the feeling that peace had been swept from her, that since last night and the coming of the owner of Thornby House on to her horizon peace had fled.

4

The following day was one of unrest for both Rosamund and Jennifer, partly because there was a sense of estrangement between them. Over the years they had had their tiffs, yet after sleeping on them they generally started the day clean, so to speak, but not after yesterday's scene. Rosamund knew that Jennifer had the idea that she should be whole-heartedly on her side, and she couldn't. If the man only had been in question, perhaps she might, but she could not condone her sister's attitude concerning the child.

And they had not, after all, last night strolled across to Andrew's. What had prevented them was not the tiff but the fact that the distance would be three times as long now that they couldn't take the short cut through the Thornby land. The road to Andrew's lay along the bank of the winding river, over the bridge near the Goose Pond, then through the cart tracks cutting the fields.

Usually it was Andrew who brought in the late mail, for he came by jeep to the bridge and walked along the riverbank; rarely if ever had he taken the cut across the Thornby land.

But Andrew hadn't come last night, and it was well past his time for calling now. He usually came about six, and more often than not left early to do his last round. Rosamund knew that it was Andrew's absence that was puzzling Jennifer. Perhaps puzzling wasn't the right word, she could nearly say worrying her. This was the fifth day that Andrew hadn't put in an appearance. True he had been to the show, but he would have been back the night before last, and he rarely let two days pass without visiting them. At least that had been the pattern for the last two years. Before that it had been occasional calls, shyly dropping in.

And so, Rosamund said to Jennifer, in a rather terse voice, 'I'm going to the bridge to see if there's any mail. Are you coming?'

Jennifer seemed to hesitate for a moment before replying, 'No, it's too hot – my hip's been aching all day.'

This statement usually elicited sympathy from Rosamund but not on this occasion. She merely said, 'Very well,' and went out.

As she walked along the bank of the cut she did not tonight take the usual pleasure in the activities of the river. The moorhens were darting back and forwards across the water leaving arrows of pale light in their wake, while their babies cluck-cluck-clucked in startled fright at her approach. A pair of grey, spectral-looking herons rose at intervals from the bank keeping their distance from her.

One after the other they lifted themselves into the air with surprising grace for such large ungainly looking creatures. Rosamund was never surprised at the swans' graceful flight, but the herons didn't seem made for grace. As she watched them they brought her mind from its brooding for a moment and a familiar thought was resurrected once again, and she smiled as she said to herself, I couldn't live anywhere else, nowhere else in the world. The thought took her mind in a leap to Clifford and the coming week. It was the end of June and the vac. about to begin. It was his last year at the university, but he wouldn't know the results of his finals for a week or so. Yet by the sound of things he should get a first. This being so, it would mean a year, perhaps two, in America for further studies in Physics. Not for him a travelling scholarship, he would go to a university out there and stay for as long as was necessary, and then back to Cambridge with the position of lecturer to look forward to. She gave a little shiver, of delight or apprehension she didn't question, but she did question her place in this plan. Somewhere between the results of his finals and the end of the vac., when he would leave for America, she should know, for he was going to spend most of his vacation here on the river. He had already booked a small motor cruiser from Banhams in Cambridge. He would berth it where he always did, in the Brandon at the bottom of the Cut. Would it be early in the holidays or towards the end when he asked her? Well, that would all depend on . . . well, on opportunity, and . . . and other things. But ask her he would, for the only thing, she felt, that had prevented him so far from putting the question had been the intensity of the third-year work.

An arrow of wild ducks flying low brought her head up. Their wings flapping in their agitated fashion only emphasised their sure and purposeful flight. They were making, she knew, for the piece of marshland up the Brandon Creek where the water lay beyond the wash bank in shallow lakes, and the approach, except in the spring, was impossible, being too boggy for feet and not deep enough to take the more shallow-drafted boats. It was on that marshland, and from the top of the flood bank that she had first seen the two Canada geese. It was during her first spring on the fens, and the joy had stayed with her for days.

When she came to the Goose Pond two recently paired swans were training their young, cleaning their feathers diligently as an example to their eight cygnets, who waddled among the down discarded during their parents' toilet. The mother hissed at Rosamund as she passed and she spoke to it laughingly saying, 'All right, all right, don't get flustered; surely you know me by now.' There were a family of geese on the far side of the pond and they craned their necks and raised their voices in a protesting chorus at the sight of her.

She crossed the bridge, being careful of the rotting plank in its middle, and stopped at the post to which was nailed the letterbox . . . There was no letter in the box from Clifford or anyone else. Her disappointment was keen, but she told herself it was all part and parcel of this particular kind of day . . . of the last two days.

As she turned to make her way back over the bridge she glanced up the first of the long straight tracks that led to Andrew's place, and in the distance she made out a small shape almost obliterated by a cloud of dust. That was Andrew's jeep. She smiled to herself; it would be nice seeing Andrew, he was so sane, so easy to get on with. At one time she had wished that Andrew had taken a fancy to her instead of Jennifer, but it had only been a weak kind of wish.

As the jeep came nearer she thought with an inward chuckle, I'd like to bet Jennifer isn't so cool tonight. If yesterday's business did nothing else perhaps it's made her more appreciative of what she's been turning up her nose at.

The jeep was still quite a way off when Rosamund realised that Andrew wasn't alone, and when it pulled up opposite the bridge she only half answered his 'Hello there, Rosie,' for her whole attention was riveted on his companion. Why did the sight of Janice Hooper disturb her so much that she was almost unable to return his greeting? She looked at Andrew now. His colour was higher than usual and his voice sounded different, not Andrew's voice, as he said, 'We're just off to Ely. Everything all right at the mill?'

'Yes . . . yes, Andrew.'

'That's good.'

'We . . . we thought you might be over last night.'

'Well . . . yes, er . . . but I had one or two things to see to.' He laughed. 'You know what it's like after being away for a day or so.'

'You should come to the shows, they are very interesting.' Janice was leaning forward past Andrew to look at her. And Rosamund, returning the self-assured look, answered coolly, 'We are not farmers. There could be little interest at the show for us.' It was the wrong thing to say in front of Andrew, and she could have bitten her tongue out.

Andrew straightened up and put his foot on the accelerator. The engine hummed and he turned his head once again towards Rosamund, saying quietly, 'Well, I'll be seeing you. 'Bye, Rosie.'

'Goodbye.'

She watched the car bounce away. He hadn't mentioned Jennifer . . . Janice Hooper had been to the show with him. She looked absolutely self-assured and possessive – yes, possessive, like a cat that had stolen the cream. Oh no, he couldn't be falling for her. Oh, Jennifer, poor Jennifer! She was still staring at the back of the retreating jeep when she saw it stop. She watched

Andrew climbing down and come running back up the track towards her. He did not speak until he was quite close, and then his words were preceded by a gesture that showed his embarrassment. He rubbed his hand vigorously across his mouth, then took it up over his face and the top of his head before saying on a sheepish laugh, 'Do something for me, will you, Rosie?'

'Yes. Yes, Andrew. What is it?'

'Well. . .' He looked at her under lowered brows. 'Well, will you . . . will you tell Jennifer that you saw me with Janice?' He made a slight indication with his head towards the car.

'O . . . oh, Andrew!' The long-drawn-out 'Oh' expressed only too clearly Rosamund's relief. She laughed now as she said again, 'Oh, Andrew! You had me worried for a moment. But . . . but what about Janice? She likes you Andrew.' Rosamund nodded her head with superior wisdom, 'I can tell.'

'She likes lots of others.' Andrew laughed self-consciously. 'Janice can take care of herself, I'm not worried about her.'

'Anyway, I'd be careful. But I'll tell Jennifer. Oh yes, I'll tell Jennifer.' She laughed again.

'I must be off now.' He paused for a moment before turning and said rapidly and stiffly, 'Jennifer's got to make up her mind one way or the other. I can't go on like this, Rosie. For two years now I've been asking her; four years I've been after her all together. I'll ask her once more and that'll be the last. But I want the answer to be yes, so I thought I'd give her . . . well, a bit of breathing space, so to speak. I've been too attentive; it's a mistake, Rosie.'

'I'm sorry, Andrew, if she's hurt you.'

'I must go, else Janice will take off in the jeep on her own – she's quite capable of doing it.' He laughed now, and then became serious again. Looking down into Rosamund's upturned face, he said, 'You're nice, Rosie. A fellow would know where he was with you.'

'Oh, Andrew, that's no compliment.' She screwed up her nose at him and shook her head. 'It only means I'm dull.'

'It doesn't, by gum! Many a time I've wished it had been you. But there it is. We're all a lot of fools, aren't we?'

'Oh, Andrew, go on, don't be silly.' As she pushed him there came three loud blasts from the horn of the jeep and she laughed out loud as he pulled a comically frightened face before sprinting away down the road.

'Oh, Andrew!' Again she repeated the words. He was nice, was Andrew. Yes, perhaps she might have taken him if it had been herself he had first set his cap at. She didn't love Andrew, but that wasn't saying that she couldn't have grown to love him. Kindness and consideration went a long way with her, that's why she liked . . . she loved . . . Clifford. Clifford was kind and considerate.

But Jennifer must stop playing about, Andrew was no fool. As he said, he would ask her once more and that would be the last. Perhaps he was already thinking that Janice Hooper would make a better farmer's wife than Jennifer, and undoubtedly he would be right.

She did not saunter as she returned home but walked briskly. But she stopped when she saw one lone magpie flying across the river. Closing her eyes quickly, she said, 'Let there be two', and when she opened them she saw the partner. Good. She smiled to herself. One for bad luck, two for good. Things would work out all right for Jennifer. She was still laughing at her childish superstition when she reached the mill . . .

'Janice Hooper? Andrew with Janice Hooper? Where were they going?'

'Ely, he said.' Rosie's tone could not have been more casual.

'But where? The pictures?'

'Oh, I don't know; they were a bit late for the pictures – I just don't know.'

'Stop being so damn smug. You know more than you're telling.'

'How should I? I saw them in the jeep. He stopped and said "Hello". Janice Hooper said, "Hello". He asked how everybody was at the mill and that was that.'

'Didn't he say when he was coming?' Jennifer's voice was quiet now.

'No. No, he didn't.' At least this was the truth, anyway. 'But I'll tell you one thing. I judged from what Janice Hooper said to me that she had been to the show with him.'

'At the show?'

'Yes.'

'Well, I suppose she always goes to cattle shows; she's a farmer's daughter, isn't she?'

'Yes, but I've never heard Andrew say he had been with her. Yet she made a point of putting it over. I thought it was rather odd.'

When she saw the consternation on Jennifer's face she had to stop herself from going to her and putting her arms about her and blurting out Andrew's strategy. As Jennifer passed her, her limp definitely pronounced now, on her way out of the room, she could not resist putting out her hand and touching her. 'It'll be all right,' she said.

'Why should it? You always told me this would happen. You should feel very proud of your prophetic powers.'

'Oh, Jennifer! Don't take it like that!'

'I'm not taking it like that. He's quite at liberty to go out with whom he likes. He's not tied to me, is he? I've refused him and that's that.'

Jennifer seemed to gather pride from the fact that she had refused Andrew, and, withdrawing her arm from Rosamund's clasp, she went out of the room, but with her head at too high an angle.

Oh dear, oh dear, what next? Heavily Rosamund went through the hall and took up her favourite position on the top step outside the front door. What a day! What a twenty-four hours! Everybody was being as awkward as they could be. Her father to begin with, that man over there – she looked across the river – Jennifer, and now Andrew.

The twilight was merging the colours of the fens into a soft grey sameness. On the far bank, flitting from one solitary willow stalk to another, a kingfisher was aiming to pierce the opaqueness of the coming night with its brilliant flashes of blue, but on this occasion she had hardly noticed him, for her thinking was turned inwards. Then, as if some impish genie said, 'There's still a little daylight left yet, let's give you one more thing to disturb you,' she saw the child again.

She must have watched the bobbing head above the grass for some time before she realised it was attached to anything. Swifts and swallows flitted over the reeds in such profusion that the eye became used to the changing pattern, but when the head moved into the open ground on the bank above the ferry landing she was brought to her feet with a start and an exclamation of 'No! Not again!'

She turned quickly and glanced into the hall before running down the steps. Jennifer was upstairs, thank goodness for that. She mustn't see this child again tonight; children like this needed getting used to. She could understand, in a way, her sister being repulsed. The reason she herself had not been repulsed was because, as she had told herself earlier, she had not Jennifer's artistic temperament.

She stood now on the boat landing and watched the child slithering down among the reeds at the water's edge. What was she to do? If she went across the river he might appear at any minute and then more fireworks. No, she would stay where she was. And she remained firm on this decision until she saw what the child intended to do. She was walking into the water in an attempt to cross the river, and she was dressed in what looked like her nightdress and slippers.

'Wait! Wait!' Rosamund scrambled into the boat and hauled frantically on the chain. It wasn't likely that the child could swim, and if she came a yard or so farther on she would be in a bed of silt in which she would sink in a matter of seconds.

She caught her just in time, and, leaning over the gunwale of the boat, she propelled her gently back, with her hand under her arm. When she had moored the ferry she lifted the sodden child on to the landing and was rewarded with a smile that stretched the features into still wilder disorder. Then from the slack mouth there came a sound like a word.

'Wiv.'

'Wiv?' Rosamund repeated the word softly.

The child, still smiling, pointed a thick finger towards the water and repeated, 'Wiv.'

'Wiv?' said Rosamund again. 'Wiv . . . water . . . wiv . . . river.'

The child made a laughing sound now. It was guttural and thick, but nevertheless it was a laughing sound. Again she said 'Wiv' and pointed excitedly at the water. Her mouth was wide open, her tongue hung out over her teeth, and, to add to the distressing sight, her nose was running.

A thick rhythmic swishing sound brought the child's head flopping back on her shoulders now, and as she looked up to where two swans, coming from the direction of the Goose Pond, were flying to some point up the Cut away above the mill, she said, 'Ca . . . Ca.'

'Yes, Ca . . . swans.' Rosamund said the word slowly, and as she repeated it she got to her feet. The swans were making for home, it was getting dark. What on earth was she going to do with this child? Should she take her across to the mill, then go and tell him? No, that would be silly, upsetting Jennifer again, and having him come barging over like a bull. And yet if she took her up to the house, what then? He would likely say that the child could have found her own way back. Gently now she drew her up the bank, and, bending down and pointing to the path between the high grass, she said slowly, 'Go . . . go . . .

to . . . Daddy.' The child blinked at her, then calmly took her hand and moved forward.

Reluctantly Rosamund walked along the path. There was one thing at least evident: the child could understand, up to a point, what was said to it. With this in mind she drew her to a stop, and, pointing once more in the direction of the house that couldn't be seen from this distance because of the trees, she again spaced her words, 'Go . . . home . . . Go . . . to . . . Daddy . . . Dark . . . getting dark.' The pattern was repeated. The child looked up at her and, still keeping hold of her hand, moved forward.

Oh dear! Oh dear! She would have to go on and put up with the reception she might get at the other end. There was one blessing: the night was warm and the child was not likely to catch her death of cold. Still, the quicker she had this wet nightdress off her, the better. She looked down at her now and said quietly, 'Run?'

When she broke into a gentle trot the child began to gallop excitedly and would have fallen again and again, owing to the long nightdress, had not Rosamund steadied her, and at times pulled her upright. This latter action elicited the guttural laughter; evidently the child was enjoying it as she would a game.

When at last they came in sight of the house, Rosamund, drawing the child to her and pointing to the great grey building, said yet once again, 'Go to Daddy.' The child's reaction to this was as before. She moved forward, but still retained a grip on Rosamund's hand.

They walked round the broken gate and up the drive to the front door. When they reached it the child stood with her, waiting, as if she too were a stranger, a nervous stranger; and as she stood, uncertain what to do for the moment, the child, making a sudden strange noise in her throat, drew her attention to the far end of the house. There, standing as if transfixed, was Michael Bradshaw. He had a mattock in his hand and had evidently been rooting the ground. The child did not run to him but continued to make the noise as she held on to Rosamund's hand.

His approach was slow, and Rosamund could see that he was baffled, even taken completely off his guard for the moment. She said quietly, 'I felt I had to bring her; she was down by the river again. She tried to cross.' She watched him look down at the child. Then, stepping past her, he pushed open the front door and called, not loudly, but in a voice that showed his anger more than bellowing would have done, 'Maggie! . . . Maggie!'

It was some seconds before there came the sound of a door opening, and then there shambled into view the fat old woman that Jennifer had described. She looked first at her master, and then at the child, and lastly at Rosamund, and she said, 'Mother of God!'

'Mother of God, indeed. And she could at this minute be with the Mother of God for all you care, Maggie. I asked you, didn't I, to sit by her.'

'I did, I did, Master Michael; honest to God, I did. She was in a sleep as deep as death itself when I left her. Don't you go for me like that, Master Michael; it's the truth, I'm tellin' you.'

Rosamund watched the man making a great effort to control his temper, and now his voice was almost ordinary as he said, 'Take her upstairs.'

'Come away; come away, child.' The old woman held out her hand, but the child would have none of it. Instead, she looked up at Rosamund, then, stepping over the threshold, attempted to pull her forward.

'No, not now.' Her father was leaning down to her. 'Tomorrow . . . tomorrow. Bed now . . . Susie, go to bed now . . . chocolate . . . Come.'

The child would not be influenced by this inducement either, and Rosamund, feeling very uncomfortable, bent down and disengaged her hand. The result of this was that now her thigh was clutched by the two podgy arms.

'Now this is a state, isn't it? What's come over her, anyway?'

'Be quiet, Maggie.' He turned from the old woman to the child again, and, bending down, he said sternly, 'Susie . . . Susie . . . let go.' His face was just below Rosamund's and she whispered to him, 'Would you allow me to put her to bed?'

He straightened up and it was some seconds before he answered, and then it wasn't Rosamund to whom he spoke, but the old woman. 'Get a light, Maggie,' he said. Then, moving into the large, bare hall, he went on, 'I'm getting a generator in, but it all takes time.'

'Yes, yes.' She was following him now, holding the child by the hand once again.

'The furniture hasn't arrived yet.'

She did not make any comment on this; it was evident that the furniture hadn't arrived, the whole place was bare and smelt musty with years of disuse. He was going up the stairs, she walking behind him, but slowly, for the child's step faltered when she had to raise one foot any distance from the ground.

'In here.'

They were in a small room. The only furniture was a camp bed and a chair. She watched him open a trunk, and after flipping garments here and there he took out a nightdress. Putting it across the camp bed, he said under his breath, 'Be firm. When she's in bed tell her you'll be downstairs, she'll stay then.'

'Very well.'

Left alone with the child, she had a strong urge to sit down and cry, and for a number of conflicting reasons. Taking the nightdress off the child, she dried her with the top half of

375

it, then slipped the dry garment over her head and pulled off her wet slippers, dried the podgy feet, and lifted her into the bed.

'There now.' She stroked the hair back over the hard bony cranium. 'Susie go to sleep?' She spoke her name as if she was in the habit of using it every night. Again she said, as she pressed the child gently down on to the pillow, 'Susie go to sleep.' And after looking at her for a long moment the child turned her face into the pillow and remained still. Rosamund stood and watched her for a time, then, remembering Michael Bradshaw's words, she said, 'I'll be downstairs.' When there was no movement from the bed she turned away and went out of the room, not closing the door but leaving it ajar.

When she reached the top of the broad, dusty stairway she saw down below her the figure of Michael Bradshaw. He was standing looking out of the long window to the right of the front door. As she descended the stair he turned slowly and came across the hall to meet her. What his exact feelings were at this moment she could not gauge, his face was giving nothing away. His voice sounded ordinary as he said, 'I'm afraid I have nothing to offer you in the way of a drink, with the exception of tea, that is.'

It was on the point of her tongue to say, 'That's all right, I'll be making my way home now, if you don't mind, it's getting dark.' This would have put her in charge of the situation and prevented her laying herself open to any sarcasm or rudeness which she still felt he might, at any moment, level at her. Instead, she heard herself saying, 'Thank you very much, I would like a cup of tea.'

He seemed slightly taken aback by her acceptance and he kept his eyes hard on her before turning away, saying, 'Will you come this way then?' He pushed open a door at the far end of the hall that had once been covered with green baize, and stood aside, allowing her to go through.

The room into which he showed her was a kitchen, and she took in immediately that it was also the living-room. Partly covering the wide stone floor was an old carpet, and isolated in its middle stood a white deal table. Three plain wooden chairs stood near an old-fashioned delf rack that ran the whole length of one wall, and at each side of the antiquated open fireplace there was an old but comfortable-looking easy chair. It was to one of these he pointed, saying, 'Will you sit down?'

As she made her way to the chair the old woman eased herself from a kneeling position in front of the large oven. 'It's me back,' she said. 'And wouldn't this kind of contraption break anybody's back? Is it tea you're after?' She cast a glance towards the man, adding, 'It's there on the hob.'

'We want none of your stewed brew, Maggie. Make a fresh pot.'

'Aw! Away with you!' Maggie now laughed towards Rosamund, and added, 'The English don't know how to make tea. You got her to bed then?'

'Yes.'

'It's strange how she's taken to you – isn't it?' The last part of the remark was addressed to her master, but he made no reply to it whatever. He was standing with his back to the delf rack, and Rosamund could now sense his unease. He was making an effort to be ordinary and it was evidently costing him something.

'Aye, she's taken to you.' Maggie was carrying two plain thick white cups and saucers to the table. 'And I've never known her do that since that time with O'Moore.' Maggie cocked her head towards her master, and he gave a wry laugh. Then, looking towards Rosamund, he said, 'I can assure you that is no compliment. O'Moore happened to be a sheep-dog.'

'And a grand sheep-dog into the bargain; that dog had the intelligence far above the ordinary.'

'It had indeed.'

Rosamund smiled at his reply because Michael Bradshaw had answered Maggie in her own thick Irish twang.

'Aw, you were never the one to forget the body who did you down, were you, Master Michael?'

'No, I never was, Maggie.' The voice still held the twang. But now he turned to Rosamund again and asked, 'Have you ever been to Ireland?'

'No, I've never been there.'

'Well, don't go, unless you want to be fleeced, befuddled and begoozled.'

'Away with you! Where would you have been without the Irish? Be fleeced, indeed. I've given you me whole life, that I have . . .'

'Be quiet, Maggie.'

There was a quick sternness in the words, but his tone altered as he turned yet again to Rosamund, saying, 'The child took a fancy to this particular dog and would follow it to its home. He was owned by one, Shane Bradley, the biggest scoundrel in the south of Ireland . . .'

He had successfully diverted Maggie from personalities, for she cried now, 'He wasn't that, he had to make a livin'. . .'

'Make a living indeed!' Michael Bradshaw answered Maggie as he still looked at Rosamund. 'He sold me O'Moore for five pounds . . .'

'It was a grand dog.'

'Yes, it was a grand dog indeed, as you said, a most intelligent dog.' There was a twinkle in his eye now and he flung his large head upwards as he said, 'Too intelligent. When you got him home you could chain him, bury him, chloroform him, but when you woke in the morning he would be gone, back to his master. Shane Bradley made a fine living in the summer, selling that dog to the gullible visitors. There is a tale that one fellow even got it across the border and it made its way back to home and Shane Bradley.'

Rosamund was laughing now, laughing with an ease she would not have thought possible in the presence of . . . the Fen Tiger. She saw also that he was enjoying relating the story of how he had been done, and apart from him calling this Shane Bradley a rogue he gave her the feeling that he had liked this Shane Bradley. She was wondering how long he had lived in Ireland, when Maggie gave her the answer.

'Aw, you're always on about the Irish and Ireland, but don't forget it took the devil in hell to get you away from it after two years. If they hadn't said they were going to nab your land never a foot would you've put . . .'

'You jabber too much, Maggie. Where's that tea?'

'It's right here.' Maggie handed a cup of black-looking liquid to Rosamund, another to her master.

'You take sugar?'

'No. No, thanks.' She smiled at him, then sipped at the tea. It was so strong and bitter that she didn't know how she was going to get through it.

'It's too strong for you?'

'Yes, yes, just a little.' Again she was smiling at him. He took the cup from her hand and went to the sink and poured half of the tea away, then filled the cup with hot water. Handing it to her again, he asked, 'Is that better?'

'Yes. Yes, thank you very much.'

'Water spoiled, that is.' Maggie was sitting at the other side of the fireplace, moving her body with a motion as if she were in a rocking-chair, and there now followed a space when not one of them spoke and the seconds began to beat loud in Rosamund's head. Michael Bradshaw was still leaning against the dresser, his look seeming to be turned deeply inwards. She forced herself to break the uncomfortable silence by saying, 'It's almost dark, I'd better be making my way home.'

Michael Bradshaw moved from the dresser and put his cup on the table. He did not speak as he went towards the door, but Maggie, stopping her rocking movement and raising her head, smiled at Rosamund as she said, 'Aye well, we'll be seeing more of you if she's taken to you. There's not a doubt but we'll be seeing more of you.'

Rosamund could make no reply to this, so all she said was, 'Good night.'

'Good night, Miss . . . By the way, what's your name? I didn't hear it.'

She did not say, as she usually did, 'Rosamund Morley', but used the more familiar Rosie, 'I'm Rosie Morley.'

'Aw, its's a nice name. Rosie, comfortable like. Well, good night, Miss Rosie . . . ma'am.' She laughed as if she were enjoying a private joke.

Once again he stood aside as she went out of the front door. The courtesy seemed natural to him, yet up to an hour ago she would never have coupled any kind of courtesy with this man. He walked by her side to the gate without speaking and when they were on the field path he asked abruptly, 'Do you like the fenland?'

'Yes, I love it.'

'Well, you either love it or hate it, there are no half measures.'

Yes, she knew this. Jennifer's attitude had taught her this much: you either loved or hated the fenland. They had walked on some distance before he spoke again, and then he began hesitantly, 'I . . . I don't know what to say as regards the child. I . . . we can't keep her fastened up, and now she's found her way to the river' – he didn't add 'and you' – 'she'll make herself a nuisance.'

'Oh no. Please don't think that. If you don't mind her coming I certainly don't mind seeing her.'

When he stopped she went a step ahead of him before she too halted, and as last night, they stood looking at each other. Then he said quietly, 'Except Maggie and some of the Irish in Agnestown you're the only person who hasn't shown herself to be utterly repulsed by her.'

Her throat felt tight, and she swallowed before saying, 'You . . . you mustn't think like that. It's just that people are not used . . . They are apt to stare but they don't mean . . .'

'Were you used to seeing anyone like her?'

'Well . . . I worked for a short time in a day nursery' – she did not say three days – 'and there was a child there, she was very like Susan.'

In the gathering dusk she saw his cheek-bones moving, indicating the pressure on his jaws, and then, as if forcing the words through his teeth, he said, 'It makes me mad, furious, raving, when I see the way they look at her.'

'Has she been to school?' Rosamund's voice was very low. 'A special school?'

'Yes, she's been to two. They are very good in their way, and they have an effect on some of them. Some of the children improve, but not Susan – they couldn't get through to her.' He looked away from her and she knew he was seeing the child again when he said, 'In the last place she was sitting there like a dumb animal in a cage. All the others were playing, laughing, talking their own particular jargon, but she was just sitting there, waiting, waiting for me.' He turned round to her now, almost fiercely. 'Somewhere there's a spark of intelligence, I know there is –

it's only being able to get at it – she understands some things.'

After a space of time during which she looked at him she said quietly, 'Yes, yes, I'm sure you're right.'

She watched him draw in a deep breath that pushed back the lapels of his coat, and then he said brusquely, 'You know, you've been very kind . . . after the other night. My manner, I'm afraid, wasn't very tactful, or helpful. I'm sorry about that, but . . . but not about yesterday.' His tone was rapid now. 'Oh no. I would willingly murder anyone who calls her frightful . . . you understand?'

'Yes, yes, I understand.'

They were staring at each other again when their glances were snapped apart by a far-away voice calling, 'Rosie! Rosie! Ro . . . osie!'

'I'll have to go now. They didn't know I had come; they're wondering where I've got to. Good . . . good night.'

'Good night.'

She turned quickly from him and began to run. She found that she was running, not only to relieve Jennifer's mind, but to get away from something. What, she didn't rightly know. She only knew she was now running in a sort of panic and the desire was strong in her to escape, not only from the man whom she felt was still standing where she had left him, but away from the fens, the beloved fens, the deep, secret fens.

When she came to the boat landing Jennifer and her father were on the far bank, and Jennifer cried across to her, 'Where on earth have you been?'

She did not reply but dropped into the boat and pulled herself across the water.

Her father said, 'I was worried when you weren't about – you didn't say you were going out.'

She pulled herself up the bank before she said, 'I had to take the child back, she was in the water.'

'What, again?' Jennifer's voice was high in her head. 'You should have left her alone, you don't want to encourage her.'

Rosamund's manner was so ferocious that it surprised even herself as she turned on Jennifer, crying, 'And let the child drown, or be sucked into the mud! I was just to sit on the bank and watch it happen?'

'Well, you needn't bellow at me like that.'

'Then don't be such a damned fool.'

She stamped up to the house, her body quivering with a rage that was new and startling; it was as if she had touched the Fen Tiger and had become contaminated with his ferocity.

'Rosie, wait a minute.' It was her father's voice, quiet and puzzled. She took no notice, but marched through the hall and upstairs and into her room. They could make their own supper, they could look after themselves. She had left the house for half an hour, and because she hadn't told them where she was going they were bawling the fens down. As her mind attacked them she knew that her attitude was merely a weapon warding off something else, something deeper, something that had made her run from the owner of Thornby House, the father of the Mongol child.

5

The following morning, when Jennifer brought her a cup of tea up to bed, Rosamund was embarrassed, ashamed, and a little amused at this gesture, and to cover her reaction she said, 'I'm glad of this, I've got a splitting headache.' She was looking down into the cup as Jennifer said quietly, 'I'm sorry about last night, Rosie.'

She glanced up swiftly at her sister and, putting her hand out, gripped her wrist as she said, 'It's me who should say sorry. It wasn't a good day yesterday, was it? Tempers were running high on all sides. Let's hope today will be better.'

'Father's made a good start anyway, he's been in the workshop since around six.'

'No!'

'Yes, and he's off now down to the post.'

'What on earth time is it?' She glanced at the clock on the table beside the bed. 'Nine o'clock! *Nine* o'clock?'

Jennifer smiled broadly. 'You slept on and we didn't disturb you.'

'Lord!' Rosamund leant back and handed the empty cup to Jennifer. 'Fancy me sleeping until this time, I've never done that before.'

'I'll do your breakfast. Would you like it up here?'

'Good gracious no, I'm getting up. Thanks, all the same.'

When Jennifer had left the room, she lay with her hands behind her head staring up at the ceiling. That's what crying yourself to sleep did. Slowly now she raised herself up into a sitting position. That was strange; she hadn't had her dream, not any part of it. She couldn't remember a night for years when she hadn't had her dream. It had become part of her life. She couldn't have been more surprised at this moment if she had realised that she had stopped breathing during her sleeping hours. Still, she swung her legs over the bed. The past two days had been unusual. You couldn't expect the pattern of life to remain the same.

As she entered the kitchen from the hall her father came in the back door.

'Hello, had a good sleep?' He smiled at her – he looked well this morning. As he handed her three letters she said, 'Yes, I can't remember sleeping like that for years.' She looked at the letters, two brown envelopes and one white. The white one brought a warm glow into her body and a sense of well-being. She did not open it but put it into the pocket of her dress.

Jennifer, aiming to be tactful this morning,

made no comment on this, nor did she ask the obvious question 'Who is it from?'

It took quite some willpower on Rosamund's part to eat her breakfast, then help wash up and clear away, before she allowed herself to go into the mill proper. She had always felt it was a bit childish to keep Clifford's letters until she was sitting on the platform high above her world of the fens.

Once in the mill house she raced up the rickety stairs and was tearing at the envelope before she curled her legs under her to sit on the wooden floor.

'My Dear Rosamund.' She was smiling as she began to read, but by the time she had turned over the single page of the letter her face had a stricken look, and when she came to the last words and read, 'See you when I get back,' she dropped her head until it met her uplifted hand.

She remained still for a moment, her fingers pressed on to her eyeballs in an effort to shut out the meaning of the letter. He would see her when he got back. His plans had had to be changed. His mother thought that as he was going to America, anyway, it would be nice for them all to have the holidays there. His mother had a great desire to see her cousin in Washington as they hadn't met for years – 'I'm disappointed, Rosamund, but will see you when I get back.'

When would he get back? This was June, the holidays stretched through July and August and into September. And would he come back? Her aunt would see to that — she had smelt a rat. She was clever, was her aunt, wily. She could even hear her saying to Clifford in her high nasal voice, 'Well, why go back to England? You'll only have a double journey. Why not stay on, now that you're here?'

With a sudden gesture Rosamund crushed the letter in her hand. She hated Clifford; he was weak, weak, like clay in his mother's hands . . . No, no, she didn't hate him — Clifford was nice, kind and gentle. Clifford's trouble was that he wanted to please everybody, his mother included. She remembered again that she hadn't had her dream last night and the reminder brought with it a stab of fear and anxiety, and she spoke aloud, trying to quell her fears. 'Why worry about that? Nothing has changed. You'll be here as long as father's here . . . But it isn't only that, it isn't only the mill.' And it wasn't only that, it wasn't only the mill. She wanted something else besides the mill. She wanted the kindness and the tenderness of Clifford.

She could see no beauty at the moment in the sun-drenched land below her and went slowly down the stairs and into the house.

As she entered the hall Jennifer was going into the workroom and she turned. 'Well?' She was smiling with the question.

Rosamund gave a little cough before saying,

'Clifford's not coming, he's going to America. They're all going for their holidays.'

'What! Oh, Rosie, that's Aunt Anna. But why can't he come and see you before he goes?'

'He'll be very busy; they'll be off soon.'

'But all this must have been done in a hurry. Oh, Rosie' – Jennifer put out both her hands to her sister – 'don't take it so hard.'

'Don't be silly.' Rosamund quickly warded off the sympathetic touch. 'I told you, didn't I, that there was nothing. It was you who insisted.'

'All right, have it your own way.' Jennifer moved slowly back towards the workroom now, and just before she opened the door she turned her head and remarked, 'It isn't the Morleys' week, is it – Andrew first, now Clifford.'

Rosamund made no answer but went into the sitting-room, and there she began an onslaught on the furniture. At one point, when she was rubbing vigorously, deepening the already deep lustre on a small sofa table, she spoke to it, saying, 'We must keep you at your antique best, mustn't we, for when Aunt Anna takes you over again.'

Oh dear, dear, she hated to be like this. As Jennifer said, why couldn't Clifford have come and told her. Perhaps she would have understood then – at least she wouldn't have felt so hurt. The letter in her pocket was as cold and informal as if from a stranger. If he didn't care for her why had he kissed her on his last visit? They were at the end of the

Cut – she was standing on the bank watching him as he started up the engine of the boat – and just before he let in the throttle he had jumped out of the boat and on to the bank again, and before she knew what was happening she was in his arms and he was kissing her . . . once, twice, three times. And then he was down in the boat again. She had waved to him, not just with one hand but with her two high above her head, waved until he was lost to sight. And now he was off to America.

When the sting of tears came into the back of her eyes she chided herself sternly, saying, 'No more of that, you've done enough crying lately. If this is the way things are to be there is nothing you can do about it but face up to it.'

It was about half-past eleven when her father came hurrying from the garden into the kitchen, and, speaking below his breath as if his voice could be heard across the water, he said, 'He's just taken it back.'

'Taken it back? What do you mean?'

'The child.'

'Was she . . . was she right here?'

'No, I first noticed him racing over the field. Then I saw him stoop and pick something up. It was the child.'

Rosamund shook her head. 'He's going to have his work cut out.'

'A child like that should be in a home, you know, Rosie.'

'She's been in a home, two homes. Apparently she pines. I should say she wants love . . .' She stopped and added cynically to herself, 'Don't we all?'

'She's not normal, Rosie.' Her father's voice was slightly persuasive as if trying to convince her of something, and he went on. 'She won't feel things like other children.'

'Don't be silly.' She had rounded on him angrily, and now she bit her lip. 'I'm sorry, but, Father, that type of child needs it more than the normal ones.'

'Yes; well, perhaps you're right. You nearly always are. You're a wise little bird.' When he came up to her and slipped his arm round her shoulders she wanted to cry at him, 'Don't, don't.' She wanted no sympathy today, no praise for being the little mother – she was tired of being the little mother, she was tired of playing the little mother to him and to Jennifer . . . and . . . and oh, she was tired of everything . . .

By tea-time Michael Bradshaw had come within sight of the mill three times to Rosamund's knowledge alone, and the last time she had seen him carry the child back she had thought to herself. 'This can't go on, he'll never get anything done at this rate.'

It was as they sat having tea on the lawn in

the shadow of the mill wall, out of the sun, that she said, and without leading up to the matter, 'Tomorrow I will have the child across here.'

'Oh no, Rosie, I just couldn't bear it.' Jennifer held her cup of tea poised halfway to her lips.

'Well, don't you see that the man can't spend his days trying to stop her from coming here?'

'That's his business, I should think. Why doesn't he get someone to look after her?'

Rosamund opened her mouth to make a retort, then closed it again. Why? Yes, why? Jennifer was right there. The old woman Maggie was less than useless for running after a child. There came into her mind a picture of the bare house and the scantily furnished child's room and kitchen. She had seen such furniture before in the cheapest of cheap rented rooms. Why hadn't he waited for his furniture to come before opening up the house? Why had he bought that poor stuff? And why, if he was going to farm, was there no machinery, no man to help him? Why was he grubbing out roots with a mattock? Her thinking seemed to force the next words out of her mouth. 'Well, if you can't tolerate her here I shall go over in the afternoons and see to her. Anyway, until we can get to work in the shop there's nothing to do.'

Noticing her father's uneasy movement at this statement she could have bitten her tongue out for her tactlessness.

'It'll look very like pushing, won't it?'

'Oh, Jennifer—' Rosamund bestowed on her sister a knowing side-long glance and just prevented herself from saying, 'You're the one to talk about pushing.'

'Well, you go. Go ahead, do what you like, but he'll show you the door, you'll see.'

'I don't think so.'

'Well, try it.'

'I have.'

Jennifer was silent. 'Did he ask you in last night?' It was her father asking the question.

'Yes, he did, and I put the child to bed and then he offered me a cup of tea.'

She saw Jennifer's face darken and she understood her feeling at this moment. She herself would have felt much the same in her place, but she knew she would have refrained from making such a retort as now came from Jennifer.

'It's a case of love me, love my dog.'

'Jennifer!' Rosamund was on her feet. 'The child is not a dog, she's not an animal.'

'Now, now, now. Both of you.' Henry Morley spread his arms between them. 'What's come over you all of a sudden? You've never been like this.'

'Oh, I'm sorry . . . I'm sorry.' Rosamund slumped down into the chair again, and after taking a deep breath she said quietly, 'It's this heat, it's been unbearable all day. I think I'll go down to the pond after tea and have a swim . . . and cool off.' She smiled apologetically across the table at her father and Jennifer. But it was her father only who returned the smile, saying now, 'I'd do just that. I wouldn't mind going in myself, but it's such a long trudge down to that pond.' He looked towards the river and added musingly, 'It wouldn't be a bad idea if I were to clear a part up here. It mightn't be deep enough for swimming, but you could have a dip. Down near the bend there, say. What d'you think?' He looked at Rosamund for approval, and she was just about to answer when again she saw the child. She remained still, her eyes fixed across the river, and she knew that her father and Jennifer had followed her gaze.

The head came bobbing nearer through the high grass and when the child came into the clearing above the boat landing, she stood looking across at them, her mouth open, her face spread in a wide laugh. And the sound of her voice came across the water crying, 'Wiv . . . wiv.'

She was walking quickly across the lawn when Jennifer's voice came at her, low and pleading, 'Don't bring her over here, please, Rosamund.'

She did not reply in any way, but, getting into the boat and keeping her eyes fixed on the child in an effort to hold her attention, she pulled herself swiftly towards her.

When the ferry grated against the bank Susie was standing waiting for her, and when she stepped on to the landing the child put out her hand and without hesitation made her way up the bank again towards home.

With her shambling, erratic gait she kept ahead, intent on leading Rosamund back to the house, and a sad smile came to Rosamund's lips on the thought that indeed she had taken the place of O'Moore in the child's mind.

When they reached the broken gate the child did not lead her to the drive but along by a stone wall half obliterated with dead grass and shrub, and across what had once apparently been a garden. This was suggested to Rosamund by the hard stone path her feet found every now and again, and the rose bushes struggling for existence through the undergrowth. Then round to the back of the house and the stables and out-buildings, which, with the exception of a high barn-like structure, had been conquered by the luscious undergrowth.

It was as the child drew her nearer to the barn that she heard the voices. The unmistakable one of Michael Bradshaw was saying, 'Yes, it'll take time as I'm mostly having to use sweat for money. I've got just about enough to get me started, that's if we live on the bread line. But I'll get going, never fear; if it's only to spite my dear neighbours I'll get going. Do you know that some of them were trying to get an order on the place.' The voice was harsh.

'I heard something.'

'Damned impertinence. I'd see them in hell before I'd let them have the land.'

'How you going to manage without labour?'

'Oh, I'll manage.'

'Are you going to furnish the place?'

'Furnish, huh! Furniture won't worry me. We have beds and a table, the bare necessities – they'll see us through until we get better. Maggie doesn't mind. There wasn't much else in her cottage.'

'How have you managed all this time – I mean, have you had a job?'

'Oh yes, jobs in plenty.' The voice was scornful. 'Brawn pays better than brains these days. I even managed to save.'

A laugh followed this, and then came the other voice . . . a pleasing voice, saying, 'Well, you know, Mike, my week-ends are my own. I'll come and give you a hand any time. I'm not a stone's throw away, really.'

As Rosamund pulled the child to a halt the two men came out of the barn, and she felt a wave of hot embarrassment flowing over her as they both stood looking at her without speaking.

'She . . . she was down by the river, I thought I'd better . . .' She broke off as Michael Bradshaw lowered his head for a moment, then, coming towards them, he looked down at the child before moving his gaze to Rosamund and saying heavily, 'I've brought her back six times today.'

'Yes, I know.'

'She was here just a minute ago.' It was the stranger speaking and they both looked at him, then Michael Bradshaw made the introduction.

'This is a friend of mine, Gerald Gibson . . . Miss Morley.'

'How do you do?'

Rosamund looked up at the tall fair man. She guessed he was about the same age as Michael Bradshaw, yet he had that youthful, lively-looking air that made him appear younger, not thirty even. Her first thought was, He's good looking, and then, He seems rather nice.

'How do you do?' He was inclining his head towards her, 'Morley? From Heron Mill?'

'Yes.'

'Oh, I've heard about you. You took over after the Talfords left. It's years since I saw the mill. I used to go up there, up the Cut in a little dinghy, when I was a boy. Do you like it here?'

'I love it.'

'That's odd. Most people have to be born here before they like it. I was born in Littleport, but we now live in Hockwold . . . you know, just beyond Wilton Bridge?'

'Yes, yes, I know it.'

'Come.' At the sound of Michael Bradshaw's curt syllable the child's hand was tugged from her own. As he made to walk away over the grass-strewn courtyard she said to him, 'Would you like me to . . . to see to her?'

He stopped and seemed to consider for a moment. Then going on, he said, 'No, no. We can't have that. Thank you, all the same.'

The thanks sounded grudging, and she stood for a moment at a loss, feeling embarrassed because of the other man's presence. It was bad enough to be choked off without having an audience. She was on the point of looking at the man to say goodbye when an ear-splitting scream brought her round to the child again. With her two hands holding her father's, her body arched, she was almost in a sitting position in an endeavour to stop him from going on.

'Susie! Stop that!' He had her by the shoulders now and was shaking her gently. 'Do you hear? Stop it!'

The screaming stopped and the child turned her face towards Rosamund again. She was not crying, her eyes were quite dry, but in their opaque depths there was a wild look as if another scream was imminent. Michael Bradshaw's reactions came swiftly. With a lift of his arm he hoisted the child up and, apparently deaf to her now terrifying screams, he marched with her into the house.

'Don't be upset.'

She looked up at this Gerald Gibson. His voice was kind, his eyes were kind. She said softly, 'It's dreadful, awful.'

'Yes, it appears worse when you're not used to it. He's used to it.'

'Yes.' She nodded her head in small quick jerks, then added, 'I'd better go. Goodbye.'

'Goodbye, and don't be upset.'

She hurried away, and did not slow her pace until she was beyond the wood and out of sight of the house. Then she stopped and stood looking to where, in the far distance, her father and Jennifer still sat at the table on the lawn in the shadow of the wall. And as she stood she bit on her thumbnail. It was a long, long time since she had been so emotionally disturbed as to bite her nails. Even her father's lapses had ceased to make her bite her nails. She was thinking again, Poor soul, poor soul! but, strangely, the picture in her mind was that of the man, not of the child.

Jennifer did not want to go swimming in the pool. She had changed into an attractive print, one she had made herself, and she was waiting for Andrew coming.

Rosamund tossed up in her mind whether she would go for a swim or not. She did not relish her own company this evening; she wanted someone with her to take her mind off herself. There would be time enough to think about herself when she got to bed, for then there would be no chores, no diverting incidents connected with Thornby House and its occupants to prevent her from thinking of Clifford's letter, for she was fully aware that once she was alone the feeling that

401

had been growing in her all day against Clifford would no longer hide itself under the term of disappointment but would take on its real name of resentment. Whenever she had thought about him today, and that had been often, she had resented so many things about him – the fact that he had been weak enough to fall in with his mother's wishes, that he had deliberately played on her emotions these past few months, that he had misled her with their last farewell. One could say, Well, what was a kiss, anyway? What were three rapid kisses in succession? The result of high spirits, payment for a happy day. Anything . . . Anything apparently but a promise of marriage. So, to prevent her suffering her own company and self-questioning, she stayed with Jennifer. At least, she told herself, she would stay until Andrew arrived. But when by eight o'clock Andrew had not arrived and Jennifer's nerves were showing signs of strain, she felt she could no longer be with her sister without telling her of Andrew's strategy. So she made her way alone to the pool.

The pool was strangely deserted tonight, and there was not enough breeze to stir the reeds. When the long brown head of a bulrush wagged independently Rosamund guessed the cause to be a vole sitting on its hind legs, its back against the thick rush stem, as it nibbled off its supper from among the flat blades of grass. Nor were the swans and their cygnets to be seen; likely having gone down the Cut to the main river. For this Rosamund was thankful – she had too much knowledgeable respect for their tempers to get into the water when they were anywhere about.

She unbuttoned her overall dress and threw it on the grass near the large bath towel she had brought with her, then, going to a part of the bank which was firm with sunbaked blue clay, she let herself quietly down into the pool and began to swim. The water felt beautiful, wonderful. When she reached the middle of the pond she turned on her back and, paddling gently with her hands, lay staring up into the clear sky. A group of mallard, flying high, moved across her vision, and then a little barn owl. Then nothing for a long time. When she found herself reading her own thoughts in the endless sky space above her, she swung on to her stomach again and, thrashing out with the crawl stroke, made for the far bank.

'Enjoying it?'

She jerked her head upwards as Gerald Gibson's voice came to her, and, pressing down on her feet, trod water as she blinked upwards towards the bank.

'Are you enjoying it?'

'Yes. Yes, it's lovely.'

'I wish I had thought about it – I had forgotten all about this pond.'

'It's beautiful and cool.'

'Come on out for a while.' He was squatting on his hunkers and he patted the turf at his side.

Rosamund, still treading water, was on the point of saying, 'My things are at the other side,' when she thought, How stupid! It won't be the first time he's seen anyone in a bathing costume, and this one's almost old-fashioned enough to be Victorian. When she had swum the few yards to the bank he put down his hand to her, and with a lift and a pull she was on the grass, sitting by his side, laughing.

'I remember swimming in here when I was a boy. Every other week I came.' He wiped the water from his wet hands. 'You could get up the Cut in a boat then. The other week-end I made for the Railway Bridge. You know . . . right beyond Hockwold, near Brandon. Have you ever been up that part of the river?'

'No, I can't say I have.'

'Oh, the fishing's marvellous up there. You can really put your hand in the water, tickle 'em and pull 'em out. You can. Do you fish?'

'No. I've tried, but I find I haven't got the heart for it.' She paused and laughed sheepishly. 'I hate taking the hook out of their mouths.'

'They don't feel it.'

'That's what you think, but you're not the fish.'

As they laughed together she thought of how different people were. Here she was, within a few seconds, laughing with this man she had met only that day, and then she had spoken to him not longer than a few minutes. He was the kind of man who made you feel at home right away. Easy, not like his friend. But then, he didn't look as if he had the responsibilities of his friend; he looked carefree. She felt so at ease with him that she could ask right away, 'Have you had a nice day?'

'Yes. Well, sort of. I was pleased to see old Mike again.' He turned his face full to her now. 'He's got a hell of a life, hasn't he?' He seemed to take it for granted that she knew all about the owner of Thornby House.

Her face became straight as she said, 'Well, I know very little about him . . . only the child . . .'

'That's what I mean, the child. He should put her away and keep her away.'

She did not answer for a moment, and her voice was very quiet and perhaps held a note of censure as she said, 'I don't think he'd find that easy to do. In fact, it would be more difficult than having her with him. He seems very fond of her.'

'Fond of her? It's a mania. She's ruined his whole life.'

Her eyes were wide as she looked at him.

'It's a fact, you know.'

'Have you known him long?'

'Oh yes, since we were boys. We were at school together, then in the Army. Then he went to medical college and I into the Polytechnic. We roomed together for a time too, and then . . .'

'Yes?' She spoke quietly, waiting for him to go on, hoping he would go on.

'Well, he was in his second year when he met Camilla — she was his wife, you know. He went clean mad.' He paused as he looked away from her across the pond. 'It takes some people like that.' Then on a little laugh he was looking at her again. 'I'm glad I'm not that sort — too intense.' He nodded his head at her, and as she looked at him, still thinking, He's nice, she also thought he would never be intense. Loveable, yes, but never intense. She heard herself say, 'He didn't finish his studies then?' She knew that she wanted information about their neighbour and that this pleasing stranger was quite willing to give it to her without her doing much probing.

'No. No, he didn't. But, mind you, he realised that he had been mad almost before they were married a month. She was so unpredictable — a bit unbalanced, I'd say. But a man was apt to forget that when he was looking at her.'

'She was beautiful then?'

'Yes, she was beautiful, and vivacious — auburn-haired and half-Spanish. She had her mother's colouring and her father's temperament. It was a very deceptive combination.'

He shook his head as if remembering back; and as Rosamund looked at him, still thinking he was nice, she knew that here was a loquacious individual whom she had only to prompt to know all he knew about the master of Thornby House. She did nothing to resist the strong urge. 'Is she dead?' she asked.

'Yes, drowned.' He looked at her, nodding his head the while. 'It's an awful thing to say but it was just as well, they would have driven each other round the bend if it had gone on much longer.'

'When did she die?'

'Oh' – he screwed up his eyes thinking – 'it must be around three years ago. I'd been staying with them; they were in Spain at the time in a little village on the coast. The people were poor, everybody was poor, so they accepted the child. It was the child, of course, that was the trouble. But she didn't look so bad somehow among the pot-bellied urchins who ran about the shore. I had come upon them by chance, just sheer luck. I was touring at the time – hitch-hiking would be a better word. Mike was very much in need of real company, at least someone who talked his own language. I stayed with them nearly five weeks, but I hadn't been with them two days before I saw what a set-up it was. She loathed the child. She would have killed it, I think, if she'd got the chance.' His face was sombre now as he inclined his head towards her. 'This made Mike go the other way. He pitied the thing . . .'

'Oh, please!' Rosamund had screwed her face

up and was now covering it with her hands. 'I'm sorry, but I can't bear to hear her called . . . a thing.'

'Oh.' Definitely the man was taken aback. Then he laughed. 'I meant nothing. It was . . . well after you're with her for a time you're apt to forget she's human.'

'*No! No!*'

'I'm sorry. I can see that you look at her much in the same light as Mike himself does. But in his case I'm sure it was because Camilla hated her. The more she was against the child the more he was for her. And then she goes out one day swimming and that was that, it was all over. The strange thing was, I might have been with her, but I was too lazy that day to move. She was a strong swimmer, but she must have been caught in a current and sucked under. I left shortly after – I think Mike wanted to be on his own. He became . . . well, rather strange. Things like that affect people.'

'Did they never find her?'

'Yes. I wasn't there at the time, but her body was washed up. She's buried in the little cemetery. She's got the distinction of being the only English woman to be buried there.'

'It's all so very sad.'

'Yes, I suppose it is. But there' – he laughed – 'you've got no reason to feel sad . . . Do you always come here swimming?'

'Yes, most days, weather permitting.'

'I'll have to join you sometime.'

She smiled and raised her eyebrows. 'It's a long walk for a bathe, and the river's pretty wide near Wilton Bridge.'

He laughed. 'I'm coming to give Mike a hand at weekends. I'm going to get very, very dirty grubbing that ground.'

She turned her head and looked at him seriously now, asking quickly, 'What is he going to put the land to, beet and such?'

'No. No beet for him. He's going in for flowers. Chrysanthemums in particular, I think. Strange bloke, Mike; he's always been crazy about flowers. He aims to build greenhouses.'

Yes, indeed, strange bloke, Mike. Who would have thought a man of his type and . . . manner would have had a feeling for flowers? It seemed rather ludicrous on the face of it. He had shown surprise when she had told him they did silver-smithing up at the mill. He growing flowers was more surprising still.

'But the Lord knows when he'll really get going.' He shook his head.

'He's short of money?' But she already knew the answer.

'Short is right. He's got a bit but nothing like what is needed. He should be employing labour and machines to clear the place. But he's only got enough to carry him for six months or so. His old father was a bit of a swine, you know – he must have hated his guts. Mike always loathed this place, and now he can neither sell it nor let it. The only thing he can do is live in it. He must have felt very loath to come back, for he's always said they could do what they liked with it. But some of the birds around here have been trying to get a compulsory order on the land. Well, anyway, here he is. And he's got some nice neighbours.' The smile with which he accompanied this latter was a bit too pert and it brought Rosamund slowly to her feet. She was just about to take her leave of him with a laughing remark to match his own when she saw the subject of their conversation. Across Gerald Gibson's shoulder she saw in the distance Michael Bradshaw emerge from the wood. As she watched him hesitate for a second before coming on she was filled with an uneasiness and a desire to dive into the water. Her voice was quiet as she said, 'Here's Mr Bradshaw now.'

'What? Oh!' Gerald turned and called a greeting to his friend. 'Hello there.' And as he drew nearer she shouted, 'I'm still here. I met a water sprite.'

Rosamund could not translate the expression on Michael Bradshaw's face as he came up to them; there was a blankness about it that could be hiding any type of emotion. It was, she supposed, a definite poker expression, but nevertheless it filled her with a vague unease. Whereas she certainly hadn't minded sitting next to Gerald Gibson in her bathing costume, under Michael Bradshaw's look she had the feeling that she was almost naked, and she wished heartily that she had her dress at this side. To cover her embarrassment and make light of the situation she laughed as she looked at Michael, saying, 'I'm trespassing again.'

'Yes, I see you are.'

Oh dear, dear, he was utterly humourless. Surely he couldn't mean that he minded her being on this side of the pond? He hadn't minded her trespassing to take the child back. She felt the unfairness of the situation.

'Well' – she was looking him straight in the eye as she spoke – 'I'd better get to my own side, I suppose.'

He did not answer and she turned now and looked at Gerald Gibson, and she forced herself to smile amicably as she said, 'Goodbye then.'

'Goodbye. I'll be seeing you.' His voice, high and pleasant, held perhaps just the faintest note of embarrassment. But his embarrassment was nothing compared to her own as she turned her back on them and entered the water. She felt hot with it, and with annoyance too, and this came out in her stroke, for her crawl sent the water spraying and she arrived at the other side somewhat exhausted. She suppressed the urge to turn round to see if they were still there, and, picking up her towel, she rubbed at her hair. Then she pulled her dress over her wet costume and slipped on her sandals. As she turned her face towards home, her name being called brought her around, not to look across the river but to the bridge and Andrew.

'Been havin' a dip?'

'Yes. I didn't hear the car.'

'No, I walked over.'

She waited for him to reach her side, and as she turned again she glanced casually across the pond. The two men were still standing on the far bank and looking towards her. Her sense of humour taking over, she laughed to herself. She had spoken to three men in a matter of minutes, two of them comparative strangers. This had never happened to her before. It would seem that the fenland was crowded with men.

'I'd like to bet that the burly one of those two is Bradshaw.' Andrew had given a little jerk of his head in the direction of the pool.

'Right first time.'

'Who's the other?'

'A friend of his, name of Gibson, from Hockwold. Do you know him?'

'I don't know him, but I know a Gibson, an elderly man, could be his father. By the way, are you on visiting terms with his lordship?' Again Andrew indicated the pool.

'I wouldn't say visiting terms, Andrew. I bumped into him in the wood a few nights ago. I was dashing for you – father had set the bed alight.'

Andrew stopped. 'What happened?'

'Oh.' Rosamund went on to relate her father's lapse, just touching lightly on it and also on the outcome of her meeting with Michael Bradshaw. But when she told him about the child, being Andrew he said, 'Poor devil! He has his hands full, then. I'll drop in and see him sometime. Perhaps I can lend him something. You always want the loan of something when you're starting from scratch again.'

Rosamund said nothing that would deter him from visiting Michael Bradshaw. The man's attitude to another man might be different altogether. Anyway, Jennifer would likely give him all the reasons why he shouldn't visit their neighbour.

'How's Jennifer?' Andrew kept his eyes looking straight ahead as he asked this question, and Rosamund too looked ahead as she answered, 'I don't know how we'll find her now, but she looked rather beautiful when I left her a little over an hour ago. She had put on a new dress she had made – I think she was expecting a visitor.' She glanced at him sideways and met his eyes now, and they laughed together.

'Do you think absence has made the heart grow fonder?'

'I would say it has, but don't overdo it, Andrew. She's . . .' She looked at him fully now as she said, 'She's not very happy at present.'

He nodded at her, and in silence they continued the journey to the house.

As Rosamund led the way up the steps she called, 'Jennifer! Jennifer!' and when she received no answer she went into the sitting-room, only to find it empty, then into the kitchen, saying to Andrew as she passed him, 'Sit down a minute, I'll get her.' In the kitchen she found her father making a drink and asked immediately, 'Where's Jennifer?'

'I . . . I think she went up to bed. She was a bit disturbed – in the huff, I think.'

'Bed? But it's only nine and Andrew's here. Go and talk to him, Father, will you?'

'Yes, yes, I'll do that.'

Rosamund, leaving the kitchen, went straight upstairs and into Jennifer's room.

Jennifer indeed was in bed and pretending to be sound asleep. Standing over her, Rosamund shook her by the shoulder and said, 'Come on, you can't be asleep yet. Jennifer, listen to me. Andrew's here.'

'Well, he knows his way back home.'

'Don't be silly. Don't be a fool, Jennifer.' Rosamund was hissing at Jennifer now, and Jennifer, swinging herself round in the bed and sitting up, hissed back at her. 'A fool, am I? Yes, I know I am. I've sat there all night waiting for him. And last night, and the night before. I suppose Miss Hooper is otherwise engaged tonight or he wouldn't be here.'

'Look.' Rosamund was speaking patiently now,

softly and patiently. 'Get up, Jennifer, and get dressed. I'm telling you, don't let Andrew go away without seeing you. If you do you'll be sorry for it.'

'Me be sorry? Why should I be sorry? I've been sitting here like a Victorian miss just waiting for him to condescend to come and see me. Ask yourself, has he ever come this late before?'

'He's been working.'

'He's been working other nights but he could always find time to slip across. I'm not coming down, and you can tell him that.'

'You'll be sorry, I'm telling you. You'll be sorry.'

Jennifer's voice was calm now and had a cold ring to it. 'I'll be sorry? What are you trying to tell me – that he's after somebody else and if I'm not careful they'll hook him? Well, let them go ahead. I'm not running after Andrew Gordon now, or ever.'

On a burst of swift anger Rosamund leant towards her sister as she exclaimed, 'No! But you could run after Mr Bradshaw. Why, if you could do that, can't you pocket your pride and come downstairs for a minute?'

'You're an absolute pig. Go on, get out and leave me alone.'

As Rosamund turned to go to the door Jennifer's voice hit her saying, 'Now you can go and comfort dear, dear Andrew; you've always had a sneaking liking for him. Oh, I know.'

Rosamund, filled with anger, turned and for a moment glared at Jennifer. Then, clamping her lips together, she swung round and out of the room.

She had no need to speak when she entered the sitting-room. Andrew, who was talking to her father, broke off for a moment to look at her, and then resumed the conversation – the house was not so large that voices would not carry downstairs. She left the room without speaking and went into the kitchen.

Five minutes later Andrew opened the kitchen door and, putting in his head, said, 'I'll be off then Rosie.'

'I'm making some coffee, Andrew.'

'Not for me, thanks all the same.'

She walked to the front door with him, but she did not say anything.

Her father, embarrassed for Andrew, was standing behind them. 'Good night, Andrew. Try to look in tomorrow.'

Andrew made no reply to this but simply said, 'Good night, Henry.' Then, smiling somewhat sadly at Rosamund, he said, 'Good night, Rosie.'

'Good night, Andrew.' She did not add to her father's invitation, 'Come tomorrow.' That would be up to Andrew. He was a quiet man, but a stubborn one. Jennifer was a fool.

6

It was seven long hot days later, and the occupants of the mill, each in his own individual way, was tasting unhappiness.

Henry Morley, because he couldn't get at his craft. The materials had been sent for but had not yet arrived, and Henry had found that there was only one thing that had the power to ease his craving, and that was work, even if the finished article was only an imitation of the real thing.

Jennifer was unhappy with an unhappiness that she wouldn't have believed possible, and all over Andrew Gordon. The old stick-in-the-mud Andrew Gordon. Andrew had not been near the place since a week tonight and she could not sleep for thinking of him . . . and Janice Hooper. And she was not a little puzzled at her own reactions, for she was now also full of self-condemnation over her casual treatment of Andrew during the past two years.

And then there was Rosamund. Clifford's defection had hurt her deeply, and she was filled with vague fears that she couldn't pin down but which were all mixed up with the insecurity of their lives. Their security was really no worse than it had been for years, yet in a strange way she felt that it was threatened. Life at the moment seemed very empty and purposeless. This had been added to by the fact that for the last five days she hadn't seen the child. The last twice she had taken her back from the other side of the river she had delivered her to Maggie, for Michael Bradshaw had been nowhere in sight. She just couldn't guess at what method he had adopted to keep the child in, but whatever he had done it had apparently succeeded.

She was in her room, actually on her hands and knees polishing the uneven wooden floor, when Jennifer came in. Her sister's voice was stiff and slightly sarcastic as she said, 'You have a visitor.'

'Me?'

'Yes. I would straighten your hair, you look a sight.'

'Who is it?' Rosamund asked this question as she ran her fingers through the thick coppery tumbled mass of hair.

'Our neighbour, Mr Michael Bradshaw.' The name was given stress.

'Mr . . . What does he want? Did he say he wanted to see me?'

'Well, he certainly didn't want to see me.'

'Oh . . . oh.' Rosamund pulled off her apron, and, again pushing her hands through her hair, went rather self-consciously past Jennifer.

'I've put him in the sitting-room.'

Rosamund, glancing back at Jennifer, was on the point of saying, 'What do you think he can want?' but decided against it and hurried on down the stairs.

When she entered the sitting-room Michael Bradshaw was standing facing the door as if waiting for her. She closed the door behind her and stood with her back to it for a moment before advancing towards him. She did not give him any formal greeting, but, rubbing her hands together and on a nervous laugh, said, 'I'm very untidy, I was polishing the floor.'

As he looked at her hands she felt that she wanted to push them quickly behind her back.

Reverting to formality, she said, 'Won't you sit down?'

'No . . . No, I can't stay . . . Thank you. I've . . . I've come to ask you a favour.'

'Yes?' She was looking straight up at him. 'Is it the child?'

'Yes. She's been in bed for some days now with measles. Maggie does her best, but she's too old to keep running up and down stairs and I've . . . I've been tied for days and it can't go on, I've got to get the land cleared. I was wondering . . . if you could spare a few hours in the afternoon or' – he shook his head – 'any time to relieve me. It would just be a temporary measure. I'm looking out for someone to take charge of her.'

'I would be pleased to.' She had not hesitated for a second. 'My time's my own after lunch.'

'It would only be for a short time until she's over this.'

'That's all right. I wouldn't mind . . .'

'I mean that; I don't . . .' His voice had risen a tone now. 'I don't want to impose on your good nature. I am seriously looking for someone to take charge of her. The trouble is . . .' His chin jerked sideways and he went through the motion of pushing his cuff up and looking at his watch as he went on, 'I couldn't afford to engage someone professional, say a nurse – not at present, anyway. May I ask if you know of anyone who would fit this bill around here?' He was looking at her again. 'Someone not too old and yet not too young to be . . . to be afraid of her.'

She shook her head and thought for a moment before she said, 'I can't recall anyone to mind at present. The only young ones are the Brown children, and they are too young, they are still at school. I don't really know anyone in the villages, they are too far away.'

'Yes, that's the trouble, the isolation.'

'I can ask Andrew . . . Andrew Gordon. He comes in contact with quite a lot of people, he might know of someone.'

'Thank you. I'd better state the facts whilst I'm on. I'm offering three pounds a week part time, or as much time as they will do for that amount, and I can't say for how long I'll be able to pay that, but I must have someone for the next few weeks; and again I'm not under the impression that that sum is going to entice anyone out this far. Still, there it is.'

Every word he had said was indicative of the straits he was in, but no-one would ever have guessed it from the tone of his voice. It was brusque, even haughty, as if he were proposing to make breath-taking terms, yet, strangely, she was not now adversely affected by his manner. She had the desire at this moment to pull him off his iron guard by saying, 'Come on, what are we waiting for? Let's go!' Instead she said, 'Will you have time to stay and have a drink, we usually have it about now?'

'No, thank you, I must get back.'

He was moving towards the door now when he turned and, looking at her again, said, 'I've told you before that I think you are very kind. I can only repeat it.'

His words were so stiff, his manner so proper, she felt for a moment she would rather have him yelling at her, or being rude as he had been during their first two meetings. This kind of politeness she felt was entirely unnatural to him. He was the type of man who would laugh heartily, and curse heartily . . . and love grandly. She found herself blinking as she looked away from him. She said, 'You are really doing me a favour. We're . . . we're very slack at present and there's nothing to fill one's time.'

He was staring at her fixedly, and now he said in a more natural tone, 'You want me to believe that, so I will.'

'I'll be over shortly after lunch, about half-past one. Will that do?'

'Yes, that'll do.' His hand was on the knob of the door and he was about to open it when his glance swept the room as he commented, 'You have some lovely pieces here; you are to be congratulated. It's something different from what it was in the Talfords' day.'

She was looking towards the desk as she replied, 'Yes, they are lovely pieces and they've created in me a passion for antiques, but . . .' She paused and turned her eyes to him again as she said quietly, 'They are not ours, they don't belong to us.' She was strangely happy that she was able to say this; it gave her a deep satisfaction to couple their own lot with his, and so she added, 'Everything in this house belongs to my aunt. The property is my uncle's, and we can only stay here during my father's lifetime.' She gave a little sigh here and finished on a wry smile. 'My aunt will make short work of us once my father goes.'

He seemed unable to answer her for a moment, and then a remarkably softening effect swept over his face. It couldn't be called a smile, it could be attributed rather to a slackening of tension in the muscles. 'We could be practically what you call in the same boat,' he said.

She nodded at him and smiled broadly.

'I'll see you this afternoon, then?'

'Yes, this afternoon.'

They walked into the hall and out on to the steps, and there he turned and inclined his head towards her before running down the steps with a lightness of tread which was unusual in a man so heavily built.

Jennifer, coming out of the kitchen and joining her at the front door, looked to where he was stepping into the boat and she said, 'He wants you to go and see to the child, doesn't he?'

'Were you listening?'

'No. But what else would bring him here? He can turn on the charm when he wants anything. It's a wonder I didn't slam the door in his face . . . I almost did.'

Rosamund said nothing to this, and as she walked across the hall towards the stairs Jennifer was forced to ask, 'What are you going to do?'

Rosamund, looking over her shoulder, now said, 'Finish the floor.'

'Don't be facetious, you know what I mean?

'Well, since you've guessed so much, why can't you guess the rest?' Rosamund's voice was tart. 'If you want to know, I'm going over after lunch today and every day until the child is better – she's got measles.'

'Don't be a fool. You've never had it, you'll likely catch it.'

'All right, I'll catch it.' Rosamund was half-way up the stairs.

'It's contagious, you could bring it here.'

'Well then, I won't bother coming back until she's over it, you can see to things.'

'Rosie!'

'Oh, be quiet, Jennifer! And stop it.' Rosamund had turned and was looking down towards Jennifer, 'I'm tired of your grizzling and snapping. What you want to do is go over and see Andrew, swallow your pride and you'll feel better . . . and leave me alone. If I want to use my time by looking after the child, I'm quite at liberty to do so. My main work in this establishment is the cooking and chores, and I can get through those in the morning. Now . . . have you anything more to say before we close the matter finally?'

As Rosamund watched Jennifer's lips trembling she chided herself sternly for going for her, and she was about to apologise when Jennifer, jerking her head up, went hastily towards the workroom.

When she was once again on her knees polishing vigorously at the floor, she said to herself, It's the best thing that could have happened – it will take me out of the house; we're getting on each other's nerves.

For at least the sixth time Rosamund made an effort to leave the child's room, but was stopped yet once again by her sitting up in bed and giving vent to an almost blood-curdling sound of protest.

Rosamund, pressing the hot head back on to the pillow, said patiently, 'I'm coming back, I'm just going to make you a drink.' She made the motion of lifting a cup to her mouth and repeated, 'For Susie . . . a drink for Susie.' But again there was the scream, so ear-splitting this time that she closed her eyes and screwed up her face against the sound. Then from the doorway came Michael Bradshaw's voice.

'I'm sorry . . . I'm sorry you're having a time of it. I heard her over in the field.' He advanced swiftly to the bed and, bending over the child, said sternly, 'Susie! Listen!' He held up his finger before her eyes and again he said, 'Listen! She's-not-going-to-leave-you-just-going-downstairs.' He now pointed his finger rapidly towards the floor, then said quietly, 'I'll stay with her until you get the drink.'

Rosamund took an empty jug and glass from an upturned box that served as a table to the side of the camp bed and hurried out of the room and downstairs.

In the kitchen Maggie greeted her with, 'She won't leave you be, will she? God in heaven, but you're in for a time of it. An' I've had me share. She'd wear out the devil and all his imps, she would, that one. God help her . . . You want more lemon water? . . . Give us the jug here. If that man doesn't get a break he'll end up as fey as the wee folks themselves. It's beyond human endurance, it is that.'

Rosamund made no comment. She watched the old woman pour the boiling water on to the lemon, and when she was about to hand it to her Maggie paused in the operation, and, still holding on to the jug, she said, 'She wasn't half as bad as this across the water. Two years I've had her over there. Of course I had only three bits of rooms and she was never out of our sight, and she could go out of the cottage door and play on the front and still know you were near, but in this god-forsaken house of misery, upstairs must be like another world to her. I remember back to when I first came here, I was only a slip of a girl of thirteen and I was petrified at the whole set-up – the house, the land and everything.'

She relinquished the jug, and Rosamund, saying no more than 'Thanks, Maggie,' left the room.

So Maggie had been here when she was a girl. That's what she had meant by saying the other night that she had brought him up. He must have taken the child to her in Ireland. As she climbed the stairs again she had a mental picture of a man travelling from one country to another, a child by the hand in search of what? . . . Peace? A solution to his problem? Rest? She didn't know.

At the bedroom door he was waiting for her, and he said under his breath, 'If she falls off to sleep, leave her; don't stay in the room any longer than you've got to – it's very wearing.'

She smiled quietly at him. 'Don't worry, I don't mind. I don't find it wearing. When I do, I'll tell you.'

As her smile broadened, he turned his eyes away and then his head. Looking across the wide bare landing, he said quietly, 'If I believed in God I would be thinking at this moment that for every sore in life he provides a salve.' When he brought his eyes back to her again she could not look at him. She turned from him and went into the room, and as she stared towards the child, sitting up once more, she put her hand to her throat. She was disturbed and the disturbance was creating a feeling not quite new to her. Again she wanted to run, run until there was a great distance between her and the owner of this house.

She set the jug on the box, then sat down on the side of the bed, and the child, as if at last reassured, flung herself back on the pillow and, turning on her side, stuck her thumb into her mouth and sucked on it avidly.

It was nearly half an hour later when Rosamund eased herself cautiously from the bed. The child was sleeping now, breathing noisily through her mouth. Moving quietly to the window, she stood looking down on the tangle of growth that had once been the garden. To the right of her, in the distance she could see a gleam of silver appear where the sun was reflected for a second on a blade of steel. The effect occurred with rhythmic regularity. Michael Bradshaw was hacking at the stubble. Her eyes now swept the land around her, and she shook her head as if in dismay as she thought, How on earth will he ever get through this by hand? Taking in the land as far as the pond, and to the extent of Andrew's boundary on the south side, there must be at least a hundred acres. And when the winter came, what would he do? What would the three of them do in these cheerless, damp, high bare rooms? In this moment the problem was weighing on her as much as if it were her own.

She was turning from the window when the sight of a figure hurrying round the perimeter of the wood brought her eyes wide. That was her father. What could he be doing here? Had anything happened to Jennifer? She turned now swiftly but quietly and tiptoed past the bed and out of the room. She was still on her toes as she ran down the stairs. By the time she had crossed the wide hall and had opened the front door her father was nearing the end of the stone wall. She went down the drive towards the broken gate, and while she was still some distance from him she called, 'Is there anything wrong?'

'No, no, don't worry.' He came up to her breathing rather heavily. 'It's this.' He held out an air-mail letter. 'Mr Brown brought it over. He was in the village, in the post office, and Mrs Yorke, thinking it might be important, asked him if he would send one of his girls down with it. It had just come in. It . . . it's from America.

As her father nodded down at the envelope in her hand she said to herself, Yes, it's from America, and she turned it over without opening it. She knew the writing; it was from Clifford. He was already in America. Always she had opened Clifford's letters while sitting above the world on the platform at the top of the mill, but even if she had been at home she would not have kept this letter to read at the top of the mill. Moreover, she knew that her father was waiting for her to open it. As she looked at him he smiled and said softly, 'Perhaps he's writing to ask you to go out there.' Even as she said, 'Oh, Father,' she knew that something of the same thought had flashed through her own mind, and she also knew that it had brought her no excitement. She slit open the envelope and began to read, but she had not covered more than three lines when, jerking up her head, she gazed at her father and cried, 'Uncle Edward. Oh no! Oh, Uncle Edward.'

'What's happened?'

She looked down at the paper again. 'He . . . he had a heart attack almost as soon as he left the plane.' She was moaning aloud almost as she read the remainder of the short letter. When she had finished she handed it blindly to her father and turned away, cupping her face in her hands.

'My God! He was no age. Poor Edward. And he was a good man, was Edward . . . Why? . . . Oh.' He came to her side and put his arm around her shoulders. 'Don't take it like that. There, there, don't worry. You were fond of him, weren't you? And he was the only one who ever did me a good turn in my life. Now, now. Oh, don't give way like that.' He pulled her into his arms and patted her head. 'You'll only upset yourself . . . I wonder if they'll bring him back – for burial I mean. Not that we would be invited to go, not when she's in charge. Things will be different now.'

The fear of the difference making itself felt, he released her, and, patting her shoulder, said, 'Come on, away home.'

It was some moments before Rosamund could speak, and then, drying her face, she muttered, 'I . . . I'll have to go and tell him.'

'Go on then, I'll wait here for you.'

She went in the direction of the field and Michael Bradshaw, and some time before she reached him he straightened his back and looked towards her. Then, throwing his implement aside, he came quickly to her, saying, 'What is it? What has she done?'

Rosamund closed her eyes and shook her head swiftly. 'She . . . she's all right. My father has just been with a letter for me.' The tears sprang from her eyes again as she ended, 'My uncle, he's died . . . They . . . they had just reached America.'

He did not speak for some seconds, and then he offered no condolences but asked, 'Was he the one who bought the mill?'

She nodded her head.

'Is it legally your father's?'

'What . . . what d'you say?' She raised her face to him.

'You said the other night it was your father's for his life-time. Is it in black and white?'

'Yes. Yes, I think my uncle saw to that, but . . . but it doesn't matter. He was quite young, and so nice, so nice. He was good to me.'

'That wouldn't take . . .' He cut off his words roughly, then added, 'You're going home?'

'Yes, my father's waiting.'

'Will you . . . will you be going to see them – to the funeral? Are they likely to be bringing him back?'

'No, no, I don't suppose so.'

'Will you be across tomorrow?'

'Yes, I'll be across tomorrow.'

You could not blame him for worrying whether she would come and see to the child or not – he had not known her uncle – but at this moment she could not think of the child, or him, or anyone else. Her heart was sunk deep in the loss of the man she had coupled with God. 'Goodbye.'

'Goodbye.'

He did not accompany her across the field, neither did he resume his work, but he stood watching her.

It was evening now and they were in the sitting-room. They had all been together for the last three hours, drawn close, as it were, by the shock of this tragedy, for tragedy it was in more ways than one. On the outside of her grief Rosamund was keenly aware that such security as they had enjoyed would be almost nil in the future. Even if her uncle had made a statement in black and white regarding the mill, there was the vital matter of the allowance.

It was the allowance that was on all their minds, and it was Jennifer who at last brought it into the open. She asked quietly, 'Do you think the allowance will stop, Rosie?'

Rosamund let out a small sigh before she replied, 'It's nearly sure to.'

'Yes, as you say, it's nearly sure to.' Henry Morley moved his head in pathetic little jerks.

'She never knew anything about it, that's why it wasn't paid through the bank, always in registered notes. His life was difficult enough, poor blighter, without her knowing about that. But now . . .' He spread his hands wide and looked towards Rosamund.

Jennifer, too, was looking at her, and Rosamund had the desire to turn on them and cry, 'Why look to me? There are solutions for both of you.' She was tired, tired of thinking, of feeling responsible for them all. Jennifer, if she hadn't been a fool, could have been married to Andrew by now, and her father, with just that little bit more self-control, could have been in a decent job. She was sick of thinking for both of them. Again the feeling of youth had fled. She was no longer a girl of twenty-two. The future, their future, was piling the years on her once more, and she protested inside herself. Uncle Edward had been her one support both financially and morally, and now he was gone. She was sick of being leaned on. She herself wanted someone to lean on. Oh, she was tired of it all. Rising from her chair, she forced herself to say evenly, 'I'm going to bed.'

'Yes. We'll all go.'

When they followed her from the sitting-room like lambs, still wanting to keep close to her, to the one who had always managed to work things out, she again had the desire to run. This time, strangely enough, across the river, towards

Thornby House and . . . and . . . This last thought, checked at its telling point, carried her up the stairs to her room actually at a run, and, dropping on to the bed, she clutched tightly at the pillow before burying her face in it.

7

It seemed to Rosie that from the time she had heard of her uncle's death she had never been able to get away from the close proximity of Jennifer and her father. Even when she was over the river with the child so great was their need of her that she was drawn back to them almost against her will. Of late they had both become feverishly active in the work-room and always insisted on her being with them, although they knew that her skill was negligible in this line. She looked at them now, with their heads bent over the bench that her father had constructed roughly to the pattern of the first one he had worked at. There were the two semi-circular openings with the jeweller's 'skin' attached to them. This skin, originally a receptacle for small particles of dropped filings of silver and gold and small tools, was merely a decoration in this instance, for never had her father been able to work with a piece of real silver since coming here. The space between him and Jennifer was strewn with wires of different thicknesses, and a conglomeration of imitation stones, all glass, ranging from deep rubies to emeralds. There was a hacksaw, and a range of tin-snips and shears. Pliers, both round-nosed and flat. Top-nippers and side-nippers. In fact most of the tools required for the work of a craftsman in silver. There were pieces of flat metal, showing variations of patterns done by puncher and hammer. But there was no plating vat, no gas to supply a blow-pipe. There was no modern electric drill. Henry Morley supplied the heat he needed from a furnace he had concocted in the old chimney breast of the room. But even with the lack of modern tools he could have turned out some fine work had the materials been forthcoming, and, if he hadn't been working against time, the time it takes to create a work of art in silver. Yet even now he couldn't hurry over what he termed in his own mind the trash. And Rosamund, knowing this, pitied him.

Her job in the process was to select and set the stones, and give the final burnish to the finished article before placing it on its bed of cotton wool in the little gilt cardboard box. As she now looked at the row of such boxes on the table before her she had a strong desire to jerk her hand and sweep them into the air. Her mind had been in a turmoil all morning, and not only this morning, but for days past, and she knew now that she had come to the point of decision. One of them had to go out to work, and obviously it would have to be her. There was absolutely no money in this work. She flicked a box with her finger. This kind of thing had to be mass-produced before you could make a profit, or you had to find a market that would pay well for good imitations, and that's what they hadn't been able to do. Yesterday she had wanted to shout at them both, 'Let's drop this, it's like flogging a dead horse. We can go in the fields and help; the farmers want workers.' But there lay the rub. The farmers did want workers, but could Jennifer with her limp last out a day walking, bent double most of the time, up and down the rows of beet or celery, or potatoes? And could her father, who had used his fingers as an artist all his life, numb his touch by grappling with the earth, even if he had the stamina to stand up to farm work? No. Then there was only herself left, and there was a job waiting for her. On this last thought she seemed to be pulled to her feet, and so quick was her movement that both her father and Jennifer looked at her enquiringly.

Wetting her lips, she stared back at them before saying, 'I've had enough of this. You know it's no use, I'm going after a job.'

'A job?' Her father's mouth was puckered with the word.

'Yes, I said a job.'

'But you'll have three miles to walk to the bus unless you can get a lift.' Jennifer was standing now and she added, 'Unless he' – she jerked her head – 'lets you cross his land.'

'I won't be going to the bus. Mr Bradshaw is looking for someone to see to the child, and he's offering three pounds a week. He went into Hockwold yesterday to interview a woman he had heard about. If he hasn't got her I'm going to take it on.'

'Rosamund . . . No. And three pounds a week!'

'All right! . . . I know it's practically nothing, but tell me what we're going to do for money. Profit on this—' She now actually did swipe the boxes aside. 'We've sold so little recently it won't pay for bread and milk let alone anything else. Can you think of any other way? Or you, Father?' She was now glaring accusingly at her father, and as she saw his head droop she chided herself sternly, saying, Enough. Let up.

Her voice was quiet now as she went on, 'There's no disgrace in taking such a job. Why should either of you be so shocked? What's more, I'll be doing some good, I'll be useful. And it's only part-time.'

'You're always useful, Rosie.' Her father's words were scarcely above a whisper and they cut her to the heart. She watched him turn to his work again and Jennifer with him, then saying, 'It'll be all right, you'll see,' She went out of the room.

Going straight upstairs, she changed her dress, and, standing before the mirror, combed her hair.

Then, pulling open the top drawer of the dressing-table, she took out some cosmetics and quickly made up her face. When she had finished she stood peering at herself in the mirror, and she jerked her chin at her reflection as she said: 'You look worse. You look as old as you feel.' When she gave herself the answer: 'You couldn't possibly,' she did not smile, she couldn't see the funny side of anything today.

She pulled open another drawer to take out a handkerchief and, seeing a number of letters stacked neatly one on top of the other, slammed the drawer closed again. In this moment she hated Clifford. Not a solitary word had she heard from him since the air-mail letter. She did not know whether her uncle had been buried in America or if they had brought him home.

She had written to her aunt, as had her father, at the Buckinghamshire address, but neither had received a reply. This silence too had told on her nerves. The fear was growing in her daily that in some way her aunt would undo any legal claim her father had to the mill.

There was no sun this morning. It was still very warm but dull and grey, and the weather matched her spirits. She had just lowered herself into the ferry when she saw Michael Bradshaw coming out of the wood.

'Is something wrong?' she called, before she reached him. 'Is it Susie?'

'No, No.' He shook his head vigorously.

'Oh!' She was standing in front of him, looking up at him. He appeared different somehow. Then, her eyes sweeping over him, she realised why. He was dressed in a grey lounge suit and was wearing a white shirt with a dark tie. He looked spruce, smart, townish.

'Were you coming to the house?' he asked.

'Yes.' She lowered her eyes from his. 'I was going to ask you something. It was about the job.' She stopped. Her throat felt dry. Then, jerking her head up to him and looking him straight in the eye, she demanded: 'Did you get that girl?'

'The girl? Oh.' He shook his head. 'No, the whole prospect frightened her. Me, the fens, the child, the lot.'

She drew in a deep breath. 'If it's still going, can I have it?' she asked bluntly. When she saw the laughter in his eyes she added brusquely, 'It isn't funny.'

'No, it isn't funny.'

'We are on our beam ends, else I wouldn't ask. I don't want paying for looking after the child, but – but—'

'Rosie, Rosie' – he was speaking softly as if trying to penetrate through something – 'of course, the job's yours . . . *Yours*. You understand?'

It was the first time he had called her by her name, and she had the racing feeling inside again, wanting to run away, and yet . . . She stared at him.

He was entirely different this morning. It wasn't only that he was dressed for town, there was something quite unusual about him. She said, 'Do you want me to see to her until you come back?'

He nodded again. 'That was part of the idea, but I came over to see you, Rosie. I've got news I wanted to tell you. I had a letter this morning. The gods have at last seen fit to be kind to me.'

He straightened up, and he appeared more like the man to whom she had grown accustomed, as he said, 'It would seem that we can only benefit, have our desires fulfilled, at the bitter expense of others. And yet' – he gave a little smile now – 'I'm not going to be a hypocrite about this, Rosie. I didn't know him, I only met him once.'

The smile became a laugh and he shook his head. 'You don't know what I'm talking about, do you? Come on.'

He took her arm almost roughly, turning her about, as he said, 'I'd nearly forgotten. I've only an hour to get to Ely and catch the train. Do you think I'll manage it?'

She did not reply; she was slightly bewildered by his whole attitude and in some way apprehensive.

'Look, I'll give it to you briefly. Maggie will fill in the details, with many additions of her own, no doubt, before I get back. It's like this. My father had one brother older than himself and they fought like cat and dog – that's nothing to be surprised about, my father fought with everyone.

I sometimes think I've inherited some of his qualities.'

He turned his head and looked at her for confirmation of this, and when she gave it with a twinkle of her eye and a small nod of her head, he burst out laughing. He still had his hand on her arm as they walked along, Rosamund's amazement growing every minute.

'I only saw my uncle once,' he went on, 'and he liked me as little as my father liked me. Quite honestly, I don't believe I've thought of the old fellow half a dozen times over the years. I didn't even know he had married and had three children, two of them sons. This being so, it's understandable, I suppose, that he would make no provision against me inheriting. Who would have dreamed, least of all him, that they would all be wiped out together?'

Rosamund drew to a halt. 'They were all killed together?' Her face expressed her horror.

'Yes. He had a yacht apparently. I don't know the ins and outs of it yet. I only know that the eldest son and the mother were found in the lifeboat . . . and they died shortly after.'

'Oh, how terrible.'

'Yes. Yes, it is.' They were walking on again now. 'When you let yourself think about it, it is terrible, and I should, I suppose, put on an armour of mourning, but I'm not a hypocrite. I'm sorry, naturally, but that's as far as I can go.'

'When did it happen?'

'Five, six weeks ago, I think. In the mean-time, they have been trying to trace my aunt's people, only to discover that she hasn't any. Apparently she was my uncle's ward when he married her – I don't know the facts yet.'

They had reached the broken gate and he stopped. 'I'll have to run now. You go and have a natter with Maggie. You'll hear all the family history, she knows it better than I do myself. Oh, Rosie—'

She found her shoulders gripped in his two big hands, and he whispered softly, 'You're the sweetest thing this side of paradise, Rosie. Remind me to tell you that again when I get back.' He touched her on the chin with his finger, a playful, caressing touch, and then he was gone.

She watched him running with great strides across the fields towards the main road, her heart thumping so loudly that it reverberated through her ears. When she turned to walk up the drive she realised she had the fingers of her two hands pressed tightly across her lips.

Did he – did he mean . . .? But there had been nothing, nothing to lead up to it, except gratitude for her being able to handle the child so well. By the time she reached the front door she was telling herself not to be silly, he was excited over coming into this money. In his position, she would have been drunk with excitement. That's how he was feeling. You couldn't hold him to anything he said, even if you wanted to. The sweetest thing . . . the sweetest thing this side of paradise . . . It was just a saying. Translated, it could mean what had been said to her before, 'Rosie, you're the kindest person on earth'; 'Rosie, you are the most understanding being in the world'; 'Rosie, you are nice to know'. But did they ever say, 'Rosie, you are beautiful'; 'Rosie, I love you', 'Rosie, will you marry me?' No, no, they scuttered off to America and sent a weak apology for their absence. But Michael Bradshaw was no Clifford Monkton, there was no weakness in him. What he said he would mean. And yet . . . There were so many 'and yets'. There definitely were weaknesses in Michael Bradshaw and she had proof of them, and under the intoxication of an inheritance could he be held responsible for anything he might say?

She did not enter the house, but turned and looked across the fen. To the right of her for a space that covered about an acre, the earth was black. It had taken him over a month to clear that part. Suddenly she wished that things need not change, that he would go on clearing the land, by hand, that there would be no swift alteration. Jennifer's words came back to her. 'He's not the one to stay put, he would travel.'

Yes, when he had the money he would certainly travel. He hated the fens, he had said so. She was filled now with a strange sadness. She would never, she knew, love any part of the earth as she did the fens. This was her land. She had adopted it with the same tenacity as would a nature-starved woman take a child into her life. He hated the fens and she loved them. He would go and she would stay.

The child had played quietly, but always in sight of Rosamund until shortly after two o'clock, when she fell asleep, and Rosamund took advantage of this to run back to the mill and tell her father and Jennifer that she would be staying up at the house until Michael Bradshaw returned. She did not pass on anything that he had told her. Her reticence on this occasion centred around Jennifer. If she knew the Fen Tiger was now a man of means it would not increase her liking for him but, under the present circumstances, would likely make her feel that she had been deprived yet once again of something worth while. What she did tell them was that she had got the job, and to this neither of them said a word.

It was shortly before Rosamund was going to put Susie to bed that she heard her scream, and, rushing to the front door, she saw the child standing beyond the broken gate looking towards the wood. Her mouth was wide, and her body rigid.

'Susie! Susie! Stop it! Stop it! Do you hear? Stop it this minute!' Holding the child by the shoulders, Rosamund saw the beads of perspiration standing on the bony forehead. 'What is it? What is it, my dear?' She looked toward the wood, then back to the child again. 'There's nothing there.'

Maggie came running down the path now, crying, 'Wouldn't that curdle your blood? That's the third time she's done that this week. What is it, child?' Maggie was bending over her now. 'What are you seeing? There's nothing there. Glory be to God, there's not a thing to be seen for miles except those few trees. What is it at all?'

The child was now clinging to Rosamund, her arms around her thighs, her head buried in her waist. 'Something's frightened her,' Rosamund said. 'Perhaps it was an animal. Is she afraid of cattle?'

'Not a bit, not a bit. She would go and lie down with the cows themselves. But I'm tellin' you, this is the third time she's done it this week, and it's a different screaming.'

'When she's been looking towards the wood?'

'No, no. She was sitting in the kitchen one evening having her supper, just about this time, before she was going up to bed. And she let out such a screech that, I'm tellin' you here and now, me heart nearly stopped dead in me.'

'There, there, it's all over.' Rosamund disengaged the child's arms from her, then led her up the drive and into the house. It took much longer tonight to get her off to sleep, and the nightjar was calling from the wood and the swallows flying low in the direction of the river when Rosamund came downstairs again. The sun had gone down, and already the hall was dim.

'You've had a time of it, then,' Maggie greeted her when she entered the kitchen, 'though you can handle her better than anyone I've seen, including himself. Which reminds me, it's black dark it's going to be afore he gets here and not a torch on him. God protect him, he'll end up in one of them ditches, the like of such I've never seen, and me that's lived in the bog country. I actually saw a man swallowed up in me youth, and yet the bog didn't put the fear of God in me like them ditches.'

'I've no love for them either, Maggie. Although I like the fens, I wish they didn't have to have dykes. But, you know, that's what makes the fens, the dykes. But I shouldn't worry about Mr Bradshaw.'

'No, no. But, all the same, I wonder what's keeping him. Do you think he'll go into the village and see Mr Gerald? For he said this morning it would be a gliff he would be gettin' when he heard the news. Do you like Mr Gerald?'

Maggie looked at Rosamund with her head on one side.

'Yes, yes. He's very nice, very pleasant.'

'Well, it may be news to you or not, but he thinks the same of you, and a bit more from the way he talks. He tells me he went swimming with you one night a while back.'

'No, no.' Rosamund turned quickly to the old woman. 'No, he just happened to be passing when I was swimming and I sat talking to him for a while on the bank.'

'Ah, well, I must have got it wrong, but he's been down there a number of times and I thought he was along with you.'

'No, no, he wasn't with me, Maggie.'

Rosamund had met Gerald Gibson a number of times in the past few weeks and they had talked and laughed quite a bit, but for a reason she wouldn't allow herself to go into she had made sure that when she went swimming in the pond he wasn't there. At their second meeting she had gathered that Mr Gerald, as Maggie called him, was a bit of a philanderer, that he wanted to flirt, without being taken seriously. She liked him up to a point and that was all.

Maggie began lighting the lamp and Rosamund said, 'I don't suppose Mr Bradshaw will be long now, and as Susie hasn't wakened up I think I'll be making my way home.'

'Won't you wait and let him take you to the river? I wouldn't for the life of me cross that land in the dark.'

'It isn't quite dark yet.'

'Well, will you have one last look across the field for me and see if he's comin', for I won't feel at rest until he's here?'

'Yes, I'll do that.' Rosamund smiled reassuringly at the old woman and went out into the hall.

She had just let the green baize door swing to behind her when her hand, flying to her throat, stifled a scream. Across the dimness of the hall, beyond the great bare window, stood a woman's figure, or – she closed her eyes for a second – *had* stood, for the figure was no longer there.

One hand still gripping her throat, the other hand tightly holding the front of her dress, and, righteous anger overcoming her shock, Rosamund made her way to the front door. Why couldn't Jennifer have rung the bell instead of sneaking about the place like that? She pulled open the door, and when she stepped outside and saw no-one she stood for a moment slightly perplexed.

'Jennifer, Jennifer!' she called.

When there was no reply, she walked to the end of the house and in the direction of the back door. As she reached it, Maggie called from the kitchen, 'It that you, Miss Rosie?'

'Yes, yes, it's me, Maggie. I – I was just walking round.'

'Is he not to be seen then?'

'No, not yet. I'll go and have another look.' She hurried now, almost at a run, to the front

449

of the house again, then round to the buildings at the back, and here, keeping her voice down, she called again, 'Jennifer! Jennifer!'

She had passed the front of the house once more and was half-way down the drive when she stopped. Looking towards the wood, she saw the scurrying, dim shape of Jennifer disappearing into it.

'Well! What on earth was she up to, sneaking around? What did she expect to see?' Rosamund muttered to herself, her anger was rising still further when it was checked by the thought: But she's afraid of the dark. She wouldn't come out on the fens at this time of night . . . But she had. The face that had looked through the window was Jennifer's – she knew her sister. All this business of being afraid of the dark, afraid of the fens at night. Just wait till she saw her . . .

She made her way quickly to the kitchen again, and, taking her coat from the back of the door, she said, 'I'll be away now, Maggie. I'll see you in the morning.'

'I wish you could stay until he comes. He'll have such news to tell.'

'I'll hear it all tomorrow.'

'Yes, you will, and let me say it's glad I am that you're comin' to look after the child.'

'Thank you, Maggie. Good night.'

'Good night, me dear. Good night and God look after ye across that wild land.'

'You're stark staring mad. I tell you I've never been near the house.'

'Don't lie to me, Jennifer. Look. Look at those shoes, they've got mud on them. You wouldn't get that unless you'd been down to the water.'

'Well, I was down at the water, I was looking at the boat.'

Rosamund's eyes narrowed as she looked at her sister, and she said slowly, 'The boat was at the far side, remember? Naturally, when I went across I left it there. A few minutes ago it was on this side, I had to pull it over.'

'All right! All right! I did use the boat. I did cross the river, if you want to know. But I didn't go to the house. I went—" Jennifer turned her head away. 'I took the short-cut and went towards Andrew's.'

Rosamund blinked for a moment before she asked quietly, 'Did you see Andrew?'

'No, I didn't go that far; I only got to the pond and then I turned back.'

'And you came on to the house and had a look round.'

'I didn't! I didn't!' Jennifer had swung round. 'I tell you I never went near the house.'

'I don't believe you. I saw you peering in at the window.'

'You're mad. What would I want, peering in at the window?'

'That's what I'd like to know. You've been curious these past weeks because I've never mentioned anything about him, and it's set you wondering, hasn't it?'

The sitting-room door opened at this point and Henry Morley entered. 'What's happening now?' he asked wearily.

'She's gone stark, staring mad, Father. She's accusing me of going over to the house and spying on her and that individual over there.'

'I saw her looking through the window, Father.'

'You did nothing of the sort, I've never been near the place.'

'You were over the river, Jennifer,' Henry stated, and Jennifer, lowering her head, said almost desperately, 'Yes, yes. I was over the river; I've just told her why. I went as far as the pond and I came back. I – I intended going to Andrew's, but I didn't'

'Oh! Oh!' The second exclamation was a little louder. It said that Henry believed his daughter, and now he looked at Rosamund, adding: 'You could have been mistaken, Rosie. Perhaps it was the old woman you saw.'

'Oh, it doesn't matter, it doesn't matter.' Rosamund turned from them abruptly and went up the stairs to her room.

She was too angry to go to bed. She did not relish being tossed and turned by the turmoil of her thinking. So she sat by the window, looking out across the dark land.

She had not been sitting long before she heard her father and Jennifer coming upstairs, and when their doors had closed on them she gave a deep sigh and some of the tension left her body.

She had been sitting at the window for over half an hour when the clock on the landing struck eleven. She shivered, and, reaching out, she pulled a rug from the foot of the bed, and wrapped it round her.

The moon had come out from behind the clouds, and as the far side of the river bank became visible to her, so did the figure standing on the landing stage. The sight of him brought her to her feet, but she remained still. The house was in shadow, and he would not be able to see her. Would he come across and knock them up? She had a sudden almost passionate longing for him to do just that. But the minutes passed and he made no move from the landing.

She turned her head and looked towards her bedroom door. If she tried to go out quietly they were bound to hear. But if she went downstairs ordinarily, as if she was going to the kitchen, they would take no notice. It wouldn't be the first time she had gone downstairs to make herself a drink when she couldn't sleep.

Keeping the rug around her, she went, not too quietly, out of the room and down the stairs. She went through the kitchen, unlocked the back door and moved cautiously round the side of the house, across the garden, and to the boat landing.

He was still standing on the far landing and he raised his hand to her. She gave him no return wave, but dropped quietly into the ferry. Slowly, evenly, hand over hand, she drew the boat across the water, making scarcely a ripple, and no sound at all from the heavy chain.

His hands were ready waiting for her when she reached the far bank, and when he pulled her up on to the landing she found she was trembling so much that she couldn't even whisper a greeting.

'I willed you to come out,' he said very quietly.

'I can't stay long,' Rosamund stammered. 'I just wanted to know how you had got on.'

'You're coming back to the house, I've got so much to tell you; but, more important still, I've brought some food back, real food: chicken, ham, wine. I didn't think you'd be gone. I got back as soon as I could.'

'But it's so late.'

'Late? It's just after eleven. And what does it matter, anyway?'

Yes, what did it matter? She turned and he took her arm as he had done earlier in the day, almost lifting her along the path. The excitement that was filling him found its way to her and she asked eagerly, 'Was it very good news?'

'Ah, Rosie!' Her arm was pulled tightly against his side. 'Very good news, indeed. I can't get used to it yet, but I soon will; oh yes, I soon will. I am a factory owner, Rosie. What do you think of that? And not just one factory. I have a tannery, a bag factory, a shoe factory, shares in chemicals and heaven knows what else, and at this moment reposing in a bank in Cambridge is an advance of twenty thousand pounds. Think of it, Rosie – twenty thousand pounds.' She was pulled to a stop.

They had come to the edge of the wood now. His face was in shadow as he bent above her, and she could not see the expression in his eyes, but the tone of his voice caused her heart to race as he asked, 'Who do you think I wanted with me in London today?'

She did not answer.

'When I came out of that solicitor's office and stood in the street like someone dazed, the first thought that came to my mind was: I can get away. The house could be furnished, the roof repaired, the land tilled, and it could all be done while I, Michael Bradshaw, was taking a long, long holiday abroad. I've always wanted money to enable me to travel. That is, until I came back to this God-forsaken, blood-sucking, heart-holding land. And then I thought . . . I wish Rosie was here . . . Don't be afraid.'

'I'm . . . I'm not afraid.'

'Well, don't move away from me.'

'I . . . I . . .'

'Look! Come on, let's eat and celebrate. Here, give me your hand!' He grabbed her hand and the next minute she was flying over the moonlit fields towards the broken gate and the drive. And, bubbling inside her there was laughter and excitement – and such happiness that she had never experienced before, did not know it was in her to experience. She was being almost choked by a feeling that was new, and even a little terrifying. She had said a moment earlier that she wasn't afraid. But she was afraid, she was afraid of him. Of his strength, his compellingness, his assertiveness that swept everything before it. But she was gasping and laughing out loud when he drew her to a halt at the front door. It was wide open, and the bare hall was streaked with moonlight. Still at a trot he led her across the hall and into the kitchen. The lamp was lit, and the table was set for a meal. He looked about him, saying, 'Maggie must have gone up to bed already. She was tired, but she's tucked in, I see.' He pointed to the roast chicken and the ham. Then, turning to Rosamund he pulled her towards a chair, and, whipping the rug from her shoulders, said, 'Sit yourself down there. We'll eat first and talk afterwards, eh?'

She watched him go to the sink and wash his hands before coming to the table. She watched him slice the ham and carve up the chicken. There were two bottles of wine on the table, and as he picked up one and held it to the light he cast his eyes on her and said, 'Champagne is overrated, you can't better a good Auslese.' His face was alight now with laughter, odd, satirical laughter, as he looked towards the delf rack and said, 'Wine in teacups, thick ones at that – I never thought about the glasses. I imagined I had thought about everything, at least in the food line.' As he poured the wine into the cups he went on, 'You know, Rosie, I could have bought anything today – clothes for the child, a rig-out for Maggie, and furs' – he flicked his eyes down to her – 'real ones, and diamonds to go with them, but what did I think of? Food. Good food. A square meal. It's a long, long time since I ate a proper meal. But now we can have chickens and steaks, until we're sick of the sight of them.'

She watched him place the cups on the table, then, sweeping one arm towards her with a grandiose movement, he said, 'Supper is ready. Allow me, madam.'

One moment she was looking up at him with laughter quivering on her lips, the next she was struggling vainly to quell the choking feeling in her throat, for the lump that had suddenly lodged itself there threatened to stop her breathing. The torrent of tears washed over her with the force of a breaker, and her head was bowed under it almost to her knees as she tried to stifle her sobs with her hands across her mouth.

'Rosie! Rosie! God, don't cry like that! What is it? What have I done, what have I said? Rosie . . .' He was kneeling by her side. 'What is it? Look at me. Tell me what it is.'

Her face was now cupped in his hands, but she could see him only faintly through the blur of her tears. She could not tell him what had made her cry, she did not really know herself. The pathos in his attitude towards food perhaps. The elemental man in him who had put first things first. The boyishness so strong in the man. His strange tenderness. The derisiveness that touched everything he said. So many things had made her cry.

'Rosie . . .' He was drying her eyes and his voice was low. 'Look at me, straight in the eyes.'

Her body was still shaking with her emotions as she did as he asked.

'Will you marry me, Rosie?

His eyes were deep and dark and held hers fast; there was no way of turning from them even if she had wanted to. She almost felt herself being drawn into their depths.

When she remained mute he said impatiently, 'I'm not asking you to love me. We won't talk about love; that is something to be slopped over by the very young, and to be remembered by the old. We are in between the two and I'm past romance. But I have money now, enough to support a wife, as a wife should be supported.' The derisiveness was back in his tone again, and as she gulped and shook her head he put in, 'Oh, I know money doesn't mean all that to you, Rosie, but it's a great compensation . . . There is the child.'

'Don't . . . Don't put it like that. I would have looked after the . . . the child if you hadn't a p-penny.'

'Yes. Yes, I know that.' His voice was deep and quiet as he spoke now, and without the slightest trace of mockery, 'Yes, I know, because from the moment I saw you with her at the front door, your face full of compassion, I thought, Here is someone with a heart. And from that moment you had an effect upon me, you disturbed me greatly, filled me with restlessness whenever I couldn't see you, or know that you were near. I became as bad as the child for you. I wished at times I was like the child and you would take my hand and lead me . . . Perhaps it is a mother I want.'

'Michael, don't.' She was in his arms, her head buried in his neck, repeating his name again and again, 'Michael, Michael.'

'You will marry me, then?'

'Oh yes; yes.'

'You don't love me but you will marry me.' Was there that cold laughter in his voice again?

'But I do . . . I do love you.'

And she knew that she did. She knew that this was love. That this pain, this deep ache, this unsatisfied want, was love. She knew that this was what she had been waiting for, for days, perhaps weeks. When there was no other prospect but of living in this bare, empty-sounding house, she knew now that she had wanted to do just that so as to be near him . . . What about Clifford? She could almost laugh aloud now at the thought of Clifford and her feeling for him. She would have to confess somewhat shamefacedly that security had been the main attraction where Clifford was concerned. Keeping the mill as a home for them all had been the star on that particular horizon. That, too, had been the cause of her recurring dream. But this, this feeling, this strange disturbing want – this was love.

He was holding her face once more in his hands. It was below his own now, and when quietly his lips touched hers she put her arms about his neck and with all her strength she held him to her.

When at last he released her she was overcome with a sudden shyness, and she would have turned from him to the table had he not pulled her round to face him again.

'We'll make it soon, Rosie. Special licence.'

She nodded, unable to speak.

'It could be all fixed up in a week.'

'A week?' Now her eyebrows went up just the slightest. 'But they . . . I mean my father and Jennifer . . . they'll have to get used to the idea. I'm not quite sure whether they will like it at all; they've somehow got used to being looked after.'

'Rosie.' He pulled her down to the chair again, and, squatting on his heels before her and gripping her hands in his, he said urgently, 'Don't tell them. Don't tell anyone. Let's do it on the quiet.'

'But . . . but what'll they think?'

'Does it matter what they think, what anybody thinks? Rosie . . .' He released one hand and, putting it up to her face, stroked her cheek. 'Do this for me, will you? You see, I've got a fear on me. Yes . . .' He closed his eyes for a moment and nodded his head. 'As Maggie would say, I've a fear on me. It might appear that I'm afraid of nothing or no-one, but I am. All my life I have found that anything I've wanted, and valued, has been taken from me, or spoiled in some way . . .'

'But I won't . . . I won't, Michael. I'll . . .'

'I know, Rosie, I know.' He patted her cheek as if she were the child. 'I know I can trust you, but I can't trust fate. You see, this feeling goes a long way back with me, right to my childhood in this very house.' He raised his eyes to the ceiling. 'Some things stand out in my mind. The first was the boat. I always wanted a boat of my own. My father had enough money to buy me ten boats in those days. But no, he wouldn't hear of me having a boat, so, with the help of my mother, I saved up and bought one. I kept it at the end of the Cut. I kept it for one day at the end of the Cut. The second morning when I went to see it, it was a burnt-out shell. This kind of thing happened

461

again and again. I wanted to go in for medicine, but all my father could think of was the land and the cheapest way to work it. I was just old enough to get in at the tail-end of the war, and when I was demobbed and came back here I knew I couldn't stick it. Then my mother died and left me the little that she had, and I made the break and started my studies in London. There was nothing I wanted more in life than to become a doctor, and not just a doctor, a surgeon . . . In my second year up there I met Susie's mother.' He turned his eyes away from Rosamund at this point, and his voice went deeper into his throat as he said, 'I look back now and say to myself, "You of all people should have been able to resist fascination. You of all people should have been able to discern what lay behind beautiful shells." But apparently I couldn't, for I went down like corn under the blade.' He looked at Rosamund again. 'I'm making no excuses for myself. Everything was forgotten, I went mad. She had a little money, and with what I had left it was enough to keep us on the move abroad for a time, but long before the child was born the money was finished, and so was I. I had woken up as if from a drugged dream. Yet life was bearable in some ways, until Susan came . . . From the minute that child drew breath her mother hated her. It became so intense that it turned her brain before she died . . .' He paused and drew in a long breath before adding, 'She was drowned . . .'

After a silence that seemed to Rosamund impossible to penetrate, he went on, 'It was strange, but the more she hated the child the more I loved her – the child I mean, not the mother. In the end I hated Camilla with a hatred that equalled her own for the child. It was odd, but I'd always craved for children, and I remember thinking that I would put up with Camilla if she gave me a family . . . particularly daughters.' He smiled sadly. 'I had a fancy for daughters. The psychological answer there is that I loved my mother and hated my father. Well, I got a daughter as you know, Rosie.' He was looking at her again. 'Do you see what I mean about fate? I wish . . . I get my wish, but fate gives it a twist.' He was gripping her hands once more. 'It mustn't happen again, Rosie, you understand? . . . It mustn't happen again. Your father will put up all kinds of objections, he will point out Susie to you . . .'

'No, no, he won't; he understands . . .'

He was shaking his head vigorously now. 'Then there's your sister, she has no love for me. My manner with her was very cursory at our first meeting – you will know all about that, I suppose. She'll put her spoke in . . .'

She too was shaking her head as she checked his rapid flow, saying, 'Listen, listen, Michael. Nobody will stop me doing what I want. I want . . . I want to marry you, Michael, but . . . All right, all right.' The last words were wrenched from her by the look in the depths of his eyes, and it was she now who put out her hand and touched his cheek. 'It will be as you say – I'll tell no-one.'

He brought her hand around to his mouth and pressed his lips to the palm. A second later, pulling her to her feet again, he cried jovially, 'Let's drink to us.' But when with the cup in his hand he clinked hers, he said softly and with deep feeling, 'No, not to us; to Rosie . . . Mrs Michael Bradshaw.'

She was in her room once more, undressing as if she was still in a dream, the dream of the past two hours, when her bedroom door was thrust open and Jennifer, a candle in her hand, her face tight and almost vicious in its expression, came into the room. Rosamund looked at her sister for some time, waiting for her to speak, and when she did her words were like drops of acid.

'No wonder you were afraid of being spied upon; your guilty conscience had every right to make you furious.'

'All right! All right! You know where I've been, so what about it?' Although Rosamund's head was up and her chin high, her voice was quiet, but not so Jennifer's as she went on:

'Sneaking out of the house, and creeping across the river without a sound and him waiting for you. You needn't deny it.'

'Who's denying it?'

'You're mad. He can't afford to furnish the house let alone employ anyone. Three pounds a week . . . Huh! What is he expecting for his three pounds, I wonder?'

The cry that escaped Rosamund checked Jennifer's vitriolic words, and she turned her head away from the onslaught of Rosamund's tongue. Rosamund's anger and indignation was so great that she hardly knew what she was saying herself, but as her father appeared behind Jennifer in the doorway she was crying, 'What you're afraid of is being left here to see to Father, and that's what'll happen to you, just that.'

'What is it? What on earth is it? What is the matter with you, anyway?' Henry Morley pushed past Jennifer and stood between them.

'I've been out, Father; I've just come back. I've been having supper with Mr Bradshaw, Michael Bradshaw. Jennifer saw me go out and she likely saw me come back.'

'Yes . . . yes, I did . . . Kissing on the bank, and you haven't known him five minutes . . . and supposed to hate his guts.'

'I never said I hated his guts, not once, never . . . And yes, we were kissing on the bank. Is there anything wrong in that?' She was looking at her father now, and, apparently, if not finding it wrong, Henry Morley was finding it rather mystifying, for his voice was puzzled as he asked, 'You and him . . . Bradshaw? Oh, Rosie! And . . . and there's the child.'

'I know there's the child. I've always known there's the child, Father.'

'All right! All right, Rosie, don't shout at me. I'm not saying anything against the child. I pity it. But him . . . Bradshaw . . . What about Clifford?'

'Yes, what about Clifford, Father? I can tell you now that the only thing I wanted Clifford for was to secure this house for us all. But with Michael it's different. It was different from the beginning. I knew he had nothing. I knew he'd be no means of security. Perhaps for me because I wanted very little . . . but not with both of you added on.' She wagged her hand between them. 'It's yourselves you've thought of all along, what's going to happen to you. I was just the one who solved the problems. I've felt old before my time solving your problems. I was the go-between with Uncle Edward – Uncle Edward, who could make things happen because he had money. I liked Uncle Edward for himself, but I hated being dependent on him . . .' She just stopped herself in time from finishing, 'I could earn a living anywhere.'

'Your past problems will be nothing to your future ones.' Jennifer was about to turn away on this last cutting remark when she was stopped by Rosamund saying very quietly, 'There you are mistaken. Why he wanted to see me tonight . . .

why he came to the ferry, was to tell me the result of his visit to London. He's no longer without money. He's rich. Do you hear? Rich. He can do anything he wants.' She looked directly at Jennifer now as she said, 'He can travel.' And immediately she reproached herself for her cattiness, for Jennifer's face tightened even more. She was about to make some retort when her Father said, 'Are you serious about this man, Rosie?'

Rosie wanted to cry at them both, 'Yes, yes, I am serious. We're going to be married,' but the promise she had made checked her, and for answer she said, 'He has offered me a good post.'

'Huh!'

Her Father and Jennifer, both with their backs to her, were on the landing now and the 'huh!' coming from Jennifer angered Rosamund so much that she cried at them, 'And tomorrow morning when you get up I'll be gone.'

'What!'

They had both swung round, the same expression threaded across their faces, and the apprehension that Rosamund saw there made her want to run to them, take their hands and cry, 'Listen, listen to my wonderful news, we're all going to be all right.' But the time was not now, so, dropping her head, she modified her threat by adding, 'I'm going into Cambridge to help . . . help choose some furniture.' Her eyes too were cast down as she made this admission, but when neither of them spoke she added sharply and with a touch of bitterness, 'But don't worry, it'll be all right and proper, we're taking the child with us. That should set your fears at rest.'

When in the dim flickering candlelight she saw them go their separate ways across the landing, she went quickly to her door and closed it, and, standing with her back to it, her hands joined tightly together, she whispered aloud, 'Oh why, oh why, does it have to be like this? They're spoiling it for me.' It was just as Michael had said, if they knew she was going to be married they'd put all kinds of obstacles in her way. Or would they, now that they knew he was rich? Oh! Why was she thinking like this? It made her feel horrible.

Pulling herself from the door and undressing quickly, she got into bed, and in a few minutes her mind had left them – she made it leave them. Or were her thoughts actually lifted from her and taken over the fenlands to the bare house? He had said, 'I willed you to come out', and now it was as if her father and Jennifer did not exist. She was with him again in the kitchen, hearing him say, 'Will you marry me, Rosie?' He had not said, 'I love you, Rosie.' He had been honest and admitted he was past silly romance. But he would love her, she would make him. Even now he must love her a little, but, being of the nature he was, would not admit it. How else could he have asked her to be his wife?

She was dropping off to sleep when, the control of her thoughts slackening, the answer was flung at her as she heard his voice saying as it had done only a short while ago, 'Perhaps it's a mother I want.'

In marrying her he would not only be getting a nurse for Susan, but a mother for the little boy in him. The selfish, egotistical, demanding little boy.

8

Rosamund seemed to be swimming in a sea of uncertain happiness. When at times she was overcome by fear, as if suddenly finding herself out of her depth, she would reassure herself and say, 'Just go steadily on, it'll all come right.' She had the conviction that, once married to Michael, everything would settle into place, and she longed for the next few days to pass. Her marriage, when dwelt upon, would cause her to shiver with a mixture of delight, apprehension, and longing. But generally there was little time now to sit down and think quietly, for Michael, in a spate of spending, was transforming Thornby House. In the midst of all the bustle she would sometimes stop and try to remember what the house was like a week ago. The desolation, the emptiness, the coldness of it. Now all that was changed. Knocking and hammering seemed to come from its every corner. There seemed to be painters and paper-hangers everywhere inside the house. And outside there were now four men working on the land, and only yesterday a new machine had arrived. Moreover, there was a car turning up its long snooty nose at being housed in the old barn. Overall there was a feeling of excitement pervading the atmosphere, and rather oddly an air of happiness too. The men whistled at their work. Maggie shouted and chaffed with everyone within radius. Everybody seemed happy and natural, everyone except Michael, and herself at times, when she realised she was playing a part, the essential of which was the deception of her father and Jennifer.

Michael never touched her, not even her hand, in front of others. Not until last thing at night when he was taking her back to the river in the dark did he come closer than an arm's length of her. It was strange, she thought at times, that his manner was more stiff now than it had been before he asked her to marry him. She had hinted that she would like him to come across the river and see her father, as if on an ordinary visit, but he had not taken to this suggestion either. When they were married, yes, but not before, not before.

The men, making a concerted effort in the house, had yesterday finished one room, and when at noon today some of the furniture had arrived he had asked her to see to the arranging of it. He had spoken as if she had not seen the stuff before, as if every single piece but one had not been her choice. The workmen had been present, and he had addressed her as Miss Morley, saying, 'Miss Morley will show you where it has to go.' Miss Morley knows this, Miss Morley knows that. The only thing he himself had directed was the moving of the small baby grand. When, the piano assembled, he had run a practised hand over the keys, it had come to her that there were lots of things about this man she did not know. Evidently he played and liked playing the piano.

It was long past five o'clock, but the men were still working, and as Rosie listened to the hammering and their distant voices she thought, and somewhat sadly at this point, that it was amazing what money could do. This time last week there hadn't been enough food in the house, and now men were working overtime. In a few minutes a lorry would come, and they would all pile into it and be taken to the main road. The money had even made a rough road across two fields to allow passage for the vehicles. Not only that, it had spanned the dyke with great planks of wood, a temporary affair while the bridge was being repaired. Money was like magic, like oil, it made the wheels turn, oh, so easily. She mustn't be cynical about money, she told herself, but give it the respect due to it, that and no more.

The child came running with its unwieldly gait across the hall, crying, 'Bov. Bov.' This strange syllable was Susie's name now for Rosamund. All the child's utterances were staccato and short sounding, but 'Bov' was distinctly meant for Rosamund, and she always answered to it.

'Oh, what have you got there? Oh, aren't they lovely!' She bent down and took the extended flowers from the child's hand. They were a mixture of rag-wort, dandelion, purple grass and wild foxgloves.

'Bov.'

'Yes, dear, thank you very much. We must put them in water. Come along.'

Today the child seemed happy and contented, but last night she'd had another of her screaming fits – one so intense that it had completely exhausted her. It had taken place when she was once again in sight of the wood. It was as if she was always seeing something in the wood. Yet she had these bouts at other times too. The evening they were returning from Cambridge she had been walking between them, a hand in each of theirs, when she had pulled herself to a stop, became rigid for a moment while she appeared to sniff the air, then let out a most blood-curdling scream. Although at the time they were within their own boundary they were not within sight of the house, or the wood.

When Rosamund had seen Jennifer looking through the window that evening she had, for a time, blamed her for the child's hysterics. It was evident that Susie had taken a dislike to Jennifer and the sight of her could evoke the scream. But Rosamund had now to discard this explanation. The child screamed when there was no-one to be seen, no stranger. Yet how could they say that there was no-one to be seen. She definitely was seeing someone or something. It was as if she smelt a presence. This eerie thought made Rosamund shudder, and yet the child did not have that effect on her. Even when she had first looked at the distorted face she had not shuddered. And now she saw the child as part of Michael and her compassion was threaded with love. But she shuddered at whatever it was that caused Susie to emit that terrible scream.

They had almost reached the kitchen when a voice from the doorway brought them round.

'Well, well, well, what d'you know?'

She laughed as she greeted Gerald Gibson, and cried childishly to him, 'Surprise! Surprise!'

As he came up to her he cocked his head on one side, and, looking at her through narrowed lids, he repeated, 'Surprise? Surprise indeed. I can't get over it. Mike's just been telling me. I didn't know what had hit the place when I saw all the bustle, and at this time of night. And you . . . have you come into a fortune too? You look positively glamorous!'

'What, in this?' She lifted one end of her overall up, then, shaking her head at him, she added, 'It would take a lot of money to make me look glamorous.'

'Well, if it isn't glamour you certainly have acquired something.'

She turned her face quickly from him as she said, 'It's the excitement. And who wouldn't be excited? It's like a fairy-tale. Have you had any tea?'

'Yes. Yes, thanks. I had it before I left home.'

Maggie greeted the visitor with, 'There you are then, Mr Gerald, and what do you think of the news, eh? Who would believe that such things happen? But God's good, and He sees to His own, He does. Sometimes mind, He takes His time over it.' She laughed and pushed at Gerald's shoulder vigorously, almost overbalancing him.

'Maggie' – he now teased her – 'I think it's the worst possible thing that could have happened. You'll now eat so much you won't be able to move that carcass of yours.'

'Aw, away with you. I'll move me carcass, never you fear. Now I must go and find himself and see if he's not ready for something to eat.'

When Maggie had left the kitchen, Gerald, looking across at Rosamund, remarked caustically, 'My! My! My! Aren't we all merry and bright! Not a cloud in the sky.'

Rosamund, turning her head quickly towards him, realised that Mr Gerald wasn't too pleased at his friend's changed circumstances.

He might have read her scrutiny, for he changed the conversation from Michael to herself by saying, 'Have you got that cousin of yours staying with you?'

'My cousin? No, what makes you ask that?'

'Oh, you once remarked that your cousin used to berth his boat at the bottom of the Cut, and there's one there now. It's a Banham's hired craft. Though this one's not exactly at the bottom of the Cut, but just a little way along the bank, up near the staunch. What made me think that it might be your cousin's is that I saw your sister leaving it. I was some way off and I tried to catch her up, but she was too quick for me. I've never really met her, only seen her from across the river. She's quite a good-looking miss, isn't she? You know, you've never asked me across to meet her.'

No, thought Rosamund, and I'm not going to. There was enough trouble between Jennifer and Andrew without Gerald Gibson complicating matters still further. So she evaded the latter part of the question and replied, 'Yes, yes, she is very good-looking.'

Gerald Gibson's news about the boat was rather startling. Clifford must have come. What was she going to say to him? What could she say to him? . . . 'You are three weeks too late.' No, she wouldn't go into it. She would just say no. That's if he asked her before Monday. On Monday, when she came back from Cambridge, she would say to him, 'I am married.' The thought sent a spiralling wave of heat through her. It had the power to flush her face and bring forth comment from Gerald.

'Ah! Ah! Have I stumbled on the reason for all this gaiety? Not my friend Mike's money, but the cousin, in the cutter, at the bottom of the Cut.' His high laugh at his own joke was checked by Rosamund's voice remarking with chilling flatness. 'Whatever the reason for my jollity I can assure you it has nothing to do with my cousin.'

'Oh?' He raised his eyebrows and remained silent for a moment, then added, 'Can't blame a fellow for guessing, can you?'

Rosamund turned away. Funny, but she didn't like Gerald Gibson – at least at this moment she didn't like him. She had up to now thought he was good fun, but now she wondered. She wondered, too, about the sincerity of his friendship with Michael when he said, 'What's all the to-do about in the house? Why all the rush, anyway? It's not likely that he'll stay here if he has enough money to get away. He's a strange bird, is Mike, flying too fast and too far for anyone to keep a tab on him.'

'I don't see how he can fly very fast or very far with . . .' She cast her eyes to where the child was sitting in the corner of the chair playing with her doll. 'And, anyway, I thought you had his welfare at heart, and that you'd be glad of his changed luck.'

'I have, of course I have, and I am glad. What makes you think I'm not? What's the matter with you? Why are you on the defensive all of a sudden?'

Before she had time to answer the door opened and Maggie came in, saying, 'He's as hungry as ten buffaloes, he says. Let me get the table set. It's steak he wants, with onions and mushrooms. Oh my, doesn't it make your mouth water . . .?'

The evening that followed was not what could be termed a success. Michael, she felt, overdid the Miss Morley, and she knew that his attitude was puzzling Gerald Gibson, for he had been much more free and easy with her when poverty was his lot. Now it must appear that the money had gone slightly to his head. Yet she knew that Gerald Gibson would know more of this man than she did, and would not be satisfied that this was so.

Long before it was dark she spoke of her intention of going home. She did this because she did not want the position to arise where Gerald Gibson would surely offer to see her to the river bank, with or without Michael being there. So, making the excuse that she would like to get home early, as she thought her cousin had arrived, she prepared to go.

She had run upstairs to have one last look at the child and was quietly crossing the landing towards the stairs again, when the sound of the piano being played came to her. She stopped still at the head of the stairs listening. It was beautiful, beautiful. She did not know what it was he was playing, but it had a soothing, lulling sound. She moved quietly now down the stairs and towards the open door of the sitting-room. Michael was at the piano, his profile to her. His powerful thick fingers were moving somewhat stiffly over the keys, yet bringing from them music which she knew to be good. Gerald Gibson was lolling back in an armchair smoking a cigarette, a glass of whisky to the side of him, and his eyes were on her as she looked towards Michael. But Michael did not look at her, he continued to play.

For a moment she forgot that there was anyone but themselves in the room and, moving to his side, she asked softly, 'What is that?' He did not stop playing, nor look at her as he replied, '*Berceuse*. Tchaikovsky's *Berceuse*.' His voice was dreamy as he ended, '. . . it's my favourite. It was the first piece I ever heard played at a concert and it put me to sleep. My name for it since then has been "Sleep Music".'

'Sleep Music . . . Yes, it's like that, it's lovely.'

She remained still for a time conscious only of the melody and of his hands lifting and falling, until once again she became aware of Gerald watching her, then she said, 'I'll be going. Good night.'

When Michael did not answer she turned away, filled now with pain. All her body seemed to be aching. She had a lost, lonely, unwanted feeling, and she hated Gerald Gibson.

'Rosie.'

The music had stopped abruptly, and she turned at the doorway and looked at him. He was still sitting at the piano but half-swivelled round towards her. His eyes were dark and bright, and he said now, 'Good night, Rosie.'

The pain vanished, she swallowed, smiled, and said, 'Good night.' Then, turning her head briefly in Gerald Gibson's direction, she added, 'Good night,' and left the house . . .

When she reached the river bank and saw Andrew sitting on the lawn talking to her father, she knew an immeasurable feeling of relief. When the ferry reached the other side Andrew was there to give her a hand up.

'Nice seeing you, Andrew.'

'You too, Rosie.'

'It's been a lovely day.'

'Yes, but I think we've had all we're going to get. This can't go on for ever, you know.'

She laughed merrily. 'There speaks the farmer . . . Hello, Father.'

'Hello, Rosie. Had a nice day?' His voice was ordinary.

'Yes, a very nice day.' Her answer implied nothing other than it had been a day of familiar rounds. 'Where's Jennifer?'

'That's what we're wondering.'

'Wondering?' She looked from one to the other, then, turning her eyes from her father, she asked, 'Has Clifford not arrived then?'

'Clifford?' Her father screwed his face up at her. 'What makes you ask a question like that?'

She was looking back at him as she said. 'Oh well, Mr Gibson, a visitor, said that he saw a motor cruiser at the bottom of the Cut, a Banham's, and he thought he saw Jennifer on it. That's where Clifford always berths, and I thought . . . well . . .'

'I passed the bottom of the Cut and I didn't see any cruiser. When was this?'

'I don't know, Andrew, and I don't think it's exactly at the bottom of the Cut – a little way along towards the staunch.'

'Oh, then I could have missed it. It would be round the bend.'

'What time did he see her down there?' Her father was speaking again.

'Oh, I should have said around tea-time, judging by the time Mr Gibson arrived at the house.'

'It wasn't Jennifer.' Henry Morley shook his head vigorously. 'She never left the workroom until about an hour ago, and she hadn't left the house until just on fifteen minutes before Andrew came. She must have gone one way and Andrew come the other, or else they would have met. Whoever the fellow saw getting on that boat wasn't Jennifer.'

Well, that was that. There was someone berthed at the bottom of the Cut and it wasn't Clifford, and for this she felt understandable relief. But what began to niggle at her mind was the fact that someone else besides herself had imagined they had seen Jennifer in a place where she couldn't possibly have been . . .

When an hour later Jennifer had still not returned, Andrew, about to take his departure, said quietly, 'Do you think she's purposely avoiding me, Rosie?'

'No, no, Andrew, get that out of your head. She's definitely been waiting for you coming, and she's been worrying. Oh, she's been worrying, Andrew, I can tell you that. She's likely gone the river way, and you, braving The Tiger' – she laughed at this – 'cut across by the pond.'

'Well, I thought I would have more chance of coming up with her that way.'

'How is our friend Janice?' She looked at him with an amused twist to her lips.

'Oh . . . Janice. Janice is still going strong.'

'Still on the chase?'

'Well, I wouldn't exactly say that, but she visits us at times. She's very interested in cattle, you know.' He nodded his head as he returned her twinkle.

'I bet she is.'

'Oh, Rosie, now don't be feminine.' He gave her a gentle punch with his fist, then, stepping back and surveying her, he said, 'You're liking this job across there, aren't you?' He motioned with his head across the river.

Her lids dropped for a second as she replied, 'Yes. Yes, Andrew, I'm liking it very much.'

'I knew you were. You look different. When I saw you coming across earlier I said to myself, Something's happened, Rosie looks . . . well . . . different. I don't mean that you have changed fundamentally . . .' He laughed. 'You'll always be the same, Rosie. But – well – mind, I'm not just saying this – for a moment you looked every bit as beautiful as Jennifer.'

Her head was back, and her laugh was ringing high; she was both pleased and amused as she said, 'You qualified it, Andrew. "For a moment" you said, and that's true.'

'Come now, you know what I meant, Rosie. And it's the truth, I do mean it. Well, anyway, if you looked like a sack of rotten beet you'd still have your personality left, Rosie, and that's everything.'

Her laughter went higher and higher. 'A sack of rotten beet. Oh, Andrew, you are funny.'

'I suppose I am.' His voice was quiet and he nodded to himself. 'I'm not a bloke for paying compliments – that's why Jennifer got so fed up, I suppose. I could tell her with my eyes that she was beautiful, but I couldn't get it out of my mouth.'

'You're going to change all that, aren't you?'

483

'I'm going to have a damned good try . . . But just the once more, mind, like I said?'

'Go on then, and go by the river. If she went that way she'll come back that way. Good night, Andrew.'

'Good night, Rosie . . . Good night there, Henry.'

Henry Morley, straightening his back, waved the hoe as he cried, 'Good night, Andrew. See you soon, I hope.'

'Yes, I'll see you soon.'

Andrew was gone, and as she went into the house she prayed that he and Jennifer would meet. Get that settled and there would be a load off her mind. There would only be her father then. Well, she had plans for him, and she felt she knew Michael well enough to be sure that he would fall in with her plans.

It was almost dark when Jennifer returned, and Rosamund saw immediately that she was in a very poor frame of mind.

'Did you meet Andrew?'

Jennifer jerked her head round and, staring blankly at her, said, 'No, I didn't meet Andrew.'

'Well, he's been here for the last hour and a half.'

'I hope he enjoyed himself.'

'Oh, don't be so childish, Jennifer. He came to see you. You must have gone one way and he came the other.'

Jennifer stood for a moment looking down, then, dropping into a chair, she buried her face in her hands and began to sob brokenly.

'Oh, don't! Don't, Jennifer!' Rosamund had an arm around her. 'Look, everything's going to be all right; he's as miserable as you are. And I'm going to tell you something. Look at me.' She raised her sister's face upwards, and, although she knew she was giving Andrew away, she felt that there was a great need at this moment to do something to lift Jennifer's moral and self-esteem. 'Now listen. You remember that night I came back and I said I'd met Andrew and Janice Hooper down by the bridge?' Jennifer made no answer, but lowered her wet lids, and Rosamund went on, 'Well, he asked me that night to tell you that he was with Janice. He was getting a bit tired of your dillying and dallying, Jennifer, and he wanted to pull you up.'

'But he was . . . he was with her, wasn't he?'

'Yes, he was, but it was just circumstantial, and I think it was very clever of old Andrew to make something out of it. You know, Andrew isn't just the quiet easy-going individual you take him for. He loves you deeply, but you mustn't play about with him any more, Jennifer; it would be too risky. Now listen . . . Tomorrow morning you're going to go across there . . . you're going to walk right to that farm and see him.'

485

Jennifer did not protest against this arrangement. There was no proud retort that she wasn't going to do any such thing. She merely dried her eyes calmly, and, saying quietly, 'I think I'll go to bed,' she went upstairs.

Well, that was that. At last Jennifer was seeing reason. Everything would be all right in that quarter . . . she hoped.

Rosamund now went into the sitting-room to say good night to her father, and impulsively she threw her arms around his neck and kissed him. And as he held her tightly to him, he looked at her and asked, 'Are you happy, Rosie?'

Her gaze was averted from him, but she nodded her head rapidly, saying, 'Very, very happy, Father.'

'Thank God for that. If anybody's deserved it you have.'

He had not asked what was making her happy, and she hadn't told him. Her father was really no fool. She went upstairs, her heart singing.

9

Andrew's prophecy came true, and Jennifer's decision to go and visit him the following morning was prevented.

Rain never comes at the right time for farmers. They want rain in one field and sunshine in another. Winter or summer, rain in moderation is nearly always welcomed by them, but when it passes this point it becomes a danger, and more so to the men who till the fenlands.

For three days and three nights it had rained, with hardly a let-up. The tidal part of the river above Erith was suffering badly; already many fields in that quarter were under water. The main River Ouse, going towards Denver Sluice, was just holding its own. But the Little Ouse River, which is the continuation of Brandon Creek, the latter a tributary of the main Ouse, had swollen in some places to three times its width. Also part of the newly made bank of the Old West River beyond Dale's Inn had been swept away, and the men were having a job to stem the flow. It was when the water flooded in from the cuts and dykes into the already swollen river that the situation became dangerous. For often the main sluice at Denver had to contend with tides that were higher than the level of the river water. Then the danger hours were when the swollen water from the river could not be released.

Even the water in the Cut had risen, and now covered the landing-stages on each bank and was moving threateningly across the garden. The old mill wheel had once coped with such a situation as this, but how effectively Rosamund, looking at the rising water, was given to doubt. For the diesel-driven machines installed in most of the wheel-houses dotting the fens now, were hard put to it to cope. The sluices were being watched night and day, and the men working on the house had said yesterday that it could be the beginning of another nineteen forty-seven. The only thing to be thankful for was it was summer, and not spring, as in that fateful year of fenland flooding and havoc . . . And it was her wedding day.

As Rosamund looked out of the window over the sodden water-soaked land, she thought, This is my day and it looks as if the whole world is weeping.

When she went downstairs she was wearing her ordinary clothes; her new clothes were over at the house waiting for her. Her father and Jennifer were just finishing breakfast, and Henry Morley turned to her and said, 'Isn't it risky going across there when it's like this?'

'It isn't any worse than yesterday.'

'It will be over your wellingtons before you get to the boat.'

'No, I don't think so.'

Even if the water was pouring into her wellingtons she would still cross the river this morning. She would cross the river if she had to swim.

When she was ready she turned and looked at them, and the desire to tell them was almost overwhelming. She wanted to say, 'Wish me happiness.' This was her wedding day, they should be with her. She felt a moment of acute guilt, and her conscience cried, It isn't a good thing you're doing, keeping them in the dark like this. Yet what could she do? She had promised Michael faithfully that she would tell no-one, not until they came back. She said now, 'I'll be going into Cambridge today. Is there anything you want?'

Both of them appeared to stop and think, and then one after the other they told her there was nothing they could think of.

'All right, Goodbye.'

'Goodbye.'

'Goodbye.'

There was nothing they could think of, but she could think of things they wanted. When Michael came over with her later today, she would bring across a drop of whisky, and all of the tobacco her father could smoke for a month. Michael had said to her only last night when she had told him a little of her father's struggle against his weakness, 'It's a bad thing, you know, to deprive a man of it altogether. A little now and again would do him no harm, and save him a great deal of torment, I'm sure.' Michael was right.

And Jennifer. What would she bring Jennifer? All Jennifer seemingly wanted now was Andrew, and by hook or by crook she'd get Andrew here tonight if they had to paddle all the way up the Cut, for she knew that she couldn't enjoy her happiness unless both Jennifer and her father were happy too.

The boat was not now attached to the chain but to a rope; and when it ground to a stop on the mud of the bank she scrambled over the side, and, paying out the rope, took it to a stake they had placed some distance away. She was in the process of tying the rope securely to the stake when the action recalled something to her mind. It had been as she was untying the rope last night that she had raised her head and seen Gerald Gibson hurrying towards her from out of the wood – not from the direction of the house, but from the path that led to the pond. He had run the last few yards to her, and when he reached her side she noticed that he was rather pale and was not his cheery facetious self. She had asked immediately, 'Is anything the matter?' and he had rubbed his hand across his mouth before saying, 'I've just had a bit of a shock.' And then he had asked an odd question,

'Is your sister in?' She had told him that she didn't know as she was just going across to the house, but with the water rising as it was she was nearly sure to be indoors. He had then asked if she would make sure. His words brought to her a feeling of fear that she could not analyse at the moment, and checked her from questioning him further. After crossing the river and finding Jennifer in the kitchen, she had come on to the front steps again and signalled to him that she was at home. She had said nothing to Jennifer about this, but it had troubled her for some time until it had become overshadowed in the anticipation of today. Now the memory was vividly back with her. She did not know when she had actually stopped liking Gerald Gibson, but she was certainly aware that she no longer was amused by him, or thought him a pleasant companion. Was it because of his implied criticism of Michael? Yes, perhaps. One thing she was sure of: Gerald Gibson was certainly not over-pleased at his friend's good fortune. She felt that he was more than a little jealous of Michael. But the question was, why had he asked if Jennifer was in the house?

Her mind was relieved of its uneasy probing by the sight of Michael coming towards her from the far side of the wood. She wanted to hold out her arms and run to him, but his manner always quelled spontaneity in her, and more so this morning. So she walked, even sedately, towards him.

'You're soaked already.' He was looking her up and down.

'I can't see that you're much better yourself.' She smiled at him, then screwed up her face as she took in his mud-spattered breeches and coat. 'You've been working?'

'Since five.'

'Where? What's happened?'

'I got the idea that if the dyke in the end field was cleared it would heighten the banks there, and at the same time it might relieve just a little water from the Goose Pond. I made a start on it and got all the men going as they arrived.'

'From the house, the painters?'

'The lot. They all came in rubber boots knowing what the road was like. Things are looking rather black in some quarters, I'm afraid. Some of the cottagers have already moved to the villages.'

She stared up at him a moment before saying, 'What about . . . will it make any . . .?'

Her words were cut off as he laughed and ended for her, 'Make any difference? Do you want it to? Come on, tell me, do you?'

'No. No, of course I don't, Michael.'

'Very well then, we'll be at that church, Rosie, at eleven o'clock even if we have to take a boat down the river.'

She felt self-conscious and a little ashamed at her apparent eagerness, but he did not appear to notice, and his dark eyes smiled at her as he went on, 'And it looks pretty much like that even now, for we can't use the car. The road isn't too bad, but I'm afraid of the old bridge. Half the bank on the far side is gone, and I doubt if it'll hold any weight. The men left the lorry on yon side this morning . . . wisely too . . . Anyway, no matter how we get to Ely, we get there, and by eleven o'clock.' With an unexpected, swift movement he pulled her close to him, and, looking down on her face, he said with mock seriousness, 'And I'm thinking of no-one but that minister. He's gone to a lot of work to hurry up this business. Special licences in churches these days take a little time. And I don't think at first the bishop was satisfied with my need for urgency, but the threat of the registry office did it.' He nodded at her, and for a second she leant her brow against his neck. She had expressed the wish that she would like to be married in a church, and he must have gone to quite a deal of trouble, and put others to the same, to grant this wish.

'You frightened, Rosie?'

'Frightened?' She brought her face up quickly to his. 'Frightened? No.' She was not speaking the truth and to give stress to her statement she added another 'No.'

Gently he wiped the rain from her cheek. 'You wouldn't like to back out? There's still time, and there's the child.'

'Oh, Michael, don't keep reminding me of the child, please. She's there and I love her. Yes, I really love her. You mightn't believe that, but I do.'

'I believe you, Rosie. The only thing is you seem . . . well, too good to be true. You love the child, and you like me . . . It seems too much to believe in all at once . . . yet I believe you.'

Abruptly now, he turned away, grabbing hold of her arm as he did so. This was a peculiar trait in him, Rosamund found. When he touched her, he always held on to her as if she were trying to escape. At times he hurt her, and when he became aware of this he would drop his hold as if she had burnt him. He said briskly now, 'I'd better put in an appearance at the dyke again before I change, but you get ready.' And then he checked their steps for a moment adding, and rather sadly, she thought, 'It'll be straight back for us. Do you mind?'

'No. No. It doesn't matter, not in the least.' She smiled up at him reassuringly. And it didn't matter . . . not in the least. The only thing that mattered was that she should marry him at eleven o'clock that morning.

Rosamund felt slightly faint as she listened to the words: 'I pronounce you man and wife.' And things weren't very clear to her after this until she stood in the vestry signing the register. It was the laughter that brought her to the present,

Michael's deep hard laugh. The little minister's chuckle. The hicky-laugh of the cleaning woman, and the definite ha-ha-ha of the verger. It was over something the minister had said, but she couldn't remember what it was.

'Goodbye, Mrs Bradshaw, I hope we'll see you in the church again soon.'

'Yes.' Her voice seemed rather hoarse. 'Yes, I'll come again . . . we'll come again.'

'And I hope I'll see you at Thornby House.' Michael was shaking the minister's hand. 'Don't forget you promised to pay us a visit.'

'I won't forget, definitely not.'

And when they stood outside the church, and the verger, pointing up at the sky, cried, 'Look, it's stopped raining, and I believe, I do believe, that the sun will be out in a minute or so — isn't that a good omen?' Rosamund could have reached up and kissed the tall gangling man. When, after thanking the woman once more, she said goodbye to her, she judged from the warmth of her farewell that Michael's generosity had been lavish, and not to the woman alone.

They walked some distance along the street past the cathedral and into an hotel without exchanging a word. Lunch had been ordered, and not until they were seated at the table did he speak directly to her.

'How does it feel?'

'Wonderful.'

'Don't tell fibs, you don't feel any different.'
His voice was a jocular whisper now.

'I do.' She joined in with his mood, it helped
to allay the fluttering uneven beating of her heart.
'I'm amazed at myself, I've married the Fen
Tiger . . .' She bit on her lip as soon as she
had said it. Then, dropping her head, she put her
closed fist to her mouth to suppress her laughter.

'The . . . What did you say?' He was leaning
towards her.

She was still laughing and kept her eyes from
him as she said, 'You heard.'

'You thought of me as a fen tiger?'

'*The* Fen Tiger . . . there's a distinction.'

He reached out and took her hand now. 'What
do you know about fen tigers?'

'Oh, quite a lot. I have listened to this one,
and that one, and I've read quite a bit.'

'So you think I'm a fen tiger . . . *The* Fen
Tiger . . . the father of them all, eh? You do
know that according to fen history fen tigers are
not supposed to be very desirable individuals? Do
you really think I'm a fen tiger, Rosie?'

She was prevented from answering this by the
appearance of the waiter, and she was vexed that
this was so, for she had the feeling that in some way
she had annoyed him by referring to him as a fen
tiger. By the time the waiter had gone it was more
difficult to answer his question, and when a silence
fell between them and he did not pick up the

conversation again she found it unbearable, and she asked quietly, 'Have I upset you by saying that?'

'No, no, you haven't upset me, but the odd thing is, and this may amuse you, I have a strong desire to appear on the good side of your estimation.'

She had her fork poised over the lobster cocktail as she exclaimed, 'But you do. It wouldn't matter to me what you had done, or what you've been, I feel I know what you are now.'

He stared at her across the small table. 'You really mean that, Rosie?'

'Yes, yes, I really mean it.'

'It wouldn't matter what I'd been or what I'd done, you'd always feel the same about me?'

'Yes.'

'Rosie, you're unique. You're unique because I know you really do mean every word you say.'

He held her gaze until she became lost to the fact that they were sitting in an hotel in Ely. She only knew that half an hour ago she had become his wife.

But not many hours were to pass before she was to remember her affirmation.

It was nearly three o'clock when they returned home. The sun was shining brightly now, and there was evidence in some fields that the water had gone down slightly. Her arm was held tightly in his as they neared the house, and his laughter now held an excited boyish note as he said, 'We haven't met a soul, and here I am bursting to show off my wife.' It was the first really nice thing he had said to her, and when, after taking a deep breath, he pulled her to a stop and looked down on her, she could not speak for a moment. Nor could she hold his gaze, for the intensity of his look brought a shyness to her. To cover her confusion, she said, 'I want to tell Father and Jennifer. Shall we go straight over now?'

'No, let us keep that for tonight. Let's bring them over here and have a sort of celebration supper, eh?'

'That will be lovely.' She said this to please him, but she would rather have gone and told them straight away.

They went on again, and now he said with brittle jollity, 'As soon as I get in, Mrs Bradshaw, I'm changing and getting down to that dyke.'

'Are you, Mr Bradshaw?' It was a pleasant feeling to know she could exchange playful banter with her fen tiger, so she made bold to add, 'So you already prefer the dyke to me?'

'Every time, Mrs Bradshaw.' He had her arm held so tightly against him that she winced and this brought him again to a stop, 'I hurt you?'

'A little.'

'I'm sorry.' His tone had changed and there was a deep solemnity to his words when he said, 'I hope I never hurt you, really hurt you, Rosie. I'll try not to, I swear I will.'

She was all at once overcome with a feeling of sadness and she moved from him, and as they walked the remainder of the way to the house, in silence now, she had the oddest feeling that he would hurt her, hurt her so deeply that she would not be able to bear it . . .

Maggie congratulated them and blessed them and fussed over them, and she kissed Rosie, and with true Irishism said, 'Well, Miss Rosie, ma'am, there's nobody I'd welcome like yourself to say to me, "Do this" or "Do that" or "Hold you hand there, Maggie."'

When their laughter settled, Michael said, 'Where is she?'

'Oh, she's asleep.' Maggie sighed, 'She's worn out. She started her screaming the minute you left the house. You couldn't have been a stone's throw away when she started. She was standing in the kitchen doorway there, out of the rain when she first let go, and she pointed this time; she was pointing at something out towards the buildings. But there wasn't a thing to be seen, only the car in the barn. But she yelled her head off as if she was seeing all the devils in hell. It was worse than usual, Master Michael, much worse. I thought I'd go off me head . . . Aw, there now, I didn't mean to tell you and upset you on this day of all days, but if I were you I'd have her seen to. This is new.'

'Yes, yes.' He nodded, then, looking at Rosamund, he said, 'I'll take her into Cambridge tomorrow. There's a man I've heard of, he specialises in her type. I was going to take her along to him in any case.'

'Will you have a cup of tea or are you too full of wine, both of you?'

'I'd love a cup of tea, Maggie.' Rosamund smiled at the old woman, then, turning to Michael, drawn by the intensity of his gaze, she asked quietly, 'What is it?'

'I was thinking it's a strange wedding day for you.'

'It's a wonderful wedding day.' Her voice was soft and kind.

'You don't really mind me going off to see about the dyke?'

'No, and I mean it. I love to know that you're going on working, and on the land, on the fens. I've had — as Maggie would say' - she whispered to him now while she jerked her head backwards —'I've had the feeling on me that you'd want to leave here and go off to foreign climes.'

'Six weeks ago nothing would have held me, at least I would have said so, and yet now I'm tied myself as if with an iron hawser.' Slowly he put his hand on her hair. 'A rust-coloured iron hawser.'

'It isn't rust, it's copper coloured.'

'It's beautiful, whatever colour it is.'

She was seeing him now through a thin mist.

'You love it here, don't you, Rosie?'

'I love the fenlands.'

He nodded, then in a low voice he said:

'Your land is my land,
Its toil and its sweat,
Its pain to come yet,
Your land is my land.
With mud in the meadow,
Water in the barn,
Pigs floating down the dyke.
The Ouse and the Cam,
Afloat with young lamb,
You've never seen the like.
But your land is my land,
For I've taken your name,
And the fens are my home,
Till God stakes His claim.

'That was the rhyme of a fenland bride. It should have come from the bridegroom, shouldn't it?'

She could not answer, her throat was so tight. She watched him turn away, and as the door closed on him her fingers were pressed to her lips. When she turned, there was Maggie standing with the kettle in her hand, her head on one side, her face abeam as she remarked, 'That was nice wasn't it? Oh, that was nice indeed. He can pay a fine compliment, he can that, can Master Michael.'

*   *   *

It was half-past six, and Rosamund, dressed in a soft grey, fine wool suit, was waiting in the sitting-room for Michael. She was sitting sideways on the piano stool dreamily touching one key after the other. Michael, changed once more into his town clothes, had just slipped out to have a word with the last of the men, who were finishing early tonight, for it had been a very strenuous day for all of them.

The sitting-room door was open, and she had a view across the hall to the green baize door of the kitchen; and when she saw it flung back and Gerald Gibson come striding through, her tapping of the keys stopped and with a surge of impatience she thought, Oh no! . . . Then, Why has he come tonight? It was odd enough that she should have seen him last night. He usually kept his visits for the weekends. But for him to come tonight of all nights . . .

She was more nervous than ever now of springing her news on her family and was desirous of getting it over as soon as possible, and here was further delay in the form of Gerald Gibson. But by the time he entered the sitting-room she was on her feet and asking, 'Is anything wrong? Aren't you well?'

'I'm all right. Where's Mike?'

'Round the back talking to the men – he'll be here in a minute . . . There is something wrong. What is it? What's happened?' She went up to him. 'There's nothing wrong with my people, not my sister?' She was remembering his enquiries of last night.

'No, it's nothing to do with you; it . . . it concerns Mike.'

She was on the point of saying, 'What concerns Mike concerns me,' but she said almost the equivalent with, 'Tell me what it is.' Her voice was quiet. 'It isn't good, whatever it is, is it?'

'Not for him it isn't.' He paused, then, looking at her closely, he said, 'You're not falling for him, are you?'

No, she wasn't falling for him; the state of her feelings could only be described in the past tense. She felt annoyed at the question and made no answer, but she continued to look at him as he went on, 'I'd be careful if I were you.' His voice was very low now. 'And I'd get away from here. You don't want to be mixed up in anything.'

'Mixed up in anything?' Her voice was cool, and he said quickly, 'Oh, I'm not suggesting that you've got involved with him or anything like that, but I'm just putting you on your guard. It's like this . . .'

'Don't go on . . . please.' She felt he was going to say something that would only embarrass them both later. 'I think you'd better know right away – Michael would have told you himself when he came in, anyway – we were married this morning.'

'My God!' His mouth was wide open and his eyebrows were pushed up towards his hair. He gulped now before going on, 'But you can't . . . you shouldn't . . . He can't marry again . . . she's . . . she's not dead . . .'

She was staring at him, and she knew that her face was expressing nothing, either of shock or surprise, for she was feeling nothing, only a slight coldness on her neck.

'It's bigamy. He should never have married you. He knew he should never have married you . . .'

'What did you say?'

They both turned to the french window, where Michael was taking a slow step over the threshold. He repeated in a deceptively quiet tone, 'What did you say?'

'I . . . I wanted to see you, Mike . . . I came straight to see you, but . . . but . . .' He thumbed crudely in Rosamund's direction. 'I . . . I have something to tell you.'

'What did you say?' Michael was still advancing towards him. His step was slow and each movement indicated a threat, and now Gerald retreated until his back was against the end of the piano and he began to splutter. 'A – now . . . look, Mike. Just wait until . . . I tell you . . .'

Michael stopped when he was about a yard from him and said, still quietly, 'I'm waiting.'

'She . . .' Gerald wet his lips. 'Rosie says you have got married, and . . . and I told her, well . . . you . . . you couldn't.'

'You told her we couldn't?'

'Camilla . . . she's not dead. You . . . you said her body was washed up. I tell you she's not dead . . .'

Rosamund let out a scream as Michael's hands were thrust around Gerald's throat, and she flung herself on him, crying, 'Don't! Don't! Listen! Please, Michael! Michael!' As she cried his name for the second time she found herself stumbling backwards across the room, and only stopped herself from falling by clutching the back of a chair.

'You dirty swine!' As Michael's fist contacted Gerald Gibson's jaw Rosamund bent her face in the crook of her arm. The next minute there was a tremendous crash as a table was overturned, and at the same time Maggie's bulk appeared in the doorway and her voice was at yelling point as she cried, 'In the name of God, what's come over yous?' Then, with amazing agility for one who was always complaining about her legs, and with strength equally surprising in so old a woman, she flung herself across the room and on to Michael, and her weight alone forced him to release his hold on Gerald Gibson.

'Is it stark staring mad you've gone?' She was pushing at and addressing her master as if he was a young boy again. 'What d'you think you're up to? Acting like hooligans.' She turned her face now towards the prostrate visitor and demanded, 'What bad news have you brought with you to cause this? I knew by your face that it was no good that you were coming with the night.'

Gerald Gibson rose slowly to his feet. The blood was running from his lip and nose. He looked to where Michael was standing as if ready to spring again at any moment, and he said bitterly, 'I came to tell him that his wife was alive, that's what I came to tell him.'

'You're mad, man! She's dead.' Maggie turned her small eyes from Gerald to Michael and repeated, 'She's dead, you said she was. You buried her, didn't you?'

'Yes, I buried her.' Michael's voice was thick and guttural now and still shaking with the rage that was boiling in him.

'You buried her, did you?' Gerald swept the blood from his mouth with his hand. 'Well, let me tell you, I saw her not half an hour ago. I was talking to her. Don't forget I knew Camilla. I saw her last night. I've seen her three times in the past week but couldn't believe it. I thought she was . . .' He turned to gaze in the direction of Rosamund. 'I thought she was your sister, she's very like her.'

'You're a liar! A damned sneaking liar.'

'I'm not lying, and you can't bluff me. You knew she wasn't dead. At least you knew the one you buried wasn't her. You hoped it might be, but you had no proof.'

'Get out before I kill you.'

'Yes, get out.' It was Maggie speaking now. 'And say no more, not another word.' She moved towards him almost threateningly.

When with a dark glare towards Michael he stumbled from the room, Rosamund slid slowly down into the armchair. She had the feeling that she was going to be sick. From under her lowered lids she saw Michael coming towards her and she turned her head away into the corner of the chair.

'Rosie, look at me. Rosie . . . I said look at me.' His voice appeared to be dragging itself up from the very bowels of the fen itself, but she did not obey his command, for, as menacing as his tone was, it could not blot out the voice of a week ago when he had pleaded with her in the kitchen to tell no-one of their forthcoming marriage, 'I have a feeling on me,' he had said, 'that dates back to my childhood. Anything I want badly is always taken from me.' He had not said, 'I've always wanted those things just out of reach, which the law forbids me to have.'

'Rosie!' Her head was jolted forward as he gripped her shoulders and pulled her into an upright position. 'Why are you believing him and not me? Rosie!' He shook her as if trying to wake her from a dream, a nightmare. 'Listen to me. My wife is dead . . . You don't believe me?' Slowly the grip on her shoulders slackened, and so quietly did he release her that she remained in the same position. He was looking down on her now, his face grey and agonisingly hard. 'My wife is dead, I buried her. I carried her up out of the sea myself and I buried her.'

'No, no.' She shook her head slowly as she listened to her own voice, strange and faraway sounding, saying, 'I've seen her. I've seen her looking through that window there.' She pointed into the hall, then watched him turn and look at Maggie, and saw Maggie shake her head as she muttered, 'In the name of God.' She brought his eyes back to her by saying 'Was she like my sister?'

'Yes.' His head moved slightly and his words sounded grudging. 'There was a resemblance, but she was older.'

'Then I've seen her.'

'Don't say that.' With a sudden movement he was on his knees before her, clutching at her hands. 'Whoever you saw, or whatever you saw, it wasn't her. Believe me, Rosie. Believe me . . .'

'Why didn't you want anyone to know we were going to be married?' Her voice was scarcely audible, and her eyes were turned from his.

'Because . . . because . . .' He screwed up his face and bared his teeth as he said, 'It was because of what I told you, this feeling, and wasn't I right? But I tell you, you are mistaken about this . . . this other . . .'

'Mr Gibson . . . he knew her?'

'Yes. Gibson knew her, and he wanted her as he wants you.' At her sudden recoil he said, 'Oh, I've no illusions about my friend Mr Gerald Gibson. I knew him long before he showed his hand as he did tonight. He's never had any love for me. He would have gone off with Camilla if she would have had him, but he had no money, and she had no use for anyone without money. I tell you, it's some story he's concocted. He guessed about us, and he was out to spoil it.'

'No, no, I can't believe that.'

'Because you don't want to believe it. You want to back out now.' He got to his feet, and she rose too, facing him as she cried, 'You know that isn't true.'

As they stood with their eyes riveted on each other, Maggie's voice came in between them asking quietly, 'How did the child react to her – your wife I mean, Master Michael?'

'React?' He was looking at her across his shoulder. 'Why do you ask that? What does it matter?'

'It might matter a lot. For the past week the child has been screaming at nothing, or supposedly so.'

'My God!' The words came slow and deep. They had a surprised sound.

As he turned his gaze from Maggie, Rosamund had the impression that he was shrinking before her eyes: she watched him shake himself, literally shake himself, as if throwing off something distasteful, something evil. He walked to the french window and looked out across the fens, and both she and Maggie stood silently gazing at him. When, after a time, he turned he found their eyes waiting for him and in tones threaded with awe he said, 'She's not alive. I know she's not alive, she can't be. But the child used to scream whenever she walked towards her in a certain way, because then she knew she was going to be thrashed. I didn't know it was happening for a long time, this thrashing business. She used to do it when I went out fishing with the men. It was when one of the fishermen's wives saw her at it and she told me . . .' He stood rigidly still, not saying anything for some minutes, and when he did go on he spoke as if to himself. 'I set a trap for her – she thought I was away. When I found her at it, I thrashed her with the same stick she was using on the child. It was the day after this that she was missing. Some people thought I had killed her, until three days later they found her clothes behind the rocks half a mile up the coast. It was then young Anthony confessed to the priest, and the priest brought the boy to me, to tell me he had watched her undress and swim out naked towards the point of rock where the waters of the bay met the open sea.'

Rosamund could not bear to look at him any longer. Her head was bowed deep on her chest. She was taking into her own body his suffering, his mental suffering over the years.

Maggie interposed, 'When her body was washed up, how did you recognise her?'

'I knew her body, Maggie, I knew Camilla's body only too well. I had been ensnared by it. The body that was washed up was hers. If she has followed me here it isn't with her body, but with her spirit. The evil in her that has taken shape. And the fens are the place for spirits.'

'Jesus, Mary and Joseph! Will you stop talking like that, Master Michael. I would rather have it that she's alive and on her two feet than imagining her spirit is abroad, and in this place of all places.'

Rosamund's eyes were tightly closed. He knew her body. The words seemed to cut through her. He came towards her once more, and slowly and gently raised her chin from her breast, and again he said, but quietly now, 'My wife is dead, Rosie.'

'Let me go home, Michael.' The request was whispered, and it was answered by a sudden shout, 'No! By God, no! I tell you this is a fantasy. Gibson saw your sister, he imagined it was her. I got a shock myself the first time I saw your sister.'

'The child's been screaming, Michael.' Her voice was trembling.

'All right, she's been screaming, she's seen something. She's seen the evil that bred her. But my wife is dead.'

'Michael . . .' She was appealing to him, holding out her hands. 'Michael, do something for me, will you? Will you go down to the boat at the end of the Cut?'

His eyes were narrowed now, telling her nothing, nor did he answer.

'Mr Gibson thought he saw my sister leaving that boat the other night. Will you . . . will you go and . . . and see who's there?'

'Yes. Yes.' He nodded his head slowly. 'I'll go to it now, this minute, if that'll put your mind at rest . . . But you'll wait here until I come back.'

She was staring at him, saying neither yes nor no.

He turned from her, went past Maggie and towards the hall door, and there he stopped, and, looking back, he said in a tone which she remembered from the first night she had met him, 'I'll expect to find you here when I get back.'

She stood by the window and watched him striding down the drive and across the field towards the wood. When he was out of sight she turned to Maggie, where the old woman was sitting on the edge of the chair rocking herself back and forwards.

'I must go home, Maggie,' she said.

'No! No! No, Miss Rosie, ma'am, don't do that. Wait as he says. For God's sake, wait.

'Maggie' – Rosamund drew in a shuddering breath – 'I believe that his wife is alive. I mustn't stay, Maggie. If I'm here when he gets back he won't let me go. It mustn't happen, Maggie.'

'Oh, Holy Mary. That this had to come upon him. He's been dogged all his life. Look, if you desert him in this hour of his need it will be the finish of him, I know it will.'

'Maggie, I'm finding it terrible, I'm finding it unbearable. Can't you see I want to stay? With all my heart and soul I want to stay. But I can't, for I know that his wife is in that boat at the bottom of the Cut. Something tells me, something in here.' She placed her hand on her breast. 'You know yourself that she is alive. The child was not screaming at a spirit, she smelt her mother. Susie may be deprived of normal sense, but she's got a sense that we haven't. People like her can smell fear. She feared her mother and she smelt her. Oh, it's dreadful, it's dreadful.' She covered her eyes with her hands, and, almost following Maggie's pattern, she rocked back and forth, before collecting herself again and saying, 'I'm going, Maggie; I'm going home. Tell him . . . tell him I'll be back in the morning.'

'I'll tell him no such thing. I won't be able to tell him any such thing, for when he gets back and finds you gone the devil himself won't be able to get near him. You don't know the man you've married. He's both God and the devil rolled into one, and that you'll find if you love him. I love him, I've loved him since he was a baby in long clothes. I know him; you've got a lot to learn yet. So start right now. Wait until he gets back.'

Rosamund made no answer to this, but, turning from the old woman's bright steely blue eyes, she ran out of the room . . . She was still running when she reached the swollen river, where, having forgotten to put on her wellingtons, she splashed through the water to the boat. She seemed to be running still as she pulled frantically on the rope, and when the boat ground against the bank she leaped out and raced into the house like someone flying from the devil himself. She was making straight for the stairs, when both her father's and Jennifer's voices checked her, and she stopped, holding on to the balustrade but not looking towards them.

'What is it, Rosie? What's happened? What's the matter?' Jennifer was by her side, a different-sounding Jennifer, the old Jennifer.

'What is it, my dear?' Henry Morley was at her other side now, his arm about her shoulders. 'What's happened? Come on in and sit down.'

She flung her head back and tried to shake them off, but her father firmly turned her about and led her into the sitting-room, where, standing on the hearth looking anxiously towards her, was Andrew.

'What is it, Rosie?' He too was bending over her. 'What's happened? Has . . . has anyone done anything?'

She could not reply. She could only shake her head and try to stop the lump in her throat from choking her.

'Your feet are wringing wet. Good gracious! Look at you. You must get those shoes off. I'll get your slippers.' But Jennifer did not go immediately to get the slippers. Crouching down in front of Rosamund, she added in deeply troubled tones, 'What is it Rosie? What's happened?' Then she asked as if the two of them were alone, 'Is it him?'

The word 'him' seemed to arouse her father to sudden indignation, for he cried, 'If he's done anything I'll go across there and I'll . . .'

Rosamund forced herself to speak. 'No. No, please. All of you.' She shook her head wearily. 'I'll tell you later. Get me a drink . . . tea . . . anything.'

'Yes, yes, of course, my dear.' Henry Morley almost ran from the room, and Jennifer, saying, 'I must get your slippers, you must get these wet things off', rushed after him.

Rosamund was looking up at Andrew.

'In trouble, Rosie?'

'Yes, Andrew. Great trouble.'

'Can I do anything?'

'I only wish you could.'

'You've only got to ask me, you know that.'

'Yes. Yes, I know that, Andrew, and you'd be the first one I'd ask.'

'You can't tell me?'

'No. No, not yet.'

As she finished speaking her father came hurrying back into the room; he hadn't the drink with him but in his hand he held a telegram form. He was endeavouring to cover his concern with a smile as he said, 'This'll cheer you. Andrew brought it over at teatime. It was addressed to you but we opened it, just in case. It's from Clifford – he's coming tomorrow.'

He forced the piece of paper into her hand, and her eyes hardly glanced at it. That's all she needed now, to know that Clifford was coming tomorrow. She flung the telegram aside. 'He can save himself the trouble.' Her voice was angry. 'He's weeks too late. Anyway, when he comes I won't be here.'

As the two men stood dumbly looking down on her, she asked herself where she would be if she wasn't here. It was silly to talk like that.

Jennifer now came into the room with Rosamund's slippers, and, taking charge of the situation with a quiet assurance that would have surprised Rosamund had she given a thought to it, she said, 'Come along into the kitchen; it's warmer there, and you're frozen. You can change in there. Come on now.' And she put her hand under Rosamund's arm and helped her to her feet. In the kitchen she pressed her into a chair and actually stripped her wet stockings off, and as Rosamund watched her doing this she thought, Everything's all right with her, anyway.

'It's him, isn't it, who's upset you?' Jennifer wasn't looking at Rosamund as she said this, and when she did not receive an answer she went on, 'Don't go across there any more, finish with him. He would have had to look after the child himself, anyway, if you hadn't been here. He's nothing but a great big bullying brute. As I said to Andrew, nothing seems the same since he came back.'

No, nothing had been the same since he came back, that was true, and nothing would ever be the same again. She wondered what Jennifer would say if she said to her now, 'I married him this morning, and an hour ago discovered that his wife was alive.' Jennifer would say, 'Well, what do you expect? That's the kind of thing he would do.' Yes, that's what Jennifer would say.

It was just on dusk and they were all in the sitting-room. The conversation was desultory, carried on mostly between Henry Morley and Andrew, with Jennifer chipping in now and again. Rosamund had scarcely opened her lips. She longed to be alone, but she knew that if she went upstairs it wouldn't be to sleep, but to sit at the window and think, and brood, and look across the fens towards the house. So she sat with them, not listening to what was said, for all the while her mind was crying out bitterly against what had happened. Consequently, when the thundering rap came on the door it startled the others but brought her immediately to her feet.

Her father, looking at her quickly, also rose. 'Stay where you are,' he said now. 'I'll see to whoever it is.'

Henry Morley had left the sitting-room door open, and the three of them stood looking towards it, listening. They heard the latch of the front door being lifted, and then they heard Henry's voice saying, 'Yes, Mr Bradshaw, what can I do for you?'

'*I've come for my wife.*' The voice was not loud, but it was deep and the words came into the room weighed heavily with arrogance.

Rosamund turned from the startled looks of both Jennifer and Andrew, and, putting her hand across her mouth, she went to the window. Her father's blustering voice followed her, crying, '*What!* Now look here, what do you mean? What's all this?'

She heard Jennifer saying, 'Oh, Rosie! Rosie!' as if she had heard she had committed a crime. And it was perhaps just that: a crime.

Jennifer was behind her when Andrew said

quickly, 'Come away, leave her be. Look, come into the kitchen.'

'But Andrew . . .'

'I tell you, Jennifer, leave her alone.'

'I don't believe you.' Her father's voice was loud coming from the direction of the hall. Then from the sitting-room doorway he demanded, 'Is this true, Rosamund?'

Could she say no? She said nothing, but bowed her head.

When the silence began to stretch her nerves still further, her father said, 'Rosie, you should have told us. You shouldn't have done this on the . . . the sly.'

'There's a reason why she did it on the sly – I asked her to.'

'Well, sir, all I can say to you is . . .'

Rosamund turned quickly on him, crying, 'Father, please, please. I'll explain later. Leave me alone, will you, please. Oh, please.' She had said me, but she meant us. She watched her father divide his amazed and angry glance between them before turning slowly and leaving the room.

She walked now from the window towards the fireplace. Her body was shaking and she averted her gaze from him. But his next words brought her round to him.

'Have you got her here?'

'You mean . . . you mean Susie?'

'Who else?'

'No. No.'

He stared at her for a long moment before speaking again and rapidly now, 'I thought she had followed you . . . and you, on this occasion, wouldn't bring her back . . . And she's not with you?' His eyes were screwed up. 'My God! Where can she be then?'

'Rosie!' He was standing close to her, his face not inches from her own and his words were tumbling out. 'Come on. I'll have to look for her, but come back with me. We'll talk this over. I'm nearly mad; you realise that, Rosie? I'm nearly mad. One thing on another piling up . . . there's a breaking point. Please . . .' He had her hands imprisoned and held against his chest.

'What did you find at . . . at the boat?'

'Nothing, not a thing. It was locked up. I waited for over an hour, there was no-one to be seen anywhere about. And another thing' – he shook his head slowly – 'Camilla loved comfort, she would never have lived on a thing like that. It's a little two-berth cruiser – the whole idea is fantastic.'

'I must have time, Michael. It must be proved.'

'Proved? I've told you. Do you think that if there was the slightest doubt in my mind I'd do this to you. Look, Rosie.' He moved now slightly back from her. 'I've been begging and praying. I've been asking and pleading for you to come back. Soon I'll stop doing that and I'll make you. I'll take you whether you like it or not . . .'

'You can't do that.'

'Can't I? You'll see. Well now, once more I'll ask. Are you coming? I've got to go and look for the child. It'll soon be dark . . . Well?'

She knew as she looked at him he was capable of carrying out his threat. If she said she wouldn't go with him she could see him quite clearly forcing her out of the house, carrying her out of the house, fighting both her father and Andrew in the process. She did not want any more scenes. Quietly she said, 'I'll come and help find Susie, then you can force me to stay in the house, that'll be up to you, but I don't consider myself married.'

'Don't say that, Rosie.'

'I do say it. I'll go on doing so until I have proof that the woman who has been on the fens these last few days is not your wife. And there has been a woman on the fens, I've told you I've seen her.'

When he did not answer but stared at her with pain-filled eyes she could not bear to look at him any longer. She could only mutter, 'I'll get my coat.'

In the hall, near the front door, her father and Andrew were waiting, and, looking towards them, she said, in a voice she tried to keep steady, 'The child is missing; he . . . he thought she might be here. I'm going to help find her . . .' Now she looked directly at her father as she added, 'But I'll be back later tonight.' She was conscious as she finished speaking that Michael was standing in the doorway behind her, but he said nothing to contradict her statement.

It was Andrew who now spoke. Looking at Michael, he said, 'Can I be of help?'

She fully expected a staccato refusal to this offer, but instead she was surprised to hear Michael say quietly, 'I would be grateful. It'll soon be dark and impossible to go far with the water everywhere . . .'

A few minutes later the three of them were going down the steps of the house, and Rosamund, pausing and turning to her father, asked him gently, 'Would you look along the river this side?'

'Yes, yes.' He nodded somewhat numbly at her, before adding, 'But I can't see that she'd be over here – she'd have to cross.'

Rosamund did not say, 'Anything is possible.' Things that were unnatural had this very day been accepted, believed, such as an evil spirit walking the fens and causing a child to scream.

Jennifer called to her now, 'Be careful, Rosie. You'll come back, won't you?'

She made no answer to this, and a few moments later they were in the boat. When they reached the other side it was she herself who said, 'It's no use keeping together, I . . . I'll go towards the Goose Pond.'

Michael was looking hard at her and he let out a deep breath before he said, 'Very well. I'll take the stretch beyond the house towards the main road.' Then, turning towards Andrew, he asked him, 'Would you mind taking the Cut bank towards the Wissey?'

'Yes, yes, I'll do that. But what if one of us comes across her? Shouldn't we have some sort of signal?'

'I suppose so.' Michael nodded briskly. 'Who-ever finds her can shout, just call out. There's no wind and the voices will carry.'

'Very good.'

Michael was the first to turn away, and before Rosamund had gone a yard in the direction of the Goose Pond she knew that he was running, and this gave a signal to her own feet. As she ran she didn't question why she had suggested that she would take the road to the Goose Pond. She only knew that from the Goose Pond she could cross a field towards the flood bank and this would bring her out opposite the sluice, and the boat was lying somewhere near there.

As she passed the swollen Goose Pond the geese scolded her and, with necks outstretched, pretended to chase her for some distance.

She didn't run across the field that led to the flood bank but walked somewhat slowly, even cautiously, and as she went she questioned herself as to whether she was looking for the child or the woman. The answer came to her that she was doing both, for from the moment Michael had said that the child was missing her thoughts had sprung to the woman. The mother of the child – the wife of Michael. For, although she felt that Michael believed he was telling the truth when he reiterated that his wife was dead, she herself knew that she wasn't. What she had seen was no spirit of evil; it might be evil, but it was in the flesh, and it was a woman.

When she had climbed to the top of the flood bank she saw that there was no boat away up near the sluice gates. To her surprise, when she looked up-river to the left, she saw that the boat was now at the end of the Cut and looking as if it was actually in the field. It must have been brought up the river recently.

She ran now along the top of the wash-bank until she had almost reached the Cut again, then going down the bank she picked her way through the flooded field until she came within a few yards of the boat. The little craft was pressed against some tall reeds which indicated the bank of the river. It was not held by any rond anchors and was slightly tilted. But its bows, held tight in the reeds, was the reason, she saw, why it was not going adrift. The boat was about twenty feet over all, and the usual type of cabin-cruiser. She was a few feet from its stern when she stopped, becoming almost rigid with an overwhelming sense of fear. In this moment all she desired to do was to turn and speed across the field and over the wash-bank. Her thoughts did not take her further; once beyond the bank she would be safe.

Forcing herself to move towards a window of the cabin, she was in the act of bending down when a voice, coming to her from the bows of the boat, transfixed her. In this moment she was incapable of moving a muscle; even her eyes seemed riveted in their sockets as the voice said, 'Don't bother looking through the window, come in; I've been waiting for you.'

When, at last, she managed to straighten her back she looked along the length of the small boat to the woman, half leaning over the bows. The woman smiled. It was a quiet smile, and she said, 'Do come in.'

The voice was beautifully modulated; it had a fascinating sound, only the slight clipping of the words betrayed the foreign accent. As if she were hypnotised, Rosamund found herself lifting one heavy boot after the other over the side of the boat into the small well, and then she was standing before the woman, looking up at her, for she was very tall. She was gazing into a face that looked neither mad nor evil. The woman now said to her quietly, 'Go in, go into the cabin.'

Slowly Rosamund went into the cabin. It was rather dim inside. It consisted of two single berths, one on each side, which formed seats. At the head of each was a cupboard; between these was a door leading, Rosamund surmised, into a tiny gallery or wash-place, without headroom. It was similar in nearly all its details to the boat Clifford usually hired.

Once in the cabin Rosamund jerked round quickly towards the woman, but she could say nothing. Words were impossible; her feelings at this moment were outraged. This was Michael's wife, and she neither sounded nor looked like anyone deranged; she had even a gentle air.

'Sit down.' The woman pointed to the bunk, and slowly Rosamund sat down. 'You're small aren't you? Not a bit like your sister. I've seen your sister.'

Rosamund, still speechless, was staring at the woman, and she saw now why she had thought she was like Jennifer – her hair was blonde. But the centre parting betrayed that it had once been brown; auburn, Gerald Gibson had said. But the bone formation of the face was exactly the same as Jennifer's. Yet there the resemblance ended, for the woman's eyes and mouth were different altogether from Jennifer's What the difference was she did not analyse – she was too disturbed, cut to the heart. Michael had portrayed this woman as a sort of demon, and yet both her voice and manner pointed to her being a gentle creature.

The woman now sat down on the edge of the bunk and asked quietly, 'So you know why I'm here?'

'No. I only know that you are supposed to be dead.' Rosamund's voice cracked in her throat. 'Why did you pretend to be drowned?'

'Why did I pretend to be drowned?' The woman looked away from Rosamund now and out of the window, and she gave a little laugh before she said, 'You don't know Michael very well or you wouldn't ask that. I would have gone mad, yes mad, if I hadn't got away, and it was no use just walking out. He would have found me and brought me back to look after . . .' She paused and turned her head away . . . Now she was looking at Rosamund again. 'Perhaps you don't know that Michael is, in a sane sort of way, mad. I didn't realise it until he began to have an obsession about . . . Susie.'

'Did . . . did you ever beat the child?' She had to ask this question.

'Did I beat the child?' The eyes were wide now, looking into Rosamund's. 'Do I look a person who would beat a child?'

Rosamund, looking back into the deep soft brown eyes, thought, No. No, you don't look like a person who would beat a child. A part of her mind was crying loudly now. Oh, Michael! Michael! And it came to her you could both hate and love a person at the same time, hate and love with an intensity that was unbearable.

'Why didn't you come openly to the house and confront him?'

'Confront Michael?' The woman laughed

quietly again and it had a sad disillusioned sound. 'It's so evident that you don't know Michael. My husband is capable of doing anything, anything he sets his mind to. He brooks no interference, he will sweep everything from his path to get what he wants . . . and at present he wants you. It is as well I realised this almost at once . . . it may have saved my neck.'

If you don't come I will take you . . . As his words came into her mind again, she was filled with a shuddering fear. And a deep embarrassment filled her as she looked at the woman whose husband she had married that morning. It was with an effort that she asked, 'Then why have you come back?

'We . . . ll.' The word was drawn out, and the woman cast her eyes sideways towards her hands which now lay palm upwards, one on top of the other on her lap. 'I might as well be truthful. I can be truthful, there's no reason to be otherwise now. Michael has come into some money, hasn't he? It is evident that I knew about it before he himself did, for as soon as I read about his uncle's yacht being wrecked I knew he would inherit. I haven't any money and I hate not having money.' She lifted a rather shy glance towards Rosamund, and Rosamund thought, At least he spoke the truth on this point, anyway. And now the woman went on, 'He used to talk to me about the house, and these rivers, until I grew tired. But my enforced listening wasn't wasted, because when I came here I seemed to know them as if I'd been born here. The only thing I was surprised about was that they're not so isolated as he said. I didn't expect anyone to see me, or to notice me, but they did, and that has been the trouble.' Again she cast her eyes downwards. 'Whoever would have thought that I would have run into Gerald Gibson? You know Gerald, of course?'

'Yes, I know him.'

'Yes, I've seen you talking to him. I thought perhaps that you and he . . . Well, well, it wasn't like that at all, was it?' She shook her head and waited for Rosamund to comment, and when she didn't she went on. 'I was really glad that Gerald was about. You see, I will be quite frank with you at this point. I really didn't know what I was going to do when I first came here, except about one thing: I had no intention of living with Michael again. Nor, I am sure, would he want me to. I was just interested to know how much money he had come into, and what he intended doing with it. With this knowledge I could gauge how much he would be likely to pay to keep me dead . . . I knew I would have to prove my identity to him, writing wouldn't do, and yet I was afraid to face him on my own in case he tried to kill me . . . Oh yes, he'd be quite capable of it; he's threatened to more than once. So then I saw that it was as well I had come across Gerald, for he could be the bearer of the news that I was alive. Also he could witness the meeting between Michael and myself, and be present while we came to some settlement, such as would keep a wife in comfort abroad. It was a better way out than playing dead really.' She paused for quite a while, staring at Rosamund, before she added, 'That's how it would have worked out if it hadn't been for you. You rather complicated things . . . Not that I hold that against you. You weren't to know that you were treading on . . . well, a sort of mine. Because Michael is a mine, you know, and he's liable to go off at any minute, for the pin to the detonator is Susan . . . You . . . you think I'm a bad woman because I . . . I deserted my child?'

'No, no.' The words struggled past Rosamund's lips. She didn't think that this woman was a bad woman; weak perhaps, vain perhaps, mercenary, but not bad. But Susan . . . The name of the child dragged her mind back from the pit of sadness and she muttered, 'Susan . . . Susan is lost. You . . . you haven't seen her?'

'Lost!' The woman rose from the opposite bunk. 'Since when?'

'This evening. She must have left the house about an hour ago.'

'Oh, an hour ago.' The woman smiled knowledgeably. 'She'll come back. She was always disappearing, but she always came back. One time she disappeared for a full day and Michael

530

went wild. He had the village out looking for her, and she walked out of a fishing hut. She had been asleep among the nets.'

Rosamund looked up at the woman. Her face had darkened, and her eyes were gazing beyond the boat into the past, and as she watched her Rosamund cried out bitterly inside herself, Michael. Oh, Michael, how could you? Her bitterness brought her to her feet, and she asked, 'When are you going to see him?'

'Tomorrow. I'll leave it until tomorrow now. Things will be more straightforward then.'

Rosamund couldn't see how they would ever be straightforward again. She said now, 'I must go. They . . . they may have found her.'

'Yes, most likely.' The woman opened the cabin door and, looking with an almost tender look down on Rosamund, said, 'I'm sorry this has had to happen to you, because you are nice. There are not many people one can say that to on such short acquaintance. Michael always went for the best.' As Rosamund jerked her gaze away, she finished, 'Don't worry about the child, she'll turn up. Never fear, she'll turn up . . . somewhere.'

'Can you manage?' The voice was quietly solicitous as Rosamund stepped up out of the well and into the half-submerged reeds.

'Yes, yes.' She wanted to say something more to the woman but she couldn't.

'Good night.'

'Good night.'

'Be careful how you go.'

Oh, dear God! Rosamund groaned the words to herself as she stumbled through the water towards the wash bank. What must she do? Go and find him and tell him, or let him wait until tomorrow, when the woman – she could not even think the term – his wife, would confront him.

By the time she reached the Goose Pond there was only one point clear in her tortured thinking. If they had found Susan when she got back she would tell him, otherwise she would leave events in the hands of the woman. She showed some knowledge of Michael in this decision, for he was unlikely to make any demands on her, even to insisting that she stay at the house, if Susan was not found . . .

It was dark when Rosamund came out of the wood and saw the lights shining from the house. Stupidly she had forgotten to bring a torch with her, and so the light was doubly welcome. Doubly because it seemed to bring warmth into her numbed being. Also, for the first time to her knowledge, she was actually afraid of the fenland in the dark.

She was stumbling in her running as she went up the drive, tripping as it were, over her twisted thinking. She wanted Susan to be found. Oh, she did. But that would mean she would have to tell him . . . If the child was still lost she would be relieved from the hateful task.

As she burst in through the open front door Maggie confronted her from the foot of the stairs and brought out, 'You haven't . . .?'

'No.' Rosamund shook her head as she stood gasping and holding for support on to the back of a new wing-chair. 'Have – have they been back?'

'Yes, Himself and a young farmer who's lending him a hand.'

That would be Andrew. Rosamund moved round the chair, still holding on to it for support, and sat down on its edge, and she did not raise her eyes to Maggie when the old woman said, 'He's nearly out of his mind. It's too much to happen to a man all at once. God knows I thought he was in for a little peace, and him getting the windfall an' all. But it's touched with the evil finger he is, for nothing's gone right for him since the day he was born. For how other would a man be confronted on his wedding night with the tale that the wife he had buried three years gone was on his doorstep . . . Did you go down to that boat?' Maggie asked this question under her breath as she moved quietly towards Rosamund.

'Yes.' Rosamund kept her head down as she murmured her reply.

'I thought you would. And, like him, you found nothing?'

'Maggie.' Rosamund was on her feet gripping

533

the old woman's arm. 'I must tell you, I must tell someone or I'll go mad. Come . . . come into the kitchen.' She looked around her distractedly before hurrying Maggie towards the green-baize door, and as soon as they were through it she faced the old woman, and in a low breaking voice she began to speak rapidly. 'She's there . . . the woman, and . . . and she's his wife, Maggie.'

'Jesus, Mary and Joseph. There are evil spirits indeed.'

'She's not evil, she's not bad, she's . . . she's nice in a way, charming . . .'

'She was a fiend.'

'No, no, Maggie.'

'He said so. Name of God, he told me all about her . . . dreadful things. Things she did to the child . . . God help her wherever she is this minute . . . he was never a liar, whatever else he was.'

'He . . . he is a liar, Maggie.' The words were dragged out of her. 'She . . . the woman told me why she had pretended to be dead. She was afraid of him. And if she had just left him he would have brought her back to look after Susie. She says he is mad where Susie is concerned.'

'Then why has she come back now? Tell me that?'

'For money. She read about his uncle's family being drowned.'

'That won't wash. If she's the same woman, why isn't she still afraid of him?'

'She is, but she wants money, she hates being poor. She was very honest, Maggie. You only have to listen to her to know that she is speaking the truth.'

Maggie, after staring at Rosamund for a long moment, suddenly raised her hands heavenwards and cried, 'Holy Mother, sort this out, will you? Will you sort this out?' Then, bringing her eyes as quickly down to Rosamund again, she demanded, 'What of the child? Had she seen the child?'

'No. She seemed amused that I was worrying as Susie had only been missing an hour or so. She seemed sure she would turn up on her own.'

'With the water covering everything. Yes, she'll turn up on her own . . . she'll float up . . .'

'Oh, don't, Maggie, please.' Rosamund turned away and, closing her eyes, held her head between her hands, only to turn swiftly again at the sound of footsteps coming from the hall. As she made her way towards the kitchen door, Maggie, thrusting out her hand, checked her, and the old woman's tone was beseeching as she whispered, 'Don't give him any more to carry the night, will you.'

'I won't, Maggie, if Susie isn't found, but if she is, I must. Listen. There's someone knocking.'

'Standing in the hall doorway she saw Andrew, and before she could speak he said, 'Any news?'

'No, Andrew.'

'Has – has he been back?'

'No, I don't think so, not since you came together.'

'This is serious, Rosie; unless she has wandered on to the main road . . . well . . .'

He left the sentence unfinished and they stood looking helplessly at each other.

'What's that?' Andrew had turned to the door again. 'There's a light.'

Rosamund, standing at his side, looked towards the oncoming bobbing light and before she could make any comment her father's voice hailed them saying, 'Hello there.'

As she and Andrew hurried to meet him he killed any spur of hope by shouting, 'Have you got her?'

Neither of them answered until they came up with him, and it was Andrew who said, 'No. No sign of her,' and then, seeing who was with him, 'You shouldn't have come out, Jennifer.'

'I . . . I had to. And look I found this.' She held out a mud-covered slipper. 'It might not mean anything, it could have been lost some time ago, for it was half buried in the mud.'

'Let me see.' Rosamund grabbed the slipper from Jennifer's hand, and, holding it close to the lantern, examined it. Her fingers touched the pompon on the front, and separating the wool she disclosed a tiny clean core of blue.

'It's one of a pair she was wearing tonight. They

were new last week. Where . . . where did you find it?'

'On the far side of the wood, just off the path leading to our place.'

'Near . . . near the water?' Rosamund asked the question quietly.

'No, quite some way off, although it was in a puddle.'

'This means she was making her way to the mill . . . to me.' Rosamund looked from the dim outline of her father's face to Andrew, and then to Jennifer, and she ended quietly, 'We'd better go in and wait.'

Andrew, taking the lantern from Henry Morley, now led the way back to the house, and as they entered the hall again, Andrew, turning to Rosamund, said, 'He should know about this.' He pointed to the slipper in her hand. 'But if I go out and call he'll imagine we've found her, for that was the arrangement.'

'We'd better just wait. Come into the kitchen, it's much warmer in there.' As Rosamund spoke she startled Jennifer, who was looking around the large hall, surprised no doubt at the elegant pieces of furniture standing out against the undecorated walls.

In the kitchen Rosamund quietly introduced her family to Maggie . . . She thought of Andrew as one of her family. And she realised that she knew much more about Andrew than she did about the man she had married that day – at least, more good things.

There seemed nothing good to remember about Michael Bradshaw except for the fact that he loved his handicapped daughter. And had not this feeling been created in the first place as a form of taking sides against his wife? If his wife had loved the child, then more likely than not he would have hated it.

But all this reasonable deduction was swept aside a few minutes later when, crossing the hall into the sitting-room, a lamp in her hand, there showed up in the perimeter of light the figure of Michael. He was stretched out in a chair just within the french window, and on her involuntary exclamation of surprise he turned his head heavily and looked towards her.

'You . . . you startled me. I . . . I didn't know you were back.'

He did not rise but said, 'I've just got in.' And it was the tone of his voice that, for the moment, swept all reasoning and cool thinking aside. There was not a trace of arrogance in it. It was a defeated, dead voice and it drew her to him. His tone did not alter as he added, 'I heard voices in the kitchen. I couldn't go in.' And then, looking up to where she now stood in front of him still holding the light, he ended flatly, 'None of us had to shout, had we?'

'My sister found a slipper. It . . . it is Susan's.'

'Where?' It was as if he had been shot from the chair, and he had to grasp both her and the lamp to steady them.

'The other side of the wood, but . . . not near the river.'

'But she must have been going that way . . . You went as far as the Goose Pond?'

'Yes, as far as the wash bank.' She was not looking at him.

He released his hold on her and turned from her before he said, 'And your friend Andrew?'

'He went towards the Wissey right up to the second cattle barrier.'

When he did not speak for some time but stood staring down towards his feet she asked softly, 'Can I get you a drink?'

For answer he said, 'They can't do any dragging until daylight.' He was gazing fixedly at the carpet as if seeing there a map of the action he must take to fill in the time until daylight, and he went on in the same dead tone. 'I'll follow the river to the pond – there's thick reed along there – then cut over to the dyke, come out at the bridge, then towards the main road, skirt the back of the house here, and down to the river again.' He raised his eyes to her. 'Would you ask him if he would phone the police . . . and tell them?'

'Yes.' She inclined her head slowly and there was a catch in her voice when she added, 'He'll go with you . . . Andrew'll go with you.'

'I want no-one with me. No-one.' For a moment there was his old self speaking, arrogance in every syllable. He was facing her squarely now, staring at her, and in only a slightly modulated tone he said, 'Do you remember what I said about valuing anything? Once I put any value on a thing it is wrenched from me. "It'll be all for the best," they'll say. Can't you hear them? "Poor thing, it's a happy release," they'll say . . . A happy release to lose one's conscience. To lose the only thing that touched the good in you.'

She was trembling so much she had to hold the lamp in both hands, and as she turned to put it on the table his voice, although low-toned, seemed to bark at her as he demanded, 'Are you just playing the usual female part or are you sorry she's gone?'

'Oh!' She was crying bitterly now. 'That's unfair.'

'Unfair? How do you make that out? You were, and still are, ready and willing to saddle me with a wife that I know is dead. As sure as I know that I'm reluctantly breathing at this moment, I know she's dead.'

She closed her eyes and joined her hands tightly in front of her.

'Look at me.'

She looked at him.

'You went to that boat, didn't you? That's why you jumped at taking the path to the Goose Pond . . . Well, what did you find?'

She gulped in her throat and twisted her fingers together as she stared through her tears into his grim tortured face. And she knew that if Susan was standing by her side at this minute she could not have said to him, 'I met your wife in that boat, and tomorrow she is coming to see you.'

The look that he now cast upon her was full of scorn. And the untranslatable sound he made indicated his feelings. When she watched him move quickly towards the french window again, grabbing up the torch from the arm of the chair as he went, she remained as mute as if she had been deprived of speech.

A few minutes later, when she picked up the lamp, she had forgotten entirely what had brought her to the sitting-room. She only knew that Michael must not be left alone this night. Andrew must go with him. She was calling Andrew's name before she left the room. 'Andrew, Andrew . . . Andrew, Andrew.'

It was four o'clock in the morning. The kitchen was stuffy, even hot, and Maggie was asleep in a cramped position in the arm-chair. Sitting opposite to her, Rosamund had succumbed to an overpowering feeling of drowsiness; and although she was sitting upright as if still on the alert for any sound, her head was lolling back against the head of the chair.

Only an hour ago had her father and Jennifer left

for the mill. She herself would have gone out then and aided in the search but for Maggie who now expressed real terror at being left alone. 'Don't leave me, Miss Rosie, ma'am,' she had pleaded, 'for I've got the strangest of feelings on me. Like when somebody walks over your grave, you know.' So she had pacified the old woman with the promise that she wouldn't leave her until daylight.

Andrew had come hurrying in for a moment around two o'clock when he had asked if there was any whisky in the house. When she had told him yes, he had said, 'Let me have some. He'll snap if his nerves are not eased.' He also told her they had met the police, who had answered the call almost immediately, but, as they said, there was little that could be done until daylight. And Andrew had ended, 'I wish he would believe that and ease up.' He had also told her that he had alerted Arnold Partridge from the Beck Farm and he had been with them for the past hour.

It was odd how things turned out, Rosamund thought. Arnold Partridge had been one of the men who had tried to get an order on Michael's land. But for the pressure of this farmer and Mr Brown from 'The Leas', Michael would likely still be in Ireland. And from the bottom of her heart she wished that this was so. For how simple life would have remained if he had never come back to this house.

Rosamund's head lolled to the side now, and

her limbs jerked as she began to dream. She was dreaming that she was stepping through the reeds towards the bows of the boat, and when she reached it she turned her back to the little porthole as if to stop someone looking in. It was quite light in the dream, and when a coot began to swim about her feet she felt a surge of pleasure. Coots were rare around here. The bird appeared so friendly that she was stooping to pick it up, when she was pushed forward by a hand coming through the porthole. This brought from her only a mild gasp of surprise, but a sudden startling scream coming from inside the boat made her jump right into the heart of the reeds.

Rosamund was on her feet now. Her eyes blinking dazedly with sleep. 'What is it, Maggie?' she cried, grasping the old woman by the shoulders. 'Why did you scream? Wake up. Oh, please wake up.'

'Oh, God in heaven. Oh, have you got her? She's in there. Oh, Miss Rosie,' gasped Maggie, clinging to Rosamund as she strove to draw breath. 'It must have been dreaming I was. Oh, but Mother of God, it was real.'

It must have indeed been real, Rosamund thought, for the scream still seemed to be reverberating round the kitchen.

'Miss Rosie . . . that boat, I saw that boat, the boat with the woman in it. I could describe it plank for plank. I can see it now, about so big.'

543

She pointed to the width of the kitchen. 'And two beds it had in it, and then in a cubby-hole of a place at the far end, where I got stuck 'cos I couldn't raise me back, so low it was, there was the child, on a bed affair, not longer than me arm. And I was for picking her up when some fiend-like hands grabbed me round the neck and I was struggling for me life. I screamed an' I screamed and all the while I was aware that the child hadn't moved or spoken. She seemed like dead.'

'Now, now, Maggie. Don't distress yourself. Sit back and I'll make you a cup of tea.'

'No, no. I want no tea.' Maggie edged herself out of the chair and stood gazing towards the curtained window. And as Rosamund looked at her she realised that the dream must have made a very strong impression on the old woman for her to refuse a cup of tea.

'When will it be light?'

'Around about five, I think, Maggie.'

'It's no use waiting till then, it might be too late . . . Miss Rosie.' Maggie turned and came slowly towards Rosamund. 'That wasn't only a dream I had. It was a warning. I've had it twice before in me life. On the night before me mother dropped dead, and her hale and hearty. And almost to the very hour me James was drowned. I dreamed I went down with him into the depths of the ocean an' I screamed; when the boats came back me timing was right . . . And now I know, as sure I am as there's a God, that the child is in that boat with . . . with its mother. But it won't be there for long – no, it won't be there for long.'

'Oh, Maggie, don't. I . . . I was in the boat. There was no place to hide Susie. The bows are so small there is just a little washbasin and lavatory in there.'

'She's on that boat, Miss Rosie.'

Rosamund saw that Maggie's eyes were not looking at her, but through her, as if she was actually seeing the boat, and her voice matched her eyes with that far-away quality as she went on, 'And I saw an omen of death . . . a bird, black with white on its head. It flew away through a little porthole as if it was bearing the child's soul with it.'

The coot. The gasp that Rosamund gave brought Maggie's vision back to the present and she said now in her normal voice, 'We've got to get himself to that boat. You've got to find him – if not him, then one of the others. For God's sake get into your things and find him.'

Rosamund was pulling on her wellingtons even before Maggie finished speaking. The coot and the porthole in the bows of the boat. She was remembering and clutching at the fading points of her own dream. It was strange that both of them should dream about the bows of the boat, the porthole, and the coot. It might just be coincidence; but no, people like Maggie, so near to the earth, had unexplainable experiences. She must find Michael, or someone, and get them to go to the boat.

As she pulled her coat on she said to Maggie, 'You won't be afraid to be left?'

'No, not any more. The fear has lifted from me and now I know why. It is no longer round the house, but it is out there, make no mistake about it – it is out there. Go on now, and God be with you . . . And . . . and tell himself to be careful, will you? And be with him if you can when they meet up.'

Rosamund did not answer, for she was already hurrying around the side of the house to the drive.

The darkness now seemed blacker than it had done last night. And the cold was intense enough to suggest winter rather than late July. Rosamund stopped where the broken gate had once leaned and turned her head from right to left. There was no sign of any glimmerings of light. Which way should she go? Towards the mill? That was where they would likely be. Obeying her thinking, she hurried now along the well-known path to the wood, but when she had passed through it and came within sight of the river, there were no flashing torches, or steady beams from Tilley lanterns, indicating the searchers. Nonplussed, she stood for a moment agitatedly questioning. Were they up near the Wissey, or down in the direction of the Goose Pond? If they were near the latter, all to the good, it would be no distance at all to the boat. Would she tell Michael straight away about the woman or tell him of Maggie's strange dream? She didn't know. She wouldn't know what she would say until she met him. One thing she did know. He would not laugh at this tale of Maggie's, for he had a strange faith in Maggie.

When, stumbling in her running, she reached the Goose Pond it was to find it as deserted as the river bank. Where were they all? What must she do. She couldn't go to that boat alone. But why not? She had been alone before. But that was different. If the child was really in that boat it meant . . . What did it mean? She shuddered and walked on, actually towards the wash bank. She would just look down from the top of the bank and see if there was a light in the boat.

There was no light coming from the reeds to indicate the position of the boat, and the distance was too far away to pick it out with the light from her torch.

She went against every warning feeling in her body when she quietly slid down the wet surface of the wash bank facing the river, and when she was in the water-logged field she directed the torch towards her feet. Sometimes she slipped into a hollow that brought the water almost to the top of her wellingtons, at others she could see the toecaps glittering in the torch light. It was as she stood on one such piece of raised ground that she knew she was near the boat. Slowly she moved the torch to reveal the reeds, and there, just showing above them, was the superstructure of the little cruiser. Even the hairs on her neck indicated her fear as, lifting one heavy foot slowly after the other, she made her way, not towards the well, but to the point of the bows where the port-hole was. She was about four feet away when she realised that either the boat had moved its position, or that the water had risen; for she was standing on, or rather sinking into silt, and another step might bring the water into her wellingtons. This could prove serious, as she only too well knew. Caution directed her step to the side, and it was as she slid her foot tentatively into the reeds that the bird rose squawking almost into her face. As she thrust out her hands to ward it off, and at the same time to keep her balance, its fluttering, petrified body was revealed for a second in the light of the torch, and the marking on its head brought a convulsive shiver to her whole body . . . A coot. Both Maggie and she had dreamed of a coot, and here it was. She had pressed her hand over her mouth to prevent any sound escaping her, and now she waited, the torch switched off, listening for any movement from the boat. . . . There was no movement, no sound, except for the coot, that was still spasmodically expressing its fright from the far side of the river. The woman, if she had been on the river for some time, was likely to be used to night noises and they would no longer startle her, or even disturb her sleep.

Rosamund shivered now with both cold and fear as she stood in the water peering towards the darker blackness of the boat. Now she had got this far she couldn't go back – not now, not after seeing that bird. But she must get her wellingtons off. Slowly she wriggled her foot out of first one, and then the other boot, and she was on the point of stepping forward when the sound came to her. It was a sound she had become used to in the past few weeks. It was the half-moaning, half-whimpering sound that Susie made in her sleep. It stopped, then after a second or two it came again. The child – the child was in there, in the bows of the boat. It was unbelievable, fantastic . . . Maggie was right . . . But the woman? The mother? She could not be evil; she could mean no harm to the child. Perhaps she had found her later. Then why hadn't she brought her to the house? Well, how could she? She was just keeping her until daylight . . . Oh, she didn't know what to think.

'What do you want?'

The voice coming out of the blackness startled her more than the coot or the sound of Susie had done, and she almost fell forward into the water.

'It's me . . . Rosamund Morley.'

'Yes. I know it is. What do you want?'

'The question, repeated so flatly, so unemotionally, left Rosamund entirely at a loss. Automatically she picked up her wellingtons, then, pushing through the reeds, made her way towards the voice. She knew that the woman was standing in the well of the boat, and she played the torch over the deck into the well, and not on to the woman's face, before saying quietly, 'I've come for Susie.'

There was no retort from the woman. It must have been a full minute before she even moved. Then she said as she had done last night, 'Come in.'

Rosamund found herself hesitating. She wanted to say, 'No. I'm not coming in. Hand the child out to me.' But then, as if impelled to obey this flat-sounding voice, she waded towards the deck and pulled herself over into the well. And now she did play the torch light on the woman's face, and what she saw turned her shivering into a violent shudder. The face was no longer the one she remembered. The brown eyes held a blank dead look that was in some way akin to the voice. The curving mouth was now a thin tight line, and the cheeks seemed to have sunk in, like those of an old woman.

'Put that out.'

After a slight hesitation Rosamund switched off the torch and the woman now opened the cabin door to reveal a night-light burning.

'Don't stand there. Come in.'

When Rosamund slowly entered the cabin, the woman clicked the door shut behind her, then in a subtly soft tone she murmured, 'Sit down . . . dear, dear Rosie.' Both the words and the voice had a really blood-chilling effect. 'You know you are very foolish to come back here, don't you?'

It was not in Rosamund's power to make any answer, and after an agonising pause the woman went on, 'It means that I've got to deal with you. You've complicated things for me. When I first saw you, I thought, "She's harmless," and I decided to leave you alone . . . That was a very difficult thing for me to do, knowing you were after Michael. But I thought, "In the end she won't matter, she'll be of no account." But I misjudged you, didn't I, dear, dear Rosie? That's what he calls you, doesn't he? Dear, dear Rosie. He wants to marry you, doesn't he? Don't get up. You're not going anywhere.' The hand that gripped Rosie's arm was like a fine steel band. 'I've had to think very quickly in the last few minutes or so. You see, it was Michael I expected to come for Susie, not you. All this talk of waiting until tomorrow was just talk. I expected you to tell him and this would bring him tearing over here. I was to placate him and offer him a drink . . . Oh yes, I would have placated him. I was going to plead with him. Michael could never withstand a woman pleading with him. It always made him feel extra big, and tough. And once he had taken that drink the rest would have been easy. If he wouldn't drink, I had another way. In any case the result would have been the same – we would, all three, have been found in the boat suffering from an overdose of phenobarbitone, but in the case of Michael and Susie the dose would have proved fatal. It would have come out later that, rather than have me back in his life he had poisoned us . . . What does the stigma of a bad wife matter when you are the widow of a rich man, and rid of that . . . that freak?' She turned her eyes towards the door leading into the bows. Then, looking back into Rosamund's horrified face, she went on, 'She was here, all the time. I met her when she was on her way to the mill and you. The sight of me, close to, was quite sufficient to paralyse even her screaming – for long enough, anyway, to enable me to do what was necessary. I used to be quite adept at gagging her in the old days. She helps a lot; she opens her mouth wide.'

'Leave go of my arm.'

'Sit down then.'

'I won't sit down. Leave go.'

'There you are, I've let go. Now what are you going to do?'

'I'm going home and I'm taking the child with me.' The words sounded simple, even a little silly as she said them. It was as if she were saying to an avalanche, 'I'm going to push you out of the way,' for the woman before her was an avalanche of terror, of fear . . . yes, of evil. Rosamund was only too fully aware now, and too late, that this was no ordinary woman by whom she was confronted – this was a female Jekyll and Hyde. She had set a trap to catch Michael and she herself had walked into it. Terror mounted as she realised that she was utterly at a loss how to deal with this woman. She had no experience of bad people. She felt gauche, naïve, as she realised that she had little experience of people at all. She had lived almost like a cloistered nun for six years in the mill on the fens. Who was she to cope with a woman of the world, a fiend of the world? For the face before her now had a most fiendish expression. She felt totally inadequate. The only thing she could do was to scream. At the pitch of her lungs she would scream.

There were no portholes in the main cabin, the windows being modern sliding ones, and one of them, Rosamund saw from the slightly fluttering curtain, was slightly open. There was a chance that her voice might carry, for both Michael and Andrew would be on the alert for any unusual sound. She opened her mouth, but her scream was strangled before it even reached her lips. The woman acted as if she had been prepared for just such an emergency. She sprang at Rosamund, and, with a blow that caught her on the shoulder, knocked her flying against the corner of the cupboard that acted as a head to the bunk.

The impact seemed to split her head in two; blackness whirled around her, and she was aware of nothing but searing pain for a moment or two. When the worst of the pain lifted she knew that she was lying flat on the bunk and that there was something running over her face. When dazedly she put up her hand to wipe it away she saw the woman standing tall and straight by her side.

'You're bleeding. But don't worry, that won't bother you for long, and it's saved me a job. Here, drink this.' She bent over Rosamund now and offered her a cup.

Slowly Rosamund raised herself on her two hands until her back was supported against the cupboard, and she asked weakly, 'What is it?'

'Something that'll do you good. It'll make you feel good, I promise you. Drink it up.' She pushed the cup towards Rosamund's lips.

'I don't want it.' With a slow movement of her hand Rosamund warded the profferred cup away. The woman placed the cup on the cupboard, and the next instant Rosamund found herself pinioned against the head of the bunk, with the woman's knee across her legs and her two hands imprisoned within bony fingers. She was pulled upwards into a sitting position, before being flung backwards, bringing her head in contact with the bunk head again. The effect was to knock her almost senseless. The next thing she knew the cup was at her lips, and as she took a gasp of breath some of the liquid went down her throat. It was bitter and vile tasting. She spluttered, trying to cough it up, but when she drew in a breath she again swallowed the bitter, foul-tasting stuff. She did her best not to cough again, but became still when the cup was tilted up to her lips for the third time, and she let the liquid run into her mouth. Then, forcing herself to close her lips and breathe evenly through her nose, she relaxed her body and slumped sideways.

When the woman released her hold Rosamund fell over on to the cushions and slowly she let the liquid trickle from the corner of her mouth. When she was pulled roughly round again there was still some left in her mouth, and she spluttered and coughed, and the woman laughed quietly as she said, 'Cough that lot up if you can.'

She now brought her face down close to Rosamund's, and, looking into her eyes, she said, 'You're going to sleep now. Soon you'll be like her, beyond caring. It won't matter much to you what happens. Are you feeling nice now? It's a quiet feeling inside, isn't it? Nice and quiet inside. I've really been very kind to you, you know.'

Rosamund forced herself to close her eyes. Whatever she had taken she could feel no effects of it yet. The woman released her hold and she fell back once more against the head of the bunk, but her head had no sooner touched the wood than she opened her eyes wide, for she was experiencing the most odd sensation. There was a whirling in her stomach, and in her head. There was a weird feeling running down the veins in her legs. The feeling urged her to get to her feet, to get into the open air, but her common sense told her to remain still.

How long she remained still she couldn't tell. It was almost dark in the cabin now. Things were hazy, but she knew that there was a floorboard up, and the woman was on her knees, her hand groping to the bottom of the boat. Then she was standing up again, a torch in her hand, but before it had flashed over the bunk Rosamund had closed her eyes. When she opened them again the cabin was empty. The boat lurched once, and immediately Rosamund knew that the woman had left.

She waited, almost counting the seconds, and as she waited she became aware that she wasn't worrying. As the woman had promised, she was quiet inside. She had a desire now to lie still and not bother; there was a dizzy feeling in her head, her body was numb.

Get up! Get up! Get up! It was Michael's voice, but Michael wasn't here. Get up! Get up! Get up! Somebody was shouting at her. The words were coming only faintly through the thickness in her brain. Get up! Get up! Get up! She was sitting now on the side of the bunk and her feet were covered with water. The boat was sinking. She felt the slightest stir of panic, she had taken out the bung, the woman had taken out the bung. Where was she? Where was the woman? She had gone now, gone to find Michael. Get up! Get up! Get up!

She groped slowly around the door of the bows until she found the handle, then her hands were feeling around in the space before her, but it was her feet that found Susan. Her body, lagging heavy and relaxed against the bulwark, was already half submerged. When she pulled her forward the child fell into the water with a quiet, plonk sound, and then she had her by the back of her dress dragging her towards the main cabin door. She turned the handle and the door opened, but slowly against the pressure of the water. The woman had been so sure of her work that she hadn't bothered to lock the door. The water was over her knees now and round the child's neck. The bows of the boat were almost covered. She tried to lift the child up by the arms, but she couldn't. She felt too dizzy, too dazed. She held on to Susie's collar and supported her against the deck as she peered through the darkening night towards the reeds which were more than three yards away from the boat now.

She never fully remembered how she eased the child over the deck and on to her back in the water. But she did remember the thankful feeling when after only two or three weak strokes her legs and stomach slid against the mud of the bank. She remembered, too, that when she was dragging the child into the reeds she saw that her head was under water, and that she had difficulty in turning her on to her face, and more difficulty still in pulling her along this way, for she couldn't keep her head up, and she had to put her on her back again.

There was a great slow thudding in her head now as if she were going under gas, thud-thud-thud-thud-thud; and with each thud came the words, Quiet inside. Quiet inside. Quiet inside. And she was quiet inside. She just wanted to lie, lie and sleep, but she still went on crawling, tugging the child after her inch by inch. It was the child's sudden spluttering that made her stop. Susie was making sounds as if she was choking. Slowly she pushed her on to her face again and as she did so she thought, stupidly, Poor dear, she's sick.

She lay with her head resting on the crook of her arm. She was so sleepy, so sleepy . . . Get up! Get up! Get up! Michael's voice again. Get up! Get up! Get up! Do you hear? Get up! Get up! Get up! At the last command she pulled her knees up under her and groped towards the child, who was lying on her side. The ground was soggy, but there was no depth of water here.

She must get to Michael . . . Michael . . . Michael. But she was so tired. She stumbled away from the child through the field, but instinctively in the direction of the wash-bank. She was staggering like someone drunk when she reached the top, and as she tried to descend her wavering feet slipped and she slid down the blue clay bank into the field. Again she lay with her head resting on her arm. The thudding was regular now, coming with every beat of her heart. Thud-thud-thud. Get up! Get up! Get up! When she staggered past the pond the geese set up their protest again, and several families of moorhens clucked away in fright from their nests in the reeds.

Michael. Michael. She began to mutter his name. But she must shout it. She must shout . . . She shouted, 'Michael! Michael!' She could hardly hear her own voice, it was so faint and far away. She staggered on, still calling, until quite suddenly she was standing still, and straight. Her head up and her nostrils dilated. She was smelling something. She had never smelt anything like it before. It swept away the quiet feeling inside of her and brought from the dark, dark elemental depths a fear, so tearing, so shattering that she knew that she was no longer herself. It seemed as if her entire being had been shattered, splintered into fragments, all except the core, the elemental core that went back into times dark with forbidden things, times before the soils of the fens ever saw the light of day. In this split second of time she knew why the child had screamed. In this second of time she was the child, and possessed of a sense too keen to be borne. From every pore in her body sound was oozing, screams were shrieking forth, yet there was no sound, no sound at all. Only the presence of the woman, her arms clutching her shoulders, leading her from the path across the fields towards . . . what? She knew where the woman was leading her; she was leading her towards the dyke, towards the end that had been cleared of reeds, because her feet were now dragging and tripping themselves in the cut reeds. The silt in the dyke here would be soft and deep. If you lay still you would sink right down into it . . . There was no room in her for further terror – she had reached the point where suffering ends.

When the woman pushed her she clutched at the air and fell forward into space and the scream came with her. She could sleep now.

Quiet inside, quiet inside, quiet inside.

10

Quiet inside. Quiet inside. Quiet inside . . . Oh, she felt sick. So sick.

'Drink this, my dear.'

Rosamund shook her head and closed her lips tightly.

'There you are. Open your mouth. That's a good girl.'

'I'm sick.'

'Yes, you're sick, but you'll soon feel better. Go to sleep now.'

Quiet inside. Quiet inside. Quiet inside . . .

She opened her eyes and saw the woman again and screamed.

'Rosie! Rosie! It's me. Jennifer.'

It wasn't the woman. It was Jennifer; Jennifer who had different eyes, and a different mouth, and whose hair was really blonde; it was her sister Jennifer.

Quiet inside. Quiet inside. Quiet inside . . .

When next she opened her eyes she saw her father, and behind him the sun was shining through the window. He stroked her hair back from her brow and said, 'Oh, Rosie, my dear.'

Quiet inside. Quiet inside. Quiet inside . . .

'Come along, try to drink this cup of tea. Come on now, open your eyes . . . Wider now. That's it.'

Quiet inside. Quiet inside. Quiet inside. The voice was fainter now but still there. She looked at the bright face of the nurse bending over her, and this time asked, 'Where am I?'

'You're in hospital.'

'Hospital?'

'Yes. Don't worry. Come along, drink this. You feel better now?'

'Yes . . . yes.' Her voice sounded dreamy and far away. Slowly she put her hand up towards her head, and, feeling the bandages, she said, 'My head?'

'That'll be all right. You had a nasty cut. It had to be stitched. There now, is that better?' The nurse put the cup on the locker, then pushed up the pillow under Rosamund's head.

'My . . . my father. He was here?' Rosamund looked round the small room. 'And . . . and Jennifer.'

'Oh, you remember them being here? But is that all you remember?'

Rosamund tried to think, but it was a painful process trying to think. The voice was still drumming in the back of her head. Quiet inside. Quiet inside. Quiet inside. Why was it saying 'Quiet inside' like that all the time . . .? With a sudden movement that sent a stabbing pain streaking through the backs of her eyes, she was sitting upright. 'Where is Michael? Michael! . . . Where is he?'

'Now! Now! Don't get excited. You must lie quiet.'

'But Michael?'

'He'll be back. He's been here all night and most of the day. He's a perfect nuisance.' The nurse's smile softened her words. 'He's just gone along to the children's ward. Never fear, he'll be back.'

'Susan. Where's Susan? Is she . . .'

'Now don't ask so many questions and excite yourself. You must lie quiet.'

'But tell me, is she . . .?'

'The little girl is all right. I've told you, she's in the children's ward.'

Slowly Rosamund sank down into the bed. The child was safe, Michael was here . . . Oh, Michael was here. Quiet inside. Quiet inside. Quiet inside . . . She was sound asleep when Michael next came into the ward.

It was a week later when Rosamund returned to the fens, and to Thornby House. The sun was shining, the water had drained away from the land, and as Michael drew the car up in front of the house door, there was Jennifer and her father, Andrew, and the child, and Maggie, all waiting to greet her. It was too much, too much happiness all at once, and she cried, and everyone was quiet for a while. But at teatime Maggie brought laughter to them all with her humour and quaint sayings, and Rosamund, sitting in thankful peace, was more than grateful to her; oh, more than grateful, and for so many things. If it had not been for Maggie and that something that went beyond the veil of reasoning, they would not all be sitting here now.

In her heart too she was grateful to Jennifer, for now and again Jennifer spoke to Michael, and when this happened Rosamund noticed that he met her sister more than half-way; in fact Rosamund would have said that his manner was charming. She looked at her husband. There was nothing of the fen tiger about him today; he had a gentle, even subdued air about him. Another thing that added to the sum of her happiness was that Michael liked Andrew, and this feeling she knew was reciprocated.

The tea over, she was ordered firmly into the lounge chair facing the front door, and it was from there that she later watched Jennifer and Andrew, their figures getting smaller and smaller as they walked arm-in-arm over the fields towards Willow Wold Farm; and from her seat she watched her father take the child by the hand and go in the direction of the mill. Apparently he had become a second O'Moore to Susie. Lastly, she brought her eyes back to Michael where he sat by her side, her hand lost in his.

'Hullo, Rosie.'

'Hullo, Michael.' They smiled at each other. This was the first time they had been alone together except for the journey in the car.

'Happy to be home?'

'Yes, Michael, very happy.'

'Not afraid any more?'

'No, not any more.'

He looked away from her now into the shadowless fen, and his voice was very quiet as he said, 'Before we close the subject for good and all, Rosie, I want you to believe that I spoke the truth when I said that I thought she was dead.'

'I know that, Michael.'

Gently he withdrew his hand from hers, and, leaning forward, rested his elbows on his knees. 'I've been over it a thousand times' – he shook his head slowly – 'and I still can't believe that I made a mistake, although the proof, God knows, was only too evident. But the body that was washed up on that shore was as like her body as to be it. I couldn't go by the face, it was . . .' He shook his head vigorously. 'What's the use? I made a mistake . . . perhaps I wanted to make a mistake . . . But who was that other woman? That's a question that will haunt me from time to time all my life.'

When he felt her hand on his shoulder he put up his own and gripped it.

'The past is gone, Michael. Don't let's ever refer to it again.'

Even as she said this, Rosamund knew that it would be a long long time before she herself was able to wipe out the memory of the night she was drawn towards the motor cruiser lying at the end of the Cut. And she shuddered now with the thought that, but for a miracle, she would not be here, sitting in the warmth of the evening sun, but suffocated in the silt at the bottom of the dyke.

Why the woman had fallen into the dyke would always remain a mystery. Had Rosamund herself clutched at her in the last desperate moments when she was being flung into space? Or had the bank on which they were standing given way? They had found part of it broken down. Whatever had happened, the woman had been the first to hit the bottom of the dyke, and it was her last terrible scream that had brought Michael and Andrew flying to the spot . . . and only just in time.

It was her father who had given her, very briefly, a summary of the events of that dreadful night. The woman had been dead when they got her out, and she herself almost suffocated by the silt. But she could remember nothing at all from the time she realised that the boat was sinking, and only vaguely did she remember holding the bitter liquid in her mouth and letting it drip into the pillow of the bunk. But she knew now that except for this action she would have lain drugged with the phenobarbitone, as was the child, and been drowned as the boat sank.

'Look at me.' Gently she pulled at his ear, and when he turned to face her she made an endeavour to lift his mind from the past events by saying, 'Tell me, what did you say to Clifford? Father tells me he came to see you.'

He looked at her as a slow smile spread over his face. 'Oh, I said a lot to your cousin. I told him he was a fool to have let the grass grow under his feet.'

'Don't be silly. You said no such thing.'

'Didn't I though? He was a very sad young man when he left here. He's a bit of a fool.'

'He's not; he's nice, is Clifford.' She could think that now.

'I repeat, he's a bit of a fool — more than a bit, to have ever let you go. Anyway, I made a bargain with him . . . a deal.'

'A deal with Clifford? What about?'

'He's selling me the mill.'

'No!' She was sitting up now. 'Oh, Michael, that's sweet of you.'

'Sweet nothing. I've got a business head. We are going to fit that place up into a first-rate factory. Your father and I have it all planned.'

'Oh, Michael . . .!'

'Don't you, "Oh Michael!" me in that tone of voice. It's merely a business deal.'

'Kiss me, Michael.'

Bending forward, he kissed her tenderly on the lips, then said softly, 'It will keep him occupied. But he must stay here with you, live near you, because he needs you.' He now took her face between his two hands. 'Life isn't going to be too easy for you, my Rosie. It's not fair, in a way, because you're starting handicapped. There's not only your father, there's the child, and . . . there's me. And I'll be your biggest problem, Rosie. Oh yes I will.' He moved his head slowly, 'I'll not let you alone – I know myself – I'll claim your attention like a sick cow . . . or rather bull.' He laughed. 'And with it all I'll be bumptious, arrogant, loud and demanding. This present quiet demeanour of mine, which is the outcome of shock, won't last. You see, if nothing else I'm my own doctor. Moreover, there's a poison in me that I pour over people I dislike, and the result is that everybody is very uncomfortable, to say the least.'

She was smiling tenderly, her head on one side, and her voice had a serious tone as she said, 'I know. I agree with everything you say about yourself, and as Maggie would add, "That's not the half of it."' She now put up her hands and covered his with them where they cupped her face as she went on, 'But you forgot to say that the Fen Tiger is kind and generous. He is also compassionate, and loyal, and very, very loving . . . Dear, dear Fen Tiger . . .

The last words were cut off and smothered against his coat, and his lips, moving in her hair, kept repeating, 'Oh, Rosie. Oh, Rosie,' and then softly he said, 'That morning when I stood outside the solicitor's office and realised I was a rich man I also realised something else, something that hit me with the force of a bullet in the head. It was that all this money, all it stood for . . . comfort, security, travel, even the best attention for the child . . . meant nothing . . . less than the muck under my feet without you, you and your love for me. And I became terrified from that moment of losing you.'

'Well, you didn't darling.'

'You'll always try to keep on loving me, Rosie, even at my worst?'

'I'll love you best at your worst.'

'Oh, Rosie. Things will never be easy for you, you're made that way.'

In the darkness behind her closed lids she saw a picture of the coming years. As he had said, things would never be easy for her. Money in her case would not make all that difference, for money could not lessen the demands he had mentioned. The demands of her father, of the child, and . . . of himself – her Michael. They all wanted loving, mothering, but Mike most of all. Would she, if she could, change the picture that she saw threading the years? No, not one little iota of it. She had been made to give. That's what brought her the most happiness – giving.

She had been made for others to lean on, but the burdens she had now to bear would be light. Life would be light, for she had an overwhelming compensation – she had the unstinted, passionate, demanding love of this man . . . her Fen Tiger.

THE END

THE GOLDEN STRAW
by Catherine Cookson

The Golden Straw, as it would be named, was a large, broad-brimmed hat presented to Emily Pearson by her long-time friend and employer Mabel Arkwright, milliner and modiste. And before long it was to her employer that Emily owed the gift of the business itself, for Mabel was in poor health and had come to rely more and more on Emily before her untimely death in 1880.

While on holiday in France, Emily and the Golden Straw attracted the eye of Paul Steerman, a guest at the hotel, and throughout his stay he paid her unceasing attention. But Paul Steerman was not at all he seemed to be and he was to bring nothing but disgrace and tragedy to Emily, precipitating a series of events that would influence the destiny of not only her children but her grandchildren too.

The Golden Straw, conceived on a panoramic scale, brilliantly portrays a rich vein of English life from the heyday of the Victorian era to the stormy middle years of the present century. It represents a fresh triumph for this great storyteller whose work is deservedly loved and enjoyed throughout the world.

0 552 13685 9

JUSTICE IS A WOMAN
by Catherine Cookson

The day Joe Remington brought his new bride to Fell Rise, he had already sensed she might not settle easily into the big house just outside the Tyneside town of Fellburn. For Joe this had always been his home, but for Elaine it was virtually another country whose manners and customs she was by no means eager to accept.

Making plain her disapproval of Joe's familiarity with the servants, demanding to see accounts Joe had always trusted to their care, questioning the donation of food to striking miners' families – all these objections and more soon rubbed Joe and the local people up the wrong way, a problem he could easily have done without, for this was 1926, the year of the General Strike, the effects of which would nowhere be felt more acutely than in this heartland of the North-East.

Then when Elaine became pregnant, she saw it as a disaster and only the willingness of her unmarried sister Betty to come and see her through her confinement made it bearable. But in the long run, would Betty's presence only serve to widen the rift between husband and wife, or would she help to bring about a reconciliation?

0 552 13622 0

THE MALTESE ANGEL
by Catherine Cookson

Ward Gibson knew what was expected of him by the village folk, and especially by the Mason family, whose daughter Daisy he had known all his life. But then, in a single week, his whole world had been turned upside down by a dancer, Stephanie McQueen, who seemed to float across the stage of the Empire Music Hall where she was appearing as The Maltese Angel. To his amazement, the attraction was mutual, and after a whirlwind courtship she agreed to marry him.

But a scorpion had already begun to emerge from beneath the stone of the local community, who considered that Ward had betrayed their expectations, and led on and cruelly deserted Daisy. There followed a series of reprisals on his family, one of them serious enough to cause him to exact a terrible revenge; and these events would twist and turn the course of many lives through Ward's own and succeeding generations.

0 552 13684 0

THE WHIP
by Catherine Cookson

Emma Molinero's dying father, a circus performer, had sent his beloved daughter to live with an unknown grandmother, not realizing that he had sentenced her to a life of misery.

But the graceful Emma, mistrusted by the local people for her beauty and her 'foreign blood', nevertheless became a woman who mystified and fascinated men because of her fiery independence and her skill at performing with the whip – her father's only legacies.

0 552 12368 4

THE YEAR OF THE VIRGINS
by Catherine Cookson

It had never been the best of marriages and over recent years it had become effectively a marriage in name and outward appearance only. Yet, in the autumn of 1960, Winifred and Daniel Coulson presented an acceptable façade to the outside world, for Daniel had prospered sufficiently to allow them to live at Wearcill House, a mansion situated in the most favoured outskirt of the Tyneside town of Fellburn.

Of their children, it was Donald on whom Winifred doted to the point of obsession, and now he was to be married, Winifred's prime concern was whether Donald was entering wedlock with an unbesmirched purity of body and spirit, for amidst the strange workings of her mind much earlier conceptions of morality and the teachings of the church held sway.

There was something potentially explosive just below the surface of life at Wearcill House, but when that explosion came it was in a totally unforeseeable and devastating form, plunging the Coulsons into an excoriating series of crises out of which would come both good and evil, as well as the true significance of the year of the virgins.

'The power and mastery are astonishing'
Elizabeth Buchan, *Sunday Times*

0 552 13247 0

A SELECTION OF OTHER CATHERINE COOKSON TITLES AVAILABLE FROM CORGI BOOKS

THE PRICES SHOWN BELOW WERE CORRECT AT THE TIME OF GOING TO PRESS. HOWEVER TRANSWORLD PUBLISHERS RESERVE THE RIGHT TO SHOW NEW RETAIL PRICES ON COVERS WHICH MAY DIFFER FROM THOSE PREVIOUSLY ADVERTISED IN THE TEXT OR ELSEWHERE.

All Transworld titles are available by post from:

Book Service By Post, P.O. Box 29, Douglas, Isle of Man IM99 1BQ

Credit cards accepted. Please telephone 01624 675137,
fax 01624 670923, Internet http://www.bookpost.co.uk or
e-mail: bookshop@enterprise.net for details.

Free postage and packing in the UK. Overseas customers allow
£1 per book (paperbacks) and £3 per book (hardbacks).